Note from the Author

    This novel is divided into three chronological books. Each individual book tells a smaller part of the overarching plot. While this novel focuses predominantly on a few individual characters, it is intended to be known that many characters have importance, and that many will return later even if they seem relatively minor initially.

    This world — Thrella — is designed to feel as much as possible as though it is a breathing and living world, with people in all corners of it that are existing simultaneously; furthermore, in writing this I intended to leave no character as an archetypal hero or villain. A man or woman who appears to be inherently evil or good could later change or could be revealed to be much more complicated than they first seemed.

    This is an attempt at creating unique individuals with multiple goals and ideals.

    Each book will begin with a piece of lore that was written similar to an informative prologue. If one is much like me, and often skips the prologues of novels (if one is much like me they might not be reading this at all), then that will be fine. These pieces of lore are designed to enhance some understanding and give information that will be relevant to the story. By not reading them, one would not miss the plot of the series, but may miss pieces of history that could be of use or of interest.

    All that being said, it is hoped that you dive into the story with fresh interest and that you enjoy the novel for what it is.

    Thank you for reading my work, I will always feel grateful to be able to share such stories as these.

- James Lytton

The Stillness in the Air

First Novel of the Series: "A Splintering World"

By: James Lytton

Copyright © 2019 James Lytton

All rights reserved.

First, A Few Words

Thank you to everyone who offered support in getting this story to where it is now. Whether you offered support by purchasing or reading these books, or whether it was through a simple word of encouragement or by liking posts on social media. I wanted to say a thank you for all the help that I have received. I am very honoured to be able to share this tale with you.

Book One - The Darkness Within

Book One of the Series: "A Splintering World"
Part One of the Novel: "The Stillness in the Air"

By: James Lytton

Piece of Lore - The Third Era

The third era began as one of peace and rebuilding of rubble. The people of Thrella — on the continent of Estrand — took time to restructure their fractured society after the events of the Malachi Crisis. The horrific events of the recent past had ripped whole towns to dust and plagued the world with a seemingly unstoppable sea of undead. After pulling themselves back from the brink, people and races from across the land banded together and put back much of what was lost in the turmoil.

The formation of the Council United allowed the denizens of the civilized world to share resources and build a system of reparation between all the great ruling powers: The Republic of Vruyoth, The Dabarisian Kingdom, and Krunix - the heartland of the dwarves and gnomes.

After the first decade was spent reconstructing, the peoples of Estrand were not finished with their cooperation and drive to fill the world once more, and to build it greater than it had ever been. They set off down the continent to the southern tip, where they had not yet been, and across Wrofyhx's Expanse — the eastern sea — to find the new continent of Streboya, which had been largely untouched until then.

The Dabarisian King, Benedict II, was placed almost entirely in charge of the new colonies of Southpoint in Southern Estrand; and of Stormbreaker's Bay on Streboya. He did his best to see them through to prosperity for the remainder of his life.

On Estrand, the south thrived under Benedict's reign, as they founded three new towns and split into two separate townships, which worked together to bring new resources north and become nearly self sustaining. Streboya built The City of Krosa on the mountain near the bay, and spread out along the southern half of this new continent.

The Streboyan natives, consisting of large Goliath tribes and another, taller race of elves (dubbed Streboyan Elves) did not take kindly to the colonies on their continent. For just over thirty years however, there was relative peace between the opposing forces. It was after Queen Eleanor Dabaris took the throne from her father upon his death in 3E035 that tensions began to boil over.

A war raged on Streboya, starting officially in 3E044 and ending in 3E051 when the colonists, the army of house Ironheart, won against the opposing house Whiteguard, led by the natives and their supporters. There were many casualties on both sides and only the supplies and reinforcements from Estrand turned the tide.

Eleanor died in 3E050 and her son, Benedict III began his reign by overseeing the peace treaties of the civil war, and continued by immediately increasing taxes. His new laws and regulations affected the south and Streboya more than the heartland, but he has kept his mind firm since he pushed collections forward to undo the debt caused by the Streboyan conflict.

The five years since his ascending to the throne has seen much of the peace on Estrand slip away; bandit attacks have increased, orc raids in the Council Lands below Krunix have doubled in intensity and frequency, and general unrest has began to seize the known world. While much of this is not a direct result of the new king, blame from outside the Dabarisian Heartland is largely directed towards his name and the royal family.

Within the centre of the empire however, things remain calm for the moment. With only bandits and the day to day struggle for the commonfolk to worry about, many of those with money to travel north, and no ties, have uprooted. A plethora of new faces and interesting people can be found throughout the Dabarisian upper territory now, in the form of tourists or long term immigrants.

Magic has increased in frequency as well, with studies at a near record high, and gifted children seeming less of a miracle as numbers rise. The church collective has been working on imposing stricter laws on the practice of the arcane arts, but has yet to release any bill against it.

With everyone busy doing their own, the world appears — at least on the surface — to be holding together well. Those with eyes that pierce this facade, however, can see the mechanisms beginning to break down, and the fractures in the foundation. But as the fifty-fifth year of the third era winds to a close, things are falling into place for something big. Something threatens to break from the shadows and destroy the glass pane that has become the world of Thrella.

- An Excerpt from Ran-Levyr's "In Hindsight - A View of the Third Era"

Chapter One - An Unlikely Group

3Eo55, 19th of Echo's Stay

The township of Taernsby is prosperous and industrious. The outlying villages provide most products necessary for comfortable living, and the town proper is a widespread centre for trade and travel within the known world. This heart of trade and commerce is situated along the eastern coastline, bordering the calmer of the two known oceans: Wrofyhx's Expanse. Taernsby is busy and lively through all seasons from the coming and going of ships and caravans, but it is spacious enough that the walls are never quite bursting at the seams.

These walls, surrounding the aforementioned proper, are built of thick stone. They are not higher than a storey and are often left widely undefended, as the third era has ushered in widespread peace and cooperation. This calm is largely attributed to the formation of the Council United at the end of the second era, and the treaties signed by the Dabarisian and Krunixian Kings, along with the New Republic of Vruyoth.

The end of winter is fast approaching, though spring appears to be in the mood to meander. Snow has kept the whole township under a blanket of white for months now. Locals and travellers alike have been bunkered in homes and inns the whole while, keeping busy with their jobs and paying out their saved coin for warm beds, and hot, fresh meals. Taverns and restaurants have had food shipped in from the centre of Estrand where temperatures are still high enough for widespread hunting and varied farming.

Prices have been high for basic goods since midwinter, when trade caravans became less available. As such, everyone, especially those staying in inns and hostels, have had to cough up much of their stored currency to stay in comfort.

The East Air Inn and Tavern is one of Taernsby's smaller but more homely locales. Its upstairs has only ten rooms, each with two beds, dressers and desks. These rooms are comfortable and kept clean by the proprietor, Laura

Tennebaun, and her small staff. As such, they have been booked all winter long.

The tavern downstairs is quaint, simple, and designed to be lively. It features sturdy oak wood tables set just far enough away from one another that patrons can have their own conversations within their groups, but close enough that it feels warm and crowded when full.

The staircase is made of birch wood, providing a light contrast to the deep brown of the tables and walls of the tavern it leads down to. At the foot of the stairs in the north-west corner of the room is a sitting area. There stand couches and chairs stuffed with sheep's wool, and a fireplace that seems to have been seldom extinguished the whole season. The floor of the tavern is carpeted intermittently by thick, simple grey, cloth rugs which help to accentuate the browns and trap the heat from the fire and candles set on the tables.

The bar is set against the east wall. Smooth and dark stone counters topped with sanded birch — accompanied by the shelves of wines and kegs of ale — sit below beautiful stained glass windows. On this morning — the 19th day of Echo's Stay, 55th year of the 3rd Era — the sun shines through the stained glass, painting the bar in splashes of red and gold, along with the natural light from the other windows bordering the tavern.

The room is jovial, with inn-stayers attending for their complimentary breakfast, and regular citizens visiting for their morning coffees. People sit in groups. At this point most of the patrons know each other even if they aren't locals. There is chatter in the air and a pair of bards have taken a bench to stand on against the north wall, and play a merry tune on a lute and a set of hand drums.

Voss Hallehwell sits at the bar on a high stool. He is tall for a human. Even while seated, he towers nearly half a foot above the elvish Ms. Tennebaun who stands behind the counter. Voss is not paying attention as the woman complains about the cold and the more rowdy patrons. Instead, he is listening to the room. The woman continues speaking regardless, unable to see his disinterest through the black and silver helmet he wears.

Most of the patrons are dressed in thick clothing to help buffer the chill. The fire helps heat the room greatly, but with people frequently entering for food and drink, and exiting for work, the cold creeps in against the flame.

Voss stands out from the crowd. He not only wears winter garb, but a full suit of armour. His thick cotton clothes are covered by a complete shirt of dark-dyed scale mail, covered by plate bracers, gauntlets, and greaves; smaller, fused-steel pauldrons; and his matching solid steel helmet, all of which glint in the morning light. Around his neck sits a ring of dark fur, attached to which is a long, burgundy cloak. The cloak was once a banner for house Ironheart, the house Voss fought for during his days as a soldier on Streboya. Now the house symbol has faded to patches of white paint against the deep red, and the banner has been fashioned to the man's back as an accent to his otherwise monotonous appearance.

His helmet is Streboyan design. It is sleek, with hints of elvish, human, and even goliath smithing techniques imbued in the crafted product. It has two horn-like protrusions that wrap around the crown. The faceplate is a black painted visage that resembles a grinning skull or demonic face, though the craft is as immaculate and interesting as it is frightening. The armour he wears, however, is not of Streboyan make; it was a gift from a job as a mercenary near the Krunixian capital. His old armour was left behind when he began his journey to Estrand, on a ship called 'Weathered Light', now just under a decade ago.

He finished his breakfast alone in his room twenty odd minutes ago, before returning to the tavern for some background noise. While he sticks out amongst the crowd in the tavern, he is paid little attention, as many of the other patrons have seen the figure before and learned to ignore — or accept — his presence. Voss is listening for any news through the din in the room. This is difficult without turning around, but his ears have always been perceptive and other forces help to hone his senses.

Since his arrival on Estrand he has worked as a bodyguard, mercenary, and with smaller adventuring and exploring guilds to keep the gold flowing into his pockets. His physique and training as a soldier have made him an asset in these situations and, until this winter, he has not had difficulty keeping himself eating reasonably well.

The cold months this year have hit everyone hard though. The first snowfall was early and, since then, green has not yet managed to fully pierce the white sheet. Voss' coin purse is lighter than it has been in several years.

This is the main reason he is listening so carefully to the room, and has been for several days now.

Across the area sits Peren Siannodel. He is positioned regally on one of the couches near the fire. His elven heritage is clear to any observer; his long black hair, slightly pointed ears, and sharp jawline and cheekbones give it away. His human parentage is less obvious, but — to someone who really looked at him — his face does not seem to be one or the other in terms of race, as the deep, brown eyes and well kept stubble are not often present on a pure-blood elf.

He is a half-elf. His father is Arryn Siannodel, mayor of Runehaven and Magistrate of the Runehaven township, which includes the outlying villages and the smaller town of Benton. His mother was a human noblewoman from Daroonga City whose name Peren never learned. His father treated him well enough, but he was an outcast among his siblings who were pure-blood high-elves born under his married mother Selussa.

Even within the elven homeland of Vruyoth to the west it is not uncommon for half-elves to be raised and treated as true-born children. It is due to elvish nature that one pure-blood elf can have no more than three pure-blood sons or daughters, and so both male and female elves tend to often take secondary, human lovers to birth children beyond what their nature allows.

Outside of Vruyoth, though, in The South and other such areas where pure-blood elves pride themselves more heavily on their unsoiled heritage, half-elves are not always treated with the same kindness by their parents, even if the laws state differently.

So, despite his 'equal' standing in Runehaven, he sought a better life for himself and left Southern Estrand in the summer, travelling by one of the few working airships to Krunix, then further north in search of a way to make a name for himself. He landed in Taernsby just before winter.

Peren is watching the room as Voss is, and for the same reason. He is nobility among the south, but here he is just a patron and — while he has retained enough gold to get him through another year — the creeping fear of poverty has struck his heart as well.

The half-elf has taken notice of the armoured human across the room. He has, in fact, been keeping an eye on the man all winter, noting the way he keeps to himself and hides his face. Normally this would strike Peren as someone who is untrustworthy, but for some reason the nobleman sees it as a sign of honour, or perhaps a sign of modesty instead of a show of power.

Voss noticed the half-elf as well. He saw him when he entered to get breakfast, when he returned from his room with his dish, and he has seen him frequently throughout the winter months. They have both stayed in the East Air since snowfall.

The relative stillness of the tavern is broken as a burly looking man rises from his chair near the centre of the room. His table is situated between the two log pillars that hold up the second floor. It is a long table with no head seats, their absence is replaced by the supports, as four chairs line either side. This table has been full of locals all morning, regulars to the tavern whose names have long been carved on the underside of their favourite wooden slab.

The man who stands is a balding fellow with a thick, dark grey beard. His stomach extends out beyond the buckle of his black, leather belt. He is holding a hammer in one hand and a bound stack of papers in the other. There is a brown satchel slung over his left shoulder that jingles with nails as he speaks.

"Alright, lads!" He exclaims, there is something in his voice that Voss and Peren can't quite pin. "I'm off to the day's work." The sentence is accompanied by a supportive chorus from two other men at the table and Ms. Tennebaun beginning to walk towards the group to clear his empty plate.

Peren and Voss both hear this exchange. Peren grabs a finely made, dark, woolen tunic that was folded nearby, and throws his arms through the sleeves as they both leave their individual seats. Voss has been eavesdropping on this group for a notable part of the morning and Peren is observant of clothing and posture. They both know that this man works for The Magistrate. He hangs official notices on message boards around town. The notices come from both The Magistrate himself, Harold Brenspire, or the town guard which has interesting job requests sent through Brenspire's staff.

The man walks towards the door of the tavern. Voss and Peren turn and begin following, each keeping their distance. They all exit the building, Peren just ahead of Voss.

The air outside is brisk. It fights through the layers of clothing that Voss and Peren are both wrapped in. Despite the end of winter drawing ever closer, there seems no signs thus far of warmth's return.

The man walks to the main street along a thin indent in the snow caused by the heavy foot traffic of the tavern-goers. The road has been kept clear, as well, of most snow; now it bears only a thin layer of ice and white fluff.

Peren and Voss continue to pursue the man as he sets foot onto the spacious roadway and begins to head towards the gate to Taernsby's town proper, where the closest notice board is located.

The East Air is positioned just outside of the town proper, and the southern wall, which wraps around the town centre. Only the thick wooden gate breaks the curtain of stone.

The surrounding area is lined with houses, varying in size and shape, that jut from the snow like islands in a sea. They are similar in material, all a mixture of local quarry-stone and woods, and wattle and daub, but their design and architecture shows stories of different races and families taking long term residence near this trading hub of the modern world.

When Voss is twenty paces away, with Peren just ahead, the door to the tavern opens again.

In the dining area was a figure wrapped in thick brown and black robes. He had been sitting near Voss at the bar, but his body language and garments were unassuming. Neither Voss nor Peren had paid him much attention despite doing their best to observe the whole scene.

This figure exits the building, following Voss. His face is only partially visible as Peren turns slightly to the sound of the door brushing through the snow and creaking on its hinges.

The pursuer is male. His skin is a deep burgundy, darker than Voss' cloak by a shade or two, and it has a leather-like appearance. Wrapped around his right leg is a long and thin tail that he is clearly not trying to hide. His eyes, visible from under the brim of his hood, are pure black orbs.

He is Thervos Kanuun. He is an demi-imp, a demon-born, a hell-spawn. His kind have many titles, none of them flattering. They are rare and, even now, they are feared by many people. It is for this reason among others that he has opted for a life full of isolation, and is not quite accustomed to being in a large town.

He comes to the Taernsby township from his small cabin to the northwest for most winters. He often stops in the villages nearby for supplies and spends the colder months in cheap inns, but this year even those are full and the only place he could find was the East Air near the proper. He booked it for the whole winter and has been working as a dock hand and clerk for a small goods shop to cover the cost. Recently, though, he was wrongly accused of thieving and was fired from both jobs, as no one would support his innocence.

Observing the same event as the others, he followed Voss from the bar and now slinks quietly along behind the large figure, who appears apathetic, which would be preferable to intolerance.

Behind Thervos, before the door can fully close again, exits a fourth. He stands slightly taller than the demon-born, but just under Peren's height of five feet and several inches. This last man wears a white cloak with a green patterned inside, reversible to camouflage in both wooded and winter environments.

This is Brael Silviari. Blonde hair and ice-blue eyes are visible past the hood he has placed over his head to block the wind.

Thervos watched him follow and now, with all four silently aware of each other, they continue after the man with the hammer and stack of papers. The man pays little attention as he leads them to the thick wooden notice board.

The board stands about seven feet tall, with the top foot devoted to public announcements that are not meant to be removed.

The notice man hammers a single message to the board, creating a new hole in the fresh wood, which was replaced at the end of summer due to heavy usage.

The four men watch patiently until The Magistrate's servant has finished his job and walks away from the board, whistling through his beard as he heads towards the south gate.

Peren moves first, briskly stepping towards the notice and promptly tearing the fine parchment from the wood, leaving the nail embedded.

He reads for several seconds before Voss approaches to stand over his left shoulder.

This makes Peren unnerved. "Can I help you?" the half-elf noble asks in an elegant and calm voice.

"What does it say?" Voss' voice is deep and only contains a hint of his Streboyan accent that has been slowly leaving him for the last decade.

"Nothing important," Peren responds, turning his body so the notice is further out of Voss' view.

"That's a public notice board, I believe I am allowed to view anything posted upon it."

"It's nothing important," Peren repeats, feigning disinterest. He crumples the notice into his pocket and begins to walk away. He gets ten paces before he stops, hearing the other three crunching through the snow after him. He turns to face them. "I will have you know that, as a member of nobility, my birthright alone allows me to act assume priority over this situation. This notice is none of your business as soon as it becomes mine."

"The note stated that The Magistrate was requesting aid on a personal matter and would like anyone with experience as a tracker, adventurer, or investigator to report to his manor during daylight," states Brael. His voice is monotonous and slow; he carefully articulates each word.

Voss looks to Brael. "How did you read that?"

Brael does not respond.

"This man is not incorrect, however it is still clearly not your business. I have experience and training with tracking and adventuring, and I will speak with The Mayor alone."

"I have experience in both as well," Brael says, once again carefully pronouncing each word.

"As do I," Voss agrees.

"Fine," Peren finally gives. "Accompany me if you wish, but I am the most qualified to speak with The Mayor and Magistrate of Taernsby as an emissary for Runehaven."

"Sure," Voss says. Peren begins to walk away. The others wait several seconds before following. Thervos turns to Voss as they drift to the back of the order.

"Kind of an ass, isn't he?" the demon-kin asks the armoured figure.

"I wouldn't let him hear you," responds Voss. "Something about him seems more than a simple nobleman. That does not mean I disagree however."

"He is," Brael speaks suddenly, nearly interrupting Voss, and a little too loudly. Voss is certain Peren heard, but the dark haired noble says nothing.

They pass in silence through the southern gate. The large wooden doors have stood open continuously since a few years into the third era.

The streets in the proper are wide and sporadic. Many areas, especially those closest to the walls, are not divided into blocks and streets, and are closer to bundles of houses and family owned shops.

They stick to the main roads, which are cleared of snow and cut through the jumble of buildings around them like jagged scars. They catch a wagon through the town centre where there isn't too much traffic. Their driver talks for the first few minutes about the winter and the interesting travellers he's met recently, but, as no one responds much, he grows quiet as well. They pass a large bonfire burning near the winter skating rink. It crackles loudly and is surrounded by a cluster of people staying warm. Near the fire the town guard has set up a collection of tables and chairs where people are making and serving hot food and drink.

The trip through town takes just under an hour and a half and soon the wagon drops them off for a silver piece near the western gate.

The lands outside of the westernmost wall are largely devoted to farming. Small houses, barns, and fenced fields span the area almost to the horizon where woods envelop civilization again.

It is another twenty minutes of walking from the western gate to The Magistrate's manor. They move without speaking. They pace along the dirt and gravel roads, covered with snow, listening to the crunching their boots make. Many of the farm plots that they pass by have been cleared of snow so that growing winter crops can continue, but some have remained unattended and blend seamlessly into the rolling hills of white that drape over the countryside.

The log walls that encase Harold Brenspire's manor draw ever closer, beginning to loom far above their heads as they climb the small rise upon which the compound is built.

The gate to the manor stands closed, but a figure can be seen atop the wall. Before they reach close enough for the gatekeeper's identity to be discerned, Peren holds his hand into the air, signalling a stop. The group obeys this command.

"Since you have decided to trail along against my best wishes, please offer me the sympathy of letting me do the speaking," the half-elf pleads to no answer.

They continue their approach. The figure on the wall is wrapped in thick hides and furs, but is clearly small in stature.

"Hail!" the man calls in a squeaky voice, forcing volume. "Who approaches?"

"Peren Siannodel!" the noble calls back.

"Accompanied by Voss Hallehwell!" adds the soldier.

"What is your business with The Mayor?" the person, likely a gnome, asks when no one else calls up.

"There was a notice posted this morning. I am here in response!"

"*We* are here," Voss adds quietly as the gate-keeper disappears behind the wall.

"Listen," Peren says, still refusing to face the others, "if you want any hope of working with me on this, I am going to need you to begin respecting my authority." The half-elf explains this calmly, as though addressing a child.

"If you want to command my respect, you will need to earn that right, as anyone else would," Voss responds with an equally relaxed tone.

"This notice is free to be seen by anyone," a voice that no one recognizes interjects from behind them all. The tone is articulate and commanding.

The four turn suddenly to face the new voice. Thervos, then Voss, then Peren. Brael turns last despite being closest. Standing before them is a pale man with bleached-white hair. He is clad is scale mail, similar to Voss' in protective ability, but with a design reflecting its manufacturing in the Dabarisian capital of Daroonga City, as opposed to in Krunix by dwarven smiths.

The man looks slowly at the other four, who peer back at him, confused.

"How long have you been standing there?" questions Peren.

"Several minutes now, same as you," he answers. "I have been walking with you since near the western gate. You seemed content in silence however, I wouldn't wish to break that."

"What is your name?" Brael asks suddenly.

"Evandur Angelthorn," the man calmly responds.

"Unimportant," Peren decides. "On your chestplate you display the insignia of Valkronus, you carry an ornate longsword on your side, and you stand with pride. You are a paladin. I wish not pick a fight, and would be happy to have proper company."

"We are not proper company?" Thervos is appalled by this.

"How did you get the notice?" Brael asks, ignoring the others.

"I was informed by the church, and happened to travel the same way as you. I was not even sure that we had the same destination until you began to walk up the slope to the manor," the paladin replies.

Before anyone else can speak, the sound of the wooden gate creaking shatters the silence. The group turns again to face the log walls as the doorway opens, shoving thin layers of fresher snow aside, even revealing some stone tiles of the road beneath.

"You may enter!" the gate-keeper calls out. It is a high and nasally voice. He has removed his hood and is clearly a gnomish man. He smiles politely at the group as they make their way through the walls.

Peren has regained his composure, and despite the arguments, the others push on after him into the outside courtyard of the manor.

The courtyard is made of a centre square of tiled stones, with a small birdbath and several benches around it. Outside this square are small plots of dirt for growing herbs and flowers and an open yard likely used to host summer parties. There is a long building near the gate that is most obviously designed to house The Mayor's servants, though it looks to be well constructed and insulated.

There are several guards, who have stood straight and alert at the presence of guests, but beside several of them are small tables with steaming mugs, and the beards of two men are coated with the sheen of tea or ale.

They walk in line. Peren at the front, Voss, Thervos, and Brael following, and finally the new face of Evandur Angelthorn bringing up the rear.

Evandur is a paladin of the God of Life and Rebirth, as Peren correctly described. He has been with the church of Valkronus for his entire life, being left as an orphan on the steps of one of the God's churches in Layefayre as an infant.

He moves frequently, doing missions for the church across Estrand, but has had some time to himself this winter being stuck in Taernsby like everyone else. He has taken it upon himself to be helpful to the citizens here and The Mayor's notice intrigued him, and the church, like it did the other four.

The gnome beckons them onward down the stone pathway towards The Mayor's manor itself. The building looks large, but is only two storeys and was hidden beneath the log wall from the outside. The walls are a white painted wood, which blend into the snowy yard surrounding it save for the corners, which are round logs painted a near black in contrast.

They climb a short set of three white and grey marble stairs to the porch, a foot off the stone patio area. On the porch, the gnomish servant uses a metal door knocker to sound their arrival.

From within the house comes the sound of heavy footsteps on stairs. They descend towards the ground floor until they draw level with the group. Six more footfalls until the handle on the door begins to rotate clockwise, and then the door is pulled open, inward.

Standing in the frame behind the gnomish servant is a dwarven man. He is thickly built with large arms and legs, and wears finely made brown woolen pants and a white cotton shirt which displays his beer gut. He stands roughly four and a half feet in height and peers up at the group through weary, but alert eyes.

His dark hair has been put in a tight ponytail down his back and his beard was clearly recently trimmed, but is slowly growing ragged again.

"You are all here in response to the notice?" the dwarf asks in a deep and steady voice.

"Indeed," Peren speaks elegantly, hiding distaste. "You must be Mayor Brenspire."

"I am. And you are?" he asks. The gnome stands aside to allow Brenspire to step onto the porch. His hairy feet are uncovered but he does not appear bothered by the cold of the stone.

"I am Peren Siannodel, these are my associates."

"Siannodel?" The Mayor asks thoughtfully. "I believe I recognize the name, but I cannot quite place it."

"My father is-"

"South!" The Mayor exclaims, cutting Peren off, and confusing him slightly. "You are from The South. Not Southpoint though, I make regular correspondence with The Mayor and Magistrate there, so your family must run Runehaven."

"You are correct," Peren responds, smiling. "My father is magistrate of the Runehaven township."

"I have heard great things of Runehaven from my friend Favren," The Mayor smiles at Peren. It is one of relief. "Please, come in, all of you. There is much to discuss, and we shall not do it in the cold." The Mayor turns and heads into the house again. The others look to each other briefly, then follow.

Chapter Two – A Quest

3Eo55, 19th of Echo's Stay

The Mayor leads them into his home. Everyone — especially Voss and Evandur, who are wearing heavy armour — can feel the shift in temperature. The fire pulses through the building in waves, warming the frozen hands and feet of the five visitors.

The building is well insulated. Its thick walls are stuffed with sheep's wool, sawdust, and hay, and built two layers thick. The inside is spacious, with the main hallway — which runs down the length of the first floor — being wide and tall enough for someone larger than Voss by a foot to stand in comfortably.

They follow Mayor Brenspire down this hall. The first door on the left stands ajar to a comfortable looking sitting room. In there are several chairs and a couch, all dyed a forest green leather, with wooden accents made from the same fine mahogany as the low table between them. The table holds an ornate metal candelabra and several books. On the wall farthest from the hallway is set a large hearth. Within, a fire is burning furiously to bat away the chill that climbs through the closed windows in the room. The hall narrows after this sitting area, still tall but not wide enough to walk more than two by two. The change comes from the stairs that branch upwards to the left of the space, and are cut off from the rest of the house on either side by the sitting room wall on the left and a simple dividing wall on their right.

Further down, on their right, are two more doors. The closest is the one they enter, emerging into a dining room decorated with paintings of dwarven men and women, likely The Magistrate's family, and natural scenery including the ocean and the unmistakable trees of the Vruyothy woods. The table in the room is long, made to hold up to sixteen people, with seven chairs on each side and one at each head. As they enter they can see and smell, through a set of swinging doors, the kitchen, which adjoins the room and would be accessible through the second door in the hallway. Food is being prepared, as evidenced by the stream of flavours wafting into the dining hall through a small, white door between the chambers.

"It is near time for brunch," The Mayor speaks. He has walked to the table head closest to the kitchen doors. He pulls the chair away and sits himself down. "Can I offer anyone tea or a serving of soup and bread? I am certain there will be enough."

The group declines politely, having already eaten their own meals earlier. They sit themselves at the table however, feeling obliged to join The Mayor. Peren walks to the other head of the table, taking a position of power and balancing the room, Voss and Evandur sit opposite each other closest to The Mayor, Thervos sits beside Voss, and Brael takes a seat between Evandur and Peren in the middle of the table.

Soon an elven man dressed in white cloth enters the room through the thin door between the kitchen and dining area, and brings The Mayor a tray topped with steaming soup of an orange colour, a cup of green tea, and servings of milk and sugar. As he enters, Brael visibly shifts his posture away, reaching below the table. Peren watches the blonde man's hand find the hilt of a dagger and debates saying something, but instead favours letting it play out. Soon the elven servant withdraws calmly from the room and back into the kitchen, causing Brael to relax only slightly. The Mayor does not seem to notice, nor does anyone else but Voss, who only witnesses the change in attitude, and Peren's subtle reaction.

Brael keeps his hood over his face, and Voss does not doff his helmet, but the others politely remove their hoods and cloaks. Even Thervos fully reveals his leathery face. His dark black eyes watch the others with mild suspicion.

The Mayor is not taken aback in the slightest by anyone's actions. He has added the milk and sugar to his cup while the others sat. Now he calmly takes a sip from his tea, places his bread in the soup with his other hand, lets it soak, and removes it again before taking a bite. He does all this with a natural politeness and regal nature that doesn't seem forced.

"I would be content with knowing your names," The Mayor breaks the silence.

They introduce themselves, to the benefit of both The Mayor and each other, as they have not yet made their own official greetings either.

Knowing the identities of one another, The Mayor takes another short sip of his tea, adding a half spoon of sugar to it, and stirs while he continues speaking.

"Are you certain you don't want a cup of tea? It's quite nice."

"Yes, Mayor Brenspire," Peren answers for the group from across the table. "We simply wish to offer aid to you and your town while we are staying here. I personally have been taking a spot in the East Air Inn and Tavern all winter, and I know that Voss here," he gestures to the dark, scale-armoured man, "has done the same. We feel it right to help with any matter that troubles a town that has been so generous to us in such a harsh winter."

"And I need coin," Voss states plainly. He feels Peren's glare, but does not acknowledge it.

"Both valid reasons," The Mayor says after a spoon of soup which trickles slightly into his growing beard. "I thank you for your kindness, sir Siannodel, and for your honesty, sir Hallehwell. You are all in my home and you have come to my aid. Please do me the favour then of calling me Harold, it would be less formal and the matter I need assistance with is devoid of much formality."

"Should you call me Peren, sir, I would happily oblige that request," The noble says.

Harold nods slowly. "Pleasure to make your acquaintance, Peren, and all of you. I can assure you that what I ask of you will help both the community and your coin bags."

"I must now ask," Evandur joins the conversation, much to the dismay of Peren, "what is this trouble you face?"

"We are certainly willing to keep this all discreet, as I assume that is of importance," the dark haired half-elf adds.

"It is. Thank you," The Mayor says.

Harold takes a moment to pick his words while he chews another bite of bread. After he swallows it, with another short sip of tea, he addresses the group again.

"My servants' quarters have in them ten double bunks, room for twenty," his words are quiet, but loud enough to reverberate through the room.

"There is a fireplace and chests large enough for all of one's belongings if they're organized well. It's a comfortable place where my workers live without rent or tax and are paid a silver a day for farm work and two a day for skills beyond that. Enough to live by and save." He pauses. "At the end of fall, all but one bed was taken. A month ago I had seventeen servants checking in for everyday work, and now I have twelve," The Mayor finishes.

"We can safely assume they did not simply quit then?" Voss asks rhetorically.

"Indeed. My servants may quit as they please, and none have done so since late summer when I went from twenty to nineteen. If they had run for any reason they would be free to go, but the guards or other servants would have told me. If they were hurt or worse they would have been found by the watch," he is speaking calmly, but there is worry in his deep voice. "They simply disappeared. I have been so busy organizing trade and keeping the town simply running that I have not had time to organize outside help until now. The guards were notified but none have reported anything."

"So you want us to find them?" Evandur asks.

"If the guards have searched the town then they would have found anything we could have," Voss argues.

"The guards searched the town and kept an eye out, but I asked that they not go breaking down doors or investigating on my behalf as it could cause suspicion," Harold responds.

"You suspect foul play," Brael interjects thoughtfully.

"I do. I have no evidence, but I simply cannot see them all deciding to leave one by one. I think something is happening to them. The other servants are worried as well, but they have not seen anything. The ones who went missing either vanished overnight despite watches being kept, or went out for a normal days work and never returned. Missing persons reports have increased since autumn as well, but I had not thought it linked until recently, as the increase was marginal at most."

Voss and Peren think back to the man with the notices. They thought there was something about the way he discussed work. It was worry. The way he walked with them following him, not speaking or making eye contact. He was afraid he was being tailed.

As they continue, Brenspire begins scrawling on several pieces of parchment that he pulls from a pocket in his pants.

"So you want us to be the ones breaking down doors instead of the town watch?" Voss asks bluntly, returning to his original question.

"I want you to dig something up," The Mayor responds coolly, understanding the positives of going straight for the point. "I was hoping the problem would be solved in a less complicated manner, but it's growing dire, and I need closure. Preferably you can gather leads and evidence without causing a scene," Harold explains further. "If you decide to help, I will pay this group an advance of fifty golden lions to help with the investigation. When you find something, or, if after two weeks time you turn up nothing, I will give a minimum of fifty more gold pieces."

They stare at The Mayor in silence, thinking the same thought. One hundred golden lions would easily be enough to carry them through the rest of winter comfortably, even if the coins were divided between all five of them.

"Your discrepancy and utmost care would be vastly appreciated," The Mayor says soberly, "but you will carry documents allowing you to act on my behalf if and how you see fit."

"I will treat this professionally," Peren says.

"We will," Evandur corrects, solidifying everyone's participation in the job.

"Then it is settled," Harold says. "I have no need to continue looking. I have found my detectives, and Roahl will take down the notices he just put up. You also have my permission to search my own property and question my servants, though I have searched every inch of this manor myself."

Then, one by one, led by Peren, the group stands. Harold rises to meet them. He hands each of them one of the small squares of parchment he had been writing on. Every piece bears his wax signet and a small message stating their ability to work with his authority. They each shake Harold's hand on their way from the dining room. Evandur is the last to leave. He is given a pouch full of coins and a weary smile. They then return to the porch. Thervos shivers as the cold hits his face and his breath paints the air briefly with steam.

"We should start by talking to the servants in the quarters. We'll see if they have noticed or seen anything they didn't admit to The Mayor," Voss states, grey wisps breaking through the thin openings in his helmet with every word.

"I disagree," Peren states.

"Of course you d-" Voss begins, but he is interrupted.

"With what?" Brael asks, confused.

"Did you not hear the armoured giant speaking?" Peren looks incredulously at the blonde half-elf, still wearing his cloak over his head.

"No," Brael responds plainly.

There is a bewildered silence for a few moments.

Brael takes his hands to either side of his hood and pulls it down off his head, revealing a lack of ears. Instead, where they would be is covered by scarred and stitched layers of skin which have been tattooed over with black ink in the shape of eyes, complete with staring red pupils where the holes should be.

"You're deaf?" Voss asks bluntly.

Peren sighs. "You're deaf?" he restates.

"Yes," Brael nods.

Everyone is quiet for a moment. Peren shifts his head so only Brael can see and mouths the following: 'I need you to wait at the gate for me. I am going to ask the chef some questions.'

Brael nods.

"You may go on ahead," Peren says to the others. "I wish to speak with The Mayor for a little longer, I will catch up with you somewhere afterward."

"Alright, we will start at the servants' quarters," Voss says. "If you aren't done by the time we are, we may leave without you."

"That is fine with me," Peren responds, reserved.

"Then it's settled, let us be on with it," Evandur says. "The cold is not something I wish to stand still in any longer."

They split, Peren returning through the door into the white home of The Magistrate, and the others descending the marble steps back onto the stone patio in the yard. With the thought of gold in everyone's minds, and a question that genuinely intrigues them to accompany, they set off for answers and to seek reward for solving this mystery.

Chapter Three – An Investigation

3Eoss, 19th of Echo's Stay

Peren strides through the hall again, stopping near the dining room door. The Mayor looks up in surprise from his nearly finished meal.

"Did you need something else?" Harold asks.

"I wish to search the main floor of your house, and perhaps ask the cook a few questions as well," Peren does not hide his intentions. He levels his gaze to The Mayor's eyes, a rare occurrence for the half-elf.

"You think you will find something?"

"It's a possibility that I believe we cannot quite ignore yet," Peren responds.

Harold thinks. "That is reasonable," the dwarf admits. "Try to avoid creating a mess while you look around, but you have my permission certainly, as I have already stated," The Magistrate smiles politely and pulls a book from beside his chair, pushing his tray aside.

Peren nods and continues down the hallway. He stops quietly in front of the kitchen door. He collects his thoughts for a minute and decides what to say before drawing a deep breath and entering calmly.

He pushes steadily against the door, which swings smoothly open to reveal a large and well composed room. There are plenty of counters, a preparation table in the centre, and the tiles are a deep brown to contrast the white furniture, similar to the outside walls. At a large and burning wood stove stands the elven man who brought Brenspire his soup and tea. He is dressed in the white outfit befitting a chef of some degree.

He has set aside some soup in a metal container with a handle and is now in the process of cleaning the room.

"The meal was quite good," Peren states, trying to sound enthusiastic.

The cook spins around, surprised by the voice. "Th-the meal? The soup?" he asks. He has soft brown hair that is tied behind his head in a bun, and his stubble is short, barely noticeable, even shorter than Peren's in length.

"Yes, the soup," Peren responds condescendingly, then changes gears again. "You made it quite well."

"I didn't set you a plate," the cook says, then, seeing Peren's obvious disgust in the comment: "S-sorry sir, just confused. Thank you very much." The man bows low.

"I was curious about the sauces and spices you added. Would you show them to me, or tell me about them?" Peren asks, straining to make the smile on his lips seem natural. He is trying to obscure any hint of prying.

"Oh! Sure! I didn't pin you for an avid chef, if you don't mind my saying so," the cook replies as he hurries to a cupboard to the left of the metal stove. He opens it and begins sorting through bottles and jars.

"I am not proficient in the art, but I was taught well by my father and my own servant staff when I was younger," Peren explains, using his words to further authority over the man. "I know basics and enough about seasoning and flavour. I simply noted, even by smell, that your soup is no average broth."

"Well," the cook is flattered, "I added some thyme, rosemary, and crestleaf oil." He pulls the ingredients, two small herb jars and a bottle, from the cupboard and sets them on the counter.

"Crestleaf oil?" Peren asks. This time his interest is genuine.

"Indeed. You know of it?"

"Of course, I just didn't expect the addition."

The chef chuckles. "I add plenty of unexpected twists to my dishes. It's why Magistrate Brenspire chose me as the head chef and butler."

"Crestleaf is a dangerous plant though, is it not?" Peren asks, seeming to make conversation.

"Not in small amounts. It has an excellent, if not intense, flavour when boiled in a broth. If you drank a mouth full of the extract in this bottle you could be seriously ill, quite rough off without attention, but a spoonful can really be a benefit," the chef explains as he brings the bottle to Peren. "Here, breath it, and then tell me it isn't beautiful."

Peren indulges the man by inhaling the scent. It smells of mint and lavender, if it were comparable to any common plants. The aroma is intense and almost overbearing, especially to his acute half-elven sense of smell, but it is also quite lovely in some regards. Peren can genuinely see the elf's knowledge of cuisine.

The nobleman simply nods in response before continuing. "Does The Mayor treat you well?"

The elf pauses for a moment, but finds his answer quickly. "He treats me with respect. He pays well enough and the living conditions are better than they well could be, if not a little cramped."

"Cramped?" Peren asks.

"Indeed. I mean, I am not sure if you've ever had to spend every night with twenty other-" the cook pauses again. Then, slowly and quietly: "Well, with a group of other people in the same room, as it were."

"Do you cook for them?" Peren asks, acting oblivious to the man's pain.

"Who? The other servants?"

Peren nods.

"Occasionally, yeah. We usually rotate or just eat whatever leftovers I made so they don't go to waste or so we don't have to buy ourselves groceries."

"You buy your own food sometimes?"

"Indeed, there are plenty of shops in town. There are even some good general stores, and fresh vegetable stands outside, mixed about the farmland."

"Did you buy any of these ingredients yourself?" Peren questions.

The cook musters a smile. "Yes, actually, I bought all of them. I get paid an extra two coppers a day and I don't let that go to waste. I like my job, and I love my family."

"Family?" Peren is confused.

"Friends, family. To me, I never had much blood family, but I grew with the others here for nearly ten years now and, well, I'm sorry, it's not much important."

"I'm sorry," Peren states, being as empathetic as he can.

"Thank you," the man grimaces as tears threaten his eyes. He tilts his head downward.

"Listen," Peren says softly, "I would like to buy that bottle of crestleaf oil off you. I have a gold coin with your name on it if you pass it right now, and don't mention it to anyone else."

The cook looks up, life in his eyes. "Deal. Done."

"Buy your family, or yourself, something worthwhile," Peren says. He trades a coin from his coat pocket for the near full bottle of extract. "Thank you."

"No, thank *you*, sir," The cook stumbles, enveloped by the shiny circle of metal in his hands.

Peren turns and leaves quietly. His suspicion proved infantile and fruitless. He hoped this lead would circumvent the need to speak with the other servants entirely. If the chef had nothing to do with it — and Peren was fairly certain now that he didn't — then he had only succeeded in wasting time, and also missing out on being able to question the other servants. Poison is the most common weapon in a large town like Taernsby. It is harder to trace and versatile enough to debilitate a person enough to remove them quietly.

He could follow up by checking the shops the cook had mentioned, but the way the man acted and spoke made Peren believe that there was no foul play involved within the servants themselves, at least not to the elf's knowledge. The lack of surface level information to be gained in private means that the investigation will likely be more difficult, and require more stops, and digging through town is not befitting of a noble.

The promise of gold could be invaluable, though, and while Peren does not want to appear desperate, he does need a boost to his purse. The added bonus of forming a trusting relationship with the magistrate of a prominent township, one that has two separate port locations in regular trade routes, makes the deal all that much sweeter. Peren steels himself, reclaiming his calm and stern expression from one of annoyance. He struts back onto the porch to see Brael standing near the gate, alone.

"Great," he mutters. "They have gone already."

The half-elves meet each other in the centre, near the frozen fountain.

"What happened?" Peren speaks, though the deaf companion only tracks his lip movements.

"They entered the servants quarters, asked their questions, and left," Brael responds.

"What did they ask?" Peren is annoyed by the lack of clear description and detail, and even does his best to over exaggerate his words to make reading them easier.

"They asked a human with dark brown hair what he knew about the disappearances. The response suggested he knew nothing, and that they all left at some point seemingly ordinarily. They have been disappearing since the end of fall, and more recently they have been going almost at regular intervals of two to three weeks. Just enough time to begin relaxing." Brael is not quite done talking when Peren ask his question.

"Did he notice anything at all?"

"Yes. He thinks some of them may have been sick, feeling ill. Stomach pains, he thought. He had heard groaning several nights from the last two to go missing, but they had all been with the flu this winter."

"Do any of the servants feel sick now?"

"No."

"Where are the others?"

"They went to town. The paladin, Evandur, said something about a clinic near the north-western square, thirty minutes from the docks," Brael is still speaking as Peren walks by him towards the manor gate.

The noble turns his head so Brael can see his mouth. "Let's go."

It is possible that the stomach pains could relate to the crestleaf oil, and that maybe Peren was not wrong about the poison. But the thought is once again dismissed by how full the bottle is, and that The Mayor would have also felt ill. Peren shrugs his suspicion of the staff once again, but keeps his knowledge of poisons present in his mind as he starts a brisk walk down the hill towards the farmland.

Nearly fifteen minutes later — and several minutes down the road from the pair of half-elves — Voss, Evandur, and Thervos are approaching the town proper.

"Do you think this doctor Eralius really has something to do with it?" Thervos asks. With the gate still a good ten minutes away, he is trying to bridge the silence. The human they spoke to mentioned hearing the name, but Thervos would barely consider it a lead.

"I think it's worth a brief stop. We have two weeks until we are paid regardless," Voss says.

"I pinned you for the type to take the money and run," Evandur says.

"I don't have the money," Voss responds, eyeing the new bag on the paladin's belt

"You plan on investigating regardless is what I meant," Angelthorn speaks.

"I got paid for a job; I will do what I was paid for."

"That's honourable."

"It shouldn't be. It should be commonplace."

They walk in silence for a few more minutes.

"Evandur," Voss suddenly begins, something different in his voice, "If we are working together, I feel I should know more about you. Therefore, I must ask - why is your hair as it is? You do not have an old face, and yet it's white as snow."

"This is actually something I was curious about as well." Thervos echoes.

Evandur is shocked for a moment. "I was born with it."

"That's it?" Voss asks.

"There is more, but that's not something I trust to those I do not know well enough," Evandur responds.

"I respect that," Voss says, his voice returning to a flat cadence.

Evandur takes the bag from his belt, counts out ten coins for himself, ten for Voss and ten for Thervos and hands them to his companions.

"I trust you both," the paladin speaks, not making eye contact.

"I still know little about you, yet I trust you more than I trust the nobleman," Voss says. "Though, I suppose that doesn't mean a whole lot."

Evandur cracks a smile, but says nothing in response.

They pass through the western gate once more, and into the heart of Taernsby. Soon, they turn to their left and up a wide street into the open town square.

They are in the south-west corner of the large centre. Frost covered stone slabs stretch out into the distance, and beyond the edge of the square — barely visible through layers of homes and warehouses — can be seen the salt-filled, tumultuous waters of Wrofyhx's Expanse. Nearest to the investigators are a variety of churches dedicated to the Gods. One to Valkronus, God of Life and Rebirth, and one to Horan, God of Wisdom and — as some would say — Compassion. There is also a larger Polytheistic Church for general prayer or worship to any God with no established church in Taernsby.

The polytheistic churches were established in every Dabarisian town early in the second era and every town in the council lands has created one as well. They provide a means to worship all Gods without needing to devote additional resources to building a whole second church. Buildings and shrines to specific gods are common in any town - in smaller buildings or one's own home. For any additional church to be built, though, there must be funding and, in turn, a large enough following of that God in the area to warrant the construction.

"There," Voss says. His vision draws him to the clinic despite its distance. It is a large enough building nestled between the Polytheistic Church and the Church to Valkronus. They approach, nearing the front-facing wall, wattle and daub painted white, with deep-brown accents along the sills and frames of the door and two windows. From within, they see candles burning, and the sign hanging on the door reads: 'Enter.'

Evandur speaks. "When we are inside, let me do the talking. I am a paladin of Valkronus, and, because of that, the people of the town should show us respect without even needing to know our affiliation with The Mayor."

Thervos nods. Voss says nothing. He hears Evandur speak, but there is something pounding in the back of his head that steals his focus. His muscle memory simply allows him to continue following the paladin.

"Voss," comes a thin voice in the man's mind, "it could be a trap." Voss knows that this voice is not from anyone around him, and, though he knows who it belongs to, it comes from within himself. It is a man's voice; a human with a Streboyan accent. It is a wispy sound, like it is being called through a long tunnel, but it hurts Voss like a battering ram against his eardrums. Guilt racks him for a moment but he shows no sign of it.

"Give the man a break," a woman's voice responds to the first, also sounding distant and muffled.

"Oh yes, a break, Val. We've given him a damn long break already," the original voice retorts.

"He's trying, Nhasan," the woman, Val, speaks softly. Voss has heard those words before, whispered over a camp fire. He remembers them so clearly. Tears well in his eyes, but he shakes his head clear and returns to reality.

In the distance, the same bonfire that was burning on their way through the square an hour ago still glows bright with flame. The figures surrounding it have changed, shuffled as people move about their day. The square is full of folk milling about, gathering soups and warm drinks from the tables around the area and huddling by the fire to chat with the others, or simply to take a break from the piercing winds and frigid air.

Evandur leads as the three push into the clinic through the small door, escaping into a well heated room with a hearth lit to the left.

The clinic is quaint compared to its surroundings, only being a single storey with the addition of a small basement. Its supports are made mainly from wood, and no signs of masonry can be seen. There are four separate chambers for treating patients, housing a total of eight. The room they stand in now is a reception area. It is not spacious. This would remain true even if it were empty of furnishings. The group feels almost crowded by the hearth, a handful of chairs, and a big desk against the opposite wall a few meters away.

Behind the desk sits a tall, muscular man with dark green skin, short black hair and a heavy bone structure. His jaw is sharp, and from between his lips, which are pursed in deep focus, protrude two large, tusk-like teeth.

He is wearing a thick and warm looking cotton tunic over some thinner, beige, cloth garments. His clothes befit someone with a comfortable but common life, and they barely house his muscular form.

"Excuse me, sir," Evandur opens. This causes the man to look up expectantly.

"Welcome!" says the man, closing a leather bound book. He is an obvious descendant of human and orcish parents. "Are you in need of a room and treatment?" he then asks. There is worry in his gruff, bellowing voice.

"No, luckily. We are simply needing to speak with the doctor here. Eralius I believe."

"Ah," the half-orc responds. "He has been away for several days. I am looking after the patients until his return."

"Interesting, do you know where doctor Eralius went?" Voss speaks up, having recovered fully from what happened outside.

"I apologize, sirs, but what is your business with the doctor?"

Evandur answers. "I'm a paladin with the Church of Valkronus. That information is sensitive, but I assure you that it is nothing you need concern yourself with." There is silence, causing Evandur to offer more. "We have reason to believe he may have information pertaining to a crime."

The half-orc thinks. "Fine," he says. "I will help where I can. Voran went on a brief fishing trip, he does so occasionally."

"Voran?" Voss asks.

"Voran Eralius. The doctor."

"Right."

There is a pause.

"Are there any patients in right now?" Evandur asks.

"One, yes. Head wound."

"So when will Eralius return?" Voss asks.

"He should be back within a few days, he is never gone too long."

"Are you close with the doctor then?" Voss presses.

"Lots of questions," the half-orc muses. "No. He took me on as a secretary and nurse at the end of summer."

"No previous secretary?" Thervos asks.

"The clinic had been closed during spring when the older man who was running the place retired. Voran came in from Vruyoth near the end of summer and bought the place out for a good deal," there is palpable caution in the nurse's voice now.

"Hm," Thervos hums, turning to the others. He speaks in a hushed voice. "This doctor Eralius does seem to sound increasingly suspicious."

"Indeed," Evandur agrees. "We shouldn't call for an arrest, but this is worth investigating thoroughly."

The others nod.

"We should find where he went and follow, perhaps question those at the docks," Voss suggests.

"We should search the clinic too. There could be evidence around the building, or personal documents," Evandur says.

"Let's just start here and move to the docks," Thervos breaks up the discussion.

Before they can do anything however, the sound of the door opening beside them takes their attention. Shivering slightly from the cold and pulling the hoods from their heads are Brael and Peren. They enter the room as the half-orc is just returning to his book.

"You left without me, I saw," Peren notes monotonously to the group.

"We said we would," Voss replies, equally apathetic. "Did you learn anything?"

"I spoke with the cook. I have no reason to suspect any of the servants or The Mayor himself to be behind it," Peren responds quietly.

"You suspected The Mayor?" Evandur is shocked, whispering his response.

"Everyone is guilty until proven innocent. Besides, the best way to absolve yourself of suspicion is to pretend to be contributing to its solution, but I believe your lead on the doctor is well founded and so I followed suit. Is there anything to note?"

"Who are all of you, exactly?" the secretary asks. "I can let a paladin investigate and ask questions but clearly you are not all servants of Valkronus, or, if you are, this is a lot bigger than I was led to believe."

"That's not quite your business," Peren states flatly.

"It is when five men turn up in my work place to volley questions at me and then huddle in a circle by the door," the half-orc retorts, nearly getting up from his seat.

"You know not to whom you wag your tongue," Peren practically spits the words at the man.

"Peren!" Voss raises his voice. "Stand down. You're a noble from the south, but — last I was aware — the Dabarisian Empire was a free people, and this man saves the lives of those free people."

"It is not our place to hold authority over the public, lest it is for a good reason," Evandur agrees with Voss.

Peren stares around him, incredulous. He finally turns back to the secretary and, in a more reasonable voice, states: "Fine, sir, we are working with The Mayor. We need your cooperation for questioning and the searching of this building." The noble pulls his parchment square from his coat's inside pocket and, stepping forward, waves it in front of the half-orc's face.

"You have permission. I am not the doctor however, just a nurse and secretary," the man responds sternly.

"That matters not. Keep this quiet, as it's a personal matter, and in return we will not cause any trouble," Peren states. It is not a threat, but neither is it polite.

"If we want to cover the most ground, now that we're back together, it may be best to split up," Evandur says.

"It's not that big a building," Peren is confused.

"The docks. Voran Eralius may have left for a fishing trip," Voss explains.

Peren nods.

"Excellent," Evandur commands attention. "Voss, stay with me and search here, everyone else take to the docks."

"I do not wish to walk across town in the freezing cold to go searching through business ledgers and gather testimonies from drunken fishermen," Peren sounds appalled.

"And we do not wish for you to remain here," Voss retorts, grinning behind his helmet.

"I am staying. Brael and the imp can handle the docks," the noble says with finality.

"Imp?" Thervos asks, hurt and feeling angered.

"Demon-spawn," Peren corrects himself.

"Thervos," The robed man presses.

"Sure," Peren shrugs. "They can handle the docks." He turns to Brael. "Take him to the docks and find any information you can. Be back within two hours."

Brael nods and turns to leave. Thervos stares angrily at Peren for a long second. When he realizes the noble will not dignify a look back, he spins and shoves through the door with near enough force to crack it, back into the snow.

"Found yourself a servant in the north, half-elf?" Voss mutters. There is anger in his voice as well, though Peren ignores it.

"Just someone who knows a leader when he sees one, helmet," Peren replies.

"What's a half-elf doing in Runehaven's nobility anyway?" Voss presses. "Last I heard, Runehaven's hierarchy was all pure-blooded elves."

Peren suddenly spins and levels a finger to Voss' covered face. "You know nothing of what you speak. You are not-"

"Enough!" Evandur pushes between them. "Can we please just do our job so we can take our money and leave?"

"Fine," Peren and Voss say simultaneously.

The half-orc, almost afraid to say anything, speaks up. "You may search any room, including the basement and storage - so long as things are put back the way Voran left them. Please be quick and if you speak with the patient, Charles, do not disturb him long, as he needs rest."

"I will search the basement," Evandur says. "If there is anything to hide, it would be there."

"I will speak with the patient," Peren says.

"I will as well," Voss glances at Peren. Despite the look of disdain he gets from the noble, he begins walking towards the door behind the half-orc's desk marked 'Patients.'

Evandur watches as Peren reluctantly follows. He then thanks the half-orc profusely. He is shown to the door on the other side of the desk marked 'Basement and Storage.' He finds the trapdoor which leads down. It is locked.

The half-orc opens the door behind Evandur again, and hands him a key.

"Eralius didn't want me to go down there, but he leaves this in the desk," the man says nothing else, leaving the small room to return to his book.

Voss pulls open the door to the patient's room, the only one in which a fire is burning. Inside the chamber are two small beds, each with a side table. On the right of the door is a large, rough-wood shelf with some reading material. They are mostly books written by adventurers and bards, but some histories and arcane studies as well catch Voss' eye. A large mirror is hung against the ceiling opposite the beds, filling the space above the fireplace. The beds are separated by a thin white sheet hanging from the ceiling, and the one closest to Voss and Peren is empty. Light trickles into the room through a wide window against the far wall.

The pair walk around the sheet and see the thin man lying under the blankets in the other cot. His eyes are closed and around his forehead is a tightly wrapped bandage.

"Excuse me, sir?" Peren asks, his voice is gentle and soft.

The man turns over slightly in the bed at the sound of the voice. He is an old fellow with greying and slowly receding hair, and his face is wrinkled and tired. He sees the pair and smiles.

"I don't recognize you," he says. His voice is weary but present. "Am I going mad? Are you servants of Echoshan?" He chuckles at his own joke.

"No," Peren says through a legitimate smile. "My name is Peren Siannodel. This is my friend, Voss Hallehwell. We were wondering if you were feeling fit to answer some questions for us."

"I am Charles," the man smiles. "Pleased to meet you. Yes, to answer you. If you could assist me in sitting up I would be happy for the company." Voss moves to the man's side and gingerly helps sit him against the pillows. Charles' face is racked with pain for a moment but he recovers. The bandage around his head is clean save for a spot on the back where a dark liquid has dried against it.

"Alright," Voss says calmly as Charles settles.

"What kind of questions can I answer for you gentlemen?" Charles asks, looking from Peren to Voss intently.

"Well, first off, I would like you to tell me how you got that injury," Peren tells the patient.

"Oh, this?" Charles asks sheepishly, gesturing to his bandage. "I feel off my boat."

"Your boat?" Voss asks.

"Yes, well, the boat I work on. I'm no captain, but me an' my buddies bought a boat a while back. 'Old Coast' we call her," Charles responds, thinking fondly.

"So how did you fall?" Voss continues.

"Well, takes a lot to freeze over the bay, but this winter there was some ice that broke off the coastline an' drifted down near the opening to the expanse. We were coming back in from a trip and we hit a patch an' got stuck. I pitched out an' on the way into the water I cracked my head on the same damn ice that dented our girl."

"That sounds terrible!" Peren exclaims. "Glad they got you out quick. Is your boat okay?"

"Yeah, she lived. Got fixed up faster that I did, even. That was a week or so ago, though I am recovering well now. I was unconscious for the first whole day. By the time I woke up I was already put back together," Charles chuckles.

"Have you been treated by the half-orc or-?" Peren begins, but is interrupted by Charles.

"Harrock? Yeah, for the past few days, but the first few were by doctor Eralius." He explains.

"Has he been treating you well? Eralius, I mean," Peren asks next.

"Yes, quite so really. He is an odd man. Got a twitch and an accent I can't quite place, but he was kind and quick to offer me anything I asked for."

"When was the last time you talked to him?" Voss asks.

"Must have been three days ago. He did mention leaving for a while but I was having a headache and I barely remember the conversation."

"Well, do you remember anything about him? We are doing an investigation on a criminal and we believe Voran may have some insight into the man we're after," Peren says. It is a lie, but not so far from the truth that Charles questions it.

"Oh, that sounds important!" The man proclaims. "I know he talked something about having another job. He did something else around town but I can't remember what it quite was."

"That's alright, sir. Thank you for your time." Peren nods to Voss. "Harrock, the nurse, he may know something of this."

Charles smiles at the pair as they stand back. "I hope I was of help. Come back if you think of anything else to ask."

Voss nods and bows to the man. Before they leave, he recrosses the room and gives Charles a book titled 'The Journey To and From' by Ran-Levyr.

"If you get bored," Voss says as Charles takes the book.

"Thank you, sir Hallehwell," Charles says earnestly. "One of my most beloved bards."

Peren and Voss exit.

"You were quite kind in there," Voss notes.

"Sometimes the easiest way to extract information is through trust," The noble responds.

While the others were speaking to Charles, Evandur has descended into the cellar and had some time to search through the stone room. It is dark and the ceiling is low. Angelthorn struck a torch from his satchel for light and has had to bend forward slightly as he scours the area.

Most of the room is taken up by crates and barrels made of hardened wood and iron. There are a variety of labels, though most barrels read 'water' and crates read 'linens.' Some barrels are labelled 'wine' however, and there are other alcohols in vials likely used for disinfecting wounds. Some crates appear to house different plants and dried herbs for use in medicinal pastes and salves. Some even contain bottles of older and potent, magical healing liquids.

With his head pressed to the ceiling Evandur gets a clear view of the whole room. Something in the midst of the clutter sticks out to him. Over halfway towards the west wall there are a pair of larger wooden crates that bear no markings. The paladin slides between the other boxes and barrels to make his way there.

He peers around the obstruction and finds a small patch of bare stone ground, hidden from view. This square is uncovered save for some dirt, splinters of wood, and a stain from something dark. Evandur enters the space and bends down. He calmly examines the deep burgundy patch of stone. With his gauntlet he scratches away at the rock until flakes peel from the ground.

"Blood," he mutters.

"Indeed," a woman's voice responds to him, the angel Scilandra. She would not be visible or audible to anyone but him. He can see her now, though, almost as if she was standing in his peripheral vision. If he turned his head she would vanish however, reappearing just outside of his sight again.

"What do you make of this?" he calmly asks her instead, not speaking out loud, only thinking the words.

"You know I have no business in this matter. It is dried blood. Something nefarious perhaps? It could be that someone injured themselves on one of the crates and simply forgot to clean the mess."

"That seems unlikely."

"That it does," she responds. "Perhaps you should search the area and find more of the truth before asking me to make speculations."

She has been with him since his birth. His ancestry is unclear, but he aged as a normal human. The church he grew up in offered some insight into her presence, and she herself has explained in part. Scilandra and the church have told him that she is an angel created by Valkronus and bound to the man. She acts as a voice of reason, a friend, and a guide in unclear times.

Evandur stands again, smiling at her sarcasm. He contemplates the situation. The blood is not thick, nor was it a wide puddle. It would barely be noticeable without torchlight or unless someone was looking for evidence. There are no signs of struggle either.

He crouches in the empty space, letting his left arm hang to where the blood is dried. He looks around from his position and sees that every box but one is nailed shut.

"Obvious," he muses to himself, or Scilandra, if she is listening. He stands again, carefully wedges his torch between some boxes so the flame licks clean air, and pulls open the unsealed container.

Inside, there are layers of what looks to be clean sheets and clothing. However, the corner closest to Evandur's left arm is stained the same shade of dried blood. He reaches into the box, almost up to his shoulder, and at the bottom corner something hard finds his hand.

He pulls upwards, the object in his gauntlet shoves through the layers of cloth and finally his clasped fist draws into the torchlight.

It is a small shard of glass. The tip is dark with more blood and wrapped around it is a strip of cloth. Unfolding the cloth reveals words, written in the deep red liquid: "Help us, we were here. He is coming." The words take up the whole piece of fabric.

The paladin examines this carefully. The writing is neat and particular, but clearly done in haste.

"Ominous," he states aloud.

"Indeed, I stand corrected," Scilandra's angelic voice responds. "Not a simple injury."

"We should tell the others."

"You should," Scilandra responds. "I am here for guidance, not to pass judgement."

"You steered me towards becoming a paladin, Scil," Evandur argues silently as he returns to the ladder, grabbing the torch on his way.

"I gave you the facts. I shared information. You decided your own path and you can forsake it at any time," the angel whispers.

"I would not."

"I know. That's why you were chosen," she says. "Now focus, there's a mystery afoot and you doubt Voss and Peren will be able to solve it without your help."

The soldier and the noble are waiting near the reception desk when Evandur emerges from the back room. The paladin walks briskly to the front door, opens it, snuffs the torch in the snow, leaving it there, and returns to the others.

"We have found little information," Peren says, shuddering in the breeze that pushed through the door. "But Harrock here," he gestures to the half-orc who seems to not be too upset with Peren, "says that our doctor Eralius works occasionally as a clerk at the Polytheistic Church. I worry this will be a fruitless chase however."

"It bears fruit, unfortunately," Evandur says, face like stone.

"What have you found, paladin?" Voss asks.

"It's a note," Evandur passes the cloth to Voss. "The medium is blood."

Peren peers around Voss' figure as they both examine the torn piece of fabric.

"Something happened here?" Harrock asks.

"You be quiet," Peren dismisses him. "You are still a suspect."

"You honestly believe he had anything to do with this?" Evandur asks

Peren.

"Probably not, but him being in the building where a crime took place in gives weight to the suspicion," Peren responds.

"We are not placing him under watch," Evandur states, not arguing against the half-elf. "We should make haste before the day wanes to investigate the church."

They take their leave, thanking the nurse for his time. Harrock watches them go, still worried about the situation, but relieved to see them on their way.

They stop outside, several metres from the doorway.

"Should we wait for Brael and Thervos, or go without them?" Voss asks.

"They are probably not even at the docks yet, there's no point wasting time in waiting," Peren decides.

"Then we should go to the docks ourselves. It could save an hour for them, and we should all be together to follow this lead. If we work as one then we have a higher chance at finding the missing servants, and then we've no need to track down Eralius ourselves," Evandur argues.

"No need to track down the suspect?" Peren asks.

"He is responsible for the disappearances, we should find him," Voss agrees.

"It is our job to find the servants, not meddle with the business of the guard. If we prove he is responsible then the watch will mount a search," Evandur says.

"It's your job to bring justice to the world, or so I believed," Voss challenges.

"It is also my job to follow orders," Evandur responds. "Mayor Brenspire tasked us with finding the servants, not apprehending any criminals. Though, should he be there, we will take him in. We are wasting time, let us just go quickly to the docks, then double back. It should take no more than an hour. We can investigate the church when we return and if we find nothing, we can continue the search fresh tomorrow."

"Indeed," Peren settles. "Let us go get the deaf one, and the angry one with the tail and the horns. Clearly we'll need their help." The nobleman sets off towards the dock with a brisk pace before anyone can respond.

With the relative agreement in place, Voss and Evandur leave the clinic behind and march quickly after Peren towards the eastern coast.

Chapter Four - A Threat Resolved

3E055, 19th of Echo's Stay

Brael and Thervos have reached the docks and found nothing. Just under an hour has passed since they left the clinic. Several dock-hands say that they have seen Voran, and a fisherman even tells that the doctor accompanied them on a short fishing trip once. No one can say for certain where he is now, however, and no one has seen him more than a handful of times.

All describe him as an elven man with shoulder length blond hair. They say he is usually dressed in a tucked shirt with trousers of varying colours, and a fine leather belt with a golden buckle.

The pair of unlikely companions has given up. They talked briefly about the others while they had time without them and they agree on their opinions of the people they are working with. Peren is inarguably the stuck up vision of what a nobleman is to the common-folk. Voss is a soldier and, while he is intimidating, he doesn't seem horrible, though something about him and the way he holds himself puts both Thervos and Brael on edge. Evandur seems fine, like a traditional paladin, and if his only negative quality is his seemingly bland nature then perhaps he is the best of them all.

They finish their discussion over some heated coffee being poured for the dock workers that they each pay a copper for.

It is then that they begin to walk back, near certain that nothing is to be found at the docks. The others are already walking to meet them, however. Brael and Thervos can pick them out in the distance.

Voss' scale shirt, and his plated arms and shoulders glint in the sunlight, which now paints the town from the west. His helmet — with its black plated face guard — gives him the visage of death, and his burgundy cloak stands stark against the white layered backdrop like they were two separate armies clashing in battle.

Peren's jet black hair purely contrasts the snow as well, blowing gently in the thin breeze as it pours down his cloaked shoulders and spilling almost to the top of his dark, leather brigandine.

Evandur's armour shines along with Voss', and the paladin's longsword handle is wrapped in blue stained leather which gives it some attention. He also wears large gauntlets; the one on his left arm is thicker than the one over his sword arm.

Brael and Thervos approach the trio. As they get within conversation range, Peren addresses the blonde half-elf.

"Brael, did you glean any information?" he asks.

"No, not much," Brael responds.

"I was there as well," Thervos states, still angry at the noble.

"We managed to discover that the good doctor may have a second job working in the Polytheistic Church," Peren says, ignoring the demon-kin. "We also have more reason to believe that he is the culprit."

"Why is that?" Brael questions, not even realizing that Thervos spoke.

Evandur holds the cloth and glass to the light. "This is written with someone's blood. It was in the clinic's basement, hidden in a crate," the paladin explains.

"That does lend some weight to incriminating the building, and those working there," Brael agrees.

"Yes, so we have decided to collect you and go investigate the church," Peren says.

"I decided to come collect you," Evandur corrects.

"We all agreed," Peren protests.

"Eventually," Voss mutters.

"We are burning daylight, please can we just move on?" Thervos asks.

"We should return," Peren says. His lack of emphasis leaves it ambiguous as to whether or not he is even addressing Thervos.

Voss starts walking first, the others fall in line behind him. Evandur is just after, followed by the rest who are bickering about something that Voss is paying no attention to. Something else takes his focus away as a new conversation begins in his mind.

"You are admirably calm," a human voice says. It is not Nhasan's, who spoke earlier to Voss, it is deeper. "Peren seems to be pushing all the buttons that would normally make you jump at him. Arrogance was always something you struggled with."

"Please," the voice of the woman, Valindra, cuts in. "Torkurth, can we get through an hour without tormenting him?"

"It's been an hour," Torkurth argues.

"The lad is right, though, dear," a gruff, dwarven voice interjects, aiming at Valindra.

"Dadek agrees with me," Torkurth states.

"He did kill us, Val," Nhasan joins the conversation, reluctantly.

"Ten years ago, Nhasan, *something* killed us."

"And ten years ago, Val, *something* spared him."

"Stop, just stop," Voss mutters.

"As you were, captain," Nhasan's voice spits before fading.

"Let's just take the elf's side on this, eh lads?" Dadek, the dwarf, speaks to the others compassionately.

"Did you say something Voss?" Evandur asks, pulling Voss back into reality.

"No," Voss says quickly. "Nothing."

They keep walking.

The voices in Voss' head breed pain. Each word presses against his mind like a knife held to his throat, pricking blood but not doing enough to leave anything that lasts.

The conversations grew less frequent as time passed and he moved further from Streboya, but recently they have spiked again, and travelling with others only provides more opportunity for a demanded explanation. Despite knowing each voice, and the spirits they belong to, better than anyone he walks with now, he still tries to ignore them as much as he can.

The Polytheistic Church of Taernsby is a large building, larger than the Church to Valkronus by a small margin. It can sit at maximum around three hundred people, its tower reaches over the tops of the two-storey houses that surround it, and its doors are taller that Voss by nearly two feet.

The group approaches the entrance. The wood of the double doors is old, but as Evandur presses against the handles, they slide open silently. Inside there are over two dozen people lining the benches, there is a fire burning in a large hearth along the left, and light trickles through the glass windows on either wall, which are stained with the symbols and colours of the known Gods.

As each person enters, they kick snow off their boots — causing some noise — but no one turns to look; the churchgoers keep their heads down and continue muttering their prayers.

This church is a place for general worship and there is nearly no way of telling which God someone is in prayer to. Altars to individual Gods are located around the room, and several offerings lie on each pedestal, but this is no place for rituals or specific devotion. Any rituals to a certain God or any longer ceremonial worship done in private, whether at a shrine in one's own home, or at a church to that God.

The room is being watched over by a pastor who stands at the other end of the hall. He resides on a raised platform behind a podium. He wears long black robes cinched with a grey belt around his hips. He glances up. His spectacles are pushed up his nose as he observes the group in the doorway calmly, before returning to humming a hymn from a large tome on the podium.

There are two doors behind him, through which are an archives room, and the stairs that both climb up to the tower and descend into the basement storage area.

The inside is decorated with large cloth banners that cover the cold stone walls. The banners show the Gods' symbols, and the Dabarisian — and even the Holliserian — royal emblems, telling how ancient this building must be.

The whole hall is lit by the white light of the sun —slowly but surely dimming as clouds thicken above the town — and the dancing of flames from the hearth.

Peren assumes the lead, and the others follow him as they walk quietly through the aisles, and past the men and women in prayer. They reach the steps at the base of the platform. The pastor glances up again as Peren puts his foot on the first of two stairs.

"Greetings," the man says. His voice breathes authority and age. He is ancient for a human, likely sixty or even older. His face is wrinkled and his hair is nearly as white as Evandur's, but his smile seems fresh.

"Hello," Peren says. "We wish to ask you some questions, if you happen to have the time."

"I have time," the pastor says kindly. "How can I help? Are you curious about the church, or Gods? Something else?"

"The matter we wish to discuss would best be heard in private," Evandur says.

The man looks around the group. "Some of you carry arms," he says, eyeing Brael's bow and rapier, Peren's own rapier, and Evandur's longsword. "Are you with the guard? You do not look it."

Peren looks to the others.

"Truth, Peren," Voss encourages.

"We are working for The Mayor on private business." He holds his wax-stamped paper up to the pastor, who peers at it through the smudged glasses he wears. "We will discuss the details away from other ears."

The pastor thinks for a moment before responding. "Alright. Come into the stairs and we can speak." He motions for the group to follow, and they do. He takes them to the door at the right wall and unlocks it with a key he produces from his robes' inside pocket.

They follow him through the oak door and into the stairwell. They stand on the landing, where there is more than enough space for everyone to fit comfortably. On the left side of the building, the smooth stone steps wind upwards to where the trapdoor to the tower lies, and on the right side, closest to them, they lead downward into darkness. This room is much colder than the main hall, as winter presses in from above and the doors block the heat.

The old man looks between the group expectantly, the chill growing on him.

"Do you know a man named Voran Eralius?" Evandur asks at last.

"Yes. He is another pastor here. Usually he cleans at night and is the one to lock up."

"But he is gone for now, yes?" Voss asks.

"Yes. I have been taking his duties for the past few days. He should be back soon, but until then I am here for long shifts," the man says with a smile.

"Let's come clean," Thervos says. "We suspect Voran of committing crimes against the town and The Mayor himself. Brenspire's servants have been disappearing and we think that they may have been abducted."

"Hush!" Peren chastises Thervos.

"He is a pastor, Peren, it's reasonable to trust him," Evandur urges.

"Voran Eralius is a pastor too," Voss reminds the paladin.

"This is troubling," the old man ignores the bickering. "I have spoken many times to Voran. He is an odd man, but he seems a man of justice, and a doctor at that. These are serious accusations," the man says.

"And we would not be investigating further without serious evidence," Peren replies.

Evandur shows the pastor the cloth and the glass.

"Help us, we are here. He is coming," the pastor reads aloud, his face moving from confusion to muffled horror as he realizes what the note was written with.

"This was found in the basement of Eralius' clinic," Peren explains.

"That is not unreasonable evidence," the pastor nods.

"We wish to search this building for traces of the doctor's activities. It is a long shot, we're aware, but we can't pass up the chance either," Evandur tells the pastor.

"I am sorry. I don't know any of you. I am not sure I feel comfortable with you walking around my church," he says warily.

"I am a paladin of Valkronus," Evandur begins, "and by the God of Life and Rebirth himself, and by the justice I swore to uphold, no harm will come to this church during our investigation."

The pastor looks at him for some time. His eyes look drained and tired now. He breathes a sigh. "I understand, I will wait in the main hall. You have my permission to search the building. I will make sure no one gets in your way. You have one hour."

"Thank you, sir." Evandur says, and the pastor leaves. He closes the door behind himself, without locking it.

"We should start with the basement," Peren suggests.

"I agree," Evandur echoes. They begin to walk down the stairs.

The steps wrap around an empty space, so they walk close to the wall for safety. It is not a long descent, only a storey below. The room beneath the church has no door. It is small, not a quarter of the main floor's space above. Not much light filters down the stairs through the large windows above, but enough to alleviate the pitch blackness reaches the basement.

In the room there is a medium size stack of wooden boxes with their lids all loosely affixed, two large bookshelves that line the wall directly across from the stairs and boxes, and a smaller metal chest in the corner under an unlit torch in a sconce.

The group reaches the base of the stairs and scans the room.

Evandur takes his tinder kit to the torch sconce and strikes it until a flame licks the oiled cloth and light floods the room.

"I will take the chest, maybe something interesting is hidden in it. If it's locked I can open it," Peren says.

"Fine," Evandur agrees after a pause. "Brael and I will search the crates. Be respectful, Peren. Voss can you see if there are any books that were recently touched or out of place?"

"Certainly," Voss says with a sarcastic undertone. "I will read these hundred or so book covers for anything 'out of place.' Thervos, you can help! You like books, right?"

The demon-born looks at the armour-clad figure. "I read occasionally." There is not nearly as much sarcasm in the younger man's voice.

The group splits up and moves to their tasks.

"I had you pegged as the studious type," Voss mutters to Thervos, making small talk.

"I am not. I live alone, in the woods. I just read for entertainment if anything, and to maintain sanity."

"I'm sure Peren really helps maintain sanity as well," Voss whispers, smiling under his face plate.

"Most definitely," Thervos replies sardonically. "Better than the best of books."

Peren roots through the chest, which turns out to be unlocked. Within, he finds little other than a variety of holy symbols and robes similar to the ones the pastor was wearing upstairs. While no one is looking he shovels a set of the robes into his backpack that looks to be his size, as well as a necklace engraved with the symbol of Echoshan.

Evandur and Brael have even less luck. While searching the boxes, the only interesting things Brael finds are some small vials that appear to be potions and have the right colouration to be used as healing ointments, but the paladin dissuades him from keeping what is not his own.

"You think one of these books opens a secret door?" Thervos asks Voss, who has stopped looking at the books altogether.

"No," Voss replies.

"I was speaking sarcastically."

"I am aware. These walls would not be able to house the mechanical pieces necessary to be triggered by the simple movement of a book."

"That is why I was-"

"However," Voss interrupts, thought heavy in his voice, "this floor could have been much larger, and churches were used as safe havens during an attack on town. This basement would not hold more than a few dozen people."

"So?" Evandur asks, turning around.

Voss crouches to examine the floor before he continues. "So these marks on the floor would suggest something more than meets a first glance."

The group gathers around the crouched soldier, and examines the marks he points to. They are thin grooves along the floor, speckled with nearly indiscernible wooden splinters.

"These were left by the bookcase," Peren says.

"Yes," Voss agrees. "Someone has moved the cases — at least this one — either fairly recently, or multiple times."

"You noticed these in this light?" Evandur asks.

"Luck," Voss responds coolly.

"Liar," Nhasan's voice pierces Voss' ears.

"He doesn't want to explain us to these new faces," Valindra speaks. "For good reason, I might add."

"We exist, he cannot deny that forever," Torkurth says spitefully.

"He can try," Dadek jumps in. "I wouldn't blame him for trying."

"Should we move the case?" Thervos asks, breaking the awkward silence that has possessed the room.

"Keep an eye on him," Scilandra whispers to Evandur.

"Voss?" Evandur asks inwardly.

"Indeed. Something about him haunts me."

"Let's move this thing!" Peren exclaims, when no one responds to Thervos. "Voss, would you assist me?"

"Voss and I will do it. You look to see if there's anything behind it while we do the heavy lifting," Evandur directs.

"Fine," Peren nods.

Voss and Evandur grab either side of the first set of shelves and lift it slightly off the ground before pulling it from the wall. Peren sticks his head into the space they create.

"There is a hallway here," Peren informs the others. "I can barely see the end, even with my elven eyes."

"Half-elven," Voss grunts, strained under the weight of the case.

"There are some barrels at the end, another bigger room, not a lot larger than this one though. I can't see much else."

"Well, we must investigate now, regardless. If there's any danger in this mission, it is in there," Thervos says.

"So what if there is?" Voss asks, placing the shelves down again. "We should prepare for a fight regardless, but we can handle whatever awaits us in a dark basement."

"Most of us are armed. The ones who wield no weapons are you and the imp," Peren states.

"I am never unarmed," Voss says calmly. He reaches his hands forward as though he is holding something, and suddenly a pale blue light joins that of the torch in the room, emanating from his hands.

A thin mist coalesces around his hands and in between his arms, forming slowly into a single line which becomes thicker and thicker. All within two seconds, the mist materializes into the shape of a battleaxe, and soon there is a real weapon in Voss' hands. A very sharp looking, black metal armament with its haft wrapped in dark brown leather, matching the colour of his fur ring.

"I have no need for weaponry," Thervos adds as they all watch the spectacle, his hands igniting in thin flame, which burns as bright as the torch and blue light coming from Voss.

"I stand corrected, I suppose," Peren says. "Then are we ready?"

"I will take the front," Evandur says.

"Then I will stand beside you," Voss responds.

"Don't rush too quickly to your own demise," Torkurth taunts Voss.

"Why not?" Nhasan asks. "We were rushed."

"Yes, and if he goes then we go again," Torkurth responds.

"We go to rest."

"I don't know if I believe in rest anymore. I do not like to think of what torment awaits us beyond the pain we bear now."

"I appreciate the offer, sir Hallehwell," Evandur says.

"Appreciate all you want, it's for my own benefit."

"You're right. Something about him worries me," Evandur voices inward.

"I know. You will drain yourself faster with all this discussion, Evandur," Scilandra reminds him. "The more we speak the faster your light will fade."

"It will return. I will speak with you tomorrow then," Evandur replies as they prepare to head down the tunnel, "or in my dreams."

The group leaves their various bags in the room, laying them quietly on the floor. They move in single file through the space behind the bookcase until the hall is big enough to stand shoulder to shoulder. Once they are in the main passageway, Evandur holds another torch towards Thervos. The demon-born summons a thin flame from himself and ignites the oil. Light spills with warmth down the hallway on both sides, casting shadows that flicker along the floor, reaching halfway to the other room.

They move slowly, but their footsteps echo along the walls and bounce down the passage with every movement.

"If anyone is waiting for us in there, they know we are coming," Voss says at a normal level, as his metal greave scrapes along the stone wall.

"Then let us be observant," Evandur says as they reach the end of the hall and light jumps into the new room. They scan all walls of the room, getting a full view of the area.

The hallway opens up in the left corner of the new room. Along the wall closest to the group, are several barrels of both wine and water. In front of the hallway lies a pedestal that stretches nearly across the whole room. It is chipped and there is a dark liquid that has splattered the surface, but it is devoid of purposeful markings. Along the right hand wall — shocking Evandur as he scans — are three bound figures who appear to be in various stages of unconsciousness.

The rest of the room is bare of any art or furnishing.

"Prisoners!" the paladin cries out, breaking focus and, handing the torch to Voss, he rushes across the room to the figures.

Voss shoves the torch into a sconce near the entrance as the others come in behind him, fixating as well on the bound humans.

"Who are you?" Evandur asks, un-gagging one of the two women.

"Tessa," her voice is barely audible. Her eyes attempt to focus in the sudden light.

"What happened to you?"

"He did something to us."

"Who?"

"Th- the doctor," she coughs between words.

"We are getting you out of here," Evandur begins to grab her.

Her eyes grow wide suddenly. "No!" she says loudly. "Watch yourselves, it's not safe. It'll be here! It's always here!" She struggles to free herself before her eyes roll into her head and her body grows limp. She begins to breathe rapidly.

"Tessa?" Evandur asks, lying her back on the ground.

Voss, who is standing by the entrance still, holds his breath as his ears catch a noise. It sounds similar to a wet footstep hitting a floor, but it not coming from the hallway. It is coming from above him.

"We aren't alone! Watch out!" he shouts, filling the stone room with his voice. He spins to face the upper corner of the room. As he does, something lets out a strange gurgling noise and a creature drops from the ceiling.

It lands in front of the barrels, then stands to reveals itself in the torchlight. It has a human-like posture, though it is taller than Voss. It stands on two scaled legs, both long and thick. Its body is muscular and covered in the same layer of red plates, and from its torso protrude long arms affixed with talon-like claws where fingers would be. Its head looks like some sort of grotesque frog. It is wide, its eyes are black and peering, there are no ears, its nose is flat, and its wide, gaping mouth, houses a row of fangs. A line of black protrusions that arc down its back become visible as it prepares to lunge towards Voss.

The group has their weapons at the ready, however.

"Give this *thing* no mercy," Peren spits, nocking an arrow.

Voss rushes forward, seemingly without any fear. He raises his axe and slashes toward the nearly eight foot tall beast. The creature attempts to block the swing with its thick scaled arm. The axe blade collides with the natural armour, but manages to cut though and draw a thick and dark strand of blue blood from the toad.

The creature lashes out at Voss in retaliation, but Voss is quick as well as strong, he gets his body out of the way and pushes the thing's arm aside with his axe haft as its claws reach for his face.

Peren and Brael loose arrows, both of which hit the creature's chest, but scrape outward and fly to the stonework as thin lines of blood escape the small wounds.

Thervos builds energy into his hands and suddenly a solid bolt of fire erupts through the air and connects with the beast's face. The creature leaps backwards onto the wall and sticks, preparing to pounce at Voss, who is still standing closest.

Voss throws his axe to the side. Before it hits the ground it bursts again into pale blue mist. The soldier jumps from the ground and grabs hold of the assailant. He finds grip on the thing's left leg and, putting his own feet to the wall, pulls it free. They both slam into the floor again.

Evandur sees this opportunity and rushes forward through the archers and mage. He thrusts his longsword into the beast directly where its heart would be if it were human. The creature only screams a howl of pain in response however, writhing beneath the blade and Voss' grip.

The beast's right leg shoots towards Voss, and the foot claws through the plating on Voss' arm, rending through skin and sending a spray of red onto the stone.

Voss grunts as his own blood splatters his helmet, using the force of the kick to stand up again. While the frog is still unable to gain its footing, Voss acts. He raises his empty hands above his head and swings them with full force towards the beast. Just before the swing reaches halfway, the mist congeals again and begins to form his blade. As the swing draws closer, the axe fully reforms and embeds itself in the thing's massive neck. Severing the head partially from the body.

The beast howls again, trying to lash out at Evandur who sidesteps. Voss grunts in pain as he swings the axe up again and then, with gravity aiding him, he plunges the head of his weapon back into the neck of the beast, cutting clean through and into the stone below.

The body goes still.

Voss throws his weapon back into mist and wobbles backward, away from the creature's corpse.

"What in the Gods' power was that?" Peren asks as Voss and Evandur catch their breath and the collective heart rate returns to normal.

"I've not the faintest idea," Thervos replies.

"I have studied monsters to an extent," Peren adds, "but even I have not seen this before. Orcs, goblins, beasts of nature.Never giant, killer frogs."

"We need to get these people out of here," Evandur urges.

They nod.

They approach the three prisoners at long last. Voss grunts, clutching his arm.

"Voss!" Evandur turns to the soldier.

"I'll live."

"Let me heal you. I can draw on the light."

"I can draw on bandages."

"Voss, please."

"Fine," Voss responds. He holds his arm out for the paladin to examine. Evandur presses his hands against the wounded area through the torn steel and the blood flow subsides. A white light emerges from Evandur's hands and eyes, illuminating the room even further.

The wound closes and the pain numbs, the only proof it happened is the ruptured armour and drops of red on the metal.

"Thank you," Voss says earnestly.

"That is all I can do. I am spent for the day," Evandur says wearily.

They view the three bound figures, two women and a man.

"If your arm is healed, you can take one." Evandur begins, speaking to

Voss, who nods. Before they can continue however, a lump appears through the tunic of the man, under his left arm. It appears to be moving, and evokes a choked sound of pain from the man.

"What is-?" Thervos begins, but is interrupted.

The lump grows suddenly, accompanied by a horrific ripping noise. The man screams in agony as his eyes open and bulge in their sockets.

The lump wriggles in his tunic, soon falling from the fabric and onto the floor. It is a blue, worm-like creature that has emerged, covered in blood. Its body is under a foot long and its face has no eyes, only a wide mouth full of fangs. Before anyone else can react, Voss slams his metal boot onto the beast, crushing its head and knocking out several teeth.

The worm creature stops moving immediately, and the sound wakes Tessa again, she looks around, terrified.

Thervos moves to examine the hole that the creature bore through the man's ribcage and insides. Voss kicks the crushed spawn against the wall opposite the entrance. Peren and Evandur both crouch down in front of Tessa and the other woman.

"Do you have these in you as well?" Peren interrogates her.

"I don't know!" Tessa cries in fear, struggling in her bonds.

"We cannot risk it," Peren calmly tells the group.

"Risk it?" Evandur asks incredulously, standing once more. "We have to help them!"

"What if we can't?"

Tessa whimpers in pain.

"It's happening," Voss says, turning to face the remaining prisoners. His mist begins to reform his weapon.

"We can stop it!" Evandur exclaims.

"They will die regardless!" Peren shouts.

"Please," Tessa moans, a mixture of fear and fever wrapped in the word.

"We can do something!" Evandur pleads.

Peren plunges his rapier through Tessa's neck. Her blood splashes the stones behind. He rips his sword free and plunges it then into her stomach. Evandur draws his own blade on Peren. Voss' battleaxe reappears, angled toward the paladin. There is silence in the room.

Peren has his sword now angled to the other woman, who is still unconscious. Evandur does not remove his own from the half-elf's neck. Voss places his axe head on the stone floor, keeping hold of the haft.

"Peren is not wrong, Angelthorn," Voss says solemnly.

"I promised to protect the vulnerable, to forbade Echoshan's claim on souls before their time," Evandur spits.

"Right now, it's not about stopping their passing, but easing it. What is better, when on death's door already? To die slowly and in pain or have life ripped suddenly from you?" Peren asks, motioning to the male human whose body is still twitching in shock.

The last survivor lets out a sudden pained cry, her eyes opening briefly.

"You want justice? You want to do the right thing? Let me end her suffering," Peren tells Evandur.

"No," the paladin says. He steps by Peren, standing between him and the woman. "I will do it." He slashes his own blade through the woman's throat cleanly, then pushes the longsword quickly through her chest.

There was no time for pain.

Both Evandur and Peren then say a brief prayer under their breath before the group steps away from the prisoners.

"You did the right thing," Peren assures the white haired man.

"Maybe," comes the response.

After assuring that the prisoners are all dead, and nothing else is coming from them, they do one full sweep of the room.

Nothing interesting is found on the altar pedestal, nor in the barrels, but they do take into memory that the prisoners all bear strange incision marks on their arms and legs.

Not knowing what these small injuries mean, but certain that they are important, the investigators meet back in the centre of the room.

"Let's go," Brael says quietly. "We will tell The Mayor what happened, he will know what to do."

No one argues. They exit the room in a line. On the way out, Evandur grabs the torch, and Voss bends down to grabs the head of the creature. He carries it with him back through the hallway and out into the main basement.

From his bag, Voss pulls a linen shirt and wraps the frog's head in it before tying it to his pack and shouldering the gear. The deep, dark blue blood of the monstrosity oozes into the fabric of the wrap, but Voss seems not to worry.

The group repositions the bookcase roughly and ascends the staircase back to the main floor of the church.

They return through the unlocked door into the main room. The pastor turns to greet them. Some of the churchgoers have left by now, but one or two new faces are present to balance the numbers, coming for a late afternoon prayer.

"Welcome back," the pastor says. "I heard some noise, did you find anything out of place?"

"Yes," Peren says. "There was a hallway behind the bookcases downstairs that you did not tell us about."

"A hallway?" the old man asks, his face screwing up in a frown. "Are you certain?"

"Yes," Peren says again. "We explored it and found a creature in another room. We will spare you the details, but please do not investigate yourself, there is a gruesome scene in there and The Mayor must be informed. As agents of the aforementioned leader of this township, we ask you heed our word."

"That I shall do," the pastor says with a nod. "I won't enter the basement, and no one else will, unless they are accompanied by a letter from The Mayor."

"Thank you, sir," Evandur says. The group solemnly takes their leave.

The light coming through the stained glass windows feels devoid of any warmth now, and — as they push through the doors back to the snow covered landscape — they are greeted with an ever more pressing sense of frozen hearts, as the sky threatens rain or fresh snow.

As they pause for breath, Peren speaks. "I will go inform the orcish man, Harrock, in the clinic, of what we found. You should all return to The Mayor and explain as well. This will save time."

"He's up to something," Valindra tells Voss.

"Yes, but so what? Let's just be on with it," Nhasan chimes.

"Yes, I would like to see The Magistrate as soon as possible," Voss says. "Let's allow Peren to have his way."

"My thanks, Hallehwell," Peren nods.

The group parts, with Peren going alone to the clinic.

He reaches the building in good time. He knocks on the door twice before opening it. Harrock looks up, surprised.

"Ah, sir!" he says.

"Have you seen doctor Eralius?" Peren asks.

"No, but I was waiting for your return!" the half-orc tells him. "A messenger stopped by with a letter from Voran."

"What did it say?"

"I haven't had the time to open it. I was busy cleaning for the night and preparing to lock up."

"Hand it over then," Peren says coolly, thinking. "It could contain important information."

"Um, yes, of course," the man says, passing over the letter.

Peren opens it.

It reads:

'Dear Harrock,

I regret to inform you that I must take an extended trip. I have been invited by a close friend to stay at his home and help him in a research endeavour. This will, of course, mean that I will be unable to take care of my duties at the clinic. I leave you in charge. You have been an excellent nurse and assistant, and so in my absence I am appointing you as head doctor. You may hire others and collect payments. There will be a form delivered that will temporarily turn over all responsibility to you and you will have full control of the business.

Thank you for all of your help, I know you will be fine.

Your friend and co-worker, Voran Eralius.'

"He wants to inform you, regrettably, that you are out of a job," Peren lies. "He wants you to pack up and leave."

"What?" Harrock asks. "I thought he trusted me."

"I'm sure he did. Maybe he is afraid, or heard wind of my investigation."

"I was doing good, though, I was learning," Harrock continues, not listening.

"How about this," Peren tries to calm the man, "if you get out of here, I will inform The Mayor of all your hard work and I am certain you will get your job back when doctor Eralius is brought to justice, maybe you will even be put in charge of the clinic. This is likely a ploy by him to gain unnoticed access to the clinic."

Harrock pauses for some time. "Okay," he says finally. "If doctor Eralius is guilty, then he deserves to be caught. I packed my things already. I don't leave anything here overnight. I will get out of your way."

"I will stake out here for the night. You can leave me the key. I believe Eralius will stop here and I will try to catch him when he does."

"Okay," Harrock passes the key from his necklace to Peren's outstretched hand.

"Thank you, Harrock."

The half-orc smiles sadly. He grabs his large backpack. "Please do not do anything destructive."

"I will do my best," Peren says as the half-orc closes the door. Peren locks it behind him after he has walked away.

With the building empty save for himself and the patient, Charles, Peren sets his bag down. He opens it and removes a small black box. Inside the box — along with the bottle of crestleaf oil he bought off the cook — is an array of poisons and toxins. He uncorks a bottle and coats his thinnest dagger with the contents, leaving a sheen of dark liquid on the blade.

He enters the room where Charles lies sleeping. Quietly Peren approaches the bed. He looks at the body. The bandage is clean, and fresh water and bread have been left out on the side table. He looks across the man's arms and legs. No incisions, no markings.

Peren pauses, breathing deeply.

"I don't take chances," he whispers, both to himself and the sleeping man. "Echoshan guide my hand, and his spirit home," he continues. He covers Charles' mouth with a gloved hand. As the man's eyes open, confused, Peren plunges the blade deep into his stomach. His muffled scream is lost in Peren's hand, then the poison quickly takes effect, causing the body to grow stiff, then limp.

Peren uses a clean piece of cloth to staunch the blood flow, which is already slowed by the poison, then throws it into the smoldering hearth, blowing the wood to stoke the flame. He takes a needle and thread and uses them to stitch the small wound closed again. He then takes the blunt end of his dagger and slams it into the side of Charles' head, causing fresh blood to coat the bandage where the original injury was.

"May you find peace. May I do the same," Peren says. He bows his head slightly to the resting body.

The noble leaves the room, unlocks the front door, grabs his bag, and leaves, locking the door again behind himself once he's gone.

Chapter Five - The Red Hand

3Eoss, 20th of Echo's Stay

The girl lets out a scream as he moves towards her, but it's lost against the stone walls of the room. His laugh reverberates through the chamber, somehow overtaking her fear and forcing her into silence.

She shakes. There is no light here, yet she can see the outline of his figure. Tall and thin, cloaked in dark cloth and metal.

He smiles, though she cannot see, extending his right hand towards her, not in an offering but with his thumb spread from his fingers, as though he was choking her from metres away.

She cowers further into the stone corner, pressing into it as though somehow it will give way to freedom.

He frowns. "Disappointing," he says. His voice is like a blade, stabbing into her. It is raspy, like air rushing through woods, but calm and steady. She falls to a sitting position, drawing her knees to her chest. "You are a runner, not a fighter. I always find the fighters more interesting."

He kneels, no more than a foot away from her now. He stares at her through the veil of darkness that encompasses them, but she knows somehow he can see her.

"I take no joy in this," he speaks again. "It simply must be done. So tell me, how old are you?"

"I answer no questions for demons," she responds. She is small, thin. Frail. Braver than he first thought.

"Demons?" he responds, near a laugh. "I am no demon."

"Then what are you? Show yourself."

"Ah, an answer for an answer."

She pauses, understanding. "I am thirteen."

"They bring me a child. Insulting."

"Why?"

The crouching figure shifts, standing again. "Because I harbour no abhorrence towards an innocent soul."

"What are you?" she asks again.

"You've asked your question, it's my turn. Where are you from? I wish to picture it."

The girl looks at him. Fear still grips her heart. "Taernsby. The big town on the eastern coast. I serve The Mayor, have you not been taking the servants?"

"Someone is taking Brenspire's servants? How curious," he muses. "No, I have not been taking your people. Merely a coincidence."

"I doubt you."

"And you are welcome to," the response is curt, no empathy or emotion to it.

"What are you?" she asks a third time.

He smiles, she sees the movement even in the darkness, her elven eyes pushing away the haze and searching for his features. "You have not yet learned. You waste your questions too quickly, it's my turn again."

"Not fair!" she protests.

"Completely fair, girl. What do you fear from me?"

She thinks for a moment. "Death," she responds.

"A smart answer, but a fatal fear. Death comes for all of us one day. Even, I expect, for me."

"It's my turn," she says.

He smiles again. "Yes."

"What is your name?"

The question shocks him. "I know many titles."

"Name."

The silence that falls over the chamber weighs heavy on them both. The unknown figure stands still as stone for a long moment. He moves close to her the,. She holds her breath as his face passes her left cheek. His voice enters her ear. It's lost, even in the silence of the room, though whatever he says sends shivers down her spine.

"Impossible, how?" she squeaks. She pushes herself from the ground to kneel before him.

"My turn," he says. He strikes a fire in his hand, the arcane flame blowing the dark away. The thirteen year old elven child's eyes adjust to the new light and she sees his face. A hollow and sunken visage of something unholy, decaying. Not at all the man he named himself to be, but still in the likeness of him.

She shields her eyes, but still gathers the courage to speak. "Your question, then."

"What do you sense in me?" he asks.

"Sense?"

"What do you feel from me?" he rephrases the question.

She thinks. "Pain."

"Smart child, you are correct again."

"Are you going to kill me?" she asks.

"Certainly, yes," the man responds, still unnervingly calm.

"Why?"

"Because I must."

The girl is taken aback at his response. Not from its contents, but from something else. She does not get to voice this though, as a pain pulses from her chest. She uncovers her eyes to find the man at eye level with her.

There is something sad about his face. It is not frightening anymore, but compassionate. Something in his grey eyes sparks to life. She follows his gaze downward to his arm, which is held in front of him. From below his elbow to the end of his forearm, his pale and grotesque skin is stained a deep red. His wrist is buried in her flesh, just under her ribcage. She can feel his fingers under the wall of bone as her blood runs cold. She can see her essence being absorbed into him, she can feel it. It's not painful, but feels instead of ice, frozen.

"It was..." she trails off, confused.

"My turn," he finishes. "I know, dearest. Find peace, for one who cannot. Will you do that?"

She nods, understanding. "I will," her voice fades as her head slumps forward.

She dies then. Her body quickly becomes a husk of the girl she was. Her skin sinks and her veins empty as blood flows into him.

He wrenches his arm from her, letting her fall limp onto the stone floor. He waves his other hand. A rip forms below her and her body disappears before him, falling through the tear in reality, sent into somewhere better, somewhere with light.

He turns, pulling open another rift, forming a doorway.

"Servants going missing," he speaks to himself now. Then, looking to where the girl lay. "Are we really kidnappers now?" He shakes his head. "Have we been fishing from the same pond, getting lazy? Is is possible that my culling of the herd has been noticed? Or is something else working from my shadows?" He exits the stone room though his portal, leaving it empty and silent. No answers to his questions were to be gleaned by standing in darkness.

Chapter Six - A Friend in Need

3Eo55, 8th of Wounded Winter

The town of Railwood is little more than a village centre with some outlying farmland. Since its founding, it has developed into a thriving place in terms of community. People get along nicely and have worked together to turn the small, fertile area into a source of food and income for the citizens who settle there, and even the surrounding towns, through trade.

Being located in the council lands has its benefits and drawbacks. Since this whole upper-central section of the continent has only been colonized for around fifty years, the property prices are cheap. The Council United is still working out quirks of governing as a collective, consisting of all three major empires. The townships in the council lands have almost entirely avoided appointing magistrates for larger areas as well, and thus the towns have a lot of freedom in terms of their own decisions for the moment.

Railwood's mayor, William Greypike, has, until recently, done a commendable job of keeping the town running, growing, and safe. One of the the negative sides to living in the council lands however, is the threat of attacks.

The whole centre of Estrand has until recently remained almost completely unexplored. This fact promises chances of both riches in the form of unclaimed minerals and resources, and danger in the form of roaming monsters and the known tribes of orcs that ravage the western towns.

Railwood is situated on relatively large deposits of both silver and gold that mining companies have been taking full advantage of, as well as a sizeable grouping of small forests that supply enough lumber for the town, year round. Railwood is also built along the eastern bank of Rail Lake, which allows fishing, alongside hunting and farming for steady food supplies. This location, however, is also located close to the western swamps, which border the other shore of the lake and the rivers which flow from it. The swamps are dangerous and uncharted, housing massive sunken forests, marshland, and some of the largest of the aforementioned orc tribes.

In the past several years, orc raids on Railwood and the nearby towns have increased in ferocity, skill, and frequency. Railwood has had a strong militia, but they have been overpowered numerous times and declined in numbers over the years. Now, housing only a dozen trained fighters and whatever other men and women are willing to stand against an attack, the situation has grown desperate.

"You must ask for aid," the voice of Gorin Ingrof — the town's resident pastor for the Railwood Polytheistic Church — reaches the ear of Mayor Greypike.

"I have," William replies, not looking up from his desk. "I have sent to all the neighbouring towns. They have not responded." He speaks in a near identical accent - though his voice is deeper.

"And what of Krunix?" Ingrof asks. "I sent letters myself to the homeland."

The two dwarves look at each other. William speaks. "They have sent nothing."

"And what of-?"

"Nothing, Gorin."

There is a silence in the room again.

The past weeks have brought tremendous loss to the town. With no walls ever finished, the last attack saw thirteen men and women fall to the orcs, and the townsfolk were forced to evacuate their homes along the lake's shore and move to inns and the church for protection. Nearly a quarter of the town lies in ruins and all of the fishing boats have been burned.

Roger Hardwick is a member of the militia in Railwood, one of the few who has received a high level of training. He is versed in the spear and sword, and carries a shield made for him by his younger sister Helena, from thick and ancient hardwood, with metal bracing. He is slightly above average height, near six feet tall. He is muscular but not of thick build. His hair is a brown so dark it could be black, and he keeps its length just below his ears and small, light grey eyes.

He walks down the centre street, through the square. He views the area with reserve. The damage here is noticeable, but not severe. Several buildings bear markings from arrowheads and even axe blows, but none have fully fallen to rubble or abandonment. In his left hand he carefully holds a sealed letter. Being in the militia, while it is respected by the townspeople, does not pay as well as it should in these times. As such, Roger has taken up a job in construction, and also in assisting the local post in sorting and organizing what mail comes in and out of town. The collection of jobs allows Roger and Helena to live comfortably when the near defenceless town is not being besieged.

Roger approaches the town hall. It's a small building, similar in size to the church which it's located directly to the left of. The two buildings, while being the centrepieces of the town, are nestled in the north-east corner of it, far from the destruction and only a minutes jaunt to the wooden sign bearing the text: 'Welcome to Railwood' to the east.

The militiaman walks through the small iron gate into the town hall's front yard. He crosses the open area to the front steps where he is greeted by a lone servant. The man says nothing as he opens the door for Roger.

"Thank you," Roger says kindly to the guard as he passes by.

The servant says nothing but Roger sees his lips curl slightly into a polite smile.

"It appears a guest has arrived," Gorin says to William as the sound of the front door closing reaches The Mayor's office.

"In here!" The Mayor calls.

Roger enters the office through the open door, presenting the letter in front of himself. The Mayor nods, and takes the letter. He opens it feverishly without dismissing the carrier.

Greypike reads in silence for some time.

"Good news, sir?" Gorin asks, pushing his glasses up his nose, further away from his bushy blonde beard. There is hope in his voice but it is weak.

William smiles. "Finally, yes."

"What is it?"

"My friend, Harold Brenspire, Magistrate of Taernsby, writes that he is sending assistance."

"A platoon?" Gorin asks. "A full company of reinforcements?"

"No. A few people he trusts."

"A few people?"

"Five."

"That will never be enough," Gorin says spitefully. "Is this mockery?"

"They are seasoned soldiers, mercenaries, and even mages, some of them."

"Some of them?"

"Led by someone named Peren Siannodel."

"Heard the name, noble from the south, I believe," Roger chimes in.

"And a soldier in the Streboyan civil war. Held a command," The Mayor continues.

"Held?" Gorin asks. "Perhaps the past-tense of the word should be the focus."

"It's help, Gorin," William says earnestly. "It's more than we've gotten in awhile, and it's not our choice to turn it down now."

The priest grunts and rises from his chair. "You're right, I'd wager," he grumbles. "I just hope they get here before there is no more town to defend." The dwarf shoves past Roger and out into the lobby of the town hall.

Chapter Seven - A Raid on Railwood

3E055, 17th of Wounded Winter

Nearly a month has passed since the events in Taernsby occurred.

When the group returned to Harold Brenspire with the news that his servants were being held under the church, The Mayor had some reasonable questions.

After a short investigation, it was determined that only one of the prisoners, Tessa, was in fact his servant. The other two were civilians with no identification on them. The Mayor asked the group to keep the identities of the prisoners — and the details of the events — a secret, which they agreed to do. There were no murder charges pressed against the investigators. The evidence, the beast's body, head, and the uncovered worm remnants, dubbed *tadpoles* by Peren, ruled the execution of the civilians a necessity. The Mayor kept the whole thing under wraps regardless.

Voran Eralius evaded capture, and while a full sweep of the town revealed no new leads, the search is ongoing within the town and outlying villages.

Later, Mayor Brenspire summoned the group to pay them for their work and to discuss another matter.

"I feel as though I can trust you, as you have done me a great favour by dealing with the whole mess. I never asked you to slay a beast below my town and yet you dispatched the horror with ease," he had said.

Harold bestowed upon them then a plot of land near the town walls as a reward, as well as two hundred gold pieces to split, generously more than he promised.

There was debate on taking the land, as paying taxes did not appeal to Thervos quite much. In the end they evenly split the gold, and Voss, Peren, Evandur, and Brael signed on as quarter owners of the property. The land is two acres in size with no water running through it. It is relatively flat and located on fertile ground, but little about it provides extra value.

The two hundred golden lions, split forty each, was not enough to do much with the land however. The Mayor offered them another job though, which — while winter calms down — they agreed may be worth their time.

"I would ask of you another favour," the magistrate told them as they divvied up the coins.

"What can we do for you, sir?" Evandur asked.

"I have received a letter from a friend of mine. He is The Mayor of a town in the council lands Railwood," Brenspire told them. "He has been under siege recently by a tribe of orcs and asks for aid. I cannot spare a military force and, until now, had no way of helping him. This party is comprised of capable fighters and diplomats, and I would be more than willing to pay for your trip, and a soldier's salary while you are on this mission. He simply needs assistance until a full relief force can arrive."

Again, there was much debate. The snow would likely not fall again this winter, considering the rain that had fallen in the days after their investigation, and already it would not be impossible to travel with the right supplies. The money they had already acquired however would last them until spring and the need for coin was no longer as great.

In the end it was Peren who settled the argument.

"Listen," he whispered to the others, "Harold likes us, we are on his good side. If we can make a couple extra coins and win his favour further then there is not any tangible downside to this. Besides, if we don't do this then we are just going to be spending another month cramped in our various inns."

They decided that Peren was right, and accepted the job. Perhaps they were possessed by the adventuring spirit after their scuffle in the church basement, or perhaps they simply agreed with Peren, or even wanted fresh air and scenery. Whatever the reason, a messenger left ahead of them and they set out the day after, the first day of Wounded Winter, having bought extra clothing and rations, and borrowing horses from Brenspire for the long journey to Railwood.

Now, just over three weeks later, the group is finally approaching the town.

They have travelled through many interesting places on their way here, but had little time to stop and sightsee.

The trip took them west of Taernsby. Along the main road, they stopped in smaller villages in cramped inns to escape the cold. As the road curved south they followed it towards the Kognear Tunnel - the gateway through the Voiceless Peaks and into Krunix. There was a small trading post at the mouth of the massive tunnel that stretched as far as they could see to the south. They restocked supplies and headed onward, spending multiple days in camping areas within the long cavern, often passing other groups or travellers, who would spend the night in their camp as well.

Once through the tunnel and back into the open air, they stopped in the outskirts of the large town of Kognear before continuing west. They passed through Lo'Dorra, known for its wheat and incredible pasta. Sampling the dishes and agreeing that it should be world famous for this reason, they then pressed on with urgency. They stopped just within the walls of Azgul Hold, the dwarven capital, for two days to rest up before leaving Krunix over the Krunixian river and entering the council lands. During their stay in the capital, they saw some dwarven and gnomish technological advancements in the form of halfling sized metal servants. These creations would bring them food and drink in the tavern, and were kept animated through magic-infused gems.

Before they left, as well, and throughout their whole stay in Krunix, Peren asked around shops that sold mechanical goods, and in blacksmiths for any information pertaining to flintlock. He had heard of prototypes being worked on in the dwarven homelands of weapons that could launch metal into someone so powerfully that many spells didn't compare. He gained some ground on this, saw a basic prototype and fired it several times. His findings were that this weapon was dangerous, but loud and inaccurate. Despite its setbacks, it interested him, and he believed he could improve the design and become an entrepreneur in the industry.

Whether that was his claim to fame above politics or crime, he was not sure, but to keep options open was never a bad thing in this time of growth.

They left, and spent several days discussing the metal servants and flintlock weaponry before the excitement finally wore off.

Finally, Marsh Hold — a small town that deals in farming and mining — passed them by. They stopped to restock again, and moved onward to their final destination.

Several hours away now, they talk calmly, comfortable with one another for the most part. Peren has assumed the leadership role, organizing the others and their camps, making decisions, and generally strengthening the others' negative opinions of him.

Voss has remained mostly quiet, speaking when spoken to, and voicing his opinions usually only to contradict Peren.

Evandur has kept an eye on Voss, interested in him and his reserved nature, and attempting to unravel some knot of suspicion in his mind around the ex-soldier. Evandur has also assisted in treating a cold that jumped through the group at the halfway point in their trip.

Voss and Evandur have kept their skills sharp, knowing that there will likely be battle ahead in Railwood. They have been sparring with each other, trading blows during rests.

Peren and Brael set up archery targets at most campsites, taking shots and comparing their aim and accuracy. Though it was difficult to judge any winners, they both proved incredible bowmen.

Thervos and Brael have grown close, with the demon-born showing the deaf hunter his magic and explaining how it works for him.

"I've never studied magic," the dark-skinned creature explains. "I was born with it." Thervos tells them all that his magic was discovered at a young age, but that it is unstable. He can use it, and it can be quite powerful, but that something about it is not quite predictable, and it often goes awry if he relies on it too heavily.

In return, Brael explains to the group that he was born able to hear, and was born into a fully elven family, but with human blood flowing half in his veins. When Brael met a human man passing through his home village near Thalas-Ara, he began to learn about human culture and was interested in where his mother came from, and to hear that she was likely still alive.

When he asked his father, a member of the small town's inner circle, he was told that his mother was a mistress and nothing more, and that he was not to search for her. When Brael ignored his father and continued meeting with the human man over the next few months, Brael's father took both the man and Brael into the woods by force, and had the human slain in front of his son. When Brael did not apologize for his actions and interest in human society, his father had his ears, a symbol of his elven heritage, removed, and disowned him from the hamlet.

"If you would be a human before my son," Brael repeated his father's words to the group, the last words he ever heard, "then you are no elf."

When they asked Peren and Voss for their stories, they were mostly declined. Evandur shared little as well, only touching on his business as a paladin, and his studies.

The snow has become less and less as the group has moved further south, and now there is only a thin layer of the melting white along the grass blades. It seems intent to stay though, as despite the clear skies for the past week, a fresh layer of frost has appeared every morning.

Ahead, unbeknownst to the heroes of Taernsby, now no more than a twenty minute ride, the town of Railwood is facing another attack.

In the morning, the knell from the church cut through the peace that Railwood had had for the past week. The militia rushed to the barracks. The bell used to mean many different things, but now everyone knew it delivered only one message: "Attack."

A hunter had given just enough warning, abandoning a fresh kill and running with Maltram's speed back to the church. The twelve members of the town's defence rushed to the western edge of the square with a handful of other brave souls, ready for a fight. Their hopes had been renewed since the message arrived that help was on the way.

They bunkered down behind readied barricades in time to see a large group of figures approaching.

Since the raids began, the town has been shrinking. People have fled the houses in the western quarter of town and moved closer to the centre square, taking space in the church, inns, and others' homes.

Some citizens have simply left, and usually in groups. The orcs have killed nearly twenty people, excluding militiamen, and taken several as prisoners during the raids, but they are usually more interested in scouring the buildings for valuables unless someone is standing in the way.

Everyone has felt the tension, and the moment the ringing of the brass bell hit their ears this morning, they locked their doors and threw furniture in front.

Roger Hardwick reached the edge of the square first. The border was drawn there, where a series of alleyways would funnel the attackers if they tried to advance past their previous devastation.

The approaching figures were definitely orcs, big bodies and large shields gave that away before Roger even separated the pounding of drums from the blood pumping through his ears.

This was a war party. It was not a massive one, but there were enough of them to outnumber the militia.

"We can't handle this," Helena, his own sister, had said beside him.

"We have to; we don't have another choice," he had responded.

The militia spread through the alleys to cover as much ground as they could. They drew their bows and spears as the figures neared firing range.

"Halt!" Roger shouted towards the orcs, who did not slow down. "We will fire in three seconds!" he called, to both sides.

They waited. The orcs entered range.

"Archers, fire!" Roger ordered, they responded to his command, launching a volley. The arrows and bolts soared through the air. The orcs at the front raised huge tower shields which blocked most of the attack, but the figures behind the shield wall took some damage, one even fell to her knees.

The orcs then charged, breaking into a sprint.

From there, the fight moved quickly. After the initial clash the militia pulled back. Casualties were felt on both sides. The militia managed to wound or kill four of the orcs, leaving ten left to deal with by their count, but lost five of their own, two from the militia and three civilian fighters. Four more suffered injuries. Roger managed to get the remaining men and women back into a defensive position while the orcs started looting the houses around the square for anything of value.

The orcs are still in the town now when a scout rushes in from the east.

"There are people on horseback approaching!" he tells the guards holding position in front of the church.

"Tell The Mayor and pastor," the guard replies to the scout, who rushes inside.

The Mayor sends the scout back to urge the approaching horses to help, and the scout once again runs out of town in the direction he spied the figures.

Voss, who is riding slightly ahead of the others, sees the scout approaching.

"Help!" the man calls, out of breath. "We need help!"

"Railwood must be under siege!" Peren calls from behind Voss, and spurs his horse forward.

"Then we have come just in time," Evandur says. "Let's go!" He follows Peren as the others speed their horses up as well, and within a few minutes they find themselves looking at the small town as they crest a hill covered in frost and footprints from the scout, which barely uncovered the gravel road beneath the snow.

Railwood has smoke rising from it on the far side of town. A small house has caught flame and no one is rushing to put it out.

"We must hurry," Evandur urges.

"No, we must take stock of this situation. If this is a war we must find our army before rushing in," Peren counters.

"There are lives at risk," Evandur says angrily, taking off.

"Let him join the front line," Peren mutters. "Voss, come with me to The Mayor." The others follow as Peren and Voss ride after the angel-blessed paladin.

They pass into the town and are greeted quickly by guards outside the church.

"Are you here to help?" one asks. He sounds genuinely relieved to see the armed party.

"Yes," Evandur nods. "Where is the fight?"

"West," the other guard, a human woman, says. "It's stable for now, they aren't rushing our line but we can't seem to find any room to push back."

"Excellent," Peren says. "The Mayor?"

"In the church," the first guard, a stocky dwarf points to the building through the iron fence that's a little taller than him. Peren dismounts his horse and leaves it with the guards. Voss follows the noble's lead. The others pause to decide what to do. They settle on all following Peren and Voss. Even Evandur reluctantly goes along, after hearing the front line is stable for the moment.

They enter the church.

It is roughly the same size as the one in Tearnsby, if not a little smaller. It is the only church in Railwood, and is decorated not by artisan-made tapestries, but by wood carvings burned with holy symbols, and polished silver plaques. The decorations are clearly made by the people living here, but — despite the lack of professional craft — the feeling that the building gives off is no less beautiful.

In the hall, defended and entrapped by the stone walls and high ceilings, are nearly three hundred people. These are the ones whose homes have been compromised, those who feel safer in numbers, and those who are here to help treat and care for the ones who need assistance. They have gathered amongst the pews and in the aisles between them. They watch the group enter with a mix of fear, distrust, and hope.

Upon the raised platform, near a dwarven preacher who is giving a sermon to those listening, stands another dwarf dressed in elegant white silk. He looks to the newcomers and waves them towards himself.

They approach.

"You are from Taernsby, aren't you?" he asks.

"Yes. I am Peren Siannodel. You must be mayor Greypike."

"William Greypike, yes. This is Gorin Ingrof, my advisor," he says. "We need your help."

"I know, we saw the smoke. We are ready to fight, but we need to see your militia."

"You already saw a good quarter of it."

"The two guards outside?" Voss jumps in, sounding almost accusative.

"We took casualties. There are half a dozen trained soldiers, and some civilian volunteers - hunters and miners mostly. Others are injured."

"Six and some hunters?" Peren asks. "They will have to be coordinated."

"They have all had some training."

"Training doesn't save lives; leadership paired with training does. Where is their captain?" Peren continues pressing The Mayor.

"The last time they had an official captain was the first raid," The Mayor says somberly.

Something flashes across Peren's face. "Voss was a squad commander in the Streboyan war," Peren tells The Mayor. "He helped assure victory for house Ironheart."

"I was informed of his involvement."

"Can you gather your guards?" Peren asks. "Voss can speak with them and rally them. We could use their help and I am certain they could use some inspiration."

The Mayor thinks about this. "Inform the two outside, they will take you to the others," he tells Peren. "Please, hurry."

Peren motions for the rest to follow as he turns and leaves on The Mayor's request.

"We will push the attackers out," Evandur says, loud enough for the nearest citizens to hear, as he begins to follow. "Evil forces do not take root under my vigil."

"Thank you," Mayor Greypike calls after him. "Railwood is in your debt."

The group's footsteps echo through the hall as they march towards the wooden doors. The preacher, Gorin Ingrof, resumes speaking. His voice raises in volume and in purpose as they push out into the cold air again.

The guards greet them once more, and — when Peren explains the previous exchange — they are led along the main road to where the large makeshift barricades have been set up against the eastern side of the square. Four others stand weary and vigilant, three human men and a woman. Two archers, clearly injured and less prepared than the others, are set up on the roof of a house to the left of the barricades, beside the main road.

The militia turns and looks to the approaching group.

"Hail!" calls one of the men, shoulder length black hair and piercing grey eyes meet Peren's gaze. "I am Roger Hardwick."

"Peren Siannodel," he moves so Voss is standing in the centre and gestures towards him. "This is Voss Hallehwell."

"Greetings," Roger says, looking to Voss. "You are well equipped. I hope you're here to help."

"I am," Voss says.

"Good. We need it."

"I know."

"He was a commander in the Streboyan army, for house Ironheart," Peren assists his quiet companion.

"Oh!" Roger exclaims and bows. "I have family on Streboya. You fought for the right side, if I may say that, sir."

"I fought for my beliefs," Voss says. "And I am no sir."

"I fight for the same," Roger responds. "We'd be happy to fight with you. I am sure I speak for all of us in saying that. And, regardless of rank, I am sure you all look like the world's shiniest knights to us right about now."

"Then let us fight like we are," Voss responds. "There aren't many of us, but you look capable. If my group leads the charge and you provide us with the support we'll need, then we can easily drive these bastards out of your town."

The militia looks nervously at each other.

"We can provide support, as much as you need," Roger says. He then turns to the other guards. "He's right. If we don't learn to take a real stand, we're never going to be free of these raids."

There is a murmur of agreement.

"There are goblins with the orcs," Roger tells the new arrivals. "They came later to help pillage. They are keeping an eye on the front line as scouts while the orcs stay further back. We think they are preparing to leave."

"Then we push now, they'll know we're coming but it won't matter if we reach them as the goblins do." Voss says.

"Itching for a fight?" Torkurth asks Voss.

Dadek responds to the human voice. "Probably because you keep pissing the lad off, and he can't hit you."

"As though you're a picture perfect remnant-of-a-soul either, old man," Torkurth muses.

"Shut up," Valindra speaks for Voss. "You two sound like a bard with one tune."

"What if we help you out here, captain?" Torkurth ignores Valindra. "Let us out. Give us a chance to see the action."

"You know he can't do that," Valindra responds.

"You know he can," Nhasan says. "He lets us summon his weapon for him, like we've been demoted from his honourable soldiers to his petty squires."

"It would drain him, and frighten others," Val pushes.

"Voss," Dadek says. "We stand by you. Some of us do so because we want to, and some because we have to, but if you call on us, we will be there."

"Let's go," Voss says, coming out of his daze. The militia has readied their weapons, and Evandur now stands beside Roger with his longsword drawn. Brael and Peren have their bows readied and their rapiers on their hips. The group places their travel packs behind the barricade.

Thervos stands behind Voss as he begins to walk. The whole company watches the armoured veteran stride by the defences and out into hostile territory.

Roger makes a motion with his hands and the militia forms around him.

"Helena, stand with me," he says. "The rest of you take bows and surround the square as best you can. Eyes up, and if you get in trouble, fall for the barricades and call for aid." The men and women nod, grabbing strung shortbows from a rack near the defences. Helena shoulders a maul that was resting against the collection of wooden tables and fallen bricks from buildings that make up the low walls they built. The two wounded archers remain on the roof while the others follow Roger.

The town square is much smaller than the one in Taernsby, but is made in the same general image. It is a large open court with a well built in the middle. The area is a rough sixty feet wide and long, and surrounded by small businesses, community buildings, and several houses.

With Voss heading the group, they advance steadily into the square. For the first half minute, all is silent. Suddenly, though, the sound of breaking glass cuts through the air from the south and the company freezes.

"Move," Voss says, just loudly enough for everyone to hear. The front line increases speed to a jog. Evandur stands beside Voss, with Roger and Helena just behind them.

Peren and Brael split from the group to find positions with good cover and visual range. The archers follow them as they find alleyways to crouch in. Peren stands in the north side of the square with three of the civilian archers, in a side-street between a general store and a tailor, while Brael leads the other to an alley near the south-east corner, along the side of the town's library.

The library has suffered some extensive damage, more so than the other buildings around the square. Not to the extent the western side has, where the smoke is still steadily rising, but the main doors have been chopped off their hinges with axes to allow the dragging out of some artifacts and minerals that were on display amongst the books.

Voss, Evandur, Thervos, Roger, and Helena stop near the centre of the square, preparing for a fight near the well that stands there.

Three orcs lumber around the southern side of the library, walking on a side-street leading from the corner opposite to where Brael is peering out.

They are large creatures, bigger by a head, on average, than Harrock - the half-orc they previously met. Only the woman among them is close to Voss' height of over six feet, but still she is taller. Their bodies are human-like in nature, but much more muscular in build, and with skin tones ranging from a deep forest green to a stormy grey.

These orcs are intimidating, their tusks protrude from their lips and their hair is braided down their backs to keep it from their faces. They all wield axes in their right hands, and the men carry large hemp bags over their shoulders with their left. They are unarmoured, but wear torn clothing that looks like it was pilfered from the houses of Railwood.

Orcs are brutes, and anyone with a basic knowledge of their nature knows this. Even three can pose a serious threat to a group of the same size, but these orcs are outnumbered and almost certainly out-skilled, favouring brutality and strength to coordination and teamwork.

Voss moves from the centre, back towards the library, with haste. Evandur follows just behind. Roger and Helena scan the area and pick out another orc, standing alone, who sees the group as well and begins to advance. Thervos sticks between the pairs, ready to assist either.

"There are goblin archers setting up!" Roger calls, raising his shield to indicate the rooftops across the square to the west where a handful of smaller figures are appearing against the blue sky and dark smoke.

"Ignore them!" Voss shouts. "Focus on the ground troops!" Then: "Peren, archers!"

Immediately Peren launches an arrow that flies true through the air, piercing a goblin through the shoulder. A cry of pain is heard in the square as the silhouette dips back below the roof.

The orcs growl loudly in response and rush forward. Voss raises his arms and soon his axe materializes in his hands. As all three orcs reach him he repels their first swings with his own weapon.

Evandur raises his left arm, the one on which his gauntlet is thicker. He grabs at the metal with his right hand, even with his sword drawn, and pulls a small handle from the plating. Tugging on it in a circular motion, a thin metal buckler unfolds smoothly, extending from his armour. Two orcs have focused on Voss, the third swings at the paladin as he finishes opening his shield. He raises the arm high at the last second, blocks the attack, and slides through the dirt-mixed snow, separating the orc from Voss.

The swing should have cut clean through the thin metal of the paladin's shield, but this is something more than common iron or steel.

Voss pushes the orcs' two axes aside with his own. He slams the butt of his weapon into the jaw of the young female attacker, and swings around to cut into the chest of the larger one.

Roger and Helena stand fast against the orc running at them. Roger, with his shield raised, stands ahead of his sister. The orc swings down with a mallet at the militiaman. He blocks the impact with his shield, moves around to avoid the full force of the hammer, and plunges his spear into the shoulder of his opponent.

Evandur severs the hamstring of the orc he is dueling, effectively immobilizing him. The orc shows no sign of surrender however, so neither does the angel-blessed.

The archers engage, the militia focuses on the goblins while Peren and Brael switch to aiding Voss, Evandur, and Roger. They pick their moments, launching arrows that avoid their allies but streak along exposed sides and arms. Brael lands a shot through the cheek of one attacking Voss, but the beast still does not fall.

Just as the current enemies are beginning to lose ground, another group of orcs round the corner. There are five of them. One with a large tower shield, three carrying shortswords, and one wielding a large two-handed hammer.

They come from the south side of the square. They have clearly skirted around the outside streets to avoid the archers before advancing from a closer position. This shows some planning and forethought, but they still have to close near twenty feet of open distance.

"Thervos!" Voss calls.

"Helena!" Roger adds. "Switch!"

Thervos and Helena react, quickly rushing forward. Helena slides into the space left by Roger between the main battle and the lone orc. Thervos raises his hands and magical energy begins piecing itself together between them. A ray of fire shoots from the demon-kin's well of power and strikes one of the shortsword wielders in the thigh, evoking a deep yell of pain and rage, and causing a stumble.

Brael also switches his sights onto the new group, Peren does the same after he looses a final arrow at the original fight, which pierces the neck of the orc Voss had slashed, effectively ending the creature's life.

The three orcs who wield shortswords rush forward, though one is now limping.

"Hold her," Voss says to Evandur as he shoves the female combatant away from himself, throwing her off balance. Evandur uses the break, plunging his sword through his current target's ribcage from behind and shoving him into the ground. He then whips around in time to barely block the woman's swing with his metal buckler.

Roger and Voss rush towards the new group together.

Voss slams into the first orc, both of them running at each other with full force. She is no more than an inch shorter than Voss. She is young, but incredibly tough. They both stop in their tracks at the force of the impact, but neither is off balance. She sends her sword towards Voss' chest, but he catches the blade with his plated forearm, pushing it to the side.

Helena pulls a hand crossbow from her side and shoots a single bolt into the female orc's head, as she raises her arm to swing at Voss. It travels through her brain and sends her reeling backwards to the ground. She dies there, blood pooling through the hole and melting the snow, staining the dirt beneath a dark red.

Helena then refocuses on her own target as he swings again towards her, catching her on the shoulder as she tries to dodge. She backs up and leaves her maul on the ground, unable to wield it with the new injury. She draws a dagger and prepares for a tougher fight.

Thervos has her covered though, he launches a barrage of pure magical energy that streaks through the air like arrows and begins pelting the orc, who stumbles backwards with the force from each explosion of white light. Thervos continues the barrage, draining his energy quickly, until the orc falls to the dirt with multiple broken bones. As he finishes his attack, the young mage begins to float into the air. His cannot seem to end the stream of magical energy, so instead he points his hands downward and raises his head.

"Watch out!" the now hovering demon-born yells, nervously. "I am directing this backwards!"

Evandur, who is standing closest to the spectacle, heeds the man's warning and manages to roll forward, over the corpses of the original orcs, and around the final combatant he was fighting. As he regains his footing, a massive blast of flame engulfs the the bodies of the orcs and the still-standing female orc. She lets out a cry of pain that is soon lost in the explosive noise. Much of the heat and fire collides with Thervos and he cries in pain.

"Careful!" Brael calls, moving from his position and climbing onto the roof of the library.

"I can't!" Thervos yells back, panicked. "This isn't within my control!"

"What?" Evandur shouts.

Suddenly the demon-kin closes his eyes and is gone, vanished from the air.

Peren rushes from around the back of the library, having left his alleyway to the other militiamen, and runs quickly towards the orcs, who are about to envelop Voss and Roger amongst them. He slides through the snow and, with his dagger, he leaves a deep gash in the calves of the shield-carrying orcish man. The orc does not go down however, instead he turns quickly to face the half-elf, who struggles to regain his footing in the slush.

Voss leaves Evandur and Roger to deal with the remaining shortsword wielding orcs and rushes past Peren to the one wielding the hammer, the one clearly in charge.

While battles rage around him, Voss centres himself and locks eyes with the hammer-wielder.

"Do you have a name before I send it with you to your grave, orc?" Voss asks.

"Lazzak," the orc spits into the snow. "Yours?"

"I only give mine to those who must remember it," Voss replies. "You won't last long enough to warrant that honour."

Lazzak growls. "You won't give?" He asks. "Then I rip from dying mouth!"

Voss runs in and swings at Lazzak. As their weapons clash, the metal of Voss' axe head, against the metal of the orc's hammer, a ringing spreads through the air.

The orc pushes Voss' weapon aside and prepares to strike, but Voss pulls back. The orc swings just short, his hammer thudding through the white and brown sludge on the ground. Voss kicks the hammer aside, spinning the orc, who maintains his grip on the haft. The soldier then swings his weapon low, slamming the thick wooden handle into Lazzak's legs, which lifts them from the earth. Lazzak falls to the ground on his shoulder, rolling to face Voss.

"As I said!" Voss screams, swinging his weapon towards the orc. The blade cleaves through Lazzak's head. "You won't last long enough," he says, quieter, breathing heavily. The soldier is smiling behind his helmet.

The battles draw to a close. Evandur and Roger slay the remaining orc group, with Voss and Peren helping from behind, Helena finishes the one injured by Thervos, and the militia archers and Brael pick goblins from the rooftops until they withdraw.

"Status?" Voss asks Roger.

"A victory," Roger responds. "With the archers gone and the square secure, the orcs that remain will surely flee back to their camp."

"Do we know where the camp is?"

"Somewhere in the swampland. Likely not too far away, maybe a week at most. They probably have one set up closer though, where they could resupply and come back even within a day or two."

"Thank you. Dismissed," Voss says.

"What now, Voss?" Evandur asks.

"Where did Thervos go?" Brael breaks in, having dropped from his roof.

They scan the area. No sign of the young demon-kin.

Suddenly however, a loud scream is heard from a nearby building. The place is two storeys tall and looks to be a shop on the first floor and a home on the second. A red light begins to break through the dark windows above them.

"We have to go in there," Evandur says.

"We don't have to do anything," Peren disagrees.

"I'm going," The paladin says firmly, walking towards the building.

"He's dangerous!" Peren calls after him. To accentuate the point, just before Evandur reaches the front door, the floor above explodes. Wood splinters and sprays into the sky, raining upon the streets below. Flames lick the air and a stream of black smoke bellows into the square.

Evandur breaks through the door and rushes upstairs. The building is a scene of terror. Many walls have been ripped through, and Evandur can see several bedrooms and a dining hall which contain furniture that now glows with red flames. He reaches the room facing the square, a master bedroom. The floor is barely intact, large chunks were blasted away, and the roof is missing entirely. Whatever the demon-born did, he tried to aim it upwards.

Thervos is lying in the corner, one of the few places where the wood seems sturdy. He is covered in soot and debris. His clothing is torn and burned. He is unconscious and one of his arms looks painfully twisted, but he is breathing. Evandur gingerly steps across the floor towards his friend. There is a powerful heat in the room, coming from the walls and Thervos himself, but the paladin ignores it. He grabs the mage and lifts him carefully onto his shoulder.

He clears the weak parts of the floor by jumping over them, crouching through a hole in the wall that leads back to the stairs, and descends. He carries Thervos quickly outside and lays him in the frost, which rapidly recedes.

The others gather around as Evandur presses his gauntlets against the young man's chest, now showing bare red and black skin. A soft golden-red glow permeates the air around the paladin.

Suddenly Thervos Kanuun coughs. It's a small noise, but it sends small flecks of dirt and blood from his mouth.

"Ow," he mutters, his eyes remain closed.

"What in Echoshan's name happened?" Brael asks, causing Peren to glance at the other half-elf.

"I felt it growing," Thervos replies weakly.

"What grew?" Peren asks, anger in his voice.

"Energy, I couldn't stop it. I didn't want to hurt anyone again."

"Again?"

"Peren, let's let him rest," Evandur urges.

"Fine," Peren agrees. "Let's get him back to the church. We just helped save the town, I am sure they can spare some healing supplies or magics," Peren says.

"I agree, he could use healing and new clothing. I am sure we can spare anything he needs," Roger says with relief. "I'm just glad we all made it out alive."

"Just pray that when we get back, our demonic friend here doesn't blow the poor civilians into dust," Peren huffs as he departs.

Evandur carries Thervos like an infant as they walk back to the church. The militia is beaten and bruised, but victorious, and there is an almost celebratory feeling in the air as they pass the barricades.

"Wait here," Roger tells the other militia members. "Watch the square, get us if there's any movement. I am taking my sister and our honoured guests to the church."

The group pushes the double doors open and people begin cheering as they see who enters. Evandur puts Thervos down and the demon-born limps beside him, holding the paladin's arm for support. The sound in the hall is choral and nearly overwhelming. They walk through the people who gather around and watch them move towards The Mayor on the platform.

"You did it!" Mayor Greypike calls above the excited chatter and applause. "You pushed them from the town!" There is palpable relief in his voice. "I had our scout watch from the tower, he told us you had slain the orcs but I did not want to believe him, not until you came back safe."

"Mostly safe," Thervos says, smiling weakly.

"There are injured!" The Mayor calls to the preacher. "Gorin, please treat them!" The other dwarf steps towards the group and leads Thervos and Helena towards the back of the church where several cots have already been set up for the more injured citizens. Evandur follows, offering what magic he has retained from the day to aid the wounded.

"What's the situation like?" Voss asks The Mayor. "That was a raiding party, not an orc tribe."

"No, the trouble is far from over I fear. They will keep coming until we learn to defend ourselves." William responds.

"No, they will keep coming until they are all dead or their tribe is destroyed," Voss replies.

"That's not an option. We have no army."

"We have time, now, and we have resolve."

"What would you do, sir Hallehwell?"

"I would retake this town, fortify the western edge against attack, train civilians to defend, wait for reinforcements, and then take the fight to the orcs."

The Mayor thinks.

Voss continues. "We could scout towards them in the meantime and gather what we can in information."

"We received word yesterday that a small militia force from Centrecrest will arrive in a week's time." The Mayor informs the party.

"We can wait then, remain vigilant and active until they arrive and then mount an offensive push," Peren speaks up.

"Exactly," Voss agrees.

"You have my permission, sirs, to organize my militia," The Mayor gives. "If they follow you, then you may lead them. You helped us secure a real victory today, and that is more than we've had in a long time. I only hope you know well what you're doing."

"I do," Voss says, smiling again behind his face plating. "For the first time in awhile, I am certain that I do."

Chapter Eight – Messages Delivered

3Eo55, 20th of Wounded Winter

It proves a good decision to wait for reinforcements. Those who need it, get the rest they deserve, and — for those who don't — the days following the orc raid of the seventeenth are busy. The militia and many of the townspeople spend their time building barricades at the western and northern sides of town. The dock areas and most of the western quarter of Railwood are left abandoned, but some people move back into their homes the evening after the attack. Thervos, with much healing magic and burn-relieving salves, recovers for the most part. Everyone gets to take a breath of air after the storm.

Voss and Peren spend the days in the barracks, mostly, with some trips to the blacksmith to get their armour and weapons worked on, spending some of the gold they earned from Brenspire back in Taernsby. In the barracks, they speak to the militia, learning the names of the more prominent, still living members.

Roger and Helena Hardwick were the unofficial leaders before Voss arrived to take over.

Roger has a more extroverted personality and more training than the other members, which makes him easy to look up to. Helena is quiet, but is easily as skilled in combat as her brother. They look similar in terms of their dark hair and their light grey eyes, though Helena's hair is longer and she stands three inches shorter in height. They are each attractive in both looks and personality. They are muscular and relatively smart, though neither of them seem to flaunt any of this.

Arthur is another human. He, and an elven woman, Izella, are trained well with bows, but not suited for a close fight. They are nice and outspoken, but don't make a strong impression on either Voss or Peren, and so they largely go unnoticed.

Jitz is a mage of gnomish descent. She stands about three feet tall, with curly blonde hair. She uses mainly protective, abjurative magic. She also knows spells to create distractions and change the environment, making her very useful in a wide range of situations. She has certainly saved lives on many accounts, but has no kills under her belt. She switches back and forth between being hyper and chatty to being quiet and reserved. Voss and Peren agree that she is a useful asset, and a nice enough person to not despise.

The final member of the surviving and able militia is Dorril the dwarf. He is a thick man, who, similarly to Voss, is rarely seen without full set of armour. His is arguably nicer than Voss' in quality, and almost certainly in terms of protection, being crafted as plate mail. Dorril carries a metal tower shield — that is slightly bigger than himself — in one hand, and a short spear in the other. It seems to Voss an odd combination, but when the Streboyan catches the dwarf training, he sees just how powerful he is as the force of the shield hitting a training dummy rips its pole from the dirt and throws it on its back in the melting snow.

When the militia have time off they spend it setting up archer posts on the roofs of abandoned buildings and scouting the area. They find it a certainty that the orcs have a camp not far from Railwood, as they see smoke on two nights rising in the distance to the north, along the shore of Rail Lake.

Thervos spends his time recovering, as there's not much else he can do. Other than a token visit from Voss once, Evandur is the only one who checks on him. The paladin comes every day at noon for several hours, offering healing and to see if there is anything the demon-born needs.

Evandur also visits the blacksmith to get his sword sharpened, and as well to ask if the smith is capable of an interesting project. The angel-blessed wants his shield to open automatically. It was a gift from a talented smith up north, and has always served Evandur well, but in a fight it would be better if he did not have to manually open the shield's plates.

The smith hears the paladin out, but shrugs at the idea. He tells Evandur to try Azgul Hold. Evandur agrees, resolving to do so on the way back to Tearnsby.

Brael takes the few days to do some more advanced reconnaissance, heading hours away from Railwood in the first night after the raid. He mentally maps the area around the town and even tracks footprints to the north. He finds the forward camp of the orcs, a dozen green beasts huddled around a fire in shoddy tents made from poorly dried hides. Their camp is not being packed, and some are sharpening their weapons on hand-held whetstones.

Brael does not get close to the camp, but does report in that another attack is likely.

He goes back to Railwood and purchases three large bear traps from a hunter who lives near the north side of town. The traps are not disguised, but he sets them along the route from Railwood to the forward orc camp in the long grass.

He tracks the trail the orcs left farther north, past this smaller encampment. This takes him the second day, where he spends the night camping in a tree. Then he returns, arriving on the morning of the twentieth.

Not an hour after Brael's return, the same scout that reported Peren and the others' arrival, informs The Mayor that someone on a white horse is approaching from the east.

The horse trots along the road, through the wooden gate-like structure that bears the Railwood sign, just before midday. Upon the saddle is the figure of a woman. Her body is covered in a fine white cloth over sleek black boots and gloves which hug her arms and legs. Her presence draws some commotion as citizens lean from their windows and doors to watch her pull the reins and call her horse softly to a stop in front of the church.

She dismounts, and turns to face those who stand to meet her.

The scout has gathered the group, including the now mostly recovered Thervos. The woman produces a small leather folder from the left saddlebag of her horse. Opening the folder, she holds out into the air two pieces of parchment folded into sealed envelopes, clearly letters.

As she turns to face the group, mayor Greypike, and the scout, she reveals her face to be covered by a mask. It's made from dark wood with white markings on it that seem to shift and change slightly, suggesting some form of magic is upon it. The onlookers see the mask, but no one seems to question it.

"I have a message for one 'Peren Siannodel and Company' and one 'Voss Hallehwell'," she says, reading the backs of the envelopes. "I was told they had travelled to Railwood and was sent after-"

"I am Voss," Voss says, extending his hand towards the messenger.

"I am Emari," the woman replies.

"The letter," Voss pushes.

"That's no way to address a lady, sir."

Voss pauses for a long moment. "Please?" he asks, unconvincingly, and largely confused.

She hands him the letter, which he snatches promptly from her.

"And Peren?" she asks.

"I am here," Peren says, stepping forward. "Thank you very much."

"You are very welcome, sir Siannodel," Emari says, bowing slightly.

The letter to Voss reads as follows:

Dear Voss Hallehwell,

12th of Rainsheer, 3E055

It pains me to think that you may not even remember the name Laeabella. We met only briefly, of course, years ago, during the Streboyan civil war.

You were an honourable soldier. I was a barmaid from Aerivas who had enlisted in the church of Stren, and was shipped overseas to help treat injured. It was not a very predictable set of circumstances that led to our encounter, though, thinking back on it now, it does ring a clichéd bell.

We only met once. I do not remember the date for the life of me, but it was towards the end of the war, I know that. House Ironheart was celebrating victory early, and you were in one of the local taverns near the docks where myself and my clergy company had been staying for weeks.

I am rambling, reminiscing, I know this, and I apologize. You have a son, Voss. I don't know if this is something you ever wanted to hear, or if you already have many more, but you have a son nonetheless.

He will be turning eleven years old this new year. This is not the purpose of my letter, I am writing to you now for another reason. I knew you left, and I have been afraid to contact you for so long. I have a fair web of connections throughout Estrand still. Friends who have heard your name in the past told me you were staying in Taernsby often and I am sending this letter just hoping it somehow reaches your eyes.

You have every right to be mad at me for a multitude of reasons, but I kept this information from you out of both fear and practicality, and I come to you now out of necessity. I named him Vaeus, the elven spelling for Voss. He is a beautiful half-elven boy. He has my black hair and your eyes. I only saw you once, but I can still remember your eyes - once you took that menacing helmet you wore off and looked human, and I finished falling for you.

This is not to say you were my only and all-consuming love, of course. One meeting was not enough to spend my life as a fawn for you. I have had several lovers since. I simply have not forgotten you, and it was my hope to one day have you meet your son.

But I am sick, Voss. It's a rare condition that only affects elves of pure-blood. I know that I only have a few more years at the most, and a few more weeks at the least.

I wouldn't ask you this if I didn't have to. I want Vaeus to at least hear from his father. You do not have to take him if you do not want to, but I know it would mean the world to him even to see a letter from you and know how you feel. He knows of my condition, he is old enough to handle it. He knows that he is likely going to an orphanage but if you want to take him into your care then I would not stand against you. He is your son as much as he is mine.

I know this must be a lot to take in, and I really didn't want to burden you, and I know I should probably have written sooner or not at all but I was afraid of the fact that I know so little about you or who you have become since we met.

I trust you, though. I trust in what little I have heard and I trust in my intuition. Please, write if this reaches your hands. If you do not send anything back I will assume you never got it anyway, so there is no punishment in choosing not to, but please, if you believe me and if you care at all about this, I urge you to think about him, about taking him, or at least letting him hear from you and what kind of man you are. Any advice you would have for him. Any words of compassion. I believe that he will be a good person, and I believe that you can help him learn how to become one.

Laeabella Fairwind

51 Silverstreet, City of Krosa

Voss finishes reading.

"A good man," Torkurth says.

"Sure," Nhasan echoes the thoughts of spearman.

"He hasn't changed," Valindra says. "He is the same man and, if he's not, then that is our fault."

Peren also reads his letter. He reads silently, despite it being addressed to everyone from Taernsby.

Dear Peren and Company,

I am writing to offer you insight into the recent events that have transpired in the past several days since you and your companions have left Taernsby.

I would open by stating that I hold high hopes that you all arrived at your destination safely, and have acted with honour in both my name and your own. I have faith in your abilities and am sure that you have already been a great asset to Railwood by the time this paper arrives there.

I received two letters within three days after you left my town, and I find that highly coincidental. Regardless of the circumstances surrounding the letters however, I have decided to share their contents with you and your allies.

The first letter that I received bore upon it the seal of the Council United, and it was signed with a name I do not personally recognize, though it was written with meticulous care. The letter contained the following:

"Archaeological discovery in the Great Estrand Desert. Seeking adventurers for help in scouting and delving into a newly found set of ruins."

This letter also states that this news has been delivered to the mayor of every major town that meets a minimum population requirement. Each letter that was sent out contains a return address and place for the names of up to ten individuals, or a guild, to answer the call in the town's name. The letter further says that a sum of 750 gold coins, in council mint, will be paid to each group that participates, and more will be given depending on discoveries made there. All treasure found will be property of the ones who found it, as well.

We can discuss more upon your return, however I wished to give you time to think on this, as it would be a good opportunity, and should you want it then it is your name(s) that will be written on this document.

The second letter is something that I would only discuss in person, as its contents are sensitive, and if they fell into the wrong hands it could mean trouble. Please, finish your business in the council lands and return to Taernsby if you see fit. You have until the end of the month of Blooming to respond or return before I look elsewhere. I wish you luck and haste.

With warm regards, Magistrate H. Brenspire.

With the new knowledge filling their minds, the messenger, Emari, simply stands and waits.

"What?" Peren asks when he finishes reading, ahead of Voss.

Emari says nothing, just keeps glancing between Voss and Peren.

Peren reluctantly gives her a couple silver pieces.

"This is not the seal of Mayor Brenspire," Voss states as he folds his letter closed again.

"Pardon?" Emari asks.

"There is a seal on the parchment, but it is not Mayor Brenspire's," Voss responds. "This is a good fake, but it is a fake."

"I do not believe so," Emari responds, calmly, thinking.

A palpable tension fills the scene. Neither appear to be lying.

Suddenly, however, a smaller bell tolls across town. The sound is soon joined by the church bell loudly adding its own metallic ring to the chorus.

"Orcs!" Roger exclaims. "Please, can we set aside this debate until later?"

"Fine," Voss says, and stuffs the envelope into his backpack, which lies against the iron fence.

"I can help fight," Emari says, understanding the situation.

"Oh, can you?" Voss asks. "You better prove your use, and you better do so very quickly." With those words hanging in the air, he turns and leaves. Roger and Helena follow him with no hesitation, and the others soon fall in tow. As Emari gives chase as well, Thervos steps beside her.

"He really is not the worst of them," the demon-kin informs the messenger, "once you get to know him a little."

"Isn't that a comforting thought?" she responds with sarcasm, heading towards the sounds of brass ricocheting off the burned and disheveled buildings.

Chapter Nine – A Second Defence

3E055, 20th of Wounded Winter

The group rushes to the alleyways. The barricades facing the lakeside and the farmlands stand as low walls between the battered and disheveled buildings on either side.

There are two main alleys that are not as heavily fortified. The rest are a mess of rubble and stacked furniture. If the orcs choose a route other than the two which the militia are stationed in, they will be slowed and made into easy targets. If the beasts maneuver around the town to other entrances, it will give enough time for the defence to launch arrows and reposition.

Arthur and Izella have already climbed atop single storey houses and are calling down to the rest of the militia and those from Taernsby.

"They are half a kilometer off," Arthur says.

"How many?" Voss calls back.

"A dozen, no more," Izella says.

"That's a fair number," Dorril says from beside Voss.

"The whole forward camp," Brael confirms.

"It's nothing we cannot handle," Evandur states.

"Agreed," Voss says. Then, to archers on the roof: "When they are in range, open fire. Do not wait to see if they will speak or negotiate; we know that they will not."

"Understood," Arthur nods, spreading the instructions to the other archers and hunters who are climbing up.

"Voss," Peren begins. "Lift me, I am better with a bow, and even better with a vantage."

Voss does not question the half-elf, lifting him at the waist and tossing him upwards. Peren grabs hold on the edge of the house's roof and pulls himself onto the top with Izella. They sit across the alley from Arthur and two others.

"Roger, Helena, take the other alley," Voss orders. "If we can funnel them into the tight spaces without getting flanked we can easily win this fight."

Roger nods and grabs his sister by the arm, leading her away. She has recovered from her previous fight fully and is now ready for some revenge.

"I will go with them," Evandur says.

"You can offer healing, paladin, I may need you here," Voss responds.

"I can offer healing," the messenger pipes up.

Voss spins and stares her down for several long seconds, but she does not flinch.

"Fine. You had best not be lying," he says.

"Thank you, Voss," Evandur says. "You are more trained than them, so they need my protection more."

They split up quietly into the two alleyways.

Long seconds pass.

"The orcs are entering range!" Arthur shouts.

"Loose arrows!" Voss responds.

Four arrows fly towards the distant shapes of orcs that are just barely coming into view over a hill. The pointed wooden missiles soar into the wall of large shields that the front-most orcs are carrying ahead of themselves.

There is a snarling mixed in with the sounds of heavy footsteps as the pack begins to pick up speed towards the town, trampling through the snow-covered farm fields as they barrel straight towards the clearly visible barricades. Clearly the enemy is not acting with any planning. Whether that is an emotional response to their previous defeat, or a lack of leadership, is uncertain.

Another volley of arrows fly out, this time two of them embed themselves in an orc behind the leaders, he doesn't quite go down, but his dark blood sprays a trail across the frost covered grass as the beasts grow closer.

The orcs reach the alleys. Just as one of the shield-bearers lowers his defence for an attack on Voss, Peren launches his own arrow into the orc's shoulder.

The orc growls in anger and pain, but does not lose his grip on his hand-axe, which he prepares once again to swing at Voss.

As the orc reaches back however, Voss raises his empty hands and in them appears his own weapon amongst blue mist. The orc's axe crashes into Voss' as it finishes forming, and is shoved easily aside.

Both groups hold against the first attack. It is Evandur and Voss who slay the shield-bearers and open room for the other orcs to rush in.

One orc leaps over the corpse in front of Voss with surprising agility. Dorril the dwarf reacts quickly though, jumping ahead of Voss. He has left his own shield behind to squeeze by the large human in the narrow alley, but he manages to grab hold of the dead orc's and raises it just in time to block the attacker.

Voss sees something in the way the shield arcs through the air, but has no time to process exactly what interested him.

Peren uses the moment to catch the back of the attacking orc's neck with an arrow and end her life quickly.

Thervos launches a barrage of fire over Voss and Dorril in an arc, and it burns into the remaining orcs' skin and into the ground, which causes them to pull back and retreat briefly.

Meanwhile, in the other alley, Izella launches her own arrows at the orcs rushing Evandur and Roger. The pair of defenders manage to keep them from clambering over the low wall though, as the paladin cuts another down effectively.

Suddenly two rush at once. Evandur easily catches the axe of the first with his longsword, parrying it to the side, but Roger is less fortunate, and is knocked backwards as his shield — a gift from Helena — is brushed aside by the second orc's mace.

The orcish woman stands above Roger and raises the weapon, which looks well made and sharp, above her head.

"Roger!" Helena jumps in front, blocking the swing with her maul. She shoves the woman back and lands another blow into her shoulder, breaking bones. The orc then returns, swinging the mace with her uninjured arm, and catching Helena across her face, tearing a piece from her nose and drawing blood from her cheek and forehead. She collapses unconscious against the wall.

Roger leaps to his feet and plunges his spear through the orc's neck before she can finish the job. He then grabs his sister by her shoulder plating and drags her further behind Evandur. Jitz manages to use a burst of air magic to knock the orc away from Evandur so he can land a series of final blows.

Brael runs to the gap that Roger left and begins launching fast attacks at the remaining orcs, killing several with his dagger and shortsword.

Evandur and Brael, with the help of Izella, manage to kill the orcs on their side before moving to assist the others.

Voss is standing, with his boot on the last living orc's chest, when Evandur arrives. The soldier has been cut through his scale armour and blood is dripping down his left arm and into the snow, melting it to the dirt. The brute under Voss' boot appears beaten, unarmed, but still very conscious. He is snarling at the faces of those surrounding him.

"Casualties?" Voss asks.

"Helena is injured, status unknown."

"Deaths?"

"None confirmed on our side. Ten orc's dead, one alive."

"Good."

"Are we keeping him for questioning?" Evandur asks Voss, gesturing to the orc.

"No," Voss says. "He wouldn't tell us anything, and deserves none of our mercy."

"That is not untrue," Scilandra speaks in Evandur's mind.

"I am aware," Evandur replies inwardly. "But his lack of second thought speaks ill for himself."

"I agree."

"We should spare him," Evandur says to Voss. "He is no threat and I won't stand and watch while an unarmed attacker is slain."

"Then turn your back," Voss says, raising his axe.

"I will kill out of defence of innocents. I will kill an assailant who shows evil in his last moments, but we do now know this orc."

"We know orcs, paladin," Voss replies. "This one is no different."

The orc spits at Voss, struggling under his boot.

"Voss-"

"I am ending his life. If you will not stand by me, then stand against me, or stand aside."

Evandur glares at Voss. "Fine, but do not lose mercy."

"You do not hold power to command me! You do not know me!" Voss spits, then slams his axe through the orc's skull. Without pausing, the soldier continues speaking. "Stop acting as though you do."

"I do not know you, but I know soldiers, I know criminals. If you can profile an orc by his race, then I can profile you by your past."

"You know nothing of my past!"

"That does not disallow speculation on you future," Evandur says, turning to leave and folding his shield back into his gauntlet.

"Voss-" Emari begins.

"I am injured," Voss cuts her off. He dismisses his weapon.

"I just-"

"You have breached a sealed document of mine and I require healing magic. If you cannot provide this then-"

"I get it, I will heal you," Emari says, stepping towards Voss. Her head barely reaches above his shoulders as she places her hands against his arm. She begins to hum. It's a beautiful sound, and as it fills Voss' ears, a pale white light emanates from her fingers and the gash on the man's arm seals shut. The blood stops pouring.

"My thanks, messenger," Voss says.

"Emari." She responds.

"I could have blocked that, lad," Dadek the dwarf speaks to Voss.

"Indeed, and I could have killed the orc before the axe hit him," Nhasan protests.

"Yes and we could all get him arrested for appearing as ghosts in a public area," Valindra retorts. "You were all more rational when you were living."

"Mortal men should not be kept trapped between life and death, we have less patience than you, elf," Nhasan responds, then they all grow quiet.

Dorril and the other militiamen begin to return to town after the adrenaline begins to subside.

Voss eyes the shield as Dorril walks by.

"What was your name?" Voss asks. "Doornail?"

"Dorril," replies Dorril, offended.

"That shield is nearly bigger than you are. I will trade you five gold pieces for it," Voss offers.

"But I-"

"Will be less able to make use of it than me, and you will make a profit. Your old shield would serve you better."

"Fine," huffs the dwarf, passing the tower to Voss in return for the coins.

As he leaves, Voss examines the shield, unsure of why it caught his attention.

"There is a button along the top rim," says Valindra. "I noticed it."

"What does it do?" Voss whispers, under his breath.

"I do not know," Valindra speaks.

"Let's find out then," Nhasan nudges.

Voss hits the button and a thin golden light expands from the shield along all sides. He tries to put his hand through it and finds his fingers unable to cross through the light, hitting a solid surface instead.

"An orc with a magic shield," Emari muses.

"I wonder where he got that from," Thervos adds.

Voss leans the shield against the barricade, then looks around at the weaponry of the other orcs. He starts by grabbing one from the ground, observing it, dropping it, then picking up a second before dropping it as well.

"What is it?" Emari asks.

"That one is elvish in make," Voss says, pointing at the first one. Brael eyes the hand-axe with poorly masked distaste, despite not knowing what Voss said. "The second one is Dabarisian, and those two look Krunixian," Voss continues, pointing at the maces.

"So they stole them." Thervos says, not surprised.

"No."

"No?" Emari asks.

"They could have stolen the Krunixian ones," Voss responds. "Maybe they even took the Dabarisian one, but the Vruyothy blade would not be common around here."

"That doesn't necessarily rule it out," Thervos responds.

"No, you're right," Voss says. "But these look new, and something doesn't feel right about it at all." Voss also uses his magic to express this thought into Brael's mind. Through Voss' eyes, he sees the outline of Torkurth walk from him to the ranger and deliver the message in Voss' voice. Brael looks in surprise at Voss, hearing his words. No one, including Brael, sees the vague apparition, save for the soldier who sent it.

"What are your thoughts then?" the deaf ranger responds.

"Either they got incredibly lucky with a caravan raid-" Emari begins, catching on.

"Or someone is supplying them with the gear," Peren says, dropping down from the roof.

"Exactly. We need to hit their camp soon, before we tire out." Voss says, with Torkurth once again passing the words to Brael.

Thervos nods. "Who knows what they will manage if they get more supplies or something worse before we get there," the demon-kin begins to head back into town. Emari turns to depart as well.

"We will still need you, messenger," Voss calls after her.

"We will see. I will be helpful where I can," she responds, not stopping. "Only until this is done and my debt to you for your broken trust seems paid."

"I will scout ahead and see if I can leave a trail towards the orc camp," Brael says.

"No," Peren says. "You will alert them to our approach."

"I will be quiet," Brael responds.

"You wouldn't know; you can't hear your own footfalls regardless!" Peren retorts with anger ripe in his voice.

"I will be fine. You do not own me, half-elf."

"I am giving you my suggestion, half-elf," Peren says coldly. "Nothing more."

"I understand your suggestion," Brael sighs. "I disagree."

"Do not leave this town until we are ready," Peren spits and turns, heading back down the alley, leaving Voss and Brael alone.

There is a long silence as they watch the noble stride back towards the square.

"When you reach the lake, Voss, head north to where the river leaves and winds towards the Voiceless Peaks. I will meet you where the grass blends with the swamp," Brael explains.

"Okay, Brael," Voss sends Valindra to place the words in the deaf ranger's mind, her elven form barely visible as an outline to the human man.

Brael nods. He shoulders his backpack and quiver and sets out, over the barricade and away from the others.

"Stay safe, friend," Voss sends, though the blonde half-elf does not make any indication of receiving the message.

"Finally," Torkurth tells Voss.

"Don't get used to it," Voss responds.

"It's nice to get some fresh air, eh elf?" Torkurth asks.

"It's nice to be of use," Valindra agrees.

"We'll test your boundaries," Voss explains, addressing the spirits openly for the first time in many months. "But you are volatile. Trained in life, but not in death."

"Ai, sir," Dadek says.

"Listen for my commands, and do as I say."

"First order?" Nhasan remarks.

"Remain patient," Voss smiles. "Though not for much longer, I imagine."

Chapter Ten - An Argument

3E055, 1st of Ildonian's End

The reinforcements from Centrecrest arrive late in the next morning, a full day ahead of schedule.

The town scout announces their arrival ten minutes prior, and people begin to prepare as sunlight stretches over the town, dancing on the fresh frost.

The Centrecrest Troop is riding on a variety of horses, with a wagon of supplies in tow. Heading the group is a stout dwarven man wearing partially plated armour of average make. Behind him is a lightly armoured elven woman with a bow and a longsword strapped to her leather gear, a gnome in robes, and ten humans in a variety of armours and clothing.

The dwarf trots up to the church where The Mayor directs the group to the barracks.

Voss and Peren are waiting just outside when they arrive.

The dwarf and the elf draw close on their mounts and pull to a stop several feet away.

"Hello," Peren begins politely. "You must be the troops from Centrecrest."

"Ai, Bobrunn!" the dwarf speaks in a heavy accent, one specific to old dwarven families.

"Is that your name?" Voss asks.

"Ai."

"Well met Bobrunn. I am Voss, and this is Peren Siannodel."

"We are mounting an attack as soon as we can. Your arrival is fortuitous," Peren says. "We could push onward today, or tomorrow morning if you need time to prepare."

"Mm the timin' ain't a prublem, men'n move out whenever."

"What?" Voss asks.

"We can move whenever," the elven woman interprets. "We are tired from the day's ride, but if it is not yet over, then we won't complain. We are here to help in any way we can. We have all had troubles with orcs in the last decade, and a lot of us feel as though it's our job to help fight back and make the council lands into a safe place."

"What is your name?" Peren asks.

"Shae Vatorril."

"Peren Siannodel."

"Well met, shall we gather the troops?" she asks, seemingly disinterested.

"We will take the Taernsby group," Voss tells Peren and those listening. "The militia in Railwood will stay in case the town is attacked by anything else. They are already worn down from yesterday's fight."

"We be goin' wit' a handful o' figh'ers an' attack an orc camp by ourselves?" Bobrunn asks, incredulously.

"Ai," Voss replies.

"We will scout it first, but we should start moving as soon as we can," Peren says. "Settle into the barracks here for an hour and rest before we set out."

"Some of our men are civilians, assisting in supplies and hunting. They won't all be joining us. There are only six of us who are trained," Shae states.

"Then we will take all six. We are five. It will be enough," Voss says.

Peren eyes the gnomish man in robes with interest while they speak. On his belt is a metal contraption that looks like a flintlock pistol, one that is only slightly different from the prototypes he tested in Azgul Hold.

"What's your name, friend?" Peren asks, stepping calmly around the others.

"Haylar Stormbrigg," the gnome replies, in a confident voice.

"You are not armoured, and carry that device on your side. Would I be wrong to assume it's a flintlock weapon?"

"Indeed it is; you are well informed. It's a pistol sent from Azgul Hold for me to test."

"I am trying to break into the flintlock industry myself, actually," Peren says. "Would you happen to have any other prototypes with you?"

"No, unfortunately not," Haylar says. "However, on the trip to wherever we are going, I would be happy to let you take a few shots, though I do not have much ammunition to spare."

"I would be overjoyed to try my luck with it," Peren says, with almost earnest excitement.

"Then you may, but let us get on the road, or lack thereof, first."

They move inside of the barracks. The group from Centrecrest has their civilian workers unload the wagon while the soldiers get acquainted with the Railwood militia.

The wagon has carried goods both for the journey here and for the people of Railwood, bringing food, bedding, and boxes of arrows as well as bundles of wood and some tar for repairing stonework.

The servants pack saddlebags with dried fruits and salted meats while Voss and Peren inform the troops of the plan once more.

Shae approaches Emari, slipping away from the others. The messenger stands alone near the door, having never fully unpacked her horse in the first place.

"I know you," Shae tells the messenger.

"I doubt that," Emari responds, coolly.

"We met almost a year ago, up north. You came through Daroonga Village and played in a tavern I was drinking at."

"Vaguely rings a bell. Who are you?"

"Shae Vatorril."

Emari's body shifts. She opens up more and lowers her guard slightly.

"I do know you. It has been a long time. What are you doing here?" she asks, almost excited, but more relieved.

"I moved to Centrecrest because it was cheaper, and I am skilled enough to make a living as a guard and fletcher."

"Settling down?" Emari muses. "Last we talked we spoke of how much fun it is travelling the world."

"I've not settled yet, just," Shae thinks, "pausing."

"I guess I cannot blame you for that," Emari smiles behind her mask.

"You seem to have made good company," Shae says. "A guild of some sort?"

Emari laughs. Drawing some eyes, she quiets down again. "No!" she says. "I don't know them, they aren't the nicest bunch. I doubt I will stick around longer than I need to."

"Well, Voss is pretty tall," she says. "I bet he's handsome under that helmet."

They both laugh.

"I doubt it," says Emari finally.

"No one knows," Thervos says, walking by and overhearing. "Although, I'd bet any sum of gold he's better looking than Peren."

Emari chuckles at this as the demon-born walks outside to find his horse.

"See?" Shae says. "They don't seem all bad."

"Maybe. If anything, they might be good for a con." Emari responds. "We should go; we can talk more on the way."

Mayor Greypike meets the group as they are finished packing and nearly ready to head out. He calls Peren, Voss and Evandur over to the side.

"Before you leave," he begins, "the orcs have stolen a good deal of gold from my town. I have little to offer in terms of payment for your aid, but if you are truly going to bring their camp to ruin I see fit that you may keep fifteen percent of any wealth you find there."

"Twenty five," Peren argues.

"I cannot offer that much!" The Mayor exclaims. "I will need the money to rebuild the town."

"Then you will need a town," Voss states. Emari and Thervos mount their horses behind them. Evandur glares at the Voss and Peren.

"I-" Greypike stutters.

"We will debate it on our return," Evandur says. Peren nods, understanding. They leave, heading for their horses.

"Until then, sir," Voss departs as well.

They set off.

Evandur, Peren, Voss, Thervos, Emari, and the six new arrivals, with their saddlebags full of supplies, depart from the north side of town and veer towards the shores of Rail Lake.

The group from Taernsby, including the messenger, take the lead and follow the trail of footprints left in the thin frost. The borrowed horses from Brenspire are certainly being put to good use.

The border that runs along the lake is one of thin sand mixed with pieces of bark, branches, and pine nettles from the trees that encompass much of the land to the east, and stretch over the shore.

They pass a dead orc, who bled out from stepping in a bear trap. They keep watch for other dangers, and find two active claw traps nearby. They activate them with sticks and carry on, leaving the scene behind.

They pass the first orc camp, now abandoned. The troop stops for lunch there to use the already prepared fire pit, and it is here that Voss first works on his shield. Despite his torment, the spirits that take hold on his mind bring some benefits as well. While Voss does not quite know how much they can do, he is tempted to stretch his current abilities, and so he convinces them to allow his shield to be taken in and summoned by them like his axe, which was once a normal piece of equipment as well. Over the first camp, he manages to make the shield vanish and , while no one questions it when he returns from his tent at lunch with less equipment, he does hear some of the Centrecrest soldiers mention his name to each other.

After this, the trail is lost, but Voss leads confidently forward.

The journey takes less time on horseback than it would on foot, but not by much. Voss brings them north, following the shoreline. Peren fires the flintlock pistol off over the water to get a better feel for the power and logistics of it. Again, the accuracy is lacking, but the power is something to behold, and the noise startles the men and women of the troop as much as the horses.

Emari and Shae speak of recent times and their plans for the future, which leaves the messenger-bard feeling better than she has in many months. Evandur and Voss speak little to anyone, but do partake in discussions involving tactics with Peren and Bobrunn, who is nearly impossible to understand.

They camp two nights, and catch fish to keep their food supplies stable, despite having plenty. On the third day of travel, midway through the fourth of Ildonian's End, they see the northern bank as the lake curves into the river Vinn. The wide crack of water cuts its way from the north, running down the southern slopes of the Voiceless Peaks and then into Rail Lake. They cannot even see the mountains over the rolling hills and forests between them and the great heights. On the other side of the river they can see the clean grass turn quickly into watery, muddy swampland as reeds take over, and drowned trees begin to dot the landscape.

They travel until it's near evening, and the sound of the Vinn can be heard over their horses' breath, before Voss begins to slow pace.

"We should meet Brael near here," the soldier announces.

"Brael is likely dead," Peren states. "He probably got too close to the camp while 'scouting' and blew our approach as well."

"No, I doubt it," a monotonous voice calls from ahead and above them. Their eyes shoot upwards to view the figure of Brael nestled in the branches of a leafless oak tree.

"I told you to wait for us!" Peren shouts up at him angrily.

"There is no need to yell," Thervos reminds Peren. "The man is deaf."

Brael ignores them both, looking to Voss. "I am glad you followed my directions," he says.

"Acknowledge that this was foolish!" Peren calls.

"From here we simply march west, across the river, and through the swamps for less than a quarter day. Their camp is upon a small hill surrounded by ponds, thick reeds, and several long dead oaks that could be used as archer posts, if we are careful," Brael continues.

"Speak to me when spoken to!" Peren grabs a stone from the ground and chucks it with force towards the blonde half-elf. It thuds into his leather armour, just below his chin. Brael nocks an arrow with incredible speed and draws the bowstring tight, trained on Peren.

"I am not a servant, you arrogant prick," he says, piecing the words together with care. "I am as much indebted to you, as you are an equal match in archery to me. That is to say, not at all."

"We should have all been on the same page, instead you decided to skip ahead, going in blind," Peren says, unfazed.

"You fell behind," Brael says. "Everyone else seemed to be fine with it."

Peren looks around and begins to realize that no one seems angry, just quiet.

"Just get out of the damn tree, elf," he spits.

Brael launches the arrow, which strikes the ground inches from Peren's foot, and causes him to jump.

"I am no elf," Brael says. "You learn that, or the next shot won't miss."

Peren turns and strides angrily towards the river, no one stops him.

The company stops for the night on the eastern bank of the river Vinn. The sky is barely beginning to fade from white to a purplish grey as they strike their fire and set up the cooking pots. Tents are pitched on the side of camp farthest from the water in case any rain causes the river to rise, however unlikely that seems.

As they settle down for dinner, sitting on soft logs dragged from the wooded area nearby, a brief discussion begins on what the next move is.

Peren sits far from the group, near the bank of the wide, quickly flowing stream. He is joined by Evandur who, despite his objections to Peren's less than legal lifestyle of swindling, conning, and suspected assassinations, wishes to keep the group together.

Shae scouted quickly in the direction Brael described until she saw the light of fire in the distance, confirming the hunter to be correct.

In the centre of the semi-circle of tents, Voss and Brael now discuss options with Bobrunn.

"The camp is a large circle of leather tents on a hill." Brael explains, closing his eyes. "The hill is flat along the top, and houses upwards of a dozen orcs, with room for the ones we already killed as well. Goblins also speckle their ranks. They have a large space in the middle for cooking and fighting, and the chief's tent is the largest and farthest west, at the back of the camp." He speaks slowly, making sure each word is correct.

"So a frontal assault would be noticed," Voss says.

"Agreed," Bobrunn says, clearly for once.

"We should sneak in then?" Thervos, who is listening nearby, asks.

"Ev'n wit' a small group we'd sur'ly be spott'd," Bobrunn says.

"Brael and Peren are the only ones who could get in unseen," Voss says.

"How'd you figure that?"

"Brael is a hunter, and went unnoticed by us amongst the treetops earlier, and Peren is," Voss pauses, "quiet. I have seen him in action. He is quick and I do not doubt his abilities."

"So we send em' in alone," Bobrunn says.

"To gather information," Brael says. "I would be willing."

"Fine," Voss agrees. "If we are going to do any more reconnaissance then let us do it tonight, rest in the morning tomorrow, and attack midday. It won't matter what light level we go under, as they will know of us regardless."

"Agreed," Bobrunn grunts.

"I will get Peren," Brael says.

"No," Emari says, standing from beside Thervos. "I will get him."

Voss and Brael look at each other, share a shrug, and Voss nods.

Emari leaves the circle of firelight and approaches Peren and Evandur, who sit near their own small fire by the water. They are holding their hands to the flame for warmth.

"Peren, yes?" the messenger begins. "We haven't spoken much."

Peren turns slightly. "The messenger?"

"Emari. And I'm more of a bard, actually. This is just the job I hold for now," she rambles slightly.

"What is it?"

"Voss and," she thinks, "Bobrunn, I believe his name is, have decided that someone should sneak into the camp. Voss vouched for your ability."

"And?"

"And you should go."

"Why?"

"Because it's better than sulking outside of our camp, makes you useful in everyone's eyes, and you would be forced to work with Brael, as he is also going."

Peren stands slowly. "What does Voss deem we need in terms of information?"

"I do not know."

"Then I will decide for myself, as I would have anyway, in the end. Fine, I will leave now. Expect me back by morning. I assume we will rest and attack midday or tomorrow?"

"Midday. Will you not wait for Brael?" Emari asks.

"I doubt he'd wait for me," Peren says. He adjusts a pair of leather water boots over his normal footwear, ties them tightly at the tops, chooses a spot in the water that seems shallow, and steps calmly into the darkness, through the river's current, and into the swamps that lie beyond the western bank.

Emari and Evandur watch him depart before both rejoin the main fire where Emari hums a melodic tune and the group prepares for rest.

Chapter Eleven - A Reconnaissance Mission

3Eo55, 4th of Ildonian's End

The journey to the camp is easy for both Peren and Brael, though it takes near two hours of steady walking. The hunter left only a few minutes after Peren, but neither see each other during their approach.

Peren is dressed in his leather armour that he had not removed for the evening in case of ambush. Over his shoulders he wears a navy cloak with a grey trim that blends into the off-pitch of the night. His long black hair is now tied behind his face so he can see clearly, and hide it within the hood that has been pulled over his head. His bow is at the ready in his hands, though no arrow is nocked.

Brael has his own cloak wrapped tightly around himself. He has the forest green side facing outward, to blend in best with the dark swamp water and the brush that litters the small hills and valleys that they trudge through. As he draws closer he takes a handful of cold muck from a thin pond and applies it to his cheeks, chin, and forehead, to prevent his pale complexion from reflecting in fire light.

They reach two different hills which overlook the orcish camp.

Peren climbs a leafless tree so he can gain an even better idea of the area's layout. He is several hundred feet away and can see the majority of the interior, save for some blind spots that are hidden by larger structures.

He counts.

Fifteen tents form a circular wall around the crest of the hill. The tents look to be of well made leather that is draped and affixed to strong enough looking wooden support beams. The beams are clearly cut from dead trees or from the forests across the river, but the leather appears too artisan for a small orcish tribe like this to have manufactured. From within the circle of leather, the light from several fires dances into the sky. The grounds within the wall contain orcs moving to and from tents and crowding around the warm flames. There are loud grunting discussions happening as well all throughout the flat top of the hill.

Goblins can also be seen standing guard atop thin wooden watchtowers on the east and west sides of the camp, as well as bringing food to their larger comrades around the fires.

Neither Brael nor Peren can spot each other. After each waiting for several minutes, they gather enough courage to approach the base of the camp at the same time. Brael advances from the north face while Peren takes the south.

Brael sneaks through the shadows around the outside of the tent wall before he finally finds a break and slips towards the chief's tent. He has observed the camp for a large, collective amount of time, and knows that the orcs will likely be too inebriated to notice him at this point unless he makes any noise. His eyes flit in all directions as his mind draws a mental picture of the whole scene around him, and tracks the location of every visible orc.

Once he makes it to the area behind the chief's tent, under one of the two watch posts set up on this side of the hill, he carefully assesses the situation. Deciding the two goblins above him won't notice him over their own conversation, he begins to climb up the inside of the north-westernmost tower. He avoids the ladder for fear of being seen, and instead sticks to using the inside support beams. As he reaches a perch high enough to see the inside clearly, and one that is wide enough to crouch comfortably on, he begins to count each orc and goblin, to get a better sense of numbers.

Peren meanwhile, is now less interested in the statistics of the camp. He skirts along the south face of the tent wall and finds the equivalent of an alleyway, where the tents are not as close together. As he peers in, he sees an orc woman approaching, stumbling drunkenly from one of the fire pits inside.

Realizing he is too close now to safely back up, he sits motionless until she gets close to the edge of the hill. She turns and begins to slide her hide trousers down her legs.

Peren, seeing the opportunity, removes his hood, draws his rapier near silently from its sheath, and in one swift motion plunges it into the orcish woman's neck.

She utters a soft cry that goes unheard amidst the commotion and drums that now sound within the camp.

Peren rolls the body down the hill, where it lands hidden in a puddle thick with reeds.

He wipes the blade against the back of a tent, cleaning it of blood, before sheathing it once more and pulling his hood back over his head. He moves through the alley, taking quick stock of the camp interior for notable locations. The only points of interest that he can quickly pick out, other than the obvious pair of fire circles melting the frost along the ground, are a tent which goblins are repeatedly carrying food trays to and from, and a tent that Peren sees an orc drop a bundle of weapons into.

The chief's long-tent is interesting as well, but Peren sees a pair of sober looking orcs standing silently on guard, and decides against risking any conflict.

The noble then sees Brael behind the camp on the tower, and they lock eyes with each other. Peren nods his head in the direction of the tent in which the orc left weapons. Brael nods, barely visible from his perch atop the scaffolding, but noticeable enough that Peren sees it.

Peren skirts the camp again, going around the outside to the east while Brael climbs down the wood structure once more and sets off for the tent that the noble motioned to.

Brael reaches his target first. He slides into the tent after making sure the area is not being watched. Once inside he takes a quick stock of his surroundings. At first glance, as his eyes adjust to the darkness, it looks empty aside from boxes and bundles of weapons and tools. As Brael's eyes grow accustomed to the lighting, however, he sees several cages against the wall to the left of the entrance, hidden from view by other crates, and barely any bigger than the wood that blocks them.

There are five cages in total, made from rough looking metal bars, and three of them contain figures.

They are all human women. They are covered in dirt and their hair and clothing are all torn in several places. Brael approaches, crouches in front of the cages, and leans in. One looks up after a moment, fear in her eyes. She realizes he is no orc or goblin, and tears well up immediately, threatening to burst forth.

Brael raises a finger to his lips before speaking, doing his best to be as quiet as possible. "We are attacking in the morning. Will you be okay until then?"

She nods, holding back sobs.

"I am Brael Silviari. I am a hunter and a tracker. I am no noble or knight, but you have my word as a man, and an ally of Railwood, that I will get you out of here."

She pauses, composing herself on his words before replying. "I am Sarah. I was taken maybe a week ago, the others have been here longer," she tells Brael quietly, Brael reads her lips.

"Pleasure, my lady Sarah," Brael says. "I must go. We will get you all home." He takes three pieces of bread from his bag and gives one to each woman, each takes the gift gratefully.

Sarah nods, comforted slightly. Brael hurriedly checks outside. No orc or goblin has heard their conversation. He pulls a bundle of weapons from the back of a pile, slings them over his shoulder, and walks quietly around the structure, out of the tent ring and back into the safety of night.

Across the camp, Peren has sneaked his way behind the tent which goblins have been carrying food from.

This tent is less fine than the others, with the leather being stitched together from a variety of animals including boar, deer, and what appears to be a de-scaled snake skin. Some parts appear to be the same quality as the other tents, though they are matched in as repairs in smaller cut segments. Peren also observes that the bottom of the tent is held loosely to the ground by large rocks, whereas the others are staked into the earth.

He could likely push the tent over with minimal effort if even one of the wooden supports was weakened. The whole thing looks less professional than the housing tents.

He has no interest in demolishing the structure though, it would draw too much attention. Instead, he grabs the base of the tent in front of him. Rolling one of the rocks away from the leather and onto the lip of the hill, he lifts the tent upwards and peers inside, pressing his cheek to the frozen earth.

Inside he sees only boxes. He is behind a large supply of food he assumes. He slips under the flap, closing it behind him, then remains crouched and still behind the crates for several seconds, before peeking over the top.

In the tent he is alone other than the many wooden containers and now visible barrels. He opens several, they contain dried meats, and ingredients such as salt and spices.

'These could easily have been stolen from Railwood.' Peren thinks to himself. He continues to open boxes, finding one that contains baked goods, sweets and some fancy looking pastries. 'This was not stolen.' He thinks. 'No bakery in Railwood would make this, and they have not been raiding northern towns, as there are not enough of them.'

Peren slides around the boxes into the tent, placing himself out of view from the main entrance, behind two barrels. He opens the top of each one. The first contains water, full nearly to the top and on the brink of stagnation. The second holds a foul smelling brown liquid which Peren easily identifies as some strong homemade alcohol. He sits low on the cold ground and begins rummaging through his pack. This ale has been nearly half emptied, and the way the night is going, it will likely be gone by morning.

In his bag he finds the bottle of crestleaf oil he bought from Brenspire's cook in Taernsby. He reads the labelling carefully. Crestleaf is known commonly for its medicinal uses, as well as for its poisonous qualities by assassins and the like. The bottle is nearly full and, when boiled or used in small amounts it would be relatively harmless. Peren looks from the glass to the barrel of ale. He uncorks the oil and dumps the whole thing into the alcohol. He knows this will slightly change the flavour, but the orcs are ignorant and already intoxicated. He puts the empty bottle back into his bag and shoulders it.

As he is preparing to leave, the main flap opens and he hears a squeaky sounding voice enter along with two pairs of footsteps. Peren simply remains still, slowing his breathing as much as he can. He cannot understand the language the voice is speaking, but by the cadence he can assume it to be light banter. The pair approaches the barrels, and while he sits in his dark cloak, he can hear the ale running through a spout on the other side, and some drops of liquid hitting the dirt. This noise lasts for nearly half a minute until the voice begins to move away from the barrel again. Peren sneaks a look towards the two goblins as they leave, both carrying one side of a large tray of metal cups. He quickly seizes the opportunity to leave, exiting the tent the same way he entered.

He meets Brael, who waits for him at the base of the hill. They begin to walk quickly away from the camp, up the hill, and start the journey back to safe territory.

"Did you find anything?" Peren asks when he notices Brael looking his direction.

"I found prisoners," he responds. "I promised them we would return. This bundle of weapons as well."

"If we fight well, then we will save them," Peren responds. "I poisoned their ale. That should make them weaker when we clash."

"That is a backhanded strategy," Brael observes.

"It will work," Peren says spitefully. "Just wait and see."

"It wasn't an insult," Brael smiles, turning away.

They walk together into the darkness, their half-elven eyes and feet leading them eastward.

The hunter, Brael Silviari, and the assassin, Peren Siannodel, arrive back at camp early in the morning. The air grew frigid over the night and the thick grass is once again hewn with frost and patches of ice. The sky is not yet light, but already it threatens to burst with rain or snow, and the weary pair cannot decide which would be worse.

The two of them have wrapped their cloaks tightly around themselves to ward off the chill as the adrenaline from the encounter in the camp has faded. They return to a central fire that is still alight, but is crackling only softly. They add some drier pieces of wood to the embers and breath life back onto the pit before warming their hands against the orange flame.

The sparks and fresh light causes movement in the nearby tents as Voss and Evandur enter the dark of the morning from their individual single person tents.

"You had me startled," Evandur says softly.

"Indeed," Voss says. "I assumed you would be later."

"It did not take long to get there and back," Peren responds. "Easier to travel when you've got a clear goal. We both made good time, and we gleaned some useful information."

"Tell us in the morning. We cannot move until the sun is up, and you will both need some rest as well," Evandur says. Voss nods thoughtfully.

Brael and Evandur retreat to their tents, drawing shut the entrances in an attempt to trap whatever heat there is within.

Before Peren can go anywhere however, Voss motions him over. The noble approaches. Voss sits down upon a thick log, he is clad in his fur ring and banner cloak. He keeps his head covered by it enough that only his short, dark beard is visible in the light of the dying fire. No armour is on the man, he does not sleep in it, but he is still not showing his face.

"What have you learned?" Voss asks once they are alone. He projects the thought into Peren's mind using Valindra's energy as the medium. The half-elf gets the question. Responding using the same energy, he explains silently what they found as best he can.

Voss listens, and as Peren finishes with what he himself did to contribute, Voss responds. "So they will be weaker."

"From the crestleaf? I believe so, yes. If I am correct, which I am, then we should have an edge in the upcoming fight."

"Do you know much about orcs, Peren?" Voss asks, switching topics.

"What do you mean?" Peren asks, confused.

"Their habits, their culture."

"Culture?"

"Command, society, leadership."

"They are brutes," Peren responds. "I learned this through study and experience. They fight for whoever pays best or whoever is strongest among them. They raid towns and attack other races for superiority. They are not smart and in no way are they cultured. They are loyal only to themselves and carry strength beyond many others."

"You say that as though it's a bad thing," Voss muses.

"You say *that* as though I should believe it's good."

"A loyal and strong group is only bad when led by the wrong person."

"What have you planned?"

"Nothing, Peren, simply my thought on the matter."

"Don't do anything stupid," Peren responds bluntly, still using the silent telepathic connection.

"Something is only stupid when it does not succeed. Ambition is not bad unless driven by a fool."

"You don't seem like a fool," The half-elf admits.

"Neither do you. Rest now, I must do the same," Voss says, rising from the log and returning to his tent.

The half-elf warms his hands briefly against the once more fading flame for a few more minutes before following Voss' lead, and returning to the tent that was set up for him.

Chapter Twelve - An Assault on the Camp

3E055, 5th of Ildonian's End

The morning arrives like a bleak, slow rolling wave. By the time the sky has transitioned from black to a solid grey, people have only just begun to wake. No snow or rain is falling as they push from their tents; the clouds simply bar the sun from warming the camp in any way.

The fire is soon re-lit by Shae, and breakfast is already being prepared by the time the travellers from Taernsby have all gathered and suited themselves for battle. The soldiers from Centrecrest move to a separate fire and eat amongst themselves, listening in while everyone discusses quietly.

Between gulps of stew, and bites of dried meat and cheese, Evandur speaks.

"We know these orcs have minor fortifications on the hill," the paladin says. "We could simply set them aflame. The orcs would likely scatter and we could pick them off while they ran."

"No," Brael says.

"Why not?"

"Prisoners," Peren steps in. "He is worried for them."

"And you're right to be," Evandur agrees, taking this in. "If they have prisoners then it would be too risky."

Brael and Peren then explain once again the events that transpired in the previous night.

"I personally don't care about these pris-" Peren pauses, seeing the others' faces as they watch him carefully. "If Brael wants to save them, then I will stand by and help," he finishes.

"They are innocent in this. We will get them out alive," Evandur nods.

"Their weaponry is all of good make," Thervos interjects, viewing the bundle of arms that has been laid out beside the fire by Brael.

"Yes, someone is clearly supplying them. Maybe even supplying other orc tribes in the swamps. We've fought them while they wield these weapons before, though, and that did not stop us then," Evandur says.

"We should focus on the approach," Voss changes topics. "The hill is a good defence in itself and we have few options for the assault itself."

"We know teh grog is pois'nd fr'm teh half-elves' investigat'n," Bobrunn says. "Still, if we're to run in teh camp we shuld 'ave more of a plan."

"A full frontal assault will draw a lot of pressure to the front line," Voss says, ignoring the dwarf. "Splitting the group may be dangerous, but advantageous as well. It would pull apart the orcs' command and attention. Orcs are stronger in numbers but handling one or two at a time is not difficult for a well trained fighter."

"We don't have enough time to skirt the whole camp and attack from both sides, by the sound of it. With groups our size and watch towers, we'd be spotted before we set up." Thervos says before slurping the rest of his soup up and placing the bowl near the fire.

"No, but if we rush the centre and split along the base of the hill we could arc up either side and meet in the middle," Evandur suggests.

"Exactly," Voss responds. "They would see us coming, but hopefully they would be forced to change tactics as hastily as we do."

"Centrecrest," Peren addresses Bobrunn, Shae, and the others, "you should flank along the northern hill face while we take the southern."

"Remain within sight," Voss says as well. "If we have need of assistance, or you do, we will need to be in range to move."

"Agreed," Bobrunn says. "I'll take me group north when we see teh camp."

"Excellent," Thervos says. "I will stay back with Peren and Brael."

"No," Peren says, acknowledging the demon-born's existence for once. "Your magic is volatile and I will not allow-"

"I will keep you out of harm," Evandur cuts Peren off, giving him a sideways glance. "He is right, your magic is volatile, but it is powerful, and useful in a close fight."

"Yes," Peren agrees.

"I will also do my best to protect you," Voss pitches in, his words seem genuine.

"Where is your weapon, soldier?" Shae asks Voss, having already gathered her gear. "I've never seen you wielding one."

Voss holds his hands out over his lap, palms turned upwards. His battleaxe appears in the space, emerging — as usual — from a pale blue smoke. As soon as it fully forms, he causes it to dissipate once more.

"Impressive," Shae comments. "I have never seen that kind of magic."

"No, you haven't," Voss agrees, changing tones to one that's more serious. "Let us move." He stands and walks briskly towards his tent.

"You seem to be getting along with master Hallehwell," Scilandra speaks to Evandur as he begins to collect the last of his things.

"I am watching," Evandur thinks to himself and the angelic presence.

"You are being friendly, I was not stating there was anything wrong with that."

"He is not wrong about the strategy."

"Likely not."

"Then what is your concern?"

"A darkness clings to him. You must feel it. It is not purely evil, and yet somehow it blocks out your light."

"My light pierces all forms that dusk takes."

"Then why can we not see him clearly?"

"You did not bring all forces that you had available," Dadek states. Only Voss can hear. He is alone now, the group has packed their belongings and he is finishing his part by strapping his backpack to the side of his horse.

"He's getting soft. The all or nothing attitude has left him," Nhasan mocks.

"Can't you feel his excitement?" Torkurth asks. "He craves battle."

"We all do. We died as soldiers, we will remain soldiers," Dadek responds. "I don't think we'll get to settle down."

"It seems to be the only time we all work together," Valindra adds.

The ghostly voices flood Voss' mind then all at once. He only catches half the conversation that follows, but he knows the feelings that come with it. He is as ready as they are for a war, desperately trying to end some battle they never quite finished. His shoulders are tense, but there is a yearning in them to swing his axe and cut through his enemies. Even if it solves nothing — even though the civil war on Streboya ended years ago in victory — he cannot set down his arms just yet.

"Still, Voss," Nhasan speaks directly to his mind, "why only bring half your available troops? They would have recovered on the trip."

Voss does not answer.

"You are getting soft," the dead rogue presses again. "You are worrying about a town, about individual lives. If we fail here then the town just gets hit again and again, we will have died in vain."

"We won't fail," Voss says aloud.

"I never said we would," Peren says calmly. Voss has walked to the others without realizing it, and now they are mounting their horses. "Are you getting worried?"

"Just stating fact," Voss replies, loosely.

"Voss-" Emari begins.

"Hallehwell," Voss responds quickly.

"Hallehwell," Emari begins again, reluctantly, "should I remain with Brael and Peren during the fighting?"

"You should have remained in Railwood." Voss' angry tone startles the bard, but she quickly recovers.

"I read your letter, alright?" she admits. Silence envelops the group. She soon continues. "For the Gods' sake you have my word that your information is private. At least allow me to aid you, and prove my skill and worth if this remains a tragedy for you. I am no child in need of protection, and I can be an asset if you learn to trust me from here. I did not know you before and I did not intend to until now." She gives more of a speech than she intended to, rambling at parts but getting the message across.

"Then remain at my side," Voss says, smiling now behind his helmet. "If I am injured, heal me. If there is an orc or a goblin in your path, slay it."

Emari nods firmly. "Fine, and when we succeed, we're even."

"When we succeed, we return to Railwood, take our share of whatever gold we have found, and then away once again to Taernsby."

"If this is not enough, what will be?" Emari asks, spitefully.

"Trust is not gained as easily as it's lost. This would be a good start," Voss says as he mounts his horse and spurs it forward. "Your forgery was good but I have an eye for fraud. We will put it behind us the further we manage to move forward." The soldier rides up to where Brael is leading the group towards the swamps.

They leave their tents standing, intending to make it back here by nightfall or spend the night in the cleared camp. They take bedrolls and provisions, but the structure remains behind to make it easier to return.

"He is difficult," Emari whispers to Shae.

"In some odd way, he is suggesting you stay around."

"What?" Emari asks, confused.

"If this was a good start, that would imply that there would be something after. Otherwise, it would be the end."

"Huh," Emari falls quiet.

They cross the river and into the swamplands. They move for some time, keeping in relative silence. The land is soft and their horses are nearly swallowed by murky pools of stagnant water many times. The smell of rotten plant and animal matter is present all the while, and flies swarm above the larger ponds.

The troop slows as Brael raises his arm. They are nearly an hour away, but the ground grows increasingly uneven, and the closer they ride to the camp, the more danger they are in of being spotted. They dismount and tie their horses to a cluster of trees on a hill that rises out of the swamp with enough grass to feed on.

They walk from there, through puddles and over wet hills until Brael once again calls a stop. "The camp is on the hill over the next crest," he says audibly, without turning around.

"Gather," Evandur says quietly. People come to him. "Let us go to this crest and observe the camp, review our plan."

"I tend to trust the observations of Brael and Peren," Voss says, summoning his axe to his hands.

"I carry no mistrust."

"We have time, sir Hallehwell," Thervos says.

"Let us go, then," Voss nods, dismissing his weapon again. "And no longer am I a knight. I have said it before and I imagine I will have to say it again. Armour and training do not make a sir; a title from a prissy lord does."

Voss, Evandur, Thervos, and Emari approach the top of the hill followed by Bobrunn.

They take a look towards the camp, whisper amongst themselves for a few minutes, and then return to the others.

Once they have regathered, they address the whole group.

"Voss and myself will approach along the left," Evandur says. "We will draw their attention and fight in the thin spaces between the tents."

"An' we'll be 'ight behind em' an' attack from the 'ight side," Bobrunn says to his militia.

"This should split their focus and allow us to surround them," Emari says before anyone else speaks. Voss' gaze moves to the smaller, presumably human figure beside him and finds her mask staring back at him.

"What do you think is behind the mask?" Valindra asks Voss.

Voss realizes that he had not yet questioned the mask's presence on her face. He had simply accepted it as normal. Soon after the elven archer's question runs through his mind, however, he forgets the relevance.

Voss nods at Emari, confirming her to be correct in her description of their attack. The mask's colours change from a darker blue to pink briefly before settling on a static black. Voss, who is the only one watching her at this point, struggles to see the phenomenon as odd. He knows there is an enchantment on this mask but his mind cannot see it as unusual. He makes a note that it changes colour, but leaves it at that.

"If we know the plan, there's no use waiting until the cold stalls our muscles," Evandur says. "Let's drop our packs and move."

"Agreed," Voss says, looking off towards the hill in front of them. He drops his leather walking pack onto the base of the hill where it rises from muck. He summons his shield in the same pale mist that his axe would form from.

They spread into two groups. Voss and Evandur take the head of the Taernsby party, with Thervos and Emari right behind, and Peren and Brael at the back.

Bobrunn and a human man with brown hair and a shield that is not much smaller than the one Voss intends to use take the lead of the Centrecrest troop. They are backed by Shae and another human man, and behind them is a human woman and Haylar the gnome.

With the groups defined, they set off.

The Taernsby party veers left while the other group holds for several seconds to give them time. As Taernsby disappears over the hill, the others start towards the right.

It is not long before Voss and Emari begin to hear cries from within the camp. These growling voices are accompanied by the sound of footsteps running about. A loud and brutish voice is yelling in orcish, the cadence suggests it to be giving orders. Drums begin to rumble from the middle of the hilltop.

Both groups appear to be rushing mostly for the middle of the hill, but quickly they both cut in different directions, rushing along the base until they are nearly opposite each other before climbing the slope. Brael and Peren do not follow up the hill however, they rush for two dead trees that could provide good vantage.

When Voss and Evandur reach the top of the hill upon which the camp sits, they get a feeling for their situation as they draw in an unfortunate sight.

The orc chief has gathered his troops around the tent at the end. The chief himself is a massive, grey skinned beast and is surrounded by the twenty one orcs that Brael counted and nearly as many goblins. One of the goblins is dressed in thick metal armour, though most other figures are clad in leather and hide.

As they reach the end of the spaces between the tents and rejoin in the camp's centre, the chief issues a loud order and half of his troops rush forward.

"They aren't all charging!" Evandur calls. "That's an unusual tactic for orcs!" There is worry imbued in his voice.

"These are unusual orcs," Voss says, thinking of the impressive weaponry and armour they have had so far.

Peren and Brael have climbed atop the two trees growing out of the southern hill face leading to the plateau, and are nocking arrows. From these spots they can see the interior of the camp, but not the chief's hut and not where Voss and Evandur stand.

The other group arrives at this point, as the ten charging orcs are nearly halfway to Evandur and Voss, now backed by Emari and Thervos. The chief bellows another order and the orc group splits evenly, with half heading for each side of camp to repel both attacks.

The pair of archers loose clean shots towards the watch towers. The four towers are built along the corners of camp, and each contain two goblins aiming small, mounted crossbows. The towers are of thin wood, but sturdy enough to reach above the camp and have a much wider view of the area. As Brael and Peren start firing towards the towers they quickly manage to take three goblins down before the towers begin shooting back.

"This is not good!" Evandur calls.

"It is for us!" Voss calls back. "Less bodies in our way!"

Before Evandur or anyone else can reply, an explosion rocks the orcs as Thervos conjures a large blast of flames that collides with the ground and throws chunks of earth and fire into the five orcs. The beasts run through it, but they look pained and they move sluggishly. Whether that is more an effect of Peren's poison or Thervos' fire is difficult to judge.

The orcs are wielding a mix of well-made greatswords and battle-axes. Their weapons gleam in the midday sun as they collide with Voss and Evandur's shields.

Voss summons his axe in his open hand. The weight shifts his balance. As he teeters to the left, Thervos hurls a ball of acid over his shoulder which collides with a she-orc's face. She lets out a pained scream, drops her weapon and paws her burning flesh in vain.

Voss utilizes the change in dynamic to throw his shield into the orcs. This staggers them enough for him to start swinging his axe with both hands. His blade finds purchase in the bicep of another assailant, an orcish man with a lighter green skin that's now speckled with his own blood.

A loud crack echoes through the air as Haylar lets loose a bullet from his flintlock pistol. An orc somewhere screams in high-pitched anguish.

This noise distracts Voss from the fight for less than a second, but — as his head turns only slightly — a greatsword connects with his shoulder. The scale and chain underneath take most of the impact and cause the blade to avoid piercing his skin, but the pure force that the swing carries causes a near immediate bruising and a pained cry from the armoured man as his knees threaten to buckle.

Evandur moves in an attempt to assist, but he's countered by his own opponents pressing the attack, nearly landing a swipe at his legs.

Emari draws her blade, a rapier that is similar in make to Peren's, and runs to the front. She thrusts by Voss and pierces the orc that he injured, driving her blade through his heart. The orc falls to the ground, clutching at the wound in a futile effort to stem the blood.

The messenger bard then, under her breath, begins to sing a soothing melody. Her magic eases Voss' pain and reduces the current swelling, if little else.

"Thank you," Voss says. His genuine voice shocks her slightly. He begins to focus on the offensive, content with Emari's ability to sustain him for the moment.

The fighting continues. Not ten seconds later, the chief sends the rest of his troops forward, save for three well-armoured, larger shield-bearers.

Among the second wave are the orcs, goblins, and several worgs as well that rush into view. The wolf-like beasts are nearly the size of a small horse, and are known well through the civilized world to be vicious and only trained through the constant feeding of hunted or slain meat. Usually only large orc tribes have the beasts in their arsenal, when they have enough hunting land to supply steady game.

Voss and Evandur push their attackers back, who retreat into the oncoming rush. This gives a very brief pause to the combat for them.

"Voss!" Evandur exclaims. "Centrecrest needs aid, they are being overwhelmed!"

Voss looks and, as the paladin said, the bodies of the two human men have fallen beneath the orcs' blades.

Brael and Peren have been launching a steady stream of arrows into the second wave and the orcs attacking Centrecrest as well, since the towers have been dealt with, but now they switch fully into focusing fire on the current combat with the northern offensive. The second wave splits as the first did, the goblins and half the orcs head for Voss and Evandur's side while only the second half of the orcs move towards Bobrunn and Shae.

"Emari, go," Voss orders.

Emari does not argue, she rushes from Voss' side. A goblin hurls a spear towards her as she sprints through the centre of camp. Thervos catches the projectile in stasis, protecting her.

Emari slides neatly behind the front line, wet dirt and slush bleeding into her cloth outfit as her back brushes along the ground. As she stands up she begins to sing loudly and clearly. The symphony of sound is embellished with magic, which washes over Bobrunn and Shae. The wounds they have sustained begin to close and their weary muscles gain a new strength for the moment.

"Without her we are in a tight spot," Evandur says.

"Then let's change that," Voss replies. He throws his arm forward and a spectral hand leaps from it. The hand is a pale blue shade, same as the mist that clings loosely to his weapon. The image latches onto a goblin, evoking a cry of pain from the creature as the print from the hand is seared into his flesh.

"Do it," Scilandra voices to Evandur. "He is laying his cards down, do the same."

"Agreed," Evandur says back. Then he speaks to Voss. "Stand back from me."

Voss knows not if that statement was directed at his magic, which came from Nhasan's spirit, as the roguish ghost was partly unleashed, but soon this question is dismissed as a brilliant light begins to pulse from Evandur's body. His armour takes on the white light as well, Valkronus' symbol on the chest glowing with pure energy, as heat begins to radiate from him.

Evandur's eyes glow red and his white hair begins to stand on end and glow faintly as well, giving it a near appearance of flames.

"Feel light, vermin," he mutters to himself, though Voss hears. "Your gods are demons, and your ways are unholy," His voice rises to a scream as he finishes: "but through my blade, your sins perish with you!" He launches himself quickly towards the goblins, his blade radiating light now as well.

Voss rushes forward with him, but keeps several feet of distance between them.

The fight takes a much more aggressive turn.

Thervos moves to cover behind a rock that juts up as a chair near the centre fire-pit. The mage sets loose a steady stream of flame from his hands. The fire cuts clean through a group of goblins that gets separated from the main force, boiling skin from bone.

Evandur fights ferociously, his presence and light seem to burn those he gets close enough to, and while he looks pained by it as well, his aura seems to keep him slowly healing to combat the heat. White and red light radiates from him and continually strikes at the orcs and goblins around him.

Voss attacks with anger, throwing himself at a single enemy at a time. He swings faster than they can, his muscles working overtime as he leaves gashes across orcs' faces and chest as they fall one by one to his axe, the spirits working with him to empower his body and mind. Pale blue smoke pours from him like fog, chilling the very air around him.

"Voss, behind you!" Dadek cries in Voss' head as the leader of the goblins aims his shortsword towards the soldier's lower back.

Voss releases the spirit of Dadek. The feeling is foreign and painful, like an unused muscle. The ghostly-blue figure of a dwarf with a thick build, and long, wispy hair and beard, flies from Voss' body. The apparition wields a mace and holds a kite shield at the ready. The goblin's stab pierces the image but gets stopped by something strangely solid about the shield. The goblin is frightened by the apparition but manages to hold his ground.

No one else seems to notice the spectacle except Thervos, who makes a note of it, but says nothing through his stream of magical attacks.

Evandur and Voss continue to cut through goblins and orcs, soon drawing the chief to call out once more. He rises and marches towards the fight, with the three shield-bearers fanned out in a semicircle in front of him.

On the other side of the camp, Emari is struggling to keep her group healed. Her magical well is not infinite, and she feels drained from using it already. The gnome fires shots into the orc line every ten seconds or so, and Bobrunn lets loose powerful swings with both a war-hammer and a shortsword. Shae doubles back, dodging a swing that could have easily ended her life. The human woman fills the gap. Shae fires a hand crossbow, which fells another orc.

Only a few attackers remain. It looks to be a victory on the northern side, when a worg leaps through the orcs and crashes into the human that just swapped for Shae. The beast pins her down. Shae cries out in shock as the woman's head is ripped clean from her body. The beast then pushes towards Emari, but Shae slams into it from the side and staggers it.

Emari and Shae take the worg down before it can regain its footing. An orc cleaves through the gap however, shoving Bobrunn aside and landing a longsword swing into the Shae's right shoulder. The orc then spins and pierces Haylar through the lower gut, pushing him into a tent beside the fight which nearly falls over.

The gnome screams, and grabs a bag from his side which contains the powder for his weapon.

He cries out something in gnomish that sounds to be a mix of sadness and anger. He rips himself from the blade, eviscerating his side, and runs between the orc's legs. Soon after he disappears, a muffled explosion is heard and two more orcs disappear into the growing pile of bodies. Bobrunn and Shae cut the remaining ones down in silence with help from Emari and her dwindling magic.

Voss and Evandur fight through their assailants. The second worg rushes Voss but Brael takes it down with a clean shot through its eye.

The goblin leader rushes the soldier again, piercing his thigh and drawing blood. Voss swings at the creature, but he slides backwards and cackles. The soldier grows aggravated. He lashes out with his left hand. From it, another ghostly hand springs forth, once again latching onto the goblin, around his neck. The armoured creature cries and tries to paw the pain from his throat. Voss uses the moment and rushes the opponent, reaching him before he can react.

Voss grabs the goblin leader by the neck, trading the ghostly image for his own, and hoists him to eye level.

"Name, swine," the human spits in a voice bordering on rage.

"Grakk," the goblin spits back. Whether this is an answer or a pained noise, Voss does not care.

"You fought well, if not for the wrong side," Voss says, throwing his body forcefully to the ground in a heap before crushing his skull with his metal boot.

The orc chief bellows above the sound of metal and — for a second — the few remaining orcs draw back, leaving Evandur and Voss to catch their breath.

"You destroy my camp!" his voice comes in the common language. His shield wall parts as they stand twenty feet from the paladin and soldier. "For why?"

"For justice!" Evandur shouts back. The flame in his eyes does not dwindle, as light springs from his whole body.

"You have captives from Railwood," Voss adds. "Coin as well. We've come to relieve you of what you stole."

"You make mistake by challenge me," the chief says. "Me Grallog

Iombrakk, chief of tribe. You stand on Grallog Druum, war camp of mine."

"I make no mistake." Voss retorts. "You pillage, plunder, and rape. I fight for coin. I may not fight for justice, or higher purpose, but even I will take pleasure in ridding the world of a scum like you." Evandur smiles, his burning aura is still pulsing, but he seems to be tiring quickly from it.

"Waste no time, paladin," Voss says.

Peren has jumped from his tree, and ran up the hill to climb the southwestern watch tower. He shoves the goblins' bodies from the small platform at the top and they careen towards the ground, landing in broken heaps at the base. Brael soon joins him in the tower, and they draw their remaining arrows, placing them along the railings for easier access.

"I will take the shields," Evandur says as the orcs move forward again. "I can handle them, focus the chief."

"Gladly," Voss agrees. He would have gone after the chief regardless of the paladin's order.

"By your side," Emari whispers to herself, though — across the battle — Voss hears her words as though they were spoken to him. There is magic in them, which seems to bolster his alertness further.

They move forward, clashing with the remaining front-line orcs. Bobrunn and Shae draw bows and move to the rock where Thervos has been crouched.

Evandur and Voss burst through the orcs towards the shields. The archers land their arrows into the backs of the battle weary foes as they turn to follow the pair.

The shield-bearers meet Evandur and Voss' own defences. The paladin is strong and fast. He summons his remaining strength and shoves one aside instead of going for a direct attack. The orc was not expecting this and stumbles slightly. "Go!" he shouts to Voss, who runs through the gap. One of the shielded orcs swings a hammer at Voss, but Evandur manages to slash through the outstretched arm and pull their attention back to him as they leave their chief to deal with his own problem.

Evandur does his best to position himself between the trio of orcs and Voss. Two of them are forced to turn and face him, while one does his best to block the arrows and bursts of flame and acid that streak towards the fight.

With only two orcs for Evandur to actually deal with he manages to fend off the attacks and prevent the beasts from reaching Voss as he fight chief Iombrakk.

The soldier rushes the chieftain, his greataxe and armour to be pitted against the orc's height, strength and two handaxes.

The fight lasts only ten seconds. Voss suffers a gash in the side that draws a deep stream of blood, adding to the oozing coming from his thigh. The chief's off-hand axe becomes stuck in Voss' armour and the chief lunges forward to shoulder him. Voss smiles behind his helmet however, as he raises his arm defensively and suddenly his shield appears in a quick burst of mist, vanishing from its previous place on the ground. Grallog collides with the metal and shoves Voss backwards, but clutches his head in pain where it collided with the new defence.

Voss bends his knees. He sweeps low and, using the same technique as he did when fighting the other orc, Lazzak, Voss' swing forces the haft of his battleaxe against the strength of the chief's legs. Grallog buckles, and is thrown to the ground on his back, dazed.

The heat from his skin begins to melt the ice around him as Voss towers above.

The soldier swings down, dropping his shield to gain full strength.

The chief blocks with his other hand-axe, managing somehow to stop the blow from reaching him. With a fury in his eyes, Iombrakk begins to push back against Voss.

"Draw on me!" calls Torkurth, from within Voss. "I can end this this!" The spirit of the spear-man longs to be released from Voss' being.

"That is foolish Voss!" Valindra cries. "That could kill you, we have already pushed your mind this fight!"

"End him!" Voss screams, not thinking. Torkurth's image springs from his body. This blue spectre is a human with shoulder length, slightly curly hair. He wields a long and narrow metal spear and uses the surprise to drive the ghostly blade into the chief's face. Grallog screams as his eyes glow with the same pale light, before it fades and the body goes still.

Evandur sees this. He loses concentration for a moment and is cut by a shortsword along his hip. His blood sprays the dirt through the frost.

"Dammit!" the paladin cries, cutting through the neck of the orc. The archers bring the second shield-bearer down at last and Evandur turns to lock against the final attacker on the field. Emari sprints behind the orc and cuts through his heels, bringing him quickly to the ground, where it is Peren who launches his last arrow to finish the fight.

The chief lies still, though he is still breathing, only unconscious.

Evandur steps beside Voss, who still wields his axe at the ready. They are both injured. Evandur's light has faded and he looks exhausted, dark circles now bordering his eyes. Voss' shoulders are relaxed, and his arms look ready to give. He rests his axe on the ground, leaning slightly against it for support.

"What was that?" the paladin asks Voss quietly, concerned.

"Nothing," Voss replies.

"What was it?" Evandur pushes.

"You saw a hallucination, man of Gods." Even through the faceplate of Voss' helm, the power in his stare is enough to send chills down Evandur's spine.

"I did not."

Voss lifts his axe off the ground with a grunt, and swings it downward again, splitting Grallog's head open and spilling further brain and blood into the battlefield.

"You had no reason to do that," the paladin says, bordering anger.

"I had none not to," Voss turns and leaves. He is not halted, though Emari gives chase.

"We should aid the prisoners," Brael says, arriving beside Evandur and continuing towards the tent in which they are caged.

Evandur changes his focus. "Aye, let us go," he says, following the deaf half-elf and putting the quarrel with Voss aside.

A quick search of the camp is led by Peren and Thervos while Evandur and Brael free the prisoners. In Iombrakk's tent, Peren finds a chest and immediately checks it for gold. He finds it; the whole chest is filled to the brim with shining coins.

Thervos checks the desk. There is a disappointing lack of anything magical or valuable. He does however find a sheet of well maintained parchment, folded in half. He opens it to reveal the following, carefully transcribed statement:

"Thank to Shadow for weapon and armour. You make easy for raid and we continue to do, but this days we reach hard time. Something change. We send gold soon with small group and me ask for more help. More orc or more armour. Common language learn slow. Teaching slow. Once more thank for help, hear from me soon."

The letter, if one could call it that, is signed: *'Grallog Iombrakk of Grallog Druum. Third of name.'*

Thervos shows the letter to Peren, who reads it, nods, and takes it out to the centre of the camp where the others have gathered for a brief respite.

Brael and Evandur bring the three prisoners out at the same time. The women are all in tears now, and muttering thanks through quivering lips.

"It's okay. You are safe now," Brael assures them.

Peren tells of his and Thervos' findings, and Evandur soon drags the chest of gold from the chief's tent with the noble's help.

Voss and Emari have walked to the side of camp where Shae and Bobrunn sit. They are planted on the ground in silence, having lain their fallen companions under a sheet of leather that was cut from one of the nicer orc tents.

"I am sorry," Voss says. He sounds earnest.

"You could have brought more men," Bobrunn says articulately. The clarity of his words strikes Voss harder than their meaning.

"I-" Voss starts.

"We shall grieve," Shae interrupts. "We've all seen loss, I am certain. We do not need to point blame, for that falls on everyone." She sounds genuine, but there is still pain in her voice. She knew the fallen by name, Voss and Emari never even got that privilege, nor had the interest.

Voss is silent, though he still feels the guilt. In holding the Railwood militia back he had hoped to save lives, but now he is uncertain. Maybe bringing them would have spared more.

Peren approaches.

"The others are packing," he announces quietly. "We will search the other tents, refill food stores and return to our horses. We should try to get to the other side of the river by nightfall if we are lucky."

No one replies.

There is silence as Peren views those he is speaking to.

"Take all the time you need," Peren says at last, adjusting to the tone. "There is no point in rushing. Should we strike a fire and remain here for ceremony?"

"Briefly," Shae says. "Your kindness is well placed, but they died in honour and we can honour them at home. Let us make a quick fire, burn the bodies and set their souls free."

"Understood," Peren responds.

Shae and Bobrunn turn and begin searching the nearby tents for flint and tinder, along with any burnable wood. Brael, Evandur, and even Sarah — the prisoner — pitch in. While their backs are turned, Peren opens the leather and grabs the flintlock pistol from Haylar's burned and gnarled corpse. He stows it in the back of his pants and covers it with his cloak.

Voss watches, saying nothing.

The flames of the bodies sends the group on their way. They carry the chest of gold to their horses where they dump the contents into the saddle bags.

Though weary and burdened by death, they make good time. They camp the night at the eastern bank of the river where they left their tents, lighting a fire in their old pit to dry the water left from the crossing, and to ward the cold of the dwindling winter once more.

"My poison worked, though not as well as I had hoped," Peren says over a bland dinner of pilfered bread and old cheese.

"It helped, Peren," Voss says solemnly. "We won that battle, but barely. Any edge was one we needed."

Evandur looks to Voss at these words, but says nothing.

"We found his secret," Scilandra says.

"Yes, but what is it?"

"That is our next question."

The fire crackles as dusk pushes into night, exhaustion takes the group to their bedrolls, and sleep forces shut their eyes.

Chapter Thirteen - An Easy Trip Back

3Eoss, 8th of Ildonian's End

The journey back to Railwood is uneventful and quiet. What talk occurs is mostly related to their findings at the orc camp. Other discussion is limited to average greetings and courtesies.

The only major debate is related to who "Shadow" might be. The name appeared on the piece of parchment in Grallog's desk, and the conversation leads to the possibility that this person is the leader of Wight's Call.

Wight's Call is the largest bandit organization in the known world. They prey on travellers, merchants, and caravans that find themselves on either side of the Voiceless Peaks, and have been rumoured to be led by a man named "Shadow" or "The Shadow" depending on who is asked.

If this was the case, and the two were the same, it would explain the orcs' ability to get steady supplies of weapons, armour, and food. While most seem to agree that this is a reasonable assumption, there is no evidence other than the note to support it as fact.

The trip takes another three days. The addition of the three new bodies is offset by the four who fell in combat. No snow remains upon the ground, and having already took the trip once, they now know their way back.

They do not bother fishing, instead they opt to dig into their rations before they inevitably expire.

Shae speaks with the group from Taernsby. She tells them that although they are grieving, they carry no blame towards the others, and are still happy to have helped in securing Railwood from this threat.

The words do little to reassure Voss or absolve him of guilt, but he says nothing to betray this to Shae or Bobrunn.

They plod their way along the shores of Rail Lake, now lying to their right. The crystal water stretches far into the west, and the other side fades over the horizon as they make their way south. Finally, before noon on the third day of riding, they see the small village in the distance.

They ride until they reach the western edge of town and are greeted by Roger and the militia, who cheer and rush forward to shake their hands.

Voss and Peren explain the events that occurred in as much detail as they can while being walked across town.

They are led quickly to The Mayor's manor, where William Greypike has returned to living since the danger has receded slightly.

The returning group's horses are taken to the stables across from the church by the Railwood militia. Roger stays with the Taernsby party and what remains of the Centrecrest force.

The Mayor comes to meet them outside. He is dressed warmly and seems unaffected by the rising, but still frigid temperature. Once again they explain what occurred, a shorter version this time, only the assault events and the rescue of the women.

"Then you've succeeded!" Greypike is jovial, relief flooding his body. His tense shoulders fall as he hears about the orc chief's death.

"We suffered casualties," Voss responds calmly, with a slight nod towards Bobrunn, who stands apart from the group with Shae and the servants they had left in town.

"I see this," The Mayor adopts a less cheerful tone. He speaks louder, directing his words at the Centrecrest soldiers. "Bobrunn, I am grateful to you, and to your town. You will be compensated and you have my word as mayor that we will send aid should the need ever arise."

"Thank ye'," The dwarf replies, somberly.

"We found a chest of gold," Peren says. "We counted just under three hundred pieces." He speaks truth, they portioned it into individual leather bags, each containing one hundred, with the third containing ninety-three. "All of it is gold, no silver or copper mint." The noble adds.

"You may keep one hundred fifty. We will make do, split this with

Centrecrest and know that I am sorry and thankful to you all."

"Thank you, mayor," Peren replies, not pushing it any farther, knowing that he would have settled for less.

"We should go," Voss speaks. "Let us say our goodbyes to the people, the militia, and Centrecrest, and then set off."

"You will not stay for awhile?" The Mayor asks, disheartened.

"With all respect," Voss begins, "I am sure most of us still have business in Taernsby, and it is a long journey. We should be heading back. The threat of the orcs has diminished and we provide little use to you from here on out."

"This is true," Greypike responds, thinking. "You are welcomed here any time. I am offering you one other thing." He pulls a square piece of parchment from his coat and hands it to Peren. "This is a signed document that authorizes the bearer or bearers to stay in any church of Horan as honoured guests. You have done good deeds for this town and we see fit to issue this."

"You have this power?" Peren asks.

"It is expected that established churches make decisions out of truth and not obligation. In Railwood, the only established church is to Horan, and the God of Wisdom and History is well respected throughout Estrand. This is our first issued document, and we have no hesitation."

"We thank you," Emari says.

"You must only sign your names on the spaces left for you, and carry it with you at any time. We can reissue it should it be lost but it will take coin and communication with the Council United to do so."

"We will not lose it, thank you sir," Peren says.

"We shall be on our way in a few hours," Voss says to everyone. "It is still early, but we have not much time to waste either."

"I will be about town. Hopefully I will say goodbye officially as you leave, but— if not — then travel safely," The Mayor says. He nods and returns down the cobblestone path to his manor's steps.

The groups reconvene in the town square. Reconstruction has begun here, as people move rubble out of the area with large carts and horses. Several tables have been set up for a hasty celebration that Roger explains will occur tomorrow and be held to boost spirits after the long fear.

They sit at the tables and finally start to relax.

"Thank you for your aid., Roger says as silence begins to feel like a burden.

"I came for the coin and the favour of Taernsby's mayor," Voss states bluntly. He does not lie, but his mind still weighs heavy costing lives, and his spirits still ache for a fight.

"There is no shame in that," Roger responds. "That doesn't dispel the fact that you did good deeds here. Are you really leaving today?" He asks, noticing that already Evandur and Brael are bringing their horses back into the square.

"We are," Peren answers.

"The life of an adventurer never slows, huh?"

"Adventurer?" Voss asks.

"What would you call it? Mercenary? That fits, I think, but it's less flattering."

Voss smiles and blows air through his nose, which barely steams the air through his helm.

On the north side of the square they can see Sarah smiling as she embraces another, older woman. The other girls found their husbands and families as well, or so they've been told, though they have seen no sign of them since their return.

"If I was more confident, maybe I would leave this town and travel more," Roger says, attempting again to make conversation.

"You could. It's a dangerous world, but you fight well enough," Voss says.

"You think? This town doesn't have much of a militia if I leave, though."

"Now that it is safe, it will recover. I expect little danger for some months, and people will fight if people must," Voss responds.

"Maybe."

"No harm in staying," Voss says. "No harm in leaving either, is my message, just personal preference. In the long run it might only make a difference if you believe in what you're doing."

"Maybe," Roger repeats, this time more thoughtfully.

They sit for some time. People move about them and life breathes back into the town in small places. Food and drinks are brought out, hot soups and ciders, and all the soldiers partake in the small feast.

As a second hour passes, the cold begins to creep slowly in and the groups prepare to leave. Bobrunn and Centrecrest's civilian troupe elects to remain another night, but Taernsby has already gathered their horses and belongings.

"We are heading out," Evandur says to the others as he mounts his horse, there is finality to his words.

"Yes, let's go," Voss agrees. They have not spoken much since the attack on the camp, but there is no hostility, only tension.

"See you again one day, perhaps," Roger smiles. Voss smiles back — though Roger does not see it behind the face-plate — and then he turns.

They spur their horses and set off. Emari says a final goodbye to Shae, embracing her for some time, and follows, galloping down the road to catch up to the others as they ride through the wooden arch.

"Winter will finally be over when we return," Thervos says thoughtfully, as they pass into the council lands again.

"Indeed," Peren actually speaks to him.

"Going our separate ways?" Emari poses the question as though she cares not what the answer is, but there is still curiosity in her cadence

"I do not plan that far ahead," Peren answers. "Thus far I don't mind the thought of company. The coin has not been bad either. I could likely find more loyal compatriots, but the thought of you does not detest me."

"I am leaving," Evandur says. "I have matters to attend to in both Azgul Hold and Daroonga. I will likely leave your side in the former, but may see you again when I pass through Taernsby on my way to the latter."

"I am leaving as well," Thervos says quietly. No one seems to question why. The demon-born has come close to death several times and seems to be the butt of Peren's berating more often than he deserves.

"I may stick with you, Peren," Voss says, also sending Valindra's energy to convey the message to Brael. "If you stick with me, that is. Perhaps we can scare up some more coin and find that doctor who evaded us once, before we split up."

"I may stay as well then," Brael agrees.

"Should I have no other arrangements to make," Peren says distantly, "then we shall see."

Emari nods. "Then we have a party still. Let's not split up until we reach safety, though. There are plenty of dangers to be had on a long road, and plenty more that can easily be avoided by travelling in numbers."

They agree, and continue until light is playing with dusk, before Voss speaks again.

"Adventurer," he says, bemused.

The others look at him, thinking back to Roger's words earlier in the day.

"Is it not what we are?" Emari asks.

"What?" Brael asks.

"Adventurers," Emari responds to the deaf man.

"I guess so," Voss replies. "Soldier and mercenary are titles I have known many times, but never adventurer."

"Sir Helmet is probably a more fitting title for you, or Armoured Hard-Ass," Emari says, immediately regretting the comment.

To her surprise, perhaps because he is tired, or maybe because he is relieved to be heading away from Railwood and winter, Voss only laughs in response. The deep and dry chuckle is bolstered, as the others join in.

They continue, spirits high, towards a safe place to find camp.

Chapter Fourteen - A Decision

3Eo55, 8th of Ildonian's End

In the mountains, as frigid air blows snow from the peaks, there is anger.

"Why, sir?" a timid voice asks. The speaker and the one to whom he speaks stand alone in a large, dark hall. The room is cavernous, and lit only by several floating candles that hover near the ceiling, which is too high for the light to reach the floor other than as dancing pinpricks.

"Because that is another plan that cannot come to fruition now," the voice comes from the other figure. It is deep, particular, but sounds hollow and distant despite the mere ten feet of space that separates them.

"We have had setbacks before, my liege."

"And we will have no more, or it is my head he will want on a spike."

"Understood, sir. Should I inform Shadow?"

"Shadow needs not know. He is irrelevant now."

"Why is that, sir?"

"Because his influence only spreads so far. If I am to succeed, if we are to succeed, then I will have to claw that victory away from those who oppose me. I must do that myself, not through pawns, not from a distance."

"What would you have me do?"

"Leave me. I have plans to finish. Tell Layvaas that he has my permission to attempt his own goals, and when I call upon you next, you will have for me the means to go south."

"How far south?"

"The Beltwood. Gather willing servants, twelve of them, and — within two months — you will be called to meet me here once more. I have made my choice."

The first man nods, and scurries towards a large set of doors at the other end of the room.

The hollow man draws the candles closer to himself, and they illuminate him and the table he stands above. He takes a dark-brown leather notebook from his robes and sets it open upon the wood. Drawing his right arm forward, with a quill between his fingers, his red-stained hand sets upon a fresh page as his mind pours notes through the pen.

* * * * *

Two full days pass calmly in Railwood after Peren, Voss, and the others leave town. The third night now begins to give way to morning.

Roger lies in bed. His house is small, but big enough for him and his sister. There is a kitchen downstairs, a room for storage, and two bedrooms. The bathhouse lies across the street, and there is little Roger could complain about now. Helena remains sleeping across the hall. There has been no movement from her room, even though morning light is beginning to pierce the windows. He envies that, the ability to sleep after all that's happened for so long. Her wounds have mostly healed. She recovered fully, save for the swollen scar that reaches from her chin to her forehead, though Roger does not understand her ability to push the memories from her mind so quickly.

His thoughts do not dwell on that long. There is a shift, his bed moves as Shae rolls over.

"You awaken," she says. It's a statement, not a question.

"Yes."

"What weighs on your mind?"

"Nothing."

"You lie," Shae responds.

Roger thinks for some time. "I worry that you have stayed these nights from pity."

"Pity?" the woman almost laughs. "No, I stayed because your eyes felt comforting, I stayed because your touch felt alleviating after the losses I have had, and I stayed because you asked me to."

"I didn't ask you to."

"Last night when we were done drinking, you did," she smiles coyly.

"Those reasons, they were one for each night, weren't they?"

Shae does not respond.

"So will you not stay a fourth?"

"I may not. I have a home in Centrecrest, and obligations there as well," she says. There is a pause. "There is something else though, isn't there?"

"Voss told me that if I wanted to get away from this town, I should."

"Yes?"

"He said that I could, and something about what I wanted being ultimately more important than the reasons."

"And?"

"I want to leave, but how could I?"

"Rent, or sell your home, then make sure your horse is fed and your bags are packed."

"I mean Helena, and my friends, and my life."

"Ask if they would come with you. Even if they don't, your life goes where you go."

"Why would they say yes?"

"Why would I?"

"What does that mean?"

"Just ask them, Roger," Shae speaks. "When they say yes, start planning. Decide what you want to do. If your heart still weighs heavy then stay and recruit new militia, and then follow your plan until it has to change again."

"Is that what you do?"

"Yes."

"It seems to be working out for you."

"It is."

Roger pauses. "Thank you, Shae," he says at length. He is relieved.

"Sleep, beautiful. You still have time. We can discuss more when the sun has risen farther, and I will make you breakfast. If I can't stay another night, I will make sure your morning is as peaceful as I can."

Roger closes his eyes, and the elf's head rests upon his chest as she sees the man off to sleep once more.

Book Two - All the Standards in the Wind

Book Two of the Series: "A Splintering World"
Part Two of the Novel: "The Stillness in the Air"

By: James Lytton

Piece of Lore - Balance In the World

3E055

The Gods of Thrella were given power by the Prime Celestial in the ages before the formation of the world. There were conditions and limitations of this power.

Some of the limitations were, of course, fairly easy to understand and work with. Upon the world there could only be a set amount of power. Everything that exists draws on this limited well of energy - from rocks, to plants and animals, to people. Any excess, the Gods allowed to take the form of arcane energy, dispersed throughout the world and the realms surrounding the physical. This limitation was only set in place to balance the world, and allow life to progress in a natural way. Other than this, the Gods had free reign over the formation and foundation of the planet. This amount of power was constantly replenishing itself, as if life on the planet was only borrowing from it and, when the life had ended, the power would be returned.

The other conditions were somewhat more interesting. The world must not be safe, but it must not be so dangerous to prevent exploration and development by the beings upon it; the world needs to be populated by at least one race that has sentience; the Gods must intervene only in the most dire of situations, and must be limited in their interaction with the world; there must always be good and evil, light and dark, and chaos and order. This last condition was the most difficult for the Gods to make function. Maintaining a balance between such abstract forces took trial and error.

The Gods made a pact to create and nurture life, but they were young and needed to test carefully what life would be. They made devils and angels to serve as their examples for morality, good and evil. These beings were not all powerful, and could be destroyed. If destroyed they would soon reform in the realms of afterlife that the Gods made - which remain now as the homes for the devils and angels, even long after the creation of the world. The Gods created the large world of Thrella and made several continents. They grew plants on these bodies of land, and made animals and creatures to form cycles of life, growth, and death. They created sentient beings of low intelligence — ones that would come to be called gnolls, goblins and orcs in the common tongues — to learn the natural desires that life holds for creatures:

power, sex, love, prolonged life.

They allowed the world to develop and saw its workings. Crovosius took governance of weather and seasons, managing the world so that life would not falter where they made it, but that it should not go unchecked either.

The gods also vowed to see no creation of theirs as a mistake. They would make sentient, intelligent life, and allow it to exist without their influence.

The first true example of sentient life the Gods created was the mighty race of giants. They gave to them the world, and infinite lifespans. These beings ruled for thousands of years, in far off lands on one side of the globe, to nearer lands on another. It was a great era of expansion and development. But this was before their immortal leaders, Yaelagra the Creator and Rodath the Destroyer, slew each other and began a great war. The races of giants devolved into chaos for many tens of years before they were nearly wiped from the world. Those that remained after the near century of war went into hiding, a great slumber that has since lasted into the current ages.

After this, the Gods created other races throughout the world. They made beings such as dragons, and others in the likeness of lizards, snakes, and frogs. They made some cunning, and some strong and tempered, they made cat-folk and bird-folk, and gave them all a home somewhere in the vast expanse of seas, archipelagos and continents. All of these new species thrived in their homelands, and many vanished after several hundred years. Some died due to war, some were struck by disease, some died during ages of ice and snow. All left remnants of their once vast empires, and all still exist in the world, though now most are fragments of their once-greatness.

On Estrand and Streboya, two continents that had barely been touched by the aforementioned races, the Gods made their most recent test of life. They made the elves, with long life, and placed them on powerful sources of arcane energy in the forests of Vruyoth. They made humans to be driven and determined, and dwarves to be strong and resilient.

So far, this cycle of life has lasted longer than many, with less disasters having threatened it. The Gods have learned from their mistakes, and also learned that the condition of maintaining balance was a test. They cannot maintain balance themselves. Balance exists in the world by itself. Whenever order has taken root for too long, chaos can, and will, rise. When war wages, either peace will be found by the opposing sides, or one will win and set peace for itself.

The races of the current era have known war, and chaos, and they have known peace and order. This age has lasted half a century with only a squabble on Streboya to break the easiness of life. The Gods do not intervene, nor can they predict the course that the world drifts on. They simply wait and observe their creations, intent on learning from them, from their joy, or from their pain.

- Excerpt from Ran-Levyr's "An Account of My Meeting with the Gods"

Chapter One - Busy Rest

3Eo55, 16th of Ildonian's End,

A long journey, taken in little time at all, ends in Taernsby. The small group of allies left the council town of Railwood on the eighth of Ildonian's End, and they arrive only eight days later. This incredible feat of halving the usual travel time comes due to a priest who happens to be riding the same route.

The man, who speaks little, and calls himself Thaldor of Aerivas, is a devotee of Maltram. Maltram is the God of Speed and Assistance, and so the priest explains that he often finds himself able to help people on their travels by some sort of divine chance. Despite the man's common looking features and clothing, and his reserved nature, he demonstrates a surprising font of arcane power. He blesses the entire group's horses with incredible speed. He does not seek coin, and accepts their thanks with grace and a humble nod. His blonde hair is always tied in an intricate braid and his features are clearly elvish, though his pointed chin and nose seem less sharp than many of the faerie-folk.

The small troop of seven, consisting of Emari the Bard, Voss Hallehwell, Peren Siannodel, Brael Silviari, Thervos Kanuun, Evandur Angelthorn, and, now, Thaldor of Aerivas, make their way north in good spirits and in better time. In under two days of travel they have arrived in Azgul Hold. Evandur does not stop there, as he had planned to before their departure, instead resolving that the lesser travel time would be better than completing his side project. They enjoy the Krunixian capital and its impressive hospitality, and then continue briskly towards the Kognear Tunnel.

When they at last pass through the borders of the Taernsby township, the group begins to diverge. The snow and the frost have mostly melted. The air is still bitter, and the wind still bites, but the sun has gained some warmth back and the sky has stayed clear for the entirety of their journey.

Thervos takes his leave just past the Twin River that marks the border between the Highfell and Taernsby townships. This river runs from the southern mountains to Glass Lake. Thervos' cabin lies just north of the road, near the river, and, for a time, he wishes simply to return and lay down. He resolves to perhaps venture to the proper later to collect his coin from Mayor Brenspire, and maybe even to take another trip in the summer, but for now he bids the others farewell, leaving his horse with them.

The group wishes him well. They do not despair at his absence.

The rest of the travellers move almost all the way to the western gate together. Thaldor and Evandur both say their goodbyes as they draw near the Mayor's manor. Angelthorn heads towards the church of Valkronus and Thaldor explains his meeting with a ship captain near the docks. Both of them have their own steeds, and so they ride off toward the town walls.

The remainder of the group all find their way back to The Mayor's manor before anything else.

The estate, a ten minute ride from the western wall, stands tall upon its low hill. It is shining in the young afternoon sun, and its log walls appear manned by two figures.

The two gate-watchers are familiar faces. One is the human man named Roahl, who is the mayoral messenger. The other is a half-elf whose name the group has learned to be Fellix through their many dealings with Magistrate Brenspire.

As they approach, the gate is cranked open. Fellix leads them across the stone courtyard, which is now bordered by flowering wooden planters. They reach the stone patio and climb the steps to the main door.

Soon, they are in the sitting room on comfortable chairs. Mayor Brenspire has a new, young servant light a fire in the hearth.

The dwarf listens carefully as they give their honest account of what transpired in Railwood. The Mayor gives them each a good deal of coin for their service, as well as papers that entitle them each to a purchase from any shop in the proper for half cost, that he will pay the other half of. He explains that he wishes to support the local businesses. There are some restrictions set on the purchase of course, but it is an interesting reward nonetheless, that they all accept gratefully.

The travellers stay for tea. They talk about the warming weather, and about anything that happened while they were away. Not much seems to be newsworthy. The search for the illusive doctor Eralius has turned up no further information and the trail has grown cold. Trade is back in swing and all the shops are restocked with food and equipment. Prices are going down and people are all preparing for the spring to begin, and the new year celebrations in four days. Other than these pleasantries, nothing spikes the groups' interest.

As the day starts to mature, The Mayor states that he must return to his tasks and he bids the group goodbye. He tells them to return on the morrow, as he wishes to discuss a letter he received when there is some more time to do so.

They agree to this, but for the moment they wish for nothing other than to return to the East Air Inn and Tavern to secure warm beds for the next few days. Mayor Brenspire's servants take the horses that were lent to them back into their care, and so the journey back to the walls is made on foot.

From the western gate they observe that the streets in the proper are full of folk carrying bundles of wood and tools, and others pulling or driving wagons of trade and building supplies. While the jumble looks like it could be maneuvered, they are tired from the journey they have just finished, and opt to take the less crowded street that runs along the outer base of the wall.

They speak little on the walk, which takes close to two hours.

When they finally arrive at the inn, they find the mid-sized establishment is not at all as crowded as when they were last here.

Laura Tennebaun explains that while travellers will likely be arriving soon from farther north and west, the place has grown quite due to those who were here all winter leaving, since the snow is gone.

Voss, Peren, and Brael are more than relieved to be back. Being stuck in this inn all winter seemed an ill fate at the time, but now they look upon the familiar setting as one of comfort and rest. They each pay a gold coin, purchasing a guaranteed room for the next three nights, coupled with a warm breakfast every morning.

They sit and share a round of ilex berry mead in the sitting area near the hearth. The heat now seems less necessary, but it is no less welcomed.

Dinner is brought by Laura. She says that the plates are extra that would be otherwise thrown away, but her patrons are grateful regardless. They eye the fat cuts of pork and beef and the steaming vegetables on the side with ravenous hunger. They enjoy the meal thoroughly before the day turns late. Then, as the sun fades, the past week finally begins to catch up to the small party, and their eyes grow increasingly heavy.

One by one they retire early to their rooms. Peren, then Brael, then Emari all disappear to quarters that have been made ready for them upstairs. Voss remains seated.

Matahari and Volana, God of the Sun and Goddess of the Moons, have just begun their dance, but there is still light outside. Voss has made a plan.

"Valindra," he whispers quietly. There are several men at the bar, mostly flirting with Laura, and three women seated at the centre table, but none are near the armoured man. "I need you to find a shop selling enchanted goods."

"Are you certain that is a good idea?" the elven woman's voice responds. Already Voss' head begins to throb.

He thinks for a moment. "No, but it will speed things along for me. Search the area. Test our boundaries, and then report back. In particular, I am looking for items made with runic or crystal magics."

He feels her essence depart from his mind, as her spirit seems to split from his. No one, not even he, can see her. Voss stands and begins to walk towards the door. His body feels hot, and the cool air of the evening does little to help. His head begins to pound painfully before a minute has passed. He stands on the street outside, adjusts his cloak so it falls off only his right shoulder, and waits for the scout to return.

It takes a few minutes. His head grows increasingly distracting and pained as the time drifts sluggishly. Finally he feels her essence rejoin his. His breathing begins to return to normal. He hadn't even realized it grew rapid.

"Are you okay?" Valindra asks.

"It hurt, but it was manageable. What did you find?"

"There is a small shop in the south-eastern quarter of the proper. It's maybe five minutes from the private docks. It looked open, lit by glowing orbs," the scout reports.

"Good work, lass," Dadek joins the conversation. The new voice slams into Voss' eardrums from within.

"Yes, thank you, Val," Voss mutters as someone walks by, along the road.

He sets off with haste towards the south gate. After fifteen or so minutes of walking, and with Valindra directing him occasionally, he finds himself standing across a side-street from 'Odali's Magical Goods.' He walks briskly and confidently to the shop, seeing the open sign still in the window.

The soldier has to lean forward slightly to fit through the low door. Inside, he encounters a comfortable, if not crowded space. The single room is lit by several soft lights that seem to meander about the ceiling, gently bumping into walls and then floating back again. Four rows of shelves take up almost all of the floor space, and each row contains three distinct sections. The rows run perpendicular to a long counter at the opposite end of the store. Behind the stone top is an elvish man. He stands a good foot shorter than Voss, quite small for an elf. The man, presumably Odali, wears a pair of circular spectacles, and a finely made vest of black velvet over a white tunic.

Odali raises his hand in a quick wave. "Hello, sir!" he calls through the shelves. His voice pairs well with his looks. It is regal, and carries some age with it. The wrinkles under his eyes bear the same appearance.

Voss nods in response before beginning to scan the aisles.

The elf lets him browse for awhile before he calls out again. "Need anything?"

"Do you do your own enchanting?" Voss responds, barely turning his gaze from a set of carved figurines.

"Not often," Odali replies. "Only temporary imbuements. Party tricks, and gentle magic that clings to an object for a month or so."

"Hm," Voss hums. "I heard tales of objects that could be suspended in midair using magic."

"Ah!" the elf nods vigorously. "Indeed. Not an uncommon form of magical enchantment. I received a set of steel objects as a gift awhile ago. All were enchanted in that way. A wonder for an entertainer. Can turn a whole career around in the less wealthy parts of the world."

"Do you still have any?" Voss asks, finally turning to face the man behind the counter.

Odali appears unafraid. "Er, yes, I think," he says thoughtfully. "I had two still at this year's start, can't remember if I sold the orb."

"Can you check?"

"Of course! I will return imminently," coos the shopkeep. Odali rushes through a small archway in the back left corner, which leads into a storage room.

"You could pocket something pretty easily," Nhasan's voice suggests.

"This shop would have some protection on it. Most do," Torkurth responds.

"I think we could deal with one tiny, elderly elf," the assassin retorts.

"Maybe we could," Voss agrees. "We're not going to try it, though."

The man returns, carrying a leather-wrapped bundle. Voss approaches him. He lays the bundle open on the counter. In the wrap are two steel objects. One is a pole nearly two feet long; the other is an orb about five inches in diameter.

"These two," Odali says, pointing to the leather wrapping, "they have buttons that unite or disengage the magic circuits within the metal. Pressing one will cause the object to attach itself to the fabric of the realm, and makes it nearly impossible to move."

Voss holds his hand out, and Odali places the orb in it. "The circuits? How is this enchantment made?"

"It is a crystal magic. Taking the crystal and grinding it into dust, then inlaying it within the metal itself," Odali explains. "A much more expensive form of enchantment, but one that holds its arcane power much longer."

The soldier presses the small, rectangular button near his thumb, and feels the object change. The orb immediately resists all movement. Voss cannot budge it from the air, no matter how hard he attempts to. He presses the button again, removing the effect, and returns the orb to Odali.

"Impressive," Voss comments. "How long will this last, roughly?"

"It was made by a powerful friend from Daroonga. It will last longer than you will, likely longer than I will," says the elf, who is considered to be nearly immortal in terms of aging as long as he makes occasional trips to his homeland.

"I want the pole. Price?"

"Two hundred golden lions. No negotiation."

"One hundred fifty," Voss responds. "You won't find many entertainers wanting a two-foot long floating stick."

The elf pauses. "Fine."

Voss smiles, and pulls the paper from his pack that gives him a half off purchase from The Mayor. Odali views the parchment, shrugs, and smiles as well.

"Ruthless," he muses at the armoured human.

Voss takes his coin purse from his side-bag, and counts seventy five gold worth of coins and square shillings onto the stone counter. As Voss produces the coins, Odali fills out the paper from The Mayor with a formal request for the rest of the item's value. They then shake hands, and Voss bids the man a good evening. He leaves the store with his enchanted steel pole.

The night then passes uneventfully. Voss sleeps soundly despite the headache he has developed now for hours. In the morning, the soldier finds himself at the centre table in the tavern. Emari sits across from him.

They do not engage much in conversation. They are brought a plate each, consisting of scrambled chicken egg, and a seared slab of cow meat. The plates are delivered by a kindly man in brown linen clothing. The man glides around tables, which are slowly filling with a crowd seeking warm breakfast, and makes his way back towards the bar where Laura stands and pours warm coffees from a large metal pitcher. Life in a trade port certainly has its perks, as imported Streboyan or Southern coffee is not a cheap drink in the council lands or farther west.

Brael and Peren have not awoken. Emari picks at her eggs, pulling her mask forward to fit the utensils under, but avoids the meat. Voss does not touch his food yet. His helmet is covering his head, as usual, and he shows no signs of removing it.

Emari drifts from watching Voss sit silently to scanning the rest of the tavern as the stoic man begins to bore her and her stomach grows full. She is looking for a specific type of person, and a few do catch her eyes.

There is a small figure sitting on one of the couches near the hearth. He is thin and short. Emari would guess halfling or, more likely, of gnomish blood. He is dressed in well made robes of blue and grey. A wide brimmed hat — fashioned of dried and treated reeds — covers his face. From under this hat pokes a dark wooden pipe, and light wisps of smoke pour from its tip. The hat is a staple of Krunixian farmers, who use it to block the harsh summer sun in the wheat and rice fields.

There is a travelling pack beside him, and hooked to the side is an ornate looking wooden staff made of some kind of red painted wood. A book lies open in the man's lap, and he turns the pages every minute or two as he takes the words into memory.

"Do you see that man?" Emari asks, looking back to Voss.

"The gnome?" Voss asks, hardly moving his head.

"Yes."

The man on the couch has also been watching them. It is hard to avoid noticing Voss' armour. The company of an attractive woman does not deter from the intrigue surrounding the table either.

His name is Boe Chong. He is a gnome and, more importantly, an aspiring illusionist. His roots lie in Fairgarde, a small village outside of Lo'Dorra. His family is large and commands one of the area's more profitable spots of farmland, which grows rice from spring to late summer, and wheat through less harsh falls and winters.

His siblings showed little to no interest outside of their family's work, but Boe used what money he made to invest in arcane teachings from the small, local mages guild. He found he could pick up basic incantations and rituals with relative ease.

When he felt comfortable with his own abilities, he began venturing for several hours every evening to Lo'Dorra's centre where he would perform illusion and minor magic for small coin.

He pooled his money and, after several long years, at the respectable age of forty six, he joined up with The Velvet Compass to fund him as an adventurer and to gain passage north. He did some jobs for smaller guilds and groups, and now he hopes to find a way to increase his library of knowledge and hone his skills further.

Boe glances up from his book to find the woman at the centre table looking back. Her head is covered by a hood. She is clad all in grey with small black accents in the form of a collar and buttons, and her gloves and boots are of fine brown leather.

Her face is a dark wood — a mask — which Boe does not find odd.

"I want to speak with him," Emari tells Voss.

"Why?"

"I have a plan, and we are clearly both interested in who he is. I will return, and give you some time to eat your food in private." She stands from her seat, pushing the oak chair back under the table, and begins to stride across the room towards Boe. Voss shrugs, lifting his helmet off of his head, but still holding it in front of him so as to block any eyes.

"Hail!" the woman says cheerfully to Boe.

"Greetings," the gnome responds. He tilts his head back so he can see her and she can see him. His voice is kindly, but still on guard.

Emari struggles, pawing for the right words. "You seem to be an interesting character."

"My thanks, I think," the gnome responds. "You as well, I suppose."

"What is your name, good sir?" she asks, courtesying slightly.

"Boe. Yourself, if I may ask?"

Emari pauses, settling against giving her true name just yet. "I am Chablisienne."

"I'm sorry, what?" Boe asks, caught off guard.

"You may call me Chablise," she says calmly. She laughs then. It's a light, musical sound. "I know it is an odd name. It was given by an odd family."

"It's unusual," Boe admits, "but not of poor craft. What brings you to this tavern? Just passing through I suppose?"

"Not quite. I am part of an adventuring group. We have done some good in the council lands, and now we've returned here to rest."

"Yes," Voss calls from the table, just loud enough for them to hear, "a group of adventurers who are all absent, or have parted ways with us." His face is partially visible as he turns his head to speak, but is still covered in parts by his helmet, long brown hair, and steadily growing beard.

Boe looks from Voss back to Emari. "Is he your only companion then?"

"No," Emari responds after a backwards glance at Voss. "There are two more upstairs, but they are resting still. We are unsure of our next move now, regardless, and we have just arrived yesterday, so they can take their time in recovering. We could actually use another member to help us in lieu of the two who left us on our journey back," she proposes, her mask shifting to pink.

"Interesting," Boe muses. "Is this an offer you're making, or just conversation?"

"It's an offer if you want it to be," Emari responds.

"I have done some adventuring," Boe expresses. "For the past few months, however, I have mostly been studying, and trying to find the coin to travel west."

"I am interested in magic as well," Emari says, feigning engagement and motioning to his book, 'Components of Sound in Illusionism.'

"Really? Well, perhaps it would be nice to have a research partner for a change, someone to bounce ideas off of and learn from in turn. If you are staying around Taernsby and making some coin then perhaps I would consider joining."

"Certainly. If you aren't busy, I should introduce you to Voss."

"Lead the way!" Boe says. He closes his book on a piece of cloth to keep the page, and then tucks it into a small satchel on his left side as he stands.

They cross back to the centre table. There are fewer people now, as many have taken their leave for work.

"Zaik!" Boe speaks the Krunixian word for hello without thinking. He removes his hat in a show of respect. His appearance is soft and kind, with smooth and rosy cheeks. He has greying hair that is cut short and wild, and a wispy goatee that has grown several inches below his chin, which is no small feat for a gnome.

Voss looks down at the man, sitting still far above his short stature. Voss' head is uncovered. This is not strange to the gnome however. The human's face is square, with a wide nose, strong jawline, and studious brown eyes. He is attractive, which is neither added to nor taken away from by the speckles of dirt and the thick beard now covering his lower face. Before responding, Voss places his helmet back upon his head. "Voss Hallehwell," he finally says.

"Voss and Chablise," the gnome makes a mental note. Emari nods at Voss, signalling to not reveal her name. "I am Boe Chong. I believe I have been invited by Chablisienne to join your group. Are you a guild or just friends?"

Voss stands. His plate has been emptied. "Neither," he says. He looks down and between the pair, nods at Emari, and begins walking towards the main entrance. "Meet me at the notice board," Voss calls over his shoulder.

"He seems a bit unpleasant," Boe says to Emari when Voss has exited the building.

"Sometimes," she responds. "It is more or less frequent depending on who you are."

"So he is always like that?"

"He is a good soldier and commander, but he often seems reserved. He is not cruel, though, so don't let his demeanor and attitude frighten you. After the first few days I spent with these people, I found myself relatively comfortable, if not bossed around on occasion."

"Well I am still willing to give it a chance," Boe resolves.

"Good. I should mention that there is a fee of ten gold for joining our group," Emari finally begins to finish her plan.

"Really?" Boe muses, in slight disbelief.

"Yes. Well, it's usually ten, but I will make you a bargain and say that seven will do. You seem nice, and I would pay the other three to our treasurer for you. I am sure we will both make double that within the next few days."

"I know established orders often have entry fees," Boe says skeptically. "Despite this, and granted that I am not specifically a social creature, I have never met a group of people you have to pay in order to be friends with."

"No, no!" Emari backs up. "Friendship is free. It's a show of faith. After our first job together we evaluate your performance and decide whether we trust you as well. It's a deposit, essentially," she struggles to find a good reason.

"Right you are!" A familiar voice speaks from behind them. They turn back towards the stairs to see a half-elven man with long black hair approaching. He is freshly shaven, and dressed in a clean blue shirt and brown linen pants. "I believe you still me some of your coin as well, Emari. But, since our recent venture was a success, I suppose I can simply take it out of the total payment to you. I will count out your coins and leave them in your room."

"Peren!" Emari cries, trying to convincingly fake happiness. "I was wondering when you would wake up!"

Boe looks very confused.

"Peren is our group's treasurer and coordinator," Emari continues the lie.

"Perhaps we can waive the fee for this aspiring mage," Peren says, studying the gnome carefully. "I have business to attend to, and this may take some weeks to get everything in order. You can take over as treasurer and work with Voss until my return." Peren leans close to her ear. "Sloppy execution, work on the details before trying a new con."

"Yes sir," Emari's mask becomes white.

"I am Peren Siannodel, so that we have met officially," he extends his hand to the gnome.

"Boe Chong," he replies.

"Excellent. I must take my leave, if you'll excuse me," Peren says, turning. "If you know anything about flintlock technology, as well, I could find you a great position as a business partner if adventuring does not suit you," he adds.

"That could be interesting. I know little of flintlock, but I know some things about alchemy and chemistry, including the recipes used for the explosive oils and powders in early prototypes."

"We will discuss," Peren says with a smile. He leaves the tavern. The door swings open to reveal a bright day outside.

Meanwhile, Voss has moved across the street and towards the gate. Near the entrance to the city is a well constructed blacksmith. The forge is outside. It is still unlit, but an open sign hangs in the window, and so Voss has pushed inside.

Standing behind a small counter is a well dressed, young looking halfling man. He waves as the tall human enters.

Voss carefully places both his shield, which he took from Dorril the dwarf in Railwood, and the magical pole that he bought the night prior onto the counter.

"I want you to attach this," he gestures to the metal rod, "to this," he says, pointing at the shield, "in place of the current handle."

In a relaxed voice the halfling replies, "Well, let me see." He grabs the pole and holds it up. He notices the button and presses it curiously. Surprise fills his face when magic fills the beam. "It's magic!" he exclaims.

Voss nods.

"Oh, wow!" the halfling bubbles. He is excited, but recovers some composure quickly. "Well, I think I could do this, yes. It will not be easy, however, because of the magical qualities of the new handle. I would have to hire an enchanter, though that won't cost *too* much. I have a friend."

"Is there someone who can do it better than you?" Voss asks calmly. "For less coin or with less risk?"

"Yes," the blacksmith responds quickly. "Not in Taernsby though. Maybe Daroonga or Vruyoth. Aebarrow, as well. None close by. I would love to do this, I can do it! I just cannot promise it to be cheap."

"Okay. Then do it," the soldier responds.

The blacksmith smiles. "Alright. The hiring of the enchanter will be the expensive bit. I would estimate in the end I could get it done for a hundred and fifty gold."

"That's more than the pole itself," Voss argues.

"How much was the pole?" the halfling asks, incredulous, gesturing to the still suspended object in front of him.

"Seventy five."

"What?" he is astounded.

"I had a half priced slip from The Mayor," Voss recalls. "In total it would have been equally priced."

"Well," the blacksmith states, "it should have been more expensive. Odali is getting carried away with his low prices."

"Still," Voss presses.

"Fine, fine. I can make it a hundred. I can cut some corners, and some people owe me favours," the blacksmith caves.

"How long?"

"I can get it done by dusk if the enchanter is available, though he often isn't. If not tonight, then tomorrow night."

"I will be back at dawn tomorrow," the soldier states. Voss has been counting shillings the whole time, and now pushes several tall stacks towards the blacksmith. "I also want a spike forged to the centre of the shield."

"As in a sharp point for bashing down doors?"

"Sure."

"Thick? Material?"

"Thick. Steel."

"I will start that before the handle replacement. I will likely be able to get it done within the same time. Come at dawn in two days. It will be a few extra coins for material cost, but I will discuss price later."

"Deal."

"I need your name for the ledger," the halfling says as he turns.

"Voss."

"Thank you for your business, mister Voss," the blacksmith says as he finishes jotting it down, and the man swings the door open once more.

Chapter Two - Tool of Death and More

3Eo55, 17th of Ildonian's End

The cold would once have betrayed the warmth within Thaldor. If any heat or life yet remained, then this would still be truth. Thaldor, however, feels nothing in the brisk air of this dying winter.

The sun has not yet risen on the seventeenth day of Ildonian's End, and the elf stands on the docks in Taernsby. He is dressed now in a thick woolen coat, though he stands still in the breeze, like the world around him has no effects.

He scans the pulsing waves for a few minutes before turning back towards the town.

"Ronald," he speaks. His voice has a distant, thoughtful tinge to it.

"Ai?" a man's voice returns. A thinner human steps from the shadows under a warehouse's overhang. His short, blonde hair is bundled into a fur hood. He draws a deep breath through his pipe to keep the flame alive.

"How long have you been in Taernsby?" asks Thaldor.

"Why? Hate it here already?" The man laughs. "I've been here a year or so now. Small raids mostly, petty thefts."

Thaldor indulges Ronald in the meaningless banter, even nodding to feign attention. "No, I do not hate it here yet. I was sent to gather information." Thaldor explains. "I sought you with the hope that you could provide what I seek."

"And what do you seek, elf? Maybe I can help, maybe I can't."

The elf clenches his fist as he restrains his urge to end the life of the man before him. "I was sent to discover the source of the disappearances in Taernsby."

"Who sent you?" the human asks. "Shadow?"

"Further up the ladder," Thaldor says, followed by the whispered phrase,

"Fear cuts deeper than steel."

"Yer' fucking with me. Why would Ghostie care about some people going missing in a port city?" Ronald presses.

"Ghostie?"

"Yeah, fucking, the dead guy with the red hand."

"You'd best watch your tongue, Ronald. *Ghostie* is well aware of your family ties here, and so am I. Assuming you don't want to be sent far away from them, you would do well do learn that your master has a temper."

The human shuts his mouth for a second. "Ai, right. Well, I don't know much about the vanishings, other than the guards were workin' on it, asking about it," he says. He pauses. "Come to think of it, a notice was posted at the church not two hours ago. Tired looking man, shivering in the cold. Read something about a doctor, Voran Eralius I believe. Official mayoral seal and everything."

"You think it's connected?"

Ronald looks past Thaldor at the ocean and shrugs. "I think most things are, somehow. I wouldn't be surprised if this Voran was the current suspect. The disappearances stopped about a month ago, though. The notice made it seem like this was something new."

Thaldor hums. "You should return to your dwelling and get some rest."

Ronald nods. "Right. Well, if you have need of me while you're in town, I'll be drinking most nights. At the same tavern you found me in first."

"We shall see." Thaldor responds. Ronald takes his leave and saunters, a little shakily thanks to his whiskey intake, into town.

The elf walks back into Taernsby then as well. He diverges from Ronald's path, heading towards the square. He moves with incredible speed. This would be attributed to his devotion to Maltram, if that was remotely real.

He reaches the Polytheistic Church in just under ten minutes. The sun will be rising in a few hours or so, but that is plenty of time. Maintaining this form for another minute seems impossible however. Thaldor drops the false image. His tanned elven skin grows pale and tight against his bones, and his blonde hair becomes spindly and white. He draws his black cloak above his head and scans the message on the church board with his decaying eyes.

He thinks for a long time, longer than it took him to walk from the docks to the square.

Finally he speaks to himself. "The only way to gather answers fast enough is to seek them from The Mayor." It's a statement imbued with frustration. He reaches forward, and with his dark, burgundy arm he tears the page from the wood.

Thoughts race through his mind. Plans. Obstacles. Hunger.

He pushes from the church, gliding silently through the square. He ventures along the edge, avoiding the large area in the centre where a square of ice has been surrounded by fences. At the western side of the space, he exits through a side-street and traverses the city, heading quickly for the outer walls.

He waits near a dirty tavern beside a wide road. It takes nearly until dawn before someone enters his view. The man is a drunk - out much too late, or much too early. He is old, and he is stumbling.

The figure pushes along the side of a small glass-work store before he stops. He undoes his trousers. Looking around, and not seeing anyone approaching, he drops his pants to his ankles.

He begins urinating, steam drifting off the cold ground into the air.

The Red Hand, as his subordinates call him, glides into the street behind him. He waits patiently, though sunlight has already began to turn the sky from black to a deep navy.

The drunk pulls his pants up once more, and turns. He jolts in shock as he sees the tall figure behind him.

"Oi!" he cries.

"Name," The Red Hand demands.

"I'm John. I'm, who the fuck er' you?" he spits the question through cracked, dry lips.

"Tonight, John, I am Echoshan."

The man stops, his blood running cold. He drops to his knees on the frosted cobble. His own piss begins to soak into his pants. Tears begin to force themselves from his eyes. Above him stands the cloaked figure of death, waiting calmly. "Please," John begs, "I ain't done nothing wrong. I ain't a bad man!"

"I never made the claim that you were."

"I love my kids. I'm away too often, I know, but I care about em'. I just need time to say goodbye."

"You've had time. You were not marked by fate for death, but chance and bad luck have played you into my domain. I swear that your soul will find an afterlife. I do not know which, but that is not my decision. It was yours," comes the calm and pitying voice. The cloaked figure, Thaldor, The Red Hand, bends down. He grabs the drunk by his collar and lifts him with ease to his feet again.

"Please!" weeps John.

"Find peace, John." The Red Hand plunges his right arm into the drunk's chest. John lets out a pained cry as his blood begins rushing from his body and into the decaying arm before him. John twists and jerks for a few seconds before collapsing to the ground.

The Red Hand stares at the body. He debates leaving it for someone to find, to give closure, perhaps, to whatever family the man had. He settles on shoving the body quickly down a thin and dark alley. He places John's corpse against the wall of a bakery in a slumped position, as though he had passed out.

With new life in his eyes, and even a slight brown tint back in his dead hair, The Red Hand sets off for The Mayor's manor. Whatever information can be learned about this doctor, Eralius, will be gathered there, and hopefully soon.

Chapter Three - The Mayor's Words

3Eo55, 17th of Ildonian's End

Voss leaves the blacksmith without his shield. He sees his companions just across and up the road a ways, before the gate. He approaches. Emari has seen him summon his shield and axe at will, and she does not question the absence of such gear. In fact, should Voss wish for his shield to return to him, he could possibly still summon it from the hands of the smith.

Boe and Emari were scanning the postings on the message board before their armoured companion arrived. Now they turn to discuss.

There are a variety of new parchments nailed into the wood, though few appear interesting. Many are simple job postings, mercenary contracts, and trade or delivery requests. Now that the winter is receding, work is preparing to resume in most industries. Many notices look to offer standard coin, but after battling orcs and travelling for nearly two months, moving trade goods onto ships seems mundane, even though setting off so soon seems painful.

Boe agrees with their aversion to these jobs. He did not travel from Krunix as an adventurer to spend time doing manual labour.

There are a few papers that do seem interesting, though, and Emari points them out to Voss as he scans the board.

The first is a call for help from a trade captain by the name of Helena Sharpe, who has recently lost her ship due to a mutiny. She is asking for someone to help her retake it, or at least not leave it at the hands of "pirate filth." The ship is allegedly somewhere among a small cluster of unmapped islands a week's journey down the coast. The notice does spark some debate among the group, but their original decision to remain in town holds firm and soon the idea is dismissed, left to some other adventurers or mercenaries.

The second posting that sticks out plainly to the group is related to their old friend, Voran Eralius. The notice bears The Mayor's seal and signature and the ink is clearly fresh, so it must have been posted late in the night or early in the morning. The paper requests that anyone with information regarding the named "doctor," or anyone already involved in the case, report to The Mayor's manor during daylight hours. This notice is almost certainly directed at the group. They elect to visit The Mayor shortly. They leave the notice on the board.

There is a final parchment, however, that Emari draws Voss' attention to before he can leave. It is posted by the town guard. It states that Frederik Landston, owner of the Landston mines, has been asking for help dealing with a group of kobolds that has intruded in his quarry. With the snow melting and work scheduled to resume shortly, he needs them removed, but does not have the man power to do so. The guards attempted to assist, but were turned away by their "king" and are now stating that technically it is outside of their jurisdiction. Frederik is offering a two hundred gold value reward to anyone who does the job for them. The situation seems to appeal to Boe.

"I speak the dragon-tongue," the gnome explains. "It may vary slightly, and I would not be familiar with slang, but I would likely be able to speak rationally with the creatures."

They agree then that a trip to the mines would be no real problem. The quarries lie an hour out of town by horse, and they could perhaps even take the trip today after their meeting with Brenspire, should they feel inclined. Voss tears the message from the board.

"We may not even need to spill any blood today," Emari says. There is something likened to hope in her voice. Voss only blows air through his nose in response.

They depart the board.

Boe hands a few silver shillings to a wagon driver, parked nearby, to take them through the proper, which is growing increasingly busy as days move by. People are travelling again, returning home, or venturing away. Even the locals are out, and seem to have made a large portion of the town square into a skating rink, surrounded by temporary fences, and kept frozen with the aid of minor arcane energy.

They pass through the square, but afterward they stick to side-streets to avoid major traffic. The driver speaks with Emari and Boe while Voss watches the town roll by.

Much work has to be done in logging as well, in order to replace the wood that was used this winter, and already wagon loads are being wheeled from the woods towards the mills on the Twin River.

Soon enough, they arrive at the western gate. Emari hands the driver a few extra copper coins. They hop to the ground and begin traversing the distance between the walls and the manor hill. The fields are finally free of snow, and they appear to be in various stages of the final winter harvest, or in preparation for spring planting.

As they walk, two wagons pass them by, rolling down the muddy road. The banners on the sides identify as a trade guild bringing cloth and minerals from Krunix.

Within twenty minutes, the trio finds themselves climbing the road towards the wood-walled manor. As they approach the gate, they see it begin to open for them.

"Odd," Boe murmurs.

Voss only shrugs in response, not slowing his pace.

Behind the creaking wood, stands a familiar gnome.

"Greetings, master Hallehwell," he hails the group in a squeaky voice.

"Greetings sir!" Emari replies when Voss says nothing. They draw closer. "What is your name?" the bard continues.

"Writh," the gnome smiles and politely kisses her gloved hand.

"Well, Writh, thank you for greeting us. Is The Mayor in?"

"Yes, he has been expecting master Hallehwell."

"Good, thank you," Voss acknowledges the servant before continuing into the grounds. Boe and Emari nod at the gnome before following as well.

"Good friends of The Mayor?" Boe asks.

"Somewhat," Voss replies.

"I carried his mail for some time," Emari adds.

Boe hums thoughtfully.

They reach the door and use the large metal knocker to sound their arrival. After a few seconds, it is opened by a human man. They recognize the man as Roahl, the official messenger of The Mayor. He looks exhausted

"You're all givin' me some busy days recently, eh?" the man asks the group with a smile.

Voss glances his way, but says nothing as he enters. Emari gives Roahl a reassuring smile as his shoulders tense with unease.

"Sorry, all," Roahl speaks as they pass. "Mayor's in the dining hall."

They walk to the first door on their right, and another human man opens it into the room. Brenspire is sitting at the table head. His beard has been recently trimmed, and he is dressed in a fine looking, deep grey suit, accented by gold patterns.

Before The Mayor is a large sandwich and a bowl of steaming soup. He has already begun to eat both, along a glass of day-ale.

"Welcome!" Harold speaks to them. "I apologize for not making much time to talk last we spoke, especially as now I have even more to speak about."

The group stands in the doorway.

"Please, sit," The Mayor urges. They oblige, and enter, the servant stepping in and closing the door behind them. They sit along the side of the table closest to the entrance. "I had received a letter from a friend in Southpoint. I am sure you have all heard the rumours of civil unease, but our fears of war have been confirmed in the messages I have been sent." Brenspire passes a folded piece of parchment to Voss, who leans towards Emari so that she can read it as well.

"*Dearest Lord Brenspire,*

This is in regards to events occurring as I write this from Southpoint.

There is unrest here, my good sir, and while I do not mean you harm, nor wish you ill will, there are many people who blame The North as a whole for the position we are in.

Rumours have it that we are much worse off than our northern counterparts. Within the past five years since the "Good King Benedict III" took his reign, our taxes and support, even our trade routes, have all been put under copious amounts of pressure. I am aware that The North faces similar problems, but I urge you to not lie to yourself. You and the other northern municipalities — the other northern magistrates — have the soft side of our King's wrath.

There is much talk of war, Harold. It is not pretty. I have not yet been swept up in the torrent of idealism that wracks the south, but I hear it preached openly in the streets, and sooner or later some fools will take up arms against the north.

A part of me hopes that this rebellion will be crushed before it begins, but another hopes that the fools who stand up have enough numbers to at least make a difference. As a noble living near squalor, I can say with honesty that if I were any less educated and composed, I would join the rabble.

This letter is not a threat, nor is it a plea. It is simply my intention to warn and inform you of the situation here, and that similar noise has been heard in Streboya. If a war does break out, and I have any say in it, wrath will not be directed at you. Regardless, you should search within yourself, and find what you side you will fall on, should you need fall one way or the other.

We will be in contact, Lord Brenspire.

Sincerely and with hope, Lord Favren Gilgun-Borde."

"Mayor," Voss speaks as he reaches the end, "what information has cropped up regarding doctor Eralius?"

The Mayor bites down on his sandwich and chews while Voss is speaking. He finishes before responding. "An elven man arrived from Highfell. He spoke about how Voran came to the smaller town near a month and a half ago. Since his joining the clinic, people began to go missing. They linked the disappearances to him quickly, and then he vanished. People are still going missing however."

"Then he is likely still nearby," Boe speaks up.

"I know not. I have been having a difficult enough time keeping up on helping organize the new trade influx, and overseeing the new construction down the coast. I have had no resources to draw on in mounting a search," the mayor explains

"We will do it," Voss says. No one objects.

"I was hoping you would offer. I can respond with little reward, but I know that the elf was speaking of one."

"Where is he?" Voss asks. "We will discuss with him."

"He is staying in my servants' quarters while there is still space there."

"Then we will seek him out," Emari states. "We have your permission to act with your authority in Highfell?"

"You do have my permission. Until I declare otherwise, you can consider yourself acting in my name and with my authority in this case. Voss still bears paper with my signet on it, as do the others of your party who are absent. You may use this to further the investigation."

"Thank you, Mayor Brenspire," Emari nods.

"Find that doctor and bring him to justice," Harold responds, sipping his tea.

The others nod, and stand once more. The Mayor rises with them. He leads them to the door, as the servant seems to have left. At the entrance, he bids them a good day, and closes the door behind them when they reach the courtyard.

The tidings from the south are not comforting, but neither are they unexpected. There has indeed been talk of the south reaching for change throughout the past year or more. Word of action has even been present throughout the northern lands as well. It is because of the civil war in Streboya that taxes have been increased, and it is also common belief that the northern cities and townships are being spared the drastic changes to maintain good faith in their King.

The group does not spend much thought on this letter for the moment. If a war were to be declared, then it would be a suicide. Without the support of

Krunix or Vruyoth they would not have a chance against the might of the Dabarisian Kingdom. Regardless, they agree for the moment that this is not nearly their main concern.

Upon the stone court of the manor, the trio stops to soak in the air once more. The sky is glowing bright. The sun speaks thin holes through the cloud layer, and is met by fresh frost that shimmers in response.

They cross the yard. The servants' quarters stand alone against the fat log wall, ten metres to the left of the gate. It is a single building with a low, A-frame roof stacked on its thick wooden walls. The building looks to be made purely of winter oak wood, but as the group draws closer, they see that the corners and base are made of a dark-dyed stone.

There are two windows along the front of the building, which face west. They are covered from the inside by thick cloth curtains. The door is closed tight. The shape of the single entrance is only distinguishable by the indent along the otherwise smooth surface.

Smoke rises from a small, square, stone chimney along the gate-side of the dwelling. The housing quarters are long, stretching one hundred feet from to end. There is also twenty feet of width, which allows for a good portion of the building, the one farthest from the gate, to be devoted to sitting and eating space.

Voss leads the others to the door, which is located at the centre of the western wall. He knocks against the wood. The sound echoes through the building.

"What? Long day for you too? Yeah, come in!" a voice calls.

Voss pulls the door through the frosted tufts of grass outside, swinging it open over the gravel side path. He enters, followed by Boe and Emari.

"Oh!" the same voice speaks up, belonging to a bearded human man. The man is sitting just beside the door on a stool. He is leaning on a shelf-like counter built from the outer wall. "Forgive me, I thought you were the other guys' friend trying to skip out on work for a nap as well," he stammers, bowing his head.

"We seek an elven visitor," Voss states, unfazed.

"Of course, sir. Down at the end, taking the empty bunk. He's still asleep I believe."

They look to the right, following the man's outstretched arm. The interior of the building is warm and lit by candles set along the same, long counter. Opposite the group are beds, two bunks high, each set with a double-drawer dresser, and surrounded by thin, birch-wood dividers.

Very few people appear to be in the building, due to both the disappearances, and the day's work having begun. The only ones in the room are the visitors, the man, and two sleeping figures at the end.

The last few bunks are shrouded in darkness.

Voss nods in thanks to the man, and begins to march towards the far end of the quarters.

Emari smiles behind her mask, which changes to a joyful pink, as she pats the man on the shoulder. She feels his body relax under her touch. The bard then continues after Voss, with Boe behind.

With each step, the wooden flooring creaks against the loose stone foundation upon which it sits. There is a draft rising from the boards, but it is locked in conflict with the crackling fire coming through the open door at the north end of the building.

They reach the end of the bunks, and peer into the last section. A thin looking man is wrapped amongst a few blankets, lying on the bottom mattress. Another lies above him, but he looks too small to be an elf. The only light comes from the counter, several feet behind the group.

Emari taps Voss on his plated shoulder. He turns slightly, to find her offering a holder with a lit candle. He nods, and takes it.

Voss then places the light atop the dresser in the bunk room. It illuminates the elven features of the man in the bed. He has a thin, dark stubble that covers his lower face. His eyes slowly open in the light to reveal their grey colour and tired nature. As he sits up, they see his body is not muscular at all, but thin and bony. He wears no shirt. The clothes he was wearing the night before have been discarded to the floor.

"Who are you?" he sounds fearful as he speaks, looking into the eyes of Voss' demonic visor.

"Friends of Mayor Brenspire," Emari explains, moving to stand beside Voss.

The man takes a moment to adjust his eyes to the scene. "Oh, thank the Gods."

"We plan on heading out within a few days to Highfell," Voss tells him. "We were wondering if you would be willing to compensate our journey if we promised to rid your town of a certain doctor."

"Eralius," the elf speaks coldly. "I have not got much, but I did bring some gold with me when I left."

"We do not need much," Boe says, which pulls a sideways glance from the armoured soldier. "Just enough for the trip, and whatever else you are willing to part with."

"If you do manage to take away the threat to Highfell, then I will scrounge up enough to reward you with. I can give a handful of gold to pay for supplies now, and then when you return I can part with a chunk of the coin I got from selling my family's fletcher business," the elf explains.

"That sounds excellent," Emari agrees. Voss nods as well.

"Thank you," the elf tells them. "I will be staying here for a few weeks if The Mayor permits, or in an inn should he see fit that I move. When you return you will be able to find me, you have my word."

"When we return, I will find you," Voss says calmly. "You have my word as well."

They take a small sum of gold from the man, enough for food and to rent some horses, and begin to walk back through the quarters and out into the yard again.

Once outside, with the door shut behind them, they pause by the gate to make final decisions.

"We should leave within the week," Voss says.

"If we want, we could still take today to investigate the kobold notice for some extra coin, and set off tomorrow or after one more day of rest," Emari suggests.

"I am not opposed to that," Boe agrees. "We are, in fact, closer to the mines than to the East Air at this point."

"Then let us make haste," Voss speaks. "Midday approaches already, and I wish to be at rest by mid-evening if we are making for the road so soon."

They walk through the open gate of the manor, which begins to swing closed behind them as Writh turns the crank from the inside. Beginning down the hill towards the farmland, they turn west towards the Landston Quarry and Mines.

Chapter Four - Track to the Centre

3E055, 17th of Ildonian's End

Evandur Angelthorn wakes later than usual. He sits up in a comfortable bed — his own bed — and waits, listening to the sounds of morning. People move outside. A cart rolls through the square a few streets away.

This house he purchased a couple of years ago, in 3E053, for a discounted price, and with the help of the local church of Valkronus. It is a small home, not completely furnished even now, but comfortable. There is sun coming through the window.

Evandur stands. His body grows quickly cold, exposed in the open room, which has not remained heated all night. He throws on a pair of cloth trousers and a wool shirt from his dresser. Warmth returns to him as he calls upon his internal light to fill the clothes.

Today he will leave. He has much to do, and to discover, and no certain place to find what he needs. He will leave for the capital, Daroonga City, where the best colleges and largest churches in the land are built.

He gathers what extra clothes he can fit into his travel pack on top of the other gear he will bring. He straps his armour onto himself atop his clothing once more. He is just affixing his sword sheath to his belt when a knock reverberates through his door.

Evandur crosses his small home, through his dining room, to his front entrance. He opens the door to find Peren standing there waiting.

"Paladin," the half-elf acknowledges him.

"Sir Siannodel," Evandur maintains pleasantry.

"You have been respectful to me above the others, and I wish not lose that. I am here simply to make a business deal," Peren explains. When the angelborn does not interrupt, the noble continues. "I wish to purchase your quarter of the property here from you. I have gold that was in reserve, but I do truly believe I will profit from such an exchange, and so I am willing to break my savings to make my endeavours happen."

"I do not need you to 'break your savings' to buy my quarter, Peren," Evandur says, motioning for his friend to enter. Peren obliges, and they walk to the table. "I've not yet eaten. I was going to wait to break fast on the road, but, since you are here, can I make you some eggs and meat?"

"That would be kind of you," Peren nods.

Evandur lights a small wood stove and places an iron pan on top. As it heats, he turns back to the half-elf.

"You plan on proceeding with your flintlock project, then?"

"Of course," Peren says, "and while I have the space, most certainly, to build a small shop, I need room for testing grounds, and even to create housing for staff. I will have to purchase a plot somewhere in Highfell or up in Bellhaven for production, but for now I can purchase in bulk from Krunix."

The paladin hums. "That makes sense. You are researching new gear and spring technology then as well?"

"Yes, of course. By the time I am able to manufacture, I want my weapons to be top competitors, at least in the Dabarisian market," the noble grins.

"Then I have a proposition," Evandur tells him, throwing four strips of fresh meat into the pan.

"Let me hear."

"Assuming my quarter of the property is worth some gold, I will take one hundred in value. That should be enough to get me some new supplies and keep me afloat for some time while I do my travelling."

"One hundred is only half of what I was planning on offering," Peren admits.

"I want you to build for me a mechanism that will open my shield automatically. I meant to stop in Azgul Hold on our return, but I elected to save time and forgo it. If you are doing research into the technology, then you should be able to find some means of accomplishing this."

"Would you leave your shield with me?" Peren asks.

"I would, yes. I will be returning with the summer I expect. So if it is possible for you to begin within a few months, then you will have time."

"I can promise you an automatic shield, or another hundred gold come summer."

"I will accept this, thank you Peren."

"Thank you, paladin."

Evandur sets the meat aside on two plates before cracking three eggs into the same pan. Peren counts one hundred gold worth of coins and shillings into a cloth bag. The eggs cook for a minute before he adds them to the meat. Two for himself, one for his guest.

They eat their breakfast, talking lightly about plans.

"What are you planning in Daroonga?" Peren asks.

"I have some research matters of my own that I must seek out."

"Regarding what?"

"I wish not discuss it, this is a personal endeavour."

"I will not pry then, but I do hope you shed light on whatever you seek."

"I do too."

Peren wipes his mouth with a silk cloth from his pocket. "For a follower of a near opposite God, you are not a person that I am completely opposed to, Angelthorn."

The paladin cocks his slightly, confused. "You are a devotee?"

"Lightly," Peren responds. "I am no paladin or priest. I pray and recite blessings when appropriate, and have learned much through the study of deities."

"Near opposite God," Evandur mutters. "I thought I sensed something about you. You follow the teachings of Echoshan."

"I do. I take no joy in the killing of innocents, like the dark cults do, but I have needed to kill before. I find it better to do so knowing I have some small hand in their souls ending with rest."

"That is an honourable take on the God of Death and Darkness.," Evandur tells Peren.

"And Finality," Peren says. "We all reach an end some day. Echoshan was betrayed by Valkronus first, you know. Neither are good or evil, despite what we are all taught to believe."

Evandur is quiet.

"I must go now, Sir Angelthorn. I will see you again. Do not be a stranger, and do not distrust me."

Evandur takes his left gauntlet from the table. "Here, Siannodel. My shield folds from this. I expect it early this summer."

"I will have it done. Good day, Evandur," the half-elf says. He stands, placing his cutlery on his plate neatly. He slides the cloth coin-bag towards the paladin, then passes through the doorway, out into the late morning.

As the paladin wets a rag in the water basin and begins cleaning the plates and pan with it, he ponders the noble's words.

"Forces of good and evil are not made by the Gods, Evandur," Scilandra tells him. Her angelic voice eases his mind slightly. "The Gods do not intervene in the struggles of mortals and, as such, it should not be up to you to worry on their struggles. If you hold true to your beliefs, and listen to me along with yourself, then you have no need to fear."

"I know, Scilandra," the paladin replies. "I only think on the words of a friend. We are different, and in fact believe in different purposes. I focus on the protection of life, he instead chooses the easing of death. It is interesting to ponder the similarities between the ideals."

"It is not wrong to either. I just wish to ease your conflict."

"My conflict is with Voss," Evandur says. "I know not why, but my mind will only be eased in the finding of the truth."

"Then we should make haste, and leave before midday."

Evandur nods. He finishes the dishes, placing them in the cupboard again before shouldering his pack, and heading for the door.

He pushes outside and locks his home behind him. He unlocks his mailbox, and places eighty golden lions inside, divided into eight labelled and dated envelopes. As arranged through the church, and The Mayor, these will be collected as tax in case eight months should go by in his absence. He locks the mailbox again.

The paladin sets off towards the Green Edge Stables at the western gate. These are the stables he chooses for his horse. They are well run by a kind and hard-working staff. The company owns good grazing fields north of town, and the facilities for keeping the horses are well stocked and clean.

Evandur crosses the square, heads through the main roadways, now teaming with people moving boxes and barrels towards the docks in wagons. After a half hour he arrives at the Green Edge.

The stable manager, an old human woman, smiles as she helps him affix the gear he left with his horse to the saddle. When his tent, bedroll, and travel pack are all tied tightly, he pays her three silver coins extra and grabs the reins.

This creature, provided by the church of Valkronus several years ago, is a pure grey mount bred for riding and combat. Evandur did not take it to Railwood for fear of the danger involved, and because the snow has claimed as many horses as bandits when things go wrong.

Evandur named her Volana, after the Goddess of the Twin Moons. This name was chosen because of her resemblance in colour to the moonstone his mother left him with, set now in a necklace he wears under his armour. Having a name associated with both the higher powers and his own life, a strong riding body, and good training, Evandur has grown quite fond of this beast.

After leading Volana outside of the stables, and making sure one last time that everything is secure, he launches himself into the saddle. As his mount bears his weight, he spurs her sides with soft kicks that send the horse trotting gently forward. Evandur rides through the west gate and out from the town's walls.

He knows a store in the bordering hamlet of Thelshire that sells quality bundled rations for longer trips. He will stop there before hitting the open wilderness. After this, he will only have a chance to stop in Highfell before reaching Daroonga. If he is lucky, however, his supplies will carry him straight through the small town with no need to restock there.

He spurs his horse again, and she picks up speed. As the midday sun reaches its peak, he rides by the Landston mines towards the outer villages and hamlets surrounding Taernsby proper.

Chapter Five - The Kobold Notice

3Eo55, 17th of Ildonian's End

As the midday sun reaches the top of its arc, the trio begins their descent into the quarry. The sound of several trade wagons and a galloping horse accentuate the peak of the day receding above them.

Voss leads the small band of adventurers downward. The Landston Mines are located slightly farther north, against a grouping of rocky hills where cave systems breach the surface, whereas the quarry has been excavated straight into the earth beside the Southroad. The large, rectangular hole is surrounded at the top by a white-wood fence, made of log posts and interlocking boards. The way into the quarry is by a steep, narrow ramp carved out of the stone, which winds around the outer walls, slowly following the progress of the quarry. As of the this day, the ramp only turns once, leaving plenty of room for further digging.

They decided against walking the extra distance to find the owner of the quarry. They have the job notice with them. It was issued by the guard, anyway, and not Frederik Landston. They may not even speak with him until they need to seek their reward.

The grasslands, smaller farms, miners' houses, and outcroppings of trees disappear from view as the group continues to the bottom of the quarry. As they walk, Boe raises his hand and mutters some incantations. A small owl hoots and glides from above to perch on the gnome's shoulder. Boe sends the creature ahead of them. He then begins to walk with his eyes closed, holding Emari's arm as a guiding tool. They approach the bottom after a few minutes, and the wizard opens his eyes again.

"There is a small hole in the south face. It looks like it leads into a passage," the gnome tells the others.

They look along the walls. The rock is rough, uneven, and jagged in places, which makes it impossible to see the entrance he speaks of. Boe leads the way along the side of the canyon with purpose, however, and finds the passage with ease. It is barely six feet high, and too thin for Voss to walk comfortably through. Beyond the initial opening, the hole appears to widen, but it is difficult to be certain how deep it leads, even in the broad daylight.

"This is likely where the kobolds have made their home. From what I have heard, the smaller dragonfolk are fast tunnelers and, despite their wariness of outsiders, they should be more afraid of us than we need be of them. We have magic, and weapons. They have rocks and sharp teeth," Boe explains.

"I am not afraid of midget dragonkin," Voss tells the gnome.

"We should press on," Emari says, unimpressed. "It's likely they can hear us speaking through the passage anyway." The bard spins and plunges through the opening.

Boe follows behind her, detaching his staff from its horizontal position on his backpack. He places a small hand on the end and it begins to glow orange. The light rises until it reaches a torch equivalent. It is not too glaring, but fills the passage enough for Voss and Emari to see.

They squeeze through the tunnel, deeper into the stone. The walls grow slightly farther apart. Voss' shoulders nearly scrape the sides even once the full width is reached, though, and he has to bend slightly to avoid hitting his head at many points where the ceiling dips.

Boe gives Emari his staff, so that she can lead more steadily. The tunnel bores gently downward, and winds left, then right again, before finally reaching an opening.

The bard calls for a halt as she arrives at a small ledge in a large cavern. The tunnel has suddenly peeled back. The new space is egg shaped, with the ceiling running to a point, where it appears that sunlight is entering in a lone, thin beam. The base is wide, and relatively flat. At the bottom can be seen a small pond and what appears to be a collection of leather tents and cooking spaces.

The whole cave is just under seventy feet from top to bottom, with the ledge they stand on being located just over halfway up, and it has a width of about fifty feet. Emari scans the edge of the platform for a way down.

"There was a ladder here," she says, pointing to some broken wooden planks that appear to have been ripped forcefully from the stone. The wood is not old.

"There is no way down, then. No easy one, anyway," Voss says.

"You could jump," suggests Nhasan.

"Don't tempt him, perhaps he'd find some peace," Torkurth adds.

The spirits in Voss' mind begin arguing, making it difficult for Voss to focus.

Emari peers over the ledge again. "I can get down. I have the ability to slow my fall. I will see what I can find. If I get into trouble I can protect myself for some time." She hops over the edge and begins to float gently downward.

"I know the spell you are casting!" Boe says, excitedly. "I have not yet mastered it, though." He steps off after her. He expects to also fall slowly, but this is not the case.

He shrieks as his body tumbles from the ledge. Emari manages to catch the gnome. The impact spins her and almost causes her to lose focus as they fall together. They manage to land unevenly and roll out of any major injury.

"Ow," Boe grunts.

"That wasn't a spell, idiot!" Emari exclaims in frustration. "You could have got us both killed!"

"What was it, if not a spell?" Boe asks, confused. "I know of many magical techniques, and the major spells for slowing descent affect the whole area in which they are cast!"

Before they can continue arguing, however, a sound echoes through the cavern. The pair glances up. Along the wall of the cave below the ledge they just descended from, are a plethora of indents. They are little more than small, circular holes, and they are freshly carved into the rock face.

Standing in one of these mini-caves, about twenty feet above Emari and Boe, is the shape of a small humanoid figure. It leans menacingly towards them, wielding some form of weapon in one of its clawed hands.

It speaks, angrily, in a language that Emari cannot understand.

"It wants to know how we dare to trespass in-" Boe pauses in his translation, "New Scazgixia."

"You understand it?" Emari whispers.

"It must be a kobold. It speaks a watered-down form of the dragon-tongue," Boe explains. "What do I tell it?"

"Tell it we seek The King of the, uh, kobolds?" Emari replies.

Boe speaks audibly back to the figure, in the same language it spoke to them.

There is a pause. The figure replies.

"He says to bow then, for we stand before The King now."

"That's not going to happen," Emari tells Boe.

"I think we should bow."

"I think you're full of shit."

Boe bends at the knee and speaks up to the apparent King.

Emari reluctantly follows suit. "What did you say?"

"Oh King, won't you parlay?" Boe responds.

"If we die because you say something stupid, and ,furthermore, if Voss lives simply because he stayed back where it was safe, I will find you in whatever afterlife you end up in and-"

The figure of The King slides down the gentle slope in the wall and lands a mere ten feet from the pair. He places his weapon over his shoulder as he swaggers towards them. Looking back up, Emari and Boe see several dozen pairs of eyes glinting over the indents in the wall, watching the exchange that is soon to take place.

Emari touches a rock on the ground and hums gently under her breath. The rock glows with a soft white light that permeates the darkness. It is not harsh, but provides enough visibility to see the approaching creature.

The King is only a few inches taller than Boe. He is muscular looking, and covered in red scales from head to toe. He looks as a kobold should, with sharp teeth and beady black eyes peering from the base of his snout-like nose. His ears are simple holes in his head. He wears a crown made from what appears to be poorly-shaped copper and bone. He is dressed in some leather armour that looks to have been cut and re-sized from some pilfered gear. It bears no symbols, but is definitely Dabarisian make.

He struts towards the pair with little fear. He speaks as he reaches an equidistant point from the glowing rock.

"He asks again why we are here, standing before King Scazgix in his kingdom," Boe relays.

"We have been sent to ask why you have made this cave your home," Emari speaks to The King, with Boe acting as a translator.

"We are here because our old home was taken from us," Boe tells her.

"By what?"

"Large, hairy men," Boe says, trying not to smile.

"If we can rid your old home of these creatures, would you return there and leave this place?" Boe asks Emari's question to The King.

The King thinks on this. He speaks in a calm tone.

"He says that his old kingdom was better than this, and that if we were to help him, then his people would return to their old glory."

"Sure, whatever," Emari says. "Tell him that we will seek out his old kingdom, and that if he would send a guide with us, we can aid his people. Just make something up, I am tired of this conversation," Emari says as she grows exasperated. Boe relays the helpful part of her message.

The King responds, in very broken common-tongue. "I go."

"What?" Emari asks.

"I go with. I guide."

"Great," she says. Her sarcasm is loosely hidden.

The King speaks to Boe.

"He will have his people rebuild the ladder up, and then we can leave," Boe says. "His old kingdom is not far, an hours march at most."

"An hour? That's it? Well, I can't say I am disappointed. I wish not to walk long."

The King turns around and announces to his people that he is going to retake their homeland. The indents in the wall suddenly throng with faces that cheer and chant his name, which is distinguishable even in the dragon-tongue. There are nearly a hundred beings that appear into view. It would not have been easy to fight them. Emari and Boe are suddenly much more content in their peaceful approach.

Most of the new figures are women and children, but there are several men as well. Boe begins to wonder what could have pushed them from their kingdom.

They wait for now, though, taking in the view of the cave once again. The leather tents that border the lake are not pristinely made, but appear to be in good repair. The cooking spaces are lined with old wood and charcoal. The kobolds must hunt at night in order to sustain their population. As a handful of small dragon-folk begin affixing the wooden beams back into the patch of wall where the ladder once stood, Boe sits beside Emari.

"So, what is your relationship with Voss?" he asks.

"I have none. He is a suit of armour with an axe and a shield."

"I wonder about him," Boe says in thought.

"You may be safer if you don't."

"I am sorry for putting us at risk."

"I was reckless, and lucky you were down here with me. We can call it even."

The ladder is soon rebuilt and, to a chorus of excited voices, Boe, Emari, and King Scazgix begin to climb the rock face back towards the ledge above. The wood is sturdy, and despite the dizzying height that they soon reach, none of them encounter a problem.

As they near the top, Voss helps pull Emari up. As Boe climbs up as well, Scazgix sees the other figure and shrieks, nearly losing his balance. Boe quickly explains the situation and he helps The King to the ledge. The kobold calms slightly, but is still wary of the tall, armoured man.

Emari and Boe then explain to Voss what the plan is, and make proper introductions finally. Voss says nothing as he listens, and says nothing after for some time as well.

"Do you have a weapon?" Voss asks The King, who looks confused. Voss sighs audibly, and turns to face Boe. "Does he have a weapon?"

Boe asks The King. The kobold responds by proudly holding a club of stone forward. Emari unsheathes a dagger from her calf and passes it to Boe.

"Make him take this, otherwise he will be of no help," she tells the gnome.

Boe passes the dagger to Scazgix. After a brief explanation The King grabs the weapon with excitement.

"What did you say?" Emari asks.

"I told him that it was enchanted, and that as long as he believed in himself, he would never be slain with it in hand."

"What?" Emari is appalled.

Voss laughs loudly as he begins to walk back down the passageway, away from the ledge and the others. Emari questions why she cares at all about The King before settling on dealing with it later and following Voss. Boe and The King pursue as well, as they return through the tunnel into the outside air. The sun has only descended slightly, and still sits high in the sky.

Boe and The King talk while they traverse the base of the quarry and ascend the ramp.

As they reach the top of the quarry, they are met by an angry man, who comes striding towards them with a dagger drawn.

They pause and wait for him to reach them.

"What is this creature doing here?" he spits the question at them.

"Who are you?" Boe asks.

"I should ask you that question!" the man cries in anger. "I am Frederik Landston, and you are trespassing in my quarry, and conspiring with kobold filth!"

"We are going to clear his old home so that he and his people may return there." Voss calmly explains, fishing the folded notice from his leather side-bag.

"You would sooner slay the beast where he stands!" Frederik demands.

"We are going to clear his old home," Voss repeats, slower, "so that he and his people may-"

"I would have him dead sooner than let him take another step unharmed," Frederik fumes.

Emari looks between the two. Voss is growing angry, and there is pale blue mist surrounding his fingers. Suddenly, the bard waves her hand forwards and speaks softly. "Please sir, go back inside," she says. There is magic in the words, and it catches Landston off guard.

"Okay," he says, calmed. "I will go back inside. You go clear their old home. Thank you." With that he turns and walks back north-west, towards his manor.

"What did you do?" Voss asks, confused.

"Avoided a pointless conflict. Come now, let's go. That spell will only last a few precious moments," Emari replies, and takes the lead as they walk back to the main thoroughfare.

The smaller members of the group soon move to the front as Scazgix brings them to a bend in the road, where they diverge and make towards the forest at the edge of the farmlands.

The woods surrounding Taernsby mostly lie far to the west, as hamlets and farm fields spread along the Southroad, but in certain places — like here to the north — the forest stretches close to the farmland. This section of trees is just under an hour march through relatively flat plains, and side paths used by hunters and farmers. The area is not well developed here, though, and soon farmsteads and fields become few and far between.

"His people made the tunnel," Boe explains through puffs of his pipe, as The King begins to focus on recalling landmarks. "They sensed the cave through the stone of the quarry, and made their own passage towards it. They are crafty, and, personally, I am glad we decided to aid them instead of attacking."

"So long as we get paid, I care not who lives or dies," Voss tells the gnome. "I believe them innocent, and to kill them would be a shame, but their lives do not weigh on my conscious."

"He's got too many lives on that conscious already," Torkurth sneers in the soldier's mind.

"I count at least four," Nhasan agrees, "eight if we're counting the Centrecrest troops."

"They've been there for little over two months," Boe continues.

"Their *kingdom* within walking distance of Taernsby has been taken by a band of *large hairy men* and so they fled to a *new kingdom* and now their *King* accompanies us to *reclaim their land*," Emari scoffs. "I am a musician, an actress even, yet I do not have close to this level of flair or dramatics."

"Whatever usurped them may have long left," Voss says. "It could be that we return and there is no longer a threat. If that is the case, this may be the easiest job I've taken in a while."

They walk for a long time. The journey takes an hour, then they enter the woods, they walk for another hour, then almost a third. As Voss and Emari both grow impatient, Boe presses The King on how far they are. The King responds at last that they are here.

Boe points at a small cluster of rocks that form a broken hill, and as they walk around the mound, they make out a hidden opening that seems to lead into the ground. The opening is obscured by lichens that hang in front of it, and the natural stone pillars cut it off from being viewed at most angles. Stone slabs line the walls of the entrance, and there are stairs that — while chipped — are strongly made and lead in a gentle spiral downward.

"Dwarven architecture," Dadek tells Voss. "Ancient by the looks of it, probably all the way back to the Holliserian Dwarves. I grow excited now to see this place."

"It's a hole in the ground, old man," Nhasan expresses. "It will be dust and rubble after all these centuries."

"Not if the kobolds maintained it or did any repairs," Torkurth disagrees with the rogue for once.

"Perhaps. I suppose we will have to see," Nhasan settles.

They set their bags quietly by the entranceway, in a nearby patch of brush. Voss takes the lead, and speaks softly to the others.

"We go in quietly. If we get spotted by anything, fall back to the stairs." His axe appears through the familiar blue mist, which surprises Scazgix and Boe. The armoured man clutches the weapon tightly as they descend into the passage. The smell of smoke enters their noses as they move deeper into the ground.

Voss' greaves scrape along the wall several times, but other than that their steps do not echo loudly. As they wind further down, they begin to hear deep and guttural voices. They are speaking in a language that none of them can understand. By the tone, it appears that several creatures are having a debate, almost an argument.

Voss peers around the final arc of the stairs, and into a wide hall.

This room is nearly thirty feet wide, and almost three times as long. It appears to once have been a grand entranceway, and perhaps a garrison, or mess hall. It is adorned with ancient carvings on the walls, some of which are recognizable. The Holliserian Lion, dwarven military emblems, and even some names and song lyrics cut in the older dwarf-speech.

The whole length of the hall is also lined with stone pillars that once all stood several feet away from the wall and would have acted as supports. Most now lie in ruin and rubble. Small indents, similar to the ones in New Scazgixia, have been carved in some places behind the old pillars that still remain, and at the back end of the hall. At this far end as well is a raised platform where a staircase appears to lead farther downward.

The room is currently lit by a large bonfire near the far end, on the platform. The blaze is surrounded by four, burly looking figures. The licking flames cast shadows across the hall, which bounce off the fallen pillars. Smoke also fills much of the room, travelling up the stairs, the only apparent exit. Mixed now with the smell of burning logs, is the terrible stenches of wet dog, piss, and shit.

Voss uses Valindra and Dadek to bridge his mind with those of Boe and Emari.

"These are goblin-kin, known as govoles. They are larger than goblins, and more brutish. I have had encounters with their kind once before, when I was a caravan guard. Often they associate themselves with orcish masters, or with pure-goblin servants. They are dangerous if they get the upper hand, but we shouldn't have any difficulty if we keep our heads," Voss silently explains. "Emari and I have fought orcs, outnumbered, and those are far worse."

"We should enter while they are distracted, and set up behind that pillar," Emari thinks in reply. She points to one of the fallen stone supports that is mostly intact, and lies on its side, closer to the entrance. "We could set up an ambush and wait."

"I can create some illusionary magic that could frighten them into leaving. We could catch them on their way out, or wait for their return and have them held in the stairs," Boe adds, also using the silent connection.

"Chablise, you take the lead, and I will follow," Voss thinks. "Boe, make sure Scazgix comes along."

They move silently and with haste from the stairway, to a crouched position behind the makeshift stone wall. Scazgix follows with Boe as well.

They now notice more carvings, depicting dwarves and humans eating and celebrating. This was likely a mess hall. Thin grooves along the centre of the room add to the idea by presenting the possibility that tables may once have been there. Whatever rubble there once was has been moved to the sides or cleared out though.

"We shall wait," Voss expresses the thought once again to everyone but Scazgix.

"Thank you for not using my true name," Emari projects to Voss alone.

Scazgix whispers something impatiently to Boe, who shushes him in response and explains the plan quietly. The King nods.

"I can create an illusion. I have an idea," Boe urges. "I am confident. They are just going to take their time otherwise. We can't be sure they will even leave."

"We can handle them if it fails," Emari agrees silently.

"Fine, do it," Voss orders.

The gnome holds both hands in front of himself, pointing them towards the fire pit, through the pillar. His fingers twitch like he is strumming some invisible instrument, and his mouth mutters arcane words under his breath.

The fire begins to surge between the goblin-kin figures. The flames grow larger. The beasts grab their weapons, a mix of clubs and small, old looking shortswords. Suddenly the fire erupts against the back wall, and it its wake appears the face of an orc. This orc has long white hair, wrinkled skin, and its eyes both glow purple. The hairy beasts wield their weapons towards the face. Upon seeing its visage, however, one of them drops to a knee.

One of the govoles, wearing a chain shirt instead of simple leathers like the others, slaps the kneeling ally on the back of his head and grunts something in their brutish language. The chastised creature stands again.

"You have been summoned!" the face speaks, its mouth seemingly creating the words, though Boe mouths his own also. "Travel now, straight south, and join Chief Dakkar's camp. You will be paid for your service."

The goblin-kin begin speaking aggressively to one another.

"Go!" the face yells at the four of them. "Either accept the offer and be given gold and slaves, or decline and be given death!"

The less equipped three hurriedly begin grabbing chunks of meat and strapping it to beaten looking backpacks. They shoulder the packs as their presumed leader, the one wearing chain, holds a bundle of thin sticks to the flame and produces a simple torch.

The three lower goblin-kin begin to march ahead of their leader, with their heads down in fear. They move speedily for the stairs. The fourth walks slightly slower. He holds his torch in one hand, and in the other he has grabbed a rusted metal buckler from the ground near the fire.

As they grow nearer, the group in hiding gets a clearer view of them. They are all hairy, coated in thick fur all over their bodies. Their features are indeed goblin-like, with flat looking faces, pointy teeth, and large eyes taken up mostly by their pupils. They stand nearly six feet tall each, just shorter than Voss, and all are nearly as muscular as well. The leader and one other carry blades, but the other two, the ones at the front, hold clubs with nails and sharp stones hammered into the tops.

As the beasts walk by Voss, Emari, Boe, and Scazgix, it appears as though they will not notice anything is amiss. Just as the second goblin-kin reaches the base of the stairs, however, the light from the leader's torch catches the glint from Voss' armour, and Scazgix's dagger.

The leader calls loudly to the others, who begin to turn at the sound of the strong voice.

It's too late however, as Boe reacts before any of the enemies. He speaks a phrase in ancient elvish, strung with draconic words as well, and throws his hands forward. A small orb of pure light shoots from his palms, and streaks towards the leader.

The goblin-kin raises his metal shield, which absorbs some of the impact.

The ball of light collides with the top of the shield, and leaves a black mark on the surface. The creature is pushed backwards slightly, and some of the fur on his shoulder is singed, but he keeps his feet.

The govole then throws the torch to the ground beside himself, which splits the bundle and scatters small burning sticks along the floor. Then he draws his sword again and lunges forward, toward Voss, who has moved to put himself between the enemies and the gnome.

As the shortsword nears Voss' body, he pulls on his spirits torment, and the spectral arm of a dwarf holding a shield emerges from his chest. The blade connects with the image, and slows to a stop.

The leader growls and swings again, but this time Voss easily shoves the attack aside with his left gauntlet.

Scazgix seizes the opportunity. The small dragon-kin slides through Voss' legs and runs under the leader. As he passes under the beast he stabs upwards, piercing the goblin-kin's thigh. Blood spatters the stone floor, and the leader gives a pained cry.

Voss then uses the distraction to whip his battleaxe towards the creature. The assailant has no time to raise his shield. He jumps backwards slightly as the axe connects directly with his chest. The chain takes a large chunk of the blow, but even splinters in certain places. The wound is not fatal, but does send the leader whirling to the floor. As he begins to stagger back to its feet, there is clearly blood seeping through the matted chest hair behind the broken armour.

Emari picks a moment to lunge and finish the leader off, but as she begins her movement, she sees the other three are almost upon them. She stops just behind Voss, instead adopting a defensive position to help shield Boe.

The leader is back on his feet, but holds his position for the moment, letting his lackeys rush first. The other three beasts swarm towards Voss and Emari. The armoured man smiles behind his face guard. Emari parries one attack easily, Voss sidesteps the second, but when the third swings for him as well, he only manages to block it into his shoulder. The impact does not break his armour, but will leave a large welt.

Scazgix rushes again, back between the legs of the chain-armoured beast. He swings furiously upwards, but only lands a few small cuts. The leader swings back, but the kobold King is agile and slides out of the way.

The fight rages on. Both sides pick their moments. Emari maintains the defensive, attacking only occasionally, and focusing on healing Voss. The soldier maintains the offensive front. Boe hurls elemental energy past the armoured man and the bard, sending bursts of flame, and small orbs of acid that singe fur and melt patches of skin on the attackers.

Finally, as both sides are beginning to feel the strain of battle, the leader of the enemy manages to get the upper hand on the small dragon-kin beneath him. The beast grabs Scazgix by the shoulder, but The King clutches the dagger with all his might. The govole growls angrily and swings his blade towards the kobold, but Scazgix manages to half-block with his own weapon. The flat edge of the sword connects with the side of his head. Scazgix's body falls limp, dropping to the floor, but no blood is seen.

"You'd better do something quick," Nhasan calls to Voss. "You don't want another death under your command."

"He is not under my command," Voss spits back, quiet enough that the others don't hear.

Despite yearning for apathy, Voss does step forward. As the leader raises his blade to swing again at The King, the armoured human shoves past one of the other attackers and swings his battleaxe. The blade of the weapon cuts deep into the shoulder of the leader, whose back was turned against the assault. The sword arm goes limp as the beast shouts in pain and fear. The other three all turn to attack Voss, and manage to batter him into a kneeling position as sword and club connect with his plating.

"Nhasan, Torkurth," Voss growls, "end this!"

Four spectral arms reach from the armoured man. Their hands slam against the stonework floor, and pale blue light crackles like lightening through the spaces between the slabs. It then erupts upward and into the legs of the enemies around him. The govoles fall backwards as energy, cold, and noise overtake their senses. The force of the flash tears the leader's arm from his body at the shoulder, and he begins convulsing in pain on the ground.

Voss stands then, rising from amid the panic. He swings his axe into the skull of the beast closest to Emari. The bard then lunges past the falling body and pierces her blade through the thigh of the closest, club wielding govole.

The two remaining goblin-kin begin scrambling for the stairs, one of them tearing his flesh through Emari's rapier painfully.

As they limp to the stairs, Voss points to the wounded one.

"Val!" he calls. The spectral form of the female elven archer steps from him with her bow drawn. "Slay them."

A blue arrow soars through the chamber and embeds itself in the base of the injured one's skull. Its body falls limp at the base of the stairs. The archer begins to move for the other, but pain wracks Voss' head.

"Return!" he calls, and the archer obeys. "One fleeing coward is not worth the risk."

Silence retakes the scene from chaos. Emari walks briskly around Voss, towards the wounded King. She quickly slays the leader, ending his misery. She then kneels by Scazgix, places her hands on both his temples, and hums a soothing song. White light reaches from her palms into Scazgix's head.

Boe approaches Voss. "What magic was that?" he asks in awe.

"It was nothing," Voss responds.

"It was not nothing. You are no mage, I see no arcane reagents, or notes, or books. You used no enchanted scrolls, and you are no man of Gods," Boe speaks to himself more than to Voss, his mind trying to unravel the man's nature.

"It was none of your business, is what it was," Voss tells the gnome. "I am no danger to you, so you should not dwell long on this."

Boe says nothing further.

"Are you forgetting why we ventured here in the first place?" Emari asks the pair, holding The King now in her arms. "We are lucky he is alive."

"If he still breathes, then we are fine." Voss says. "Let him rest for now, and when we draw closer to his people, we will rouse him."

Emari huffs at his dismissive attitude, but says nothing to argue.

They begin to search the bodies and the small camp. They find a variety of decent looking weapons and armours in pilfered boxes. Why the beasts did not use them, none can say. They also find some bags of gold and silver coins. They move anything useful towards the entrance.

The other two begin to explore the second staircase while Voss is besieged with conversation.

"Finally letting us free of our cage, hm?" Nhasan seems pleased by Voss' recent usage of their power.

"We need be careful," Dadek urges, ignoring the rogue. "People don't trust necromancy, and if we aren't the dead, then I don't know what we are."

"We are bound to our captain until he dies or the Gods intervene," Nhasan counters. "It would be nice to not be so ignored."

"We will help when we can, but let us not destroy him in the process," Valindra says. "Can you not feel the strain this places on his mind?"

"He will recover," Torkurth says.

"With time to rest, maybe," Valindra pushes.

"We will be careful, but this cannot be all bad," the rogue replies.

Valindra's voice is the last one that pierces Voss' mind before the room grows quiet for him again. "Just be careful, Voss," she says. "In the end, we may need you more than you need us."

Emari and Boe explore the lower chambers of the structure. When they return they only report that it must have been a small military base. There are chambers for sleeping and storage, planning, training, and garrison. Some are collapsed, but those that still stand have been partially restored by the kobolds. Nothing of value was found there, but a small passage in the lower chambers had been dug towards the surface it seemed, though no light came through it now.

Once everything has been checked, and all valuables organized near the doorway, Boe begins to speak arcane words again. As he finishes, and moves his hands upwards in a spiral, the ground cracks apart and a near-perfect circle of stone rises up until it floats two feet above the rest of the floor with everything atop it. He directs it through the staircase ahead of himself. The disk is barely small enough to pass through the stairs, but it does fit, and soon all the group and supplies are back in the open air.

"I will barely be able to maintain the energy needed to get this back to the quarry, but we should set our bags and even place Scazgix on top as well. The weight is not what affects my abilities unless it is a great amount," Boe explains.

They agree, and, grabbing their packs from the brush, pile everything but themselves on top of the floating stone circle.

After everything looks secured, they set off at a quick march bound for Taernsby. Despite some sustained injuries that Emari does her best to heal while they walk, they make good time.

Just over two and a half hours pass before they find themselves back overlooking the quarry. They descend quickly and, at the bottom, Boe releases his grasp on the spell he was maintaining. The disk touches the floor and dissipates.

"Where did it go?" Emari asks.

"Back to where it came from. I can probably work up the energy to do that one more time," Boe tells them.

"Why don't we give the weapons and armour to the kobolds?" Voss asks.

"That seems like something you wouldn't normally suggest," Emari muses.

"We can't carry it all. Some of it won't be good enough to sell. We should just take the gold and silver, and anything we want, and leave the rest as a gift," Voss explains. "That will leave them indebted."

Boe and Emari agree. The three of them pocket a total of thirty gold worth of valuables, trade supplies, and actual coins, and leave the weapons and armour at the entrance to the tunnel.

Finally, they wake Scazgix from his sleeping state. Emari shakes him gently until his eyes peel open.

"Where am I?" he asks in common. "Daeskar?"

"Dragon-tongue for heaven," Boe smiles. He then tells The King that he is still living, and that they have brought him back to his people, victorious.

Scazgix stands, and brushes dirt from his armour. He speaks again with confidence to Boe, and sets off down the tunnel.

The King tells Boe that his people will be gone by morning, and that they will be forever thankful. "I fought well?" he then asks, in common-speech.

Boe tells him that he fought with honour.

"Good," The King smiles. They reach the ledge and The King steps to stand over the cave. He calls down in his language to the camp below. Boe translates.

"My people, I have returned victorious. Thanks to the help of these outsiders, our homeland is free from tyranny. We can return in peace and safety," The King says. Cheering comes from below as he begins to descend the ladder. The King pauses and turns to face them. Boe translates again as Scazgix speaks, "We have little to offer you for your help, but if you should ever have need of us, you will know where to find me. My people have strong memory and we will not forget you. Boe, Chablise, Voss, thank you."

Boe stops him. In dragon-tongue, the gnome tells Scazgix about their gift of weaponry and gear. The King agrees to send warriors to collect it, and again thanks them profusely.

The King then descends.

The trio is left again on the ledge. Soon they turn and head back down the tunnel, back once again into the quarry's base. By now, the sun hangs low in the sky, and the horizon has begun to bleed a faint orange.

"If we move quickly, we can meet with good Lord Landston," Voss says with cynicism in his voice. "Then we can bed down for the night, and in the morning, or the next few days, we can purchase horses and leave for Highfell."

The others agree, and they return with haste to the top of the quarry. Just north-west lies the Landston manor. The house is made of light-grey stone and accentuated with red-wood supports and decorations.

They walk along the path that runs between the two front gardens, and up to the red door.

Boe knocks. There is a long pause. Boe knocks again.

Frederik Landston himself opens the door. He appears less than pleased to see the three of them.

"Should I have the guards called?" he asks rhetorically.

"They couldn't deal with the kobolds, how could they deal with us?" Voss asks in response.

Landston huffs. "What of your little plan, then?"

Emari speaks, but is cut off. "They will be gone in the morn-"

"I did not ask you, harlot," Landston says. Emari glares daggers behind her mask, which changes colour from a calm deep blue to a glowing red.

"They are leaving in the morning, likely before you awaken. You have our word. We came for our payment," Voss tells him.

"If they aren't gone then I will have real mercenaries hired to slaughter them properly."

"I don't care. That isn't our problem, and it won't be yours. A sum of two hundred coins, is both of our problems," Voss states.

"You'll get your coins, if the runts leave."

"No," the trio responds in unison.

"We spent all day aiding your cause," Voss presses. "We got into combat, and shed blood. We risked our lives to get the kobolds from your quarry. We have now put up with your arrogance more than once. We are taking our gold and you will not hear from us again," Voss states.

"You are in no position to-" Landston begins. Emari's hand moves to her rapier, Boe conjures a small ball of lightening into his hands, and Voss simply holds his arms out to either side, as though he was keeping the others restrained.

"Clearly it is you who is in no position," Voss tells him.

"You wouldn't," Landston gasps. He takes a step back.

"Coins," Voss tells him. "Now."

Landston stammers. "I-I have a pouch of a hundred pre-counted. I will grab that now. The rest I will send tomorrow morning to your residence. I will have a servant count the pouch now."

"Fine, go," Voss urges. The man disappears into his home, leaving the door open.

By the time he returns, the group has dropped their aggressive stance. Frederik hands Voss a pouch, which jingles as Voss takes it from the lord's hand.

"The rest will be sent to the East Air by sunrise tomorrow. The name is Voss Hallehwell."

"Understood," Frederik nods. He does not wait for them to turn and leave before closing and locking his door.

"Too much?" Emari asks. She is still angered by his comment, though her mask is slowly returning to normal.

"No. Some men need force to change, some need time. He was the former," Voss says to her.

"Let's split this coin and visit some shops. If we're travelling a week westward we will need supplies, and all the gold from today will cover that cost," Emari says, leading them back towards the town proper, and the trade district.

The others follow. The day wanes, and will likely give just enough time to reach some stores before they close. The group is tired, but looking forward now to travelling once more somehow.

In Voss, a fire burns at the thought of finally tracking down Eralius and culling the source of the strange, and grotesque creatures.

With much ahead of them, they walk briskly along the road towards the western gate. Then through Taernsby proper's walls, into the fading light of winter's end.

Chapter Six - The Velvet Compass

3E055, 18th of Ildonian's End

    Mount Azgul is the second largest of the Voiceless Peaks. It is shorter than Zyban's Rise only by a few hundred feet, and the Krunixian capital, Azgul Hold, is carved out of the stone that surrounds it. The Krunixian settlers spent decades just to complete the first stage of their great city. First, they leveled a massive section, starting ten feet from the base of the gentle slopes, to the point where it became too steep to warrant work. After they had a large, flat plateau chiseled, they began to carve into the stone they had unearthed, until the surface was bored fifteen feet down, leaving a wall of rock that was ten feet thick surrounding the new bowl at its original height. They then dug the rest of the slope away — the area outside their current construction — leaving the whole foot of the mountain as a flat plane, with only the fifteen foot walls that they left sticking up.

    The dwarves, gnomes, and sparse humans were left with stockpiles of stone, that they had been been using to build homes and villages around the mountain for years by this point. Construction only truly began within the main area after it had been cleared, though. Gatehouses were built, along with housing quarters and markets. Nobles from as far away as Raeborg (on the eastern coast) took the opportunity to move to the quickly expanding city, and invested in its development. Many folk, rich and common, settled there. Azgul Hold expanded into the mountain as well, adding a mining district that brought more stone and metals, which in turn added to the trade that Azgul Hold was able to provide throughout the known world.

    By now, Azgul Hold is a bastion of dwarven and gnomish power. The city boasts incredible smiths, technological entrepreneurs, military training programs that outmatch maybe even the elves, and a trade system that spans the entirety of the civilized world, putting out minerals and gems to the other nations faster than any other city. The tops of the turrets, the roofs of nobles' houses built into the mountain face, the tall arcane studies, and higher-storey homes and shops, all glint in hues of yellow and red. They are made using gold-tinted metals and the dyes from Krunixian roses. Light from the late-afternoon sun reflects the warm colours of the city across the golden wheat fields and the open plains, painting the normally green grasses in a layer of orange.

Roger's horse trots along the cement road, leading those behind it. The farmlands around them are in rest, save for the wheat fields and some plots of cabbages and beets. With the walls of the city only an hour away, the small band of travelers increases their pace. They intend to find an inn by nightfall.

There are five of them that left Railwood. They left nearly a week of fast riding ago. Roger and Helena had grown up there. The Hardwick family moved from Helmshire just before they were born, deciding it was cheaper to raise a family in the Council Lands. They were right, of course. The Dabarisian Empire nearly fell into debt during the Streboyan Civil War, but the council lands are supported by all three major governments. Taxes have been low since their establishment, and most trade and taxation is handled by the municipalities, and rarely imposed by larger powers.

Roger has never had the inkling to leave until recently, when he found the world was more dangerous than life in his small town had led him to believe. Things were comfortable in Railwood when he was growing up, but ever since the Iombrakk tribe from the western marshes began to assault his home, he has not been able to shake the feeling that he wants more out of life than standing guard against danger until he is old and wrinkled.

Helena agreed with him on these things, and told him that she would follow him across the world. They sought to make some destiny for themselves. They could comfortably have lived out their lives in the Council Lands, but they know they're not weak, and they believe that they can do more than most others from the town they were born into.

Facts and rumours of the order known as The Velvet Compass have reached all corners of the known world, in fact the prestige and renown that it has gathered has placed it beside other famous orders like the Paladins of Horan and Order Luminescence. The Velvet Compass was formed midway through the second era, and was started as an adventuring guild led by a demon-kin named Velvet. They got lucky a couple of times, and then a couple more, and soon they came to be sitting on a vast amount of wealth and riches. Instead of simply retiring and sitting on the fortune they had amassed, they built a sizeable order hall in Azgul Hold, and changed their focus from adventuring, to aiding honourable mercenaries and new guilds, both adventurers and craftsmen, in starting up.

The Velvet Compass is now a centre for people across the world to submit jobs for wannabe adventurers to pursue. The order is trusted widely for being the most reliable means to obtain hired help, as they have small guild halls in many major cities, and a large pile of good reviews amongst nobility and the common-folk alike.

Not only, of course, are they respected from a hiring perspective, but they are also sought by anyone with little opportunities to get ahead in the adventuring world.

Such it was that before the pair of siblings left Railwood, they asked if anyone would with to join them to join The Velvet Compass. They received a mixture of sneers and support from the community after announcing their departure and their question, two weeks before they planned to leave. This would be a decision that would have to be sat on, and Roger and Helena knew this, having sat on it themselves for some time.

When the morning came and they left their home with bags packed, they had still heard nothing from friends and townsfolk other than wishes of luck. As they mounted their horses and began to pull towards the gate, however, they were met with a surprise.

Jitz, an old friend of theirs, and a mage as well; Arthur, one of the town's best huntsmen and archers, and Jaine, a human woman and apprentice priest for the church in town had all decided, separately of each other, that they would accompany the siblings. Roger questioned them each on their certainty, but none would turn back.

A week later, they are now all riding through the south gate of Azgul Hold. The sprawling plateau envelopes them. The natural stone walls, long ago reinforced with metal, take the place of the horizon. Buildings jut from the ground like a forest. The only break in the stone and metal foliage is the collection of streets that cut like deer paths through the city.

As the band of horses press into Azgul Hold, they are surrounded by merchants barking out products and services and surrounding their group. Jaine places two gold coins into the hand of a dwarven woman in return for the ornate looking silver necklace that she was holding out.

The winter's end will bring great travel back to the kingdom of Krunix. Several intrepid souls, and a variety of merchants, are already riding from the coast and the Dabarisian Central Plains, and even coming through the mountain passes from the lower towns of the human-dominant kingdom.

As of now, however, there is not enough tourism for the merchants and businesses of the dwarven capital to sit comfortably. The group buys some simple crafts, throwing enough money for a week's survival to satiate the hungry sellers.

They push further into the city, and eventually the vendors retreat, leaving the roads clear, save for the folk walking to and from, carrying trade goods and stock. They are stopped for several minutes as a caravan of ore wagons crosses the main road.

After nearly three hours of traversing the great city, the sky has grown dark behind the outer walls, gentle plains, and the mountains of Krunix. They finally reach the square of the visitor centre, the section of the city made of inns, taverns, and recreational businesses. There are many choices for lodging, but not many that are affordable. They manage to find a basic inn above a large restaurant called 'Slab's Slab.'

'The Slab', as the locals call it, is run by Angus, the youngest child of the Yewslab family. The Yewslabs are a new-blood people, having migrated from the Dabarisian Kingdom only two decades ago. Angus, his cousin Garret Boregate, and a gnome by the name of Alli, all take turns watching the business. They keep a clean and proper operation, and are praised by travelers and regulars alike.

Roger and company tie their horses to the hitching rails outside, where a guard stands watch. They enter the restaurant through large yew doors on the south wall. The air is thick with the scents of wood polish, smoking meat, and strong dwarven ale. There are clusters of patrons spread across the restaurant, sitting at the many tables and booths. The building is square, save for a section of the north end that is built outward to accommodate the kitchen. The dining area is the shape of a horseshoe, as the centre of the west wall is taken up by a spiral staircase that runs up to the inn above.

The tables are all hewn of exquisitely carved, sanded stone. The rock is a dark, onyx colour which compliments the silver-painted wooden chairs and their red cushions. The floor around each seating area is a natural looking, brown wood, but the main walking paths, the stairs, and the areas around the two bars, at the east and west walls, are all carpeted in the same red as the seats.

Candlelight from the tables causes the room to dance slightly, but four chandeliers in the corners of the floor keep a steady glow throughout the dining spaces. The kitchen is alive with noise and, as the group finally makes it all the way inside, they are greeted by a small metal creature that clanks towards them.

This creature appears to be about the shape and size of a gnome, and does not appear threatening. It is made up of interlocking plates for skin, and tiny gears that whir quietly whenever it moves. Its head is slightly larger than the average gnome's, with two eye-like holes that glow pink, and a mouth that is constantly open in a small circle.

"Are you in need of dinner this evening? Or a place to rest your head?" the creature asks. Its voice is hollow, like someone projecting in a small, empty dining hall, but it has the slightly regal accent of Krunixian nobility.

Roger pauses before speaking, "Both."

"Excellent!" the machine chirps, its metal exterior moving jovially. "I will escort you to the house-master, who will get you keys to some rooms upstairs." The metal host then turns. Its legs bend backwards, and its torso rotates to face the other way. It begins to waddle away from the group standing in the entrance.

Roger looks to his companions. The small metal figure continues its march, showing no sign of waiting. They begin to follow. Several people interrupt their journey through the restaurant, on their way to the outhouses out front. More metal figures of the same design, acting as servers, give them a wide berth while carrying trays of food and drink. The group continues to follow the host. Their metal figure is devoid of any clothing, unlike the others, which all wear black aprons around their waists.

They eventually reach the northern side of the building, where the open kitchen pitches the smell of cooking meats and sauces into the house. Behind the low counter stands a tall dwarf with white-blonde hair. He is youthful and his beard is kept tidy. He wears a deep blue shirt, trimmed with a gold accent that matches his hair.

"House-Master Garret," the metal figure speaks. Its nearly-dwarven voice echoes through its whole head as it speaks. "These five require a room and food."

"Thank ye," the dwarf responds absentmindedly. He is reading over some small paper strips on the counter. He places two plates of food and slides one of the papers forward. Promptly, one of the servants rushes forward and takes the two plates onto a tray. It seems to read the paper before waddling back into the maze of tables. Garret looks up and smiles. "Welcome to the Slab!" he says to Helena. "I can grab ye a room key if yuh want. We've got a few open. One with triple beds. Well ye all be needing separate?"

"No," Roger says, speaking over his sister's shoulder. "We are fine with sharing."

"Right!" Garret says. He makes a hand gesture and the metal host begins its journey back to the front door. "I will grab ye two keys, then." He reaches around the corner, out of view, and the guests hear a jingle of metal as Garret produces two ornate, silver keys. "Room numbers are on em'. It's seven silver," the dwarf tells them.

There is a pause. Seven silver is a high price for an inn room. Roger knows that they will not likely find a better price though, at least not one that can be trusted.

"Seven is fine," Roger agrees, producing four from his own pouch. The others cobble together a mix of silver and copper coins to make the total and pass it to Garret.

"Ai, thank ye," Garret makes another hand gesture, and a different metal servant waddles to the counter from behind the group. "Take these five to a booth by the stairs. Make em' comfortable," Garret tells the creature, which nods and begins walking away. "Follow im'," Garret says. "He'll treat ye nice, bring ye water and menus too," he adds, chuckling at their confused expressions.

Roger leads as they catch up to the servant. It brings them towards the stair case. They arrive shortly at a long table, with room for six or seven. The table is set against the the stairs as they rise from the main floor. It is surrounded by high, cushioned benches with tall backs. There are other booths towards the back wall, but none closer to the base of the stairs. The servant gestures to the table and quickly slips out of sight.

Roger and Helena sit together on the bench closest to the restaurant, while the others take the one closest to the wall. It feels good to finally sit on something comfortable.

The servant appears with menus and glasses filled with water, whirs happily, then disappears again around the side of the stairs. They begin browsing their options and discussing excitedly.

Roger looks at his sister. The candle in the centre of the table is half burned, but will likely last several more hours. It provides enough, soft light to see by.

Helena looks better. Her face will never fully recover from the blow she was dealt in defence of her town, but it has sealed and the swelling has vanished. All that remains is the scar that runs like a river along the right side of her face and forehead. Her nose is crooked and her one nostrils is ripped open. She is smiling, though, and still carries their family's natural beauty.

Helena laughs as Arthur reminds everyone of the time, on their trip, that Roger's horse kicked black mud all over Arthur's horse's shins and they both had to clean the beast using drinking water.

The servant returns and asks for their order. They only have enough coin for a week or two at most, but tonight they are done with thinking too heavily about it.

Jaine and Jitz both order salads, and split the cheapest bottle of red wine; Arthur lights up when he sees roasted duck on the menu, as that is not something that the people of Railwood have ever made, and orders it with ale; Roger has ale and chicken, and Helena orders fresh berry tea with some mutton.

Roger and Helena lent their house to family friends. When their parents passed away, the Olberson's down the street helped greatly in getting the siblings back on their feet. The Olberson children, who are only five and seven years younger than Roger, agreed to take care of the place while Roger and Helena are gone. The pair also wrote a will in case something bad happened to them, and made sure to leave their house to the family.

As the night presses onward, the conversation returns once more to The Velvet Compass. The order is a massive beacon to those seeking fortune and to see the world. The main order hall is located not far from where the group currently sits.

The visitor centre is adjacent to three important areas of Azgul Hold. The market districts that line the outside walls of the city are largely accessible from the visitor centre, with the most interesting being the district for exotic goods and magical wares. Another important location that lies nearby is the large entertainment area just south of the centre. Complete with a large arena and playhouses, there is much to do as a visitor to, or local of, Azgul Hold. The last area, and most important to the group right now, is the guild district to the north-west. This is where large companies produce products, where guild halls are built by adventurers and merchant-lords, and where many of the trade decisions between nobility is discussed. The guild district is also where The Velvet Compass' largest hall stands, at the rise of the great Mount Azgul, where its high tower can overlook most of the city.

The Order Hall is a pinnacle of wealth and history. The sheer amount of treasures, tales, and interesting people that travel through its front doors would befuddle the minds of the average citizen. As such, most people choose to pay it little attention, instead finding contentment in their own day to day toils.

The house is not closed at this hour. In fact, it rarely closes its doors fully to the public. The group knows this, but even still they have agreed to not seek entrance until the morning when they are rested and have had time to collect themselves.

For lower level members of the order, there is not a great deal demanded. The order takes requests from across the known world, and offers many contracts and opportunities to its active members. In return for completing a contract, the order will pay a posted reward, while still profiting from the person or organization that originally gave the request.

As well, even for the lower ranking members, gear and other goods can be rented for free, or only a small deposit of gold, and returned after, which makes gearing up for longer journeys much easier than operating as a freelance mercenary. There are, of course, severe punishments for failing to comply with order rules, and there are numerous tales of low ranking members stealing gear and running, but there are equally as many tales of bounty postings taken on the thieves' heads.

Regardless, it is the best bet for Roger, Helena and their companions.

Roger looks around at his friends, as they begin to dig into the large plates of food that are arriving. He grew up with many of these people. In the past few months, with the fighting and the travelling, he has found trust in all of them. Now, though he is sitting in the capital of another kingdom, seemingly so far and so different from home, Roger lets out a sigh. He finally feels the stress of the past begin to lift.

He also feels excitement, nervousness, and — for the first time in a while — genuine happiness.

Chapter Seven - Travel and Study

3E056, 7th of Renewal

Spring ebbs in like a slow tide, with warmth returning in slow, crashing waves. Green begins to take hold - first in the south, then central Estrand, and then finally moving towards The North and into the flatlands above the Voiceless Peaks. As snow finally retreats, and joy begins to bloom, the town of Taernsby seems to grow more lively. Several large caravans set off, laden with trade goods bound for other parts of the continent. What folk leave are replaced by three times that number in trade ships and wagons, and travellers from the northern townships and Krunix.

Voss, Emari, and Boe set off for Highfell on the second, following the Southroad, which they have all taken to and/or from Krunix. The Southroad connects the coasts, running all the way from Taernsby to the town of Thalas-Ara in the south-western Vruyothy woods, and the elven capital — The City of Stren — in central Vruyoth. The trio had many things to do before their departure, and so they left later than planned. In the days leading up to their departure, before the travel arrangements began, Voss picked up his shield from the blacksmith. Then, they all purchased some fresh clothes, repaired what gear had been damaged in their flight back to Taernsby, and even had enough coin left over to stash away and pay for a nice few meals in the restaurants near the square.

The day before they set out, they stopped by the stables, and made arrangements for horses. Voss purchased his own - a deep-brown riding stallion. Boe had stabled an ass for himself when he arrived in town, and spent only a short time checking his stored saddle and baggage as the others continued with their purchases. Emari opted not to buy a horse, but rent one instead for the month. This could save some money, as she was still uncertain of how much travelling she planned on doing in the near future. Horse rental is rare, usually reserved for messengers or done through a business, but as Emari is working for the mayor, it was easier to secure the trust of the stable-master, a middle-aged human man.

On the last day they spent in Taernsby, they said goodbye to Peren, who stopped to tell them that he planned to seek passage south once more, after perhaps joining in the investigation of the desert-ruins. He was not certain that he would stay any longer than he needed to, nor was he sure that he would see them again. They parted then on good terms, though, and the half-elven noble wished them luck.

The group also said goodbye to Brael at the East Air. Brael told them that he wished to remain in town for a while longer, but that he would like them to send word when they return from Highfell, and he would wish to go with them to the desert if they would have him. They agreed to do so and wished him a good rest.

Between their interaction with the kobolds and their departure, nothing of note had transpired, save for a local drunk found stabbed in an alley off Delg Lane, and a small fire near the docks that was put out before more than a few buildings were damaged.

The group rode quickly for the first day, hoping to get to the outer reaches of the township by nightfall. They had passed through the small villages around Taernsby Proper many times now, and they had picked out a relatively clean looking inn to make for on their first day of travel. It was not as close as several others, but with the snow cleared from the roads, and stopping only twice for brief rests, they made good time. As dusk had began to settle comfortably in the sky, they could see the hamlet of Eavat in the distance over another rolling hill.

Emari asked Voss during the end of this first day what the name of his horse would be. The stable-master did not give the beasts any identification. "So, you bought your horse for good," Emari had noted. "He seems a fine mount, does he have a name yet?"

"No," replied Voss.

"Shall you not give him one?"

"None."

"You must though!" the bard cried, with only some sarcasm. "Such a beautiful creature should surely not be nameless."

Voss thought then for some time. "It would satisfy you so greatly just to have a name to call it?"

"To call *him,* yes," spoke Emari. "Mine is named Rosebud," she explained, patting her chestnut mare.

"A suitable name," Voss had mused. "Mine shall be Sir Whore."

There was a brief argument between the pair, accented by laughter from both Voss and Boe.

Voss finally ended the debate by telling Emari plainly, "If you have a problem with Sir Whore's name, you can simply call him nothing."

Their beasts were tired by the time they arrived in Eavat, even though they were all of strong breed.

The small inn, Aldshire, had a hitching rail under an awning, but no stables. In fact, there were none in the town at all. They paid the housemaster extra to have someone watch the horses for the night. Aldshire proved to be a fair establishment, if not a little rowdy for the tastes of Boe and Voss. The food and drink were fine, and the local ales had a unique citrus taste that was well received by the trio.

Emari sung several songs once she had drank her fill, and another bard played along on a well-tuned lute, making the pair a good collection of copper coins.

In the morning they set off once again, knowing it would likely take another two or three full days of travel between the edges of Taernsby and the smaller townlands of Highfell. They had purchased enough supplies, and decide to not overwork their horses, opting to ride at a steady pace and take occasional longer breaks.

Nearing the middle of their fifth day of travel (the seventh of Renewal) they now see the shape of buildings over the hills and thickets of the lowlands that make up the Highfell township. They had split from the Southroad at the end of the previous day, and began to follow the Kingslane as it cut north-west towards their destination. The sky has been clouding for the last two days, and it is now darkening with a storm.

They push onward, confident that they can outrun nightfall and rain until they reach Highfell Proper.

* * * * *

Around the same time that Voss, Emari, and Boe ride through the outskirts of the Highfell villages, their old companion, Evandur, is arriving in Daroonga City. He had rode through the same township as the others, as the Kingslane runs all the way to the capital.

In contrast to the small town to the south-east, Daroonga City is immaculate and colossal. It was constructed long ago, upon the large, mushroom-like plateau in the centre of Daroonga Canyon. It is written that the canyon was discovered by Daroo Firstwright, good friend of the first Holliserian King, and that they decided together that the canyon would be the beating heart of the whole world.

This was not the case at first, as the canyon runs many hundreds of feet deep, and in the days of old, before the dawn of the first era, men and dwarves had not developed the technologies or magics to manage such a means to even cross the huge, kilometer wide gap between the canyon's edge and the plateau in the centre.

It was decided instead that they would build on the outside of the canyon. They erected Daroonga Village, which was built as a small settlement on the southern side of the canyon, where the weather and soil were fairer. It began as a collection of simple wooden buildings, built by logging nearby thickets, but soon grew to the size of a town, and over the years it expanded to wrap around most of the bottom edge of the canyon. It was not until 1E054 that the construction of Daroonga city truly started. The project was headed by the Holliserian Royals, but all the races save for the elves of Vruyoth helped to create the great city.

Now, the town outside the main city — still named 'Daroonga Village', but often simply called 'Daroonga' or 'Lower Daroonga' — has become the centre for trade and travel. The city is nearly the same size as the town, being built on a circular space of only five kilometers in diameter, but still overshadows any town or city within the kingdom, save for maybe Aebarrow Stronghold.

The slightly ovular canyon boasts an eight kilometer diameter, leaving an average of one and one half kilometers of space between the central plateau and the outside edges. The southern face, where the village was built, runs slightly inward, to only a single kilometer. The difference did not make the initial project of getting to the plateau easy, but did prove helpful nonetheless. Three bridges were built across the gap. The bridges are made purely of enchanted steel, and bore deep into the stone on both sides. This was the work of dwarvish and halfling craft. The bridges are suspended across the gap, and not supported beneath by any means. They are wide enough for the largest of wagons to be pulled across, and despite there being a maximum weight limit that the bridges can manage, it is only in the busy seasons of trade that extra bridge-guards need to be posted to regulate traffic. The bridges are built at regular intervals along the Kingslane's course through Daroonga Village, with one near the western edge, one in the central square, and one near the eastern brink. All reach towards the main gates of the city on the plateau.

By the time of the bridges' construction, there were already paths carved into the canyon walls that allowed travel into the base, as wide rivers run cool through the basin of the canyon. The rivers come from some underground cavern or spring where water has gathered — they say — since the forming of the world. There are routes that can still be taken to traverse the canyon along the bottom, but not for wagons or the faint of heart, as they were completely abandoned to disrepair when wells and mining elevators within the city were constructed to offer all the access that people need.

Evandur has been crossing the bridge for nearly fifteen minutes, with a wagon ahead, and a group of talkative half-folk behind. After his many days of fast riding, he is finally drawing close to the great gates.

The walls of Daroonga City are build of thick, pale-grey stone that stretches out of the grass atop the red earth and the yellow rock of the canyon and plateau. The walls form a ring around the entire surface, only leaving a thin strip outside for structural reasons, and a large courtyard on the south side where traffic gathers off the bridges while waiting for entrance.

At regular intervals along the wall there are built watch towers, topped with a turquoise polish that gleams brilliantly in the sun that still pierces through the gathering clouds. This colour was ground from gems found to be common in the canyon. There are many deposits of gold, silver, copper, and coal, and even other gems that are found in the canyon's base and the stem of the plateau. The plateau is not to be mined, though many gems were chipped carefully from the outer walls of the stem. There is another major source of the same kind of turquoise gem, which is in the mines of Aebarrow Stronghold, which was built even later than Daroonga.

The gate is made of black iron, but has stood open for many years. No army has marched on Daroonga City since the Malachi Crisis at the end of the second era. Before that, the elven armies at the end of the first were the only force to oppose the might of Daroonga. Even in these events, rarely has the gate closed, as no army could cross the bridges or canyon.

As Evandur's horse, much to the beast's relief, sets her hooves upon the solid ground of the stone courtyard, the paladin looks ahead into the city. He sees the turquoise roofs of the manors of nobility, the inns, and the churches where they poke out of the sea of shorter buildings that encase the streets of the city. Most of the roofs of taller structures, aside from church towers, are constructed in dome shapes, a mark of Holliserian architecture that is now mainly seen in older buildings. The main streets are bordered by thin rows of well-kept hedges, which break at every building entrance. In front of the hedges sit flower beds sowed in dark-wood planters, that are now beginning to bloom and bring further colour to the city. Most buildings are constructed of darker stone, quarried elsewhere and brought over land, and with wood supports of either birch or maple, which grow in abundance in the thickets around the canyon.

The sections of the city are divided into rings, separated by stone walls that are built ten feet in height, and two feet in width. The plateau also slopes slightly upward toward the middle, and so each ring is raised above the other, chiseled so that all the sections are flat, but stone ramps smoothly connect them. The space between the city walls and the first inner-wall is the Merchant Ring, which wraps around the entire outer edge of Daroonga City, save for a large portion of the northernmost arc, which is a walled-in rectangle of space reserved for the military district, and cuts through most of the city rings.

The next ring is mostly housing, and is named the Living Ring. Nobles reside farther north on average, closer to the military district, and the poorer folk tend to live closer to the gate. The main roads, being the ones that wrap through each ring, and the ones that move between the rings along the cardinal points, are lined with large houses and shops, regardless of their location in the city.

After the Living Ring comes the area where most of the soft infrastructure is built, referred to as the City Ring. Within this area are universities, council chambers, guild halls, safety services, and any other necessary component in making sure Daroonga runs smoothly. Of course, there are other guild halls and safety buildings spread throughout the other rings, but the heart of these workings is in the City Ring.

The innermost part of the city, built around the top of the gentle hill of the plateau and the great royal castle, is the Royal Ring. This is where the manors of the four inner houses are built. These manors are magnificent and sprawling. They are inhabited by members of many families, that all form the houses, and help take care of and govern the whole kingdom, House Talava, Farathorn, Gaelsa, and the royal House Dabaris.

Daroonga Castle, which serves as a great meeting hall and holds the throne, is topped with a dome of solid turquoise, fused with meticulous, arcane care, that gleams even brighter than any other in the city. Halfway between each cardinal road, built against the cylindrical castle itself, is a great, golden tower that reaches up nearly as far as the castle's top. Sixteen sparkling golden columns encircle the building as well, that reach up to a shining ring that separates the stone from the dome. From each of the sixteen locations that the columns reach up to, there starts an arc that leaps across the great roof and crosses under the gleaming, solid turquoise spike in the centre. The dome is ringed with royal green banners so large that the white inlay of the left-facing lion's head can be seen from the gate. The same banners are hung on major intersections, along the breaks between ring-walls, and even above many home doors. Proud are the people of Daroonga City.

Evandur rides through the gates. There are guards stationed on either side, dressed in shining, white steel armours with pure, dark-green pauldrons, cloaks, and gauntlets. Most travelers are briefly stopped to be asked their business. There is a line behind Evandur as he passes through. The midday has brought several traders from around the kingdom and many village folk as well. The paladin is not questioned much. He simply states his business as "a personal inquiry" and that he seeks counsel from his church. He is let by without a second glance.

He looks more ragged than he did two weeks ago. His white hair is unkempt and his beard has grown slightly, so that his jaw is now covered in a thin layer. He will never be able to grow a full beard, due to his nature, but a stubble is often unavoidable for him nonetheless. He keeps his face generally clean, but his journey here was one of haste, and he stopped little. He passed Highfell after four days of travel, and stopped only for a few hours to restock his food and waterskins. After that, he made haste, and it took him only another week to reach the village. He stopped there to give himself and his horse time to recover for a day before he began to ride through the town towards the bridges.

Now, through the gates of the great city, Evandur sets forth up the main street, the Southerroad. He rides for an hour. Sometimes the street seems nearly empty, sometimes he has to wait at busy intersections where wagons unload goods to shopkeepers. Finally, he finds himself being let through the walls to the City Ring. He remembers the route through this area with crystalline clarity. He turns leftward, and brings Volana to a gentle trot along the smooth stone of the City Ring Road. Not much farther lies before him, so he rides at ease.

The main roads are lined with evenly spaced lamps that tower above the paladin on horseback. They remain unlit throughout the day. The side roads do not have any, but the ring and cardinal roads stay bathed in light at all hours.

After another fifteen minutes of riding, Evandur reaches home. It is the greatest of all churches to Valkronus in the known world that was built in Daroonga City. It stands tall and wide. The first storeys is one of pews and a podium for sermons to be given. The second has several shrines, and one greater one for the eternal flame. The third is space for church rituals and council chambers, and another is above that with housing for priests and paladins like Evandur. There is an underground complex as well for storing goods and records and for garrison in the event of an attack. Two bell towers, painted the same aqua-blue as the rest of the city, rise above the church higher than any building nearby, and shine gloriously in the afternoon sun.

The paladin dismounts, and leads Volana to the stables that adjourn the church, built in the small courtyard on the right-hand side. The yard is grass with a small stone path cut through it, and is surrounded by a low cobblestone wall. Evandur grabs a small bale of hay and strips a good portion from it for his horse, laying it in a trough. He fills a bucket with water from the well in the centre of the yard, and pours it into another small basin for

Volana.

After stripping his horse of her saddle and barding, he closes the stable door and exits, crossing the yard to the church's doors, which open into the yard, not the street. As he pulls open the doors, he finds an older fellow walking to greet him. The man is slightly bent forward, and his once blonde hair has faded entirely to grey. His face retains some youth, but wrinkles have been advancing above his brow and under his eyes.

"Ewain," Evandur says softly, with a smile.

"Is that master- my apologies, sir. Is that *Paladin* Anglethorn?" the man asks.

"It is, Ewain. And by now you must know, you may call me Evandur, old friend."

"You have told me, but the title fits you well, and so you wear it - even unintentionally. I thought I heard noise the yard," Ewain says. "I thought it was a messenger, but it was you! What a welcome surprise! Now come, do not stand in the doorway like a house cat." The old friend leads Evandur inside.

The church's interior is warmer than the outside air. Flames burn in metal basins placed upon each of the small altars, four on either side of the long and wide room. The altars are also covered in various offerings and a multitude of smoking incenses, which fill the room with a relaxing mixture of floral and woody scents.

There are others in the church. A family is clustered at the back-left altar, and nearly fifty people are spread through the first floor pews and the other altars.

Tall windows of red and orange stained glass cast the appearance of warm flame upon the dark stone floor, and light the the central red rug, that runs through the main aisle, in brilliant light. There are also candles set at the ends of many pews, in holders set in the wood, and on several altars, in no clear pattern. The stairs at the far end, on the left side of the raised sermon-platform carry Evandur and Ewain upward towards the second storey. The stairs pass between the outer wall and the wall of the storage rooms behind the platform.

As they climb the second half, leading from the landing in the centre to the lip of the second storey, Evandur sees the giant, diamond-shaped, stained window come into view directly above him. The intricate detail of this window must have taken years to fully create, as every part of it shows a different image. Some show flame, some show the city being built, some show scenes of war and conflict, or the images of the first and second Holliserian kings. All come together to create the giant phoenix of Valkronus, rising through the full scope of the window. The second floor is built as a balcony that wraps around orange stained glass in the centre, which looks down into the first floor. Seven full shrines are set up on this floor as well, three on either side of the floor, and the eternal flame which burns beneath the massive window.

Evandur spent much of early adulthood here, after he was transferred from Layefayre to Daroonga City at the age of seventeen. It was here that he finished his training, and since then he has travelled between the city and Taernsby more often that anywhere else. The window has become a symbol to him of his growth into a full paladin. Ewain rounds the lip of the stairs again, not pausing at the second floor, where yet more people are gathered at the shrines, and several priests are keeping watch. He climbs the next set of steps, that runs back again, and upward into the private areas of the church. The third storey begins with a small balcony that one can stand upon to look at the second half of the great window, as it spans both the second and third storeys.

Ewain pushes open an ash-wood door and they enter the third floor. They do not stop here either. The third and fourth floors are only three quarters the size of the bottom two in length, and the fourth is thinner to accommodate the sloping roof. They do not enter the interior of the third floor, however, instead they pass up the final flight, and Ewain unlocks another door, opening it into a thin hallway.

They enter.

At the other end of the hall from the pair is a ladder that climbs to one of the bell towers. Access to the other is granted by crossing a path upon the roof from the first.

"Here we are," Ewain says, stopping.

"You knew I would be staying," Evandur responds.

"You've been gone nearly a year. I would hope you are staying for a time," the old man smiles again.

"I am staying, yes," Angelthorn tells him. "It may not be for long, but for now I have no urgent reason to leave again. I seek information."

There is a pause.

"I know it is not my place to pry, Paladin Angelthorn, but do you think perhaps I know something that could help you?" Ewain asks.

"I think not," Evandur says somberly. "There is nothing from any teaching I ever learned that would help. In fact, I do not know very much at all about what I seek. I simply need to start looking."

Ewain thinks for a moment. "There was a squire, Sir, that was deemed ready recently to train under a paladin. He is not much younger than you are now. He was a scrawny lad, and even now that he is twenty and two, he is not much bigger. He knows his way around our records and libraries in town maybe better even than I, though. Douglas is his name, Douglas Tumbolamew."

"Tumbolamew?" Evandur asks, not entirely certain that the old man is speaking truth.

"He's a dark-skin. He was rescued from the desert by a couple of paladins, near two decades back, when a tribe of the vicious savages came and attacked. He was brought to one of the churches down in Krunix for a time, before being sent north to Rockfell, and then finally to Daroonga only a few years later. Likely, he arrived long before you left, but he was reclusive by nature. I spoke with him more than others."

"Why the name?"

"Probably closer translated to Tobacai, but the church changed it. Tummas and Bartholamew found him, and his name was not properly revealed until long after they were back. The man knows everything about his past now, but he chose to remain a man of the church. He has gained our trust, though many of our members were not so sure at first of the paladins' decisions."

"I will speak with him, if you will tell me where to meet."

"He is out on business now, but he should be back within the next few days."

"I will find him then. I do not expect to depart so soon," Evandur says. "Tonight I may walk to the library on the Wessteroad."

"The room at the end of this hall on the left I shall make prepared for you. It will be with bedding, fresh clothing, and some food as well when you return from the library. You are always welcomed home, Evandur."

"Thank you, Ewain."

"Good luck, Evandur. I must write this down in the ledgers, and continue with my fueling of the flames."

Ewain leaves Evandur in the hall. The paladin trusts the old priest closely, and moves to the room at the end to set down his belongings. For fear of attack, he has travelled most of the way with his armour on, but once he reached Daroonga Village he doffed it and has taken the last leg in simple clothing, with his longsword still at his waist.

Evandur places his bag down in the room. It is a small, but homely place, with a clear window that looks out into the sky, which is still filling with clouds. He strips his sword from his body and lays it upon the uncovered mattress. The blade was a gift from the church in Layefayre when he began his paladin training. He had it re-bladed once by a half-elven smith in Daroonga City several years back, but has kept the same hilt. The hilt, pommel, and cross-guard are all inlaid with fine silver. It is truly a good blade by all standards, and has served him well many times. Despite his connection to it, he does not need it in the city. Instead he takes his shortsword and dagger before once again exiting the room.

He passes back through the church, saying another goodbye to Ewain on his way, and leaves for the library. It is not a short walk, but he is glad to stretch his legs after days of riding. It takes him just short of an hour by the sun's course. The Wessteroad runs from the Royal Ring to the Merchant Ring, and is built directly on the west cardinal point. The City Ring Road is an easy walk, built flat and set with stone tiles, devoid of gaps or unevenness. Evandur makes good time, and when he reaches the library, the sun is still pinned in the paling sky. He will have several hours before dusk begins to duel the day.

This afternoon and evening of study passes with little in the way of results. Evandur scours through books on histories of magic, and the forms of arcane energy, but finds nothing that strikes his eye relating to Voss.

Finally, when the sun has dipped low behind the city's outer walls, and the librarian, a kindly, old, gnomish woman, has told him they are closing, Evandur leaves, feeling defeated. He strides back to the church for the night, along the stone road now washed in soft, amber-white light from the arcane street lamps.

Chapter Eight - Sickness of Body and Mind

3E056, 7th of Renewal

Sir Whore leads the trio through the outskirts of Highfell. What patches of late sun manage to shine upon the small town are absorbed by the dark feeling that hangs above. The buildings and folk that pass seem pale and weary, and a weight seems to press down on the whole scene. The scent in the air is cow shit and sweat, but even this seems muted. Voss knows the feeling. He has seen it before, and felt it himself at least once. It is fear.

The buildings are constructed almost entirely of wood. There is no quarry nearby, though stone is sometimes brought in from Taernsby and the quarries along the northern face of the Voiceless Peaks. Most homes feature log supports, walls of either wood, wattle and daub, or sometimes clay or brick, and roofs of straw. Most of the woods are spruce and oak, and the clay is prominent near the river bank to the west, and Glass Lake to the north. Some of the wealthier homes and businesses sit upon a cobble or slab foundation, or even employ stone supports, but none use the material in their walls, save for the church.

The group rides through the posts that mark the border of Highfell Proper, and quickly find a small inn and tavern to stay in while in town. They march their horses across the street to a stable that looks clean enough, and pay a couple silver coins to the stable-master for his service. The human man takes their beasts and leads them into sturdy looking stalls within the barn-like building.

There are no walls in Highfell, but the buildings are built to make a kind of defence. The proper is made in two semi circles, one on either side of the Highwater River that runs through the centre of town. The outside ring of houses and shops was constructed with thick log walls facing out. A deep trench was also dug long ago and the course of the river diverts through it, starting on the south edge, and meeting back again on the north side of town. Highfell is also surrounded by large woods to the north, west, and south. Tall watch towers stick up along the bank of the moat at regular intervals, and there are few gaps between the other buildings there, so that it would be quite difficult to reach the town proper without being spotted.

The group crosses back again and walks into the inn, The Ebb in The River. The day is waning, and rain is beginning to patter down upon the gravel road outside. The night crowd — mostly locals, but with a few other travelers mixed in — looks up suddenly as the door opens. Most quickly return to their drinks, but a few eyes linger warily. Voss stares them down until they buckle as well and continue drinking and conversing quietly.

Voss takes the others through the maze of tables to the bar counter. Behind it sits a plump human man. His face is round, his cheeks are rosy, but his expression is stern, and he looks up with tired eyes.

Emari steps forward. By now, she has realized that she is most suited to speak with people.

"Hello!" she says cheerily. Her mask fades from its normal dark hues into a mixture of pink and yellow. "We are looking to book three rooms for a week or so. Maybe a few days longer, maybe a few days less."

The man gives a wary smile. "We've got two available. Lots of travel through to Daroonga and back down to the coast. Where are you headed?"

"Here," Voss states. "We are here visiting a mutual friend."

The man leans close enough that his thin stubble grows visible in the light of the small candles on the counter. "These are some dim times to comin' round these parts."

"We've heard," Emari nods. "That's partly why we are visiting. Our friend doesn't feel quite safe."

"That's kind of you," says the man, "and ain't nothing bad happened in these four walls in the past months. Nothin' worse than a fight or two - you know how local drunks are." He says the end louder, and a few slurs are thrown towards the bar. The man only grins.

"Oh, I know, certainly," Emari speaks compassionately. "We will take the two rooms, and if a third comes available please let us know."

"Of course, dear," the man seems to relax a little. "I will give you some room keys. Two silvers a night, meals aren't included, but I will send a couple ales round a table for you once or twice on the house."

"Sounds fair," Emari agrees, and gives the man a gold coin for the week.

"We may take some of those ales now."

"Or," Voss' deep voice cuts in behind her, "we might have business to attend to before settling down for the night."

"Right," Emari says, nodding. "Our friend would like us to stop by. We will be back this evening."

The innkeeper passes two iron keys to them, for rooms opposite each other on the second floor, with a polite nod. He wishes them luck, and hope that the rain stays light.

They first move to the top floor and find their two doors.

"Well, I suppose two will have to share," Emari states.

"Yes. You two," Voss says, unlocking the first door.

"That was never decided," Emari says. "That is not at all fair."

"Only a single bed," Voss says in an apathetic voice, looking into the room. "You two are smaller than I, so you two can share easier."

"I would prefer my own room," Emari argues. "Why can the men not sleep in one?"

"Can't this wait until the end? We aren't staying here now; we have some work ahead of us still." Boe speaks.

"If you don't care, then you can share with the musician," Voss tells the gnome.

Emari is about to protest, her mask growing red, when Boe speaks up.

"For all the Gods, can we just draw for it?" he asks. He then grabs three pieces of horse-straw from his satchel and cuts them so that two are shorter than the other. Boe clutches them in one hand so that they all appear equal in length. "Whoever takes the longest, gets their own room."

"Agreed," Emari chimes.

Voss stares at the straw, but reaches one hand out, picking a piece. They each take hold of one and pull. In his hand, Boe holds the long strip.

"No," Voss says.

"We can fight it out later," Boe says. He unlocks the second door. "Just throw your packs down. We may even end up posting a watch. This whole argument may not have mattered! Let's just be on with it!"

His frustration leads to the other two reluctantly putting their bags down in the first room. Boe spreads some papers and books across the floor in a semi-organized fashion before closing and locking the room.

They leave then, crossing through the tavern and out into the street, now beginning to pool with water beneath the gravel. They agree that there are two major options, trying to gain entry to the clinic in town, or getting in touch with the captain of the watch.

There is a short debate, but it seems simpler to head for the clinic. It is not far, no more than fifteen minutes by foot, and it may still be open.

So they start to walk. They travel further up the Kingslane, which cuts through the whole town, and runs over the bridge that spans the Highwater River. The river is the centre of the town's production, where several watermills are built for sawing lumber and grinding grain. The river runs north, all the way from Kognear Mountain in the Voiceless peaks to Glass Lake, almost perfectly paralleling the course of Twin River.

On the western side of the Highwater Bridge, just down a side-street lies 'Anna's Clinic.' The small herbalism-based medical centre is a single storey. It is painted white and green, and has two gardens out front, in which herbs and a variety of berries used in disinfectants and salves are beginning to grow against the fading cold.

The sun has dipped low over the trees to the east. The trio approaches the building in the fading light. An open sign hangs on the wooden door. Voss knocks loudly. A small voice calls to enter.

Pulling the door open, and kicking dirt from their boots, they walk in. Behind a low counter, sitting on a fine chair of light wood with black velvet cushions, is an older woman wearing dirty spectacles. She eyes them with a mixture of concern and fear. Her greying hair falls loosely around her shoulders and her left hand shakes slightly upon the counter.

"Greetings!" Emari says cheerfully, which does little to set the woman at ease. "We're here looking for some information."

The woman's shoulders relax a little as she asks, "Information? Are you in need of no treatment?"

"No, we are fine, save for some sore legs from riding," Boe chimes in.

"If you need, I may have some salves for sore muscles," the woman, presumably Anna, responds.

"That's fine," Emari cuts back in. "We simply wanted to ask about a doctor who was working in a clinic here, not too long ago."

Anna's shoulders tense again, and her face grows pale. "Eralius," she says.

"Yes," Emari replies.

"He left in a hurry," Anna responds quickly. "I don't know much or what any of this is about. I run an honest business, I swear! Anything I did know, I would have told the guard."

"We believe you," Emari tells her calmly. "We were sent by Magistrate Harold Brenspire of Taernsby to investigate the disappearances here. My companion, Voss Hallehwell, has been searching for this man for some time now."

Anna thinks for a moment. She nods and her breathing slows. "When he arrived, he looked like anyone you'd expect," she explains. "He wore clean clothing, and showed a good knowledge of anatomy and medical practice. His beard was short, and his shoulders were broad. He was young and fit, and I thought he would be a good help as an assistant and doctor in my clinic."

"Was he human?" Voss asks.

"Yes," Anna responds. Voss grows silent.

"We were wondering if he left anything behind, and if we could perhaps search the clinic for any clues," Emari tells the woman. "We have proof of our relationship to the mayor of Taernsby, and truly we mean no disturbance."

Anna thinks. "I would feel better if you didn't search the place," she admits, "and I don't believe the doctor left anything behind, though he did leave it a hurry. He broke in when I was home, and left the place a mess."

"We could be quick," Emari says. "If you want us to lock up, even, while you head home, we would leave it cleaner than we found it."

"No, I will stay," Anna resolves. "Do not take long, but you have my permission to look around."

"Is this the only floor?" Voss asks.

"Yes. Only two small treatment rooms to your right, a supply closet behind me, and a separate office to your left," Anna tells them. She does not appear to be lying, as four doors branch off from this room. It is not a large building.

"Boe, search the office," Voss says, "Emari, take the supply closet, I will search the treatment rooms."

"I have two patients in, and have making house calls all day as well. I am not sure if the sickness that afflicts them is contagious, but you may want to wear masks if you are entering the rooms," Anna tells Voss.

"What are the symptoms?" Voss asks.

"Clammy skin, coughing, fatigue, sweating," Anna lists. "It varies, truly, but I believe it is the same disease."

"I will be keeping my helmet on," Voss says. "Did this disease begin before or after Eralius left?"

"The first cases happened just before he left," she answers.

Voss nods. "I will be fine," he says. He leaves the others and enters the first of the treatment rooms.

Emari begins searching the supply closet. Inside she finds sealed jars full of dried and crushes herbs, as well as salves, and a variety of bandages and adhesives.

"Is this all the supplies you have? No magical reagents?" Emari asks.

"Magical?" Anna asks. "Gods, no. I play with no power, be it holy or arcane."

"Is magic truly so uncommon here, between a large port and the capital?"

"We see it in many travelling groups, and there is an old wizard living just south of here. Other than that, no, we are not practitioners of it," Anna explains. "Here in Highfell we've opted for a simple, traditional life and, until recently, it has treated us well."

"I see," Emari says. She then falls silent and continues browsing the closet.

Boe searches the office. It seems to have been used by both Anna and someone else, likely Voran. The area is an organized mess. Parchment is piled about the desk, and hangs out of various folders. Boe takes a second to glance through the leather bindings, but most appear to be patient files, and they all seem to be written in a dancing script that must belong to Anna. In the bottom drawer of the desk, Boe finds two points of interest, but neither leap out as important. The first is a letter of correspondence written from Voran to Anna detailing his immediate departure, and the other is a map that appears to have been drawn by multiple hands, and using more than one medium. The map is mostly tidy and is drawn in careful, straight lines. It is certainly of Highfell and the surrounding area, and has markings added to it on the borders and on some buildings in messier ink.

The gnome continues to look for several more minutes, but finds nothing else of importance.

Voss has entered the first treatment room. There is a woman in the bed, wrapped in white sheets. Beside her, on a table, is a plate of crackers and dried meat, and a tall glass of water. The room is dim, with dark sheets drawn across the window. The only light comes from a candle that has been recently lit and is set in a basic holder, across from the bed, on a low cabinet.

The woman jolts slightly as she sees Voss. There is fear on her face, and she seems to be having trouble focusing.

"Are you a servant of Echoshan, or a soldier of Highfell?" she asks.

"Of Highfell?" Voss asks in response. "I am neither," he says next. "I was a soldier, once, but not for this town, and not anymore."

"Then who are you?" she asks him. There is a strength in her voice, but it is faltering.

"I am Voss Hallehwell. Myself and two others were sent by the magistrate of Taernsby to provide help."

"Help how?"

"By finding and kill-" he stops himself, "-bringing Voran to justice."

"Killing him would not be justice enough for what he has done to this town," the woman says. "We are in fear through the nights, and despite the constant watch, he, or something worse, slips in uncaught. We hear noises in the woods, and houses are broken into with seemingly no fear or hesitation. We always arrive too late."

"Is there a pattern?"

"Not that has been discovered," she informs Voss regretfully. "We thought that he was targeting the south side of town, as the first few to fall ill were there, including myself. Then the attacks and abductions started to the north. Recently the guards saw something and scared if off along the western borders, but still we've made no progress."

"Who should I speak to about recent reports?" Voss asks.

"Carver Nineshield," she says. "He is the Acting Captain."

"Who was the Captain?" Voss asks.

"Myself."

"I am sorry, I did not realize."

"I do not look much like a Captain. I can hardly see, and cannot walk. No treatments have helped."

"I have seen Eralius' work in Taernsby. He was operating slower then, though, being more methodical. Do you have any injuries?"

Boe and Emari quietly enter the room, having finished their own searching.

"I was attacked in the night by two tall figures. It looked as though one had tusks, but both were broad and scaled. They had heads like animals, but distorted. I did not get a clear look, as they knocked my torch out quickly," the Captain explains.

"Heads like that of a toad or frog?" Voss asks.

"Perhaps, though one looked more like a lizard, or even a snake. The other I did not see clearly."

Voss hums thoughtfully. "And what happened?" he asks.

"They tripped me, and kicked my head. I fell unconscious. When I woke, it was morning. A full eight or nine hours had passed, and I had been dragged to the clinic. My soldiers told me they shot the creatures as they were dragging me towards the woods, south of town. My leg hurt greatly, on the left."

"May I look at it?" Voss asks, surprisingly gently.

"Yes," the Captain responds. "It was not pretty, last I heard. Now it is wholly numb."

Voss pulls back the covers. She is clad in a white gown, but it does not go far below her knees. Her left leg is covered in a bandage, but Voss can already tell that something is wrong. The area around the bandage is covered in a thin, clammy layer of rough looking skin. There is inflammation of a sickly purple colour, and further up the legs are a few small incision marks.

"It does not look good," Voss says honestly. "I have seen similar injuries in Taernsby."

"What became of the injured?" she asks the question as though she already knows the answer.

"We arrived too late. I have no idea, truly, if their deaths could have been prevented. I do not intend to give up as of yet in aiding you, but I will not lie by saying I have any garaunteed power to help," Voss tells her.

"I appreciate the honesty, Voss."

"I have not yet learned your name, Captain," Voss responds.

"Shoal. Captain Eve Shoal."

"Well, Captain Shoal, I will do my best to help your town. You can count on my word, as I have a habit of standing by it," Voss says. She thanks him as he leaves the room, with the others falling in tow.

Voss leads them straight through the clinic, pausing only briefly to thank Anna for her time. As they are reunited with the rain, they slow down. They walk quietly down the Kingslane as water patters off Voss' armour, and the others' cloaks, which they have wrapped tightly around themselves.

"You felt no need to check the other room?" Boe asks Voss.

"Captain Shoal gave me more than enough information. What of your searches?" Voss responds.

"Nothing of interest in the supply closet. This place, the whole town, does not seem to use magic. I have seen no church towers either, other than the polytheistic symbol further in the north half," Emari says.

"In the office I found a letter from Voran to Anna, but it did not seem of importance. I did also find a map, though, which was added to, maybe by him," Boe adds. "I grabbed the map just in case."

"We have enough to go on," Voss says, a determination to his voice. "I will speak with Acting Captain Nineshield and see what reports he has. It seems clear that at least Doctor Eralius, likely some of his creations as well, are hiding somewhere in the woods."

Boe and Emari nod.

"Captain Shoal mentioned she was dragged south," Voss continues, "and that is where the attacks began. I would say, though, that Voran moved when the guard moved. Likely, he moved another time when they caught him on the northern front. I would even bet that he will soon by finished with Highfell altogether."

"If what you told us of his creations is true," Boe says, worriedly, "then he may leave when those he infected within the town begin to die. It would be horrific, but smart, to leave in the chaos."

"Then it's probable that we don't have very long," Emari states.

"Right," Voss agrees, "but we can't do much tonight, unless we want to post a watch in the rain. It may be better to rest now, after our travel, and in the morning we can start a more extensive search."

"That makes sense to me," Boe says.

"Agreed. I am tired," states Emari, though her walk is still light.

They keep moving for some time. They have just crossed the Highwater Bridge when Voss speaks again. "She won't make it long," he says.

"She has a chance," Emari says, walking close beside him.

"She will die regardless," Nhasan tells Voss, causing him an immediate headache. "We mustn't focus on this, though."

"If we can save her, we will, but in the end…" Voss begins, but trails off.

Emari says something that Voss can no longer here

"We will have to be the one to end it," Nhasan finishes Voss' thought.

"Focus for now," Valindra says. "We can stop this from happening again."

"Voss?" Emari asks.

"Hm?" he asks, disoriented.

"We're here," she says. Her mask shifts to a dark shade of pink.

Voss gets the sense that she is worried. "Right," he says. He walks quickly into the inn.

They walk through the tavern. Boe stays near the bar for a few drinks. Voss walks briskly up the stairs. Without thinking, he walks calmly into the room he was assigned.

Slowly his headache begins to die down, as he sits with the base of his helmet clutched in his gauntleted hands.

The room is small. A bed, a dresser, a small desk, and a chair are the only furnishings. They are all built of hand-carved oak wood. The mattress is comfortable, if not slightly lumpy in parts, and the chair has a thick cushion placed on it. The room is clean and warm, but not too stuffy, despite the somewhat cramped feeling it gives.

Emari has been sitting on the chair for some minutes. Finally, she works up the courage to speak. "Are you okay?" her voice comes out softly.

"Yes, I'm fine," Voss responds. He does not shift.

"You do not seem it."

He shrugs.

"Voss, please," she sighs.

"What?" the response is sharp, but it does not deter her.

"If we are going to travel together, if we are going to trust each other-"

"This has nothing to do with you, bard. Emari." Voss says her name quietly at the end, as if correcting himself. "I have not trusted many people in my life, and none for some time now."

"You can trust me though," she pushes.

"A large part of me does not doubt that," the soldier says, standing. "Despite that, I cannot. Not yet. You seem to try unlocking me, as if some great treasure is within. But trust me, you would not like what you found. If you can tolerate me as I am now, then I am happy for your company. Trust and friendship however, is something I do not believe I can offer."

"Why are you standing?" Emari asks, hurt.

"I am going to take a watch on the west side of town," he says, walking to the door. He opens it.

"Voss, stay hear, sleep," Emari pleads. Her mask fluctuates between a wide array of colours.

The door closes. Voss' footsteps are heard down the hall, and then down the stairs.

Hours pass. Emari lies alone in the bed. It feels cold. She doesn't normally mind the cold. She has weathered winter storms in nothing but shorts and thin jackets. She has swam in glacier streams near her childhood home in Outton. She has lied in the grass in every season, in summer dew, and in frost, before her mask even came to her.

This is a different kind of cold.

It weight on her mind, not just her body. She feels worried, and not just about herself. She detests the feeling. As the minutes count towards the first hour, she wishes only that this feeling would leave her so she could sleep. She tosses about.

"If Boe had missed, and fell to the base of that cave, I would have mourned for the sake of my image, not for my heart or soul," Emari whispers to herself. "If Peren, or Brael, or Evandur, had been slain by orcs, I would not have shed tears. Even if it would happen now, I would hurt for a brief time. We all have pain on our shoulders, and knives in our hearts, so why is this different?" she asks. Finally, she falls asleep. Exhaustion steals the answer to her question, and makes toward the morning.

She awakens only for a moment in the early hours, before the sun has risen. There is the sound of deep breathing beside her, and a warmth in the room. She closes her eyes again, and falls immediately back into slumber.

Chapter Nine - The Plot of Eralius

3E056, 8th of Renewal

Voss rouses himself from sleep nearly an hour before the sun peaks through the high window in his room. He glances to his left. Emari is lying at peace beside him. We wraps himself in a pair of warm trousers, a thick tunic, and a dark brown cloak. He grabs one of his side-bags, with a small coin purse and towel in it.

He leaves the building quickly, sliding through the tavern without a sound, and pushes out into the street. There are few people out this early. It is a work day, but the persistent drizzle of rain is cause for a later start than usual. The few that are out seem to eye Voss warily, but in the first hour after waking, his mind is most at peace, and he manages to push their glances from his thoughts.

He walks with intent down the Kingslane and over the High Bridge. He turns northward and continues for a few more minutes down the cobbled street. The Western Bankroad, it is called, for it hugs the river wall on the west edge of the Highwater.

Voss had seen little of import during his watch the previous night. He observed the western edge of town and, while nothing was seen moving about, he did spy a bathhouse near the Highwater. The building is larger than Anna's Clinic, but not by much. It is circular, and its roof slopes gently upward into a point, and overhangs the walls by a few feet. It is mostly made of oak planks, which are painted a deep brown. It is also built on a foundation of stone.

Voss reaches the building, and enters through a set of double door that open outward.

As he steps inside, he is met with warm, wet air that quickly begins to shove the cold from his fingers and toes. Rarely when he is on the road does Voss care about keeping clean. He does not sweat much, and tries to keep his beard and hair short enough that his helmet fits properly on his head. It is such that he does not pay close attention to his hygiene. There is the chance now, however, for a proper bath. Since before he left Taernsby in the winter, he has been bathing in streams, or in Rail Lake, at night, when others slept.

He yearns now for hot, cleansing water.

He is greeted by a woman wearing a white dress. She looks him over silently, and then gestures to the curving hall around them. They stand in the outer ring of the building. There are beige doors on either side of them along the inner wall, which is painted in the same brown as the outer one. Each door is an individual bathing room. The woman leads him to the right, almost to the other side of the building in relation to the main entrance.

There is a sign above the wooden door.

'Four Silver for Hot Bath. Five Silver for Bath and Massage', it reads.

Voss fishes through his coin purse and produces three silver coins, and thirteen copper shillings. The woman accepts the change with a kind smile. She opens the door for him, and from a front-stitched pocket in her dress she produces some flint and a steel piece.

The room behind the door angles inward to a much smaller size along the back. The walls in here are made of carefully sealed stones, aside from the wall with the door, which, of course, is made of wood. At the edge of the door-sill, the floor drops to the foundation level, and then, after only a foot of bare stone, a shallow metal bin full of a liquid solution rises up, and takes up the rest of the floorspace. Above the bin stands the tub, a great metal bath with a stone bottom that hugs the walls of the room.

The woman enters the room first. She strikes the flint and steel against a candle sconce on the left wall. She then removes the candle, and lights another on the right wall. The room suddenly feels cozy. It is still dim, but now it is easy enough to see everything inside.

The woman then kneels and, facing the tub, strikes her lighting tools toward the metal bin below. The sparks from the flint land on the liquid in the basin, and a flame erupts. The fire licks the stone bottom of the tub uniformly. Voss watches for several seconds, but the flames barely flicker.

The woman stands aside. With her back to the left wall, she gestures from

Voss to the tub.

Voss pauses. He makes a motion with his head behind himself. The woman nods politely and leaves, closing the door behind her.

Voss strips his clothes from his body and places them neatly by the entrance. He steps once upon the cool stone floor, and then into the water of the tub. It is not cold, but it is hardly above the warm air of the room. It will be some time before it is hot. Voss sighs softly as he sinks to his shoulders.

When the water is warm, and Voss has been sitting peacefully for around five minutes, the door opens and the woman returns. She places a brown towel on top of his clothes.

Voss closes himself off from the door, but when it is shut behind the woman, the room is too dark for him to see below the water.

She crosses the short room and Voss sees now that she carries a ceramic jug with her. She bends over him and pours the contents into the bath. The water begins to bubble and a deep, earthy scent fills the room. It is not overbearing, but smells clearly as a fresh spring day, and pine nettles, and rain.

She then places a bar of beige soap on the lip of the metal bath and looks at Voss. There is a question on her face.

Voss, for the first time in a long while, holds someone's gaze, and answers them with his eyes alone. She nods and leaves the room again. Voss washes his body alone. Just as the water is reaching a point where it is too hot, the fire runs out of fuel.

He dries himself, dresses, and leaves into the hall. No one is waiting for him. He returns to the inn through the cold morning mist.

When Emari wakes, Voss has clad himself in his chest-piece, greaves, pauldrons, and helmet. His arms are uncovered, save for leather wrappings, and his legs are clad in leather-patched trousers and a chain skirt. The bard can see his fingers, which is more of Voss than she often is able to.

His banner-cloak is affixed by the fur ring still, though it seems to flow smoother and cleaner. There is also a pleasant, not-quite-floral scent in the air.

"Good morning," Voss speaks.

"To you as well," she responds, still tired. "Did you sleep well?"

"I slept well, yes, but not long. We have some time ahead of us today, but my mind is clearer than usual, and I have the foundations of a plan in my head."

Emari smiles, though Voss could not see it through her mask if he was watching. "Is Boe awake?" she asks.

"I do not know. I expect so, but I have not checked."

"Were you out all night?"

"No. I could not remain alert, and so I retired for sleep after four or five hours. I heard no commotion when I left this morning, though, so I believe nothing happened."

"Where did you go this morning?" the bard asks.

"For some air," Voss tells her.

Emari watches him for a few more seconds. "Shall we still go to the guardhouse?" she asks at length.

"Yes," Voss says, "I think so. If we can urge them to show us their maps, and if those contain any useful information, then I believe I have an idea."

"Does your idea relate to the map Boe found?"

"Indeed. I wonder if there are several additions that will stand out against the maps held by the guards."

"That would be a stroke of luck," Emari agrees.

They pack quickly, shoving what they need into their day-packs. They grab waterskins, their remaining rations, small blankets, and rope. Emari fits her rapier to her hip, and two daggers on her thighs. Voss checks that his paper with the mayor's signature is still in order and clean. He has taken care to make sure it remains flat and unstained since he received it several months ago.

They finish and shoulder their packs, exiting their room. In the hall they find Boe just opening his door as well. He is dressed in a cloth robe, with his unlit pipe between his lips, and looks fresh out of bed.

"Oh!" the gnome peeps, seeing the others.

"Morning, master Chong," Emari says, her mask swirling into pink.

"Are we off? I was just going to get breakfast," Boe explains.

"We need to eat still, as well," Emari says. Then jokingly, "Rough sleep?"

Boe's door pushes open and a young halfling woman emerges into the hallway. Seeing the taller figures at the end, she freezes and stands still beside Boe. She is a few inches shorter than the gnomish illusionist, with silvery-blonde hair and green, sparkling eyes. She is also dressed in a loose cloth robe.

"It was a lovely sleep, actually!" Boe says, grinning. "Voss, Emari, this is Gemm."

The women wave at each other from across the hall. Voss nods.

"Let us grab food then, and perhaps a drink even, before we set out. We cannot tarry long, though," Voss tells them politely. "We have a good amount to get done today, but it is true that I don't wish to do any of it on an empty stomach." With that, he turns and begins to descend the stairs.

The others follow him. Voss finds a medium sized table near the bar with four chairs around it. He sits down and beckons the others over. They seat themselves in the other empty seats. Their table garners some looks from the nearby townsfolk that enter for breakfast, but the young man who serves them is polite and asks no rude questions. Gemm does not ask any either. Whether Boe has explained anything about the group, or about Voss' personality — or whether the halfling is simply polite — is hard to tell.

Voss removes his helmet to eat once the food arrives, but he keeps his head bowed the whole time. Boe and Gemm discuss joyously, and Emari joins in occasionally as well. They speak of travelling to the halfling, who is truly not much younger than Boe. She has never left her home town, here, but she loves to see the travellers and those who come through. She speaks of how it is rare to see other small-folk nowadays, save for those coming with larger trade caravans, and that was why she initially approached their companion.

Soon the breakfast winds down and the coffees are brought out. The hot water is poured over crushed, local beans and filtered through a thin, pierced, copper filter. It tastes like bitter metal, and is full of coffee grain, but they all finish their cups, aware of the long day ahead.

They bid goodbye to Gemm as she excuses herself for her own day's work. Boe rushes back upstairs and returns several minutes later with a packed bag and his staff, and they walk together through the doors of The Ebb in The River.

Quite quickly the mood changes again to a serious one. The trio's spirits are high, but there are grave matters ahead, and they all sense it. The rain has let up for now, but the sky is still smothered in clouds.

On their own side of the Highwater lies the guardhouse. It is a low and long building, built all of thick wood. It was here long before the town had a chance to ship stone up, but still it stands strong against the elements.

Upon the outer walls hang the banners of House Talava, which watches over the townships of both Taernsby and Highfell, among others. Talava's banner is vertical, and is placed always to the right of the royal tapestries. The top half is the same green as the Dabarisian standards, and the lower is a deep, royal purple. It is halved by a black line, cutting diagonally from top left to bottom right. Across the whole banner is inlaid a white hawk, seen flying upward from below.

They approach along the Eastern Bankroad and find large double doors which open out to the street from the house. They are oakwood, same as the logs. Above the doors is a semi-circular window made of clear glass.

They knock, using a large brass knocker that is carefully nailed into the left-hand door. After several seconds, the doors open, and two human men stand tall before them.

"State yer' business," the one on the left says.

"We seek Acting Captain Nineshield," Voss answers calmly.

"Why?"

"We are sent from Taernsby," the soldier explains. He tells the men about his conversation with their injured captain, and further expresses the importance of haste.

The two guards eye each other before the first one nods, and beckons them inside.

They are led into a large, open room. The floor is made of panelled wood, and wraps around a great fire pit in the centre, built of brick, and surrounded on all sides by several feet of brick as well. Across from the door is a long table with many chairs, and lit by a dozen candles on the wall behind it. On the left and right, the floor runs to walls with many doors, leading to housing and storage.

There are several guards gathered around the long table, and a dwarf is upon one of the chairs. He is dressed in clean leather and a scale coat. His hair is a chestnut brown, tied back in a bun, and his beard is curly and short. He is pointing at papers on the wood. There are a few others scattered throughout the room. Some are sparring, but most are talking and drinking small mugs of coffee. The door-guard leads them toward the table. The group around it stops talking and looks warily towards the newcomers.

"What is this?" the dwarf asks.

The door-guard relays the important parts of what Voss told him. The dwarf nods.

"Gather round, then, and I will explain where we stand," the dwarf speaks with authority. He is clearly Carver Nineshield. They oblige, and intersperse with the guards. Boe hops atop a chair like Nineshield has. "Tonight, or tomorrow, we are likely to be hit again," the acting captain begins. "We have men and women stationed to the north and south, but no more than usual, and now they are spread thin, only within shouting distance. Most of us will be watching the west, as that seems the most likely. I would have more men watching the east as well, but I don't have the man power. We have already faced too many injuries pursuing whatever these creatures are." Carver then turns to Voss. "What do you think? If you have dealt with this threat before, you must bring some new information."

Voss thinks on what to tell the dwarf. Clearly he is already worried, and though Voss cares little about worrying him further, he will be more useful without added stress.

"I think the plan is fine," Voss says eventually. "It seems to be the right counter-strategy. I dealt with Eralius under different circumstances. He was acting cautiously then, and now he is stronger, and with more help."

"So what are we to do?" Nineshield asks, fear teasing his calm voice. This town has been under more stress than even Voss initially guessed, or the guard has done well at keeping it under wraps.

"If you allow me to look for a moment at the maps you have, I will find where there are any gaps, and we will try to fill them," Voss explains.

The guards stand back. One brings two additional maps and lays them upon the table. Some new candles are lit and placed in holders between the array of paper.

The maps are detailed, with every abduction marked by a small dot of black ink, and cases of sickness marked in a deep green. It seems nearly random. Voss asks at length if they can recount the order in which events occurred, and they do their best to oblige. Voss listens intently.

Voss points at last to a small alley, which runs from the western edge and curves inward to the western town square. "One of my people will watch here," he says. "Myself and the other will find good vantage points and watch out over the eastern edge, near the road, to bolster your defence."

"Thank you," Nineshield says earnestly.

"We will find our positions now, and reconvene here just before dusk."

"Understood, sir."

The guards salute them in the Dabarisian style. They return to speaking about the maps, while Voss and his companions leave them in the guardhouse to return to the street outside.

"Boe," Voss starts, "you will find a roof or vantage above the alley I pointed out. Keep a careful eye on it. Is there any magic you know that could reach us at long distance?"

"If I had something belonging closely to you then I could perhaps focus telepathy through it," Boe suggests hopefully.

"Emari, a knife," Voss says, offering her an upturned palm.

She holds back the urge to ask for courtesy, and pulls one of the daggers from her thigh-sheaths. He pulls his helmet upward, and slices a lock of hair from his head. The strand is a few inches long. Boe nods and takes it. Emari does the same. Soon Boe holds two locks of hair, roughly equal in length. One is a deep brown, and one is a mix of sky blue, white, and silver.

Voss eyes Emari's strand of hair as it is passed over.

"This should work," the gnome says.

"If it doesn't then we'll just listen for your high-pitched screaming," Emari says. Voss grins under his helmet.

"Yeah, yeah. I'll make it work," Boe says. He smiles too, and spins around.

Emari and Voss walk along the Eastern Bankroad through the square on this side of the bridge. They turn east at the bridge and walk along the Kingslane until they can see the gateposts upon which the Highfell sign hangs.

On the left side of the road, just before the posts, is a large home of two storeys. The roof is slanted towards the street, but the top flattens slightly and could be laid upon with care. Past the gateposts, only a five minute jaunt, stands a recently constructed stone silo. It would take some effort and stealth — or discussion — to get to the top, but it would offer an excellent view. Voss points these out.

"I can get to the silo," Emari says. "I can be light as a feather when I need to be."

"I have seen," Voss says. "I will struggle to the roof."

"I will not be able to speak with you unless you open the connection," Emari tells Voss before he departs. "I do not understand what powers you wield, but I know they could be of help tonight."

Voss grows rigid. Chattering erupts in his mind, despite the voices being absent all day. He grimaces behind his mask, but stays reserved. "If I see anything," he says, "I will send word. I find it draining to do so, though, and it may be a long night. If you spot something that I do not, create a spark on the west side of the silo. I will see it, and hopefully what you are watching will not."

"I can do that," she says. Her mask fades briefly from black to pink, and then to black again. "Make sure to keep an eye out every few minutes, then."

"I will. But we do not need to settle into our positions until nightfall. Let us test the vantage, then return to this road. We can debate logistics then."

Emari nods, and they split up.

Voss finds a ladder beside a house a few doors down, and borrows it to lean against the two storey home. He makes it uneasily to the rood and sets himself on his chest. He pulls the blanket from his pack and pins it to the wood using some loose stones that he subsequently gathers once the blanket is in place. It ends up being of little comfort, but if does help slightly.

They return to the road. Emari is there a few minutes ahead of Voss.

"It should suffice," Voss reports. The bard nods in response.

They rejoin Boe at the tavern just after noon. The gnome tells of a small library atop which is a bell tower that overlooks the alley. He spoke with the owner and got permission to camp there during the nights.

They eat a warm meal of fish soup and fresh bread, and drink a large mug of 'Feller's Brew', which tastes strong and is infused with something more potent than an average beer. They review Boe's copy of the map again.

In a low voice, Voss speaks to his companions. He says, "I have a thought. The description I was given of Voran during my investigation in Taernsby, from the mayor's servants, was that he was an elvish man with long blonde hair. Anna at the clinic here said that he was a human. She seemed certain."

"So either someone was lying, or the doctor is good at disguise?" Emari muses.

"Or he is a spell caster of some repute," Boe adds.

"Any could be the case. We know that either some magic, disease, or both must be at work," Voss says. "It could well be that he can change his form with magic, but is it not hard to maintain such illusions over a longer time?" he asks Boe.

"It is, certainly."

"Exactly," Voss falls into thought.

The day fades into evening, then toward dusk. The clouds above break apart slightly, but do not grow lighter. The trio takes turns resting in their rooms. They make haste as the sun begins to near the trees around the town. They walk to the guardhouse and explain their positioning and plan.

As the sky turns to a faint grey-purple, they take their positions, and begin a constant watch. Boe sits patiently in the bell tower, Voss waits uncomfortably on the roof of the house, and Emari balances on the grain silo.

The night passes with no noise.

The next day they hear no new reports from Nineshield. The sky offers little to warm their hearts, as clouds coalesce again into a sheet of darkness. Voss spends the whole day studying their map.

Once again, as dusk begins to fall, they take their positions.

This night is especially dark, as rain continues to bubble in the deep black clouds above. Hours begin to blend together, but they each rested well and so they remain alert. Cold creeps across the town. There is very little light from the Ildonian moon or stars that gets through the thick clouds. The smaller moon, Volana, shines through a small patch of clear black sky occasionally, but does not alleviate the oppressing darkness.

Soon, night has run its course. The sun has not yet begun to rise, but the air exudes the feeling of early morning. The guard and those from Taernsby are expecting to see light on the horizon at any moment, when something causes Boe to jolt. At first he is not quite sure what he witnessed. Something in the grasses just beyond the edge of town moved. There is no wind to be felt.

Boe remains motionless, scanning the area again. Then he scans it once more. Small drops of rain hit the tower above his head and the roofs of the houses across from him. He is about to shrug it off when a splashing sound resonates from just beneath his perch.

A puddle that was formed by the dumping of a chamberpot has been disturbed. No early drop of rain could have made that much noise.

The gnome takes the locks of hair from his robe and holds one in each hand. He channels energy through them and sent a silent image of what he is seeing. He imbues the thought with the words, "Something is in the alleyway." The locks of hair glow a soft amber-gold light and then they are consumed as the energy flies silently and invisibly through them.

There is no response that comes. Boe is uncertain whether they could respond using that connection, or even if the message reached them at all. The gnome remains still for a moment in hesitation. Soon, though, he steels himself and slides gracefully down the slanted roof of the library and and rolls onto the ground, which is already dampened by the increasing rain.

He focuses again, and his owl flies into the sky above him, coming from the woods just east of town.

He follows the course of the alley towards town. There are footprints that he can pick out with his gnomish eyes in the dark, and using the owl he can see an overview of the area. The prints are made by large feet. He catches glimpses of whatever he is following. He sees its shadow, or sometimes a small part of its body like a foot or hand. He soon gives his sight over to the owl completely, and uses its eyes to track the creature more clearly. Even without sight, however, Boe finds it east enough to follow. He simply follows the occasional sound of footsteps, and the horrific scent it gives off, fecal matter, wet fur, and something else, something unholy and pungent.

Boe keeps up, finding it easier than his target to creep silently. The gnome only prays that whatever is ahead of him has no better nose than himself. He switches back and forth between his owl's eyes and his own as he draws closer.

Boe rounds a corner and finds himself looking out on a small open square surrounded by low homes. It is there, in a small patch of moonlight, that Boe sees fully what he is following.

The beast stands about seven feet tall. It appears to be covered in hair that is thick, dark, and matted with a slimy substance that glints slightly in the pale moonlight. The head of the creature appears almost hog-like, with a long snout, skin that is wrinkled and pink, and two small tusks that emerge from its gaping mouth.

Boe shudders. Alone, he has no chance of taking this thing on, even if he could fully utilize his arcane power under stress. He has no choice but to wait, watch, and hope that Voss, Emari, or a patrol of guards crosses his path.

The beast sniffs the air, turns its head left and right, and sets off across the square, Boe remains in the edge of the alley until the hog-monster has crossed halfway to the other side. He then moves from his spot to crouch behind a cart that was left chained to a small well in the centre.

The creature continues. It is walking towards a house in the middle of the row on the north edge of the square. They are near the north-eastern corner of town, but far enough west that the majority of the guard is near a kilometer away.

The beast grabs the handle of the door and pulls. It does not open, locked from the inside. With a sudden movement, the hog draws its hairy arm back, and swings with force toward the wood. The door splinters around the handle. Once again it grips the handle. This time the door grinds open. The sounds of its entrance echoes through the square. Nothing responds.

The beast disappears into the building. Boe thinks he hears a scream, but it is difficult to tell over his pounding heart. Soon, though, he certainly hears glass shattering from the other side of the house.

The square returns to silence. The beast slips through a broken window. Boe can see it look around and then begin to move quickly northward. There are at least two bodies slung over its shoulders.

"We can't lose it," Voss' voice startles Boe. It is within his own mind. He turns and sees both the soldier and Emari coming quietly up behind him from a different alleyway.

It is now that Boe fully understands the plan.

Voss purposefully let the guards leave the eastern edge less watched. He never expected Voran or anything else to approach the first night, but it was better to be safe and take a watch. Likely, the doctor watched the guard patterns and tracked them. Voss, Emari, and Boe would not have been on his mind, though, and that is why they faced mostly east, with Boe watching the only gap in the western defence. It was most likely that something would approach from the less guarded side or through a place that appeared neglected.

"There were three places on the map you found in the clinic, Boe, that were not drawn on the guards' maps," Voss tells them through the collective telepathic link. "One was a small stream to the south, one was a thicket to the west, and one was a cave to the north."

"Nothing to the east," Emari adds, also without speaking.

"Which is why the creature is moving north," Voss sends the thought, reaching Boe at the cart. "We must make haste," he says aloud. "Whatever that was, it is likely moving north with some speed. I saw a hole the guards' defensive plan on the north-eastern corner. That is why I needed you to watch the alley. It is likely the same place it will exit from."

They begin to move quickly, with Voss in the lead. They wind through the alleys and side-streets back towards the library. As they reach the edge of the town, just east of the library, they see in the distance that there is a figure running for the safety of the woods that lie north of town, through a large field.

"It is heading straight for the cave," Voss says, grinning behind his face-plating.

"You knew this would be the outcome," Boe says, turning to look at Voss.

"I thought it likely," Voss admits. "I believed it would enter from the east, though. We were lucky you caught sight of it on its way in, or else we could have lost precious time."

"There is a larger garrison of guards not far south of here," Boe says. "We should go alert them."

"No," Voss says. "This was always our fight. We can handle whatever is out there. The guards should remain in the town."

"That is foolish!" Boe hisses.

"We want to catch Voran unaware," Voss responds. "If he is the cave and hears the sounds of horses, or a troop of men, then he will flee. He is a coward, in the end, even he proves to be a powerful one."

Boe thinks for some time. "Fine," he agrees reluctantly. "Let us make haste then, and remain careful."

They set off from town as the creature vanishes into the darkness of the forest. The sky is turning grey, but the rain is growing thicker to balance it.

The field is used as a pasture for cattle and, as such, the grass is short and easy to traverse. They make it from end to end in just over ten minutes. This is much slower than the beast they are tracking, but they are no longer worried about losing it, instead focusing on their surroundings in case they are being watched.

When they arrive at the woods, they can see a clear path which has been beaten through the ferns and low brush on the forest floor.

They follow this trail for nearly twenty more minutes. The east becomes warmer, and a dull grey is steadily clawing away the darkness. Rain is pattering against the canopy above, and the occasional heavy drop falls on the trio.

Finally, they come into view of a small clearing. The barer patches along the forest floor have been purposefully cut in a circle around one side of a steep and tall hill. The hill itself remains covered in long grass, moss, and four trees that grow in no particular pattern around the crest. On the side facing the circle, the hill is nearly vertical, and a large portion is clear rock. At the base of this rock there is a crack that is wide, deep, and high enough for even a larger creature to pass through.

There is no doubt that this must be the cave from the map. No sound passes through the clearing but a dim wind from the north and the growing patter of rain. A chill has fallen heavily on the trespassers.

They take extra caution in moving quietly now. They continue towards the clearing, but move around it as well so that they are facing the sheer cliff. Now, fully visible, they can see the entrance to the cave. The crack forms a point at the top, but at the bottom is opens nearly five feet wide, and stands about eight feet in height.

Beyond the initial entrance there is a tunnel that varies in width and height that leads into pitch darkness. It cannot travel far, though, for the three can hear sounds coming from within. Something scrapes along dirt, and then a loud *crack* jumps from the hill.

The three remain in the cover of trees.

"We could attempt to draw it out," Voss suggests.

The others nod. Emari unsheathes her rapier, and Boe rests his hand on the ornate looking book that hangs from his side.

They creep slowly towards the mouth. Emari stands ten feet back and to the right of Voss. Boe does the same on the left. The soldier focuses. A pale mist winds crawls up his feet and into his hands. The mist branches outward and forms a long and wide rectangle. Suddenly Voss' shield is in his left hand. His battleaxe is in the other no more than three seconds later. The shield is now fitted with a polished steel spike in the centre, which protrudes nearly half a foot past the rest of the metal. It is well attached and looks as though it was always part of the shield. The handle has also been carefully replaced by Voss' magical bar.

Voss holds the shield against the mouth of the tunnel, and steps in until it barely fits. Voss presses the button on the bar and the shield pulses with white light as it attaches itself to the air around it. The shield blocks nearly half the tunnel. Voss presses with all his strength against it to test it, being careful to cause no noise. The shield does not budge. Emari strikes a torch and plants it in the ground under the shelter of the cliff, where a rock juts out slightly, blocking the rain.

"Are we ready?" he whispers.

The others nod.

They ready themselves around the mouth of the cave. Emari stands ten feet behind Voss still, but Boe moves back to fifteen. Voss takes a stone from the ground and throws it at the shield. A loud, metallic ringing noise shoots into the tunnel and back out from it again. For a moment there is quiet. Then, a horrible, gurgling howl answers the noise, and heavy footsteps begin to scrape the dirt and mud and move towards the passage from somewhere further down. Voss stands back and waits, holding his axe in two hands.

Two beasts appear behind the shield. The first is the same one from town, with a disgusting face that resembles a hog mixed with a human. This one tries to kick the shield out of the way, but stumbles in doing so. As its balance shifts, the second arrives behind it. This one is taller, and appears to be crouching to fit through the passage. It emerges into the light of the torch, stepping on its companion and then over the shield. Voss takes a swing as it clambers over the barrier, and the blade catches its shin and draws blood. The soldier then quickly shifts back several feet. The beast walks like a bear on all fours, and is covered in scales. It does not look quite like a frog or toad, as its head features an elongated snout, which in turn features long and sharp teeth that poke out at uneven angles. It looks closer to a mixture of lizard and bear, but even that is a loose description of what now stands in front of Voss. Even on all fours, it is far taller than its opponent.

There is a second of uneasy calm as the creature eyes each of the trio. Its wound appears to be slowly healing now as well; its skin is forming a scab with incredible speed.

The beast darts forward. It is encumbered by its own weight, but it still moves with a surprising aggression and purpose. Voss barely sidesteps, but manages to cut the creature down its side while he does. The thing growls, and a green slime froths from its mouth.

The lizard then lunges again. This time, it is towards Emari. Voss' axe just catches its ankle, biting through its tendons and causing it to fall before its claws reach the bard. The beast turns back to Voss. Emari sings clear, and her voice fills the clearing. Voss feels his muscles grow lighter, and he begins to grow. As the creature swings at him, Voss manages to block it and absorb the impact with his left arm. Voss continues to grow until he is nearly double his normal size. He now stands at almost twelve feet tall, with his axe having grown as well. Emari continues to sing the same melody.

Boe focuses on keeping the other creature behind the shield. Every time it pokes its head above the metal barrier it faces a blast of lightning, fire, or acid from Boe's staff. The gnome is also working quickly with his other hand, constructing an invisible wall of energy in the entrance. His free hand draws symbols to keep the wall strong, but his attention is being maximized. The combination of offense and defence will keep the monster at bay for the moment, but Voss and Emari will need to work quickly on the first opponent.

The tangle in the middle is now an even fight. Voss delivers swing after swing, cutting deep wounds across the creature's arms and chest. They heal quickly, but slowly the creature is beginning to lose its confidence. It swings suddenly in a wide arc. Voss manages to hit it under its ribs, but it leaves a deep wound along the soldier's bicep. Emari changes pitch, and the wound on Voss' arm begins to heal, but at the same moment, he begins to return to normal size. Emari manages to continue with her original song, stabilizing his size around eleven feet.

As the fight draws to its first full minute, Voss glances at his companions. Boe is struggling to keep the other at bay, and sweat is beading along his forehead. Emari's voice is growing hoarse, and some notes crack.

Voss changes tactics. "Boe!" he cries, darting quickly towards the tunnel. Boe does not understand, but does drop the barrier as Voss reaches it. The soldier grabs his shield, which has not grown in size, and presses the button. The hog-beast leaps forward, but Voss catches it and slams it into the cave wall, as he is still larger and stronger than it. He swings around quickly as the other, more dangerous creature, reaches him. Voss slams the spike of the shield directly into its eye.

The lizard-monster screams and backs up. Voss advances just as fast, bringing his axe down on its back. The beast growls and swipes towards Voss' legs. Voss goes down on his back. The beast claws for his armour.

"Dadek! Torkurth!" Voss shouts audibly. The figure of a dwarf emerges within Voss' body, also on its back. Its spectral shield shoves from Voss' chest and deflects two of the attacks, but a third still dents Voss' scaled chest. The spectral spearman materializes behind the creature and pierces its back with his ghostly, blue weapon. The lizard-like creature screams again and turns to face the new assailant, but he is already disappearing again.

Voss pushes backward and onto his feet. He slams the spike of his shield through the beast's upper thigh, and into the ground. The creature spins back, but Voss presses the button and jumps back as it swings. It attempts to remove the shield, but it cannot.

Voss barely reaches Boe in time to intercept the other beast running at the mage. Voss tackles the hog-creature into the ground. The fight does not last much longer. Voss holds this beast down with foot before swinging his axe and severing its head from its shoulders.

The larger beast is still struggling, but its other wounds have healed. Boe turns his focus to this threat, and begins hurling orbs of acid at the pinned abomination. Voss acts as well, but as he draws near it, it wrenches its leg free, tearing flesh and bone along the spike. It stands unevenly. Emari's voice stumbles, and Voss feels heavier again suddenly. He is beginning to shrink once more.

He swings his ace and catches the lizard along its chest as it rears up. He dodges a powerful swing directed downward toward him, and manages to slam his axe into the other side of the beast's injured leg, cutting it off before it can heal.

The lizard stumbles. Voss is nearly back to normal size. He lunges for the creature's neck, and draws a stream of black blood from the wound he leaves. Boe lets loose a barrage of lightening as it tries to regain its footing. The lighting causes its muscles to tense, and it falls on its stomach. Emari leaps onto its back and pierces its scales between its shoulders. She leaves the blade in, twisting it repeatedly, and the lizard lets out a screech of pain. Voss waits. The beast cranes its injured neck towards Emari, its fangs leering from its lips, coated in green slime and black blood. Voss swings with immense speed towards the neck. His axe cuts through loose scales, flesh, and bone as it shoves its way in just above the creature's shoulders.

The creature drops again, its neck hanging limply. Still, it tries to push itself up again. Voss raises his axe again, and brings it down on the skull, splitting it in two from its cranium to the end of its snout. Boe smothers each body with a wave of fire, just to make sure neither are clinging to life.

The now-pouring rain kills the flames quickly, even putting the torch out as a puddle collects there. They wait a full minute in silence and dark. Their heart rate still does not drop. The bodies lay still. The tunnel is quiet.

"Leave them where they fell. The town can sort it out later," Voss says at last.

"Are you injured still?" Emari asks.

"Bruised, and still bleeding from my arm," Voss answers. "I will be fine for now. Let us make sure nothing else lurks in the cave. We can seek medical attention in the barracks. You are both uninjured, right?"

"Yes," Boe and Emari answer in unison.

Voss says nothing. He approaches the entrance to the tunnel. It is taller than he is now, and he easily slides into the darkness, taking his shield and axe with him. Boe stamps his staff against the mud and the top glows with a calm light. They walk into the tunnel. They are greeted with the smell of shit, piss, and blood. They are — unfortunately — smells that the trio is growing used to.

They turn a bend to the right, after walking only five feet, and then another turn takes them left immediately after. They find themselves staring into a medium-sized, circular cave. The ceiling of the cave is twelve feet high at the middle, and slants downward until it reaches an average of ten feet around the edges. The floor slopes downward as well, running on an angle until it is about a foot lower than the exit. There is a murky pool in the centre, brown liquid with green froth floating on the surface.

Boe's light illuminates much of the room, and the carnage that has taken place in it. Six bodies line the right-hand curve, all in various stages of consumption, and all with a hole in their chest where something had emerged from within. Directly across from those six are three fresh looking bodies, with their necks twisted at crude angles.

There are many bones scattered in no discernible pattern around the cave as well, even under the bodies.

"What in the name of the Gods happened here?" Boe asks, trying not to vomit.

"Voran," Voss answers. "He grows his creatures inside of people. When they burst free, they must grow quickly into the beasts we fought. There are clearly more about as well, or else they did not grow properly and died young."

"Voran is not here now, though," Emari says. "Perhaps he will return. We should move the bodies inside, so he does not suspect anything."

"Look here!" Boe exclaims, bending to the left of the entrance. He holds up a leather bag. Inside there is a book, a pen, ink, and several bottles of some shimmery, deathly-green liquid.

"This cannot be all that he had," Voss says, "but this could certainly belong to our doctor." Voss takes the book from the bag. He opens is and begins to read. It is mostly written in a language that neither he nor Boe can comprehend, but there are diagrams, and some parts are written in the general tongue.

What they gather in the few minutes they spend scouring the pages is that Voran and his creatures were already preparing to leave Highfell before Voss and the others arrived, and were just now gathering food for their next journey. Voran wrote nothing of where he intended to go, unless it is in the unknown language. He does state in the margins that he is intending on heading far away, and that his goals could not be accomplished with constant interruptions.

Voss curses and throws the book back into the leather bag. He turns back to survey the scene. "You're right, Emari," he says. "We should move the bodies and set a watch."

"I know you," a wrathful, angry voice calls from behind them. They turn just in time to see a dark shape disappearing around the bend in the tunnel. They immediately give chase, rounding the two corners and pushing back into the clearing.

Opposite them, standing just within the tree line is a horrific looking being. He is half man, half twisted and covered in hairs and scales. His limbs are contorted and long. His left arm bends three separate times.

"Who are you?" Emari demands.

The man laughs. As he finishes, he coughs bile onto the grass. "Voran Eralius," he says mockingly, and laughs again. "No, I own no name to speak of that is true. Though clearly I have been made a villain by you, I truly had no quarrel with you, save for your interference. Tonight, though, you have made yourselves my enemy. It seems you are not the only ones who are after me, though. Others came two nights ago, and stole an important book of mine. We could not catch them, whoever they were, but they did leave a nice little calling card. I thought it may have even been you." Eralius tosses a piece of thin metal onto the ground between them.

There are sounds of horse-hooves coming from the field between Highfell and these woods, a rumbling in the air.

"I must be off," Voran tells them. He chuckles, then retches. "I only came back for my final bag. If you would hand it over, that would be so kind."

"You can come with us to face justice, or die here," Voss says. "You will not get this bag back either way."

"Pity," Voran murmurs, "I thought you were smarter." The creature raises his hands towards the trio. Suddenly and intense cold takes over them, and they each fall to their knees in the slick mud. Voran strides quickly over to them. Some fierce malice burns in his eyes, but intelligence resides there as well. He rips the bag from Boe's clutching hands, then kicks the gnome in the face. Boe falls to his side, blood pouring from his nose.

Voran draws a longsword from his back as he walks over to Voss. He raises it high above his head. "I am sure I wouldn't see you again," he tells the soldier, "but I have to be certain. Besides, if I wait, I wouldn't get another chance." As his arm tenses to swing, a metal arrow pierces him through the hand. The blade clatters off of Voss' back. "Damned," Voran curses. "Well, that's a pity. Should we meet again, I won't hesitate too long." He then vanishes. Voss hears the sound of many feet approaching the clearing.

The spell finally passes, and the trio regain their mobility. Voss crawls forward and grabs the piece of metal from the short grass.

As Voss stands, Carver Nineshield and twelve other members of the guard rush into the clearing, nearly out of breath.

"A sentry saw you leaving, and we gave chase. We heard cries and the sounds of battle across the field!" the dwarf tells them. "We rushed for horses, but they were unsaddled. What happened here?"

They explain the events that occurred, but leave out most of their conversation with Voran. Carver listens carefully. They tell him of all they found in the book.

"We are no closer to catching him, but perhaps he will not bother the Dabarisian Heartland any longer," Nineshield says. "But you say they were taking citizens then to make more of those abominations, and for food? They would have had to keep them alive while they were eating, in order to keep the young intact, unless they only ate them after the young emerged." The dwarf grows dark. "I have no words. I will not sleep for many nights."

"He must be caught," Voss says. "If we hear any word of him, or if anyone does, then he must be tracked. I owe you thanks for that shot. I would be dead, or at least horribly wounded."

"What shot?"

Voss pauses. If it was not him, nor Valindra, then something else loosed that arrow. "I meant the sound of horses," he lies. "I apologize, we have had a great deal of stress thrown at us tonight, I may not be making much sense."

"Well, whatever drove him off, I am glad you are alive. I would not have traded your lives to kill him, even after what he did to our town. You did us a great deed in helping us, friends of Highfell."

Voss does not reply.

"We appreciate the thanks," Emari says, "but it is more important that everyone is safe at last."

"Not everyone," Voss says. He begins walking back towards town. "Tonight we have one last stop to make."

Chapter Ten – Farewell

3E056, 10th of Renewal

The room in which Captain Shoal lies is lit only by two candles and the grey, crawling light of the rising sun behind layers of cloud. She stirs and wakes as her hand is taken by Acting Captain Nineshield. She looks at him through glazed eyes. She can hardly focus. Sweat coats her forehead.

"The town is safe, my lady. The threat is gone," Carver tells his superior.

"That is good news," she says. Her voice is weak, and is met be silence. After waiting for a few seconds, she speaks again. "There is still bad news to tell me, isn't there?"

No one wants to respond, so Voss is the one who answers. "Yes," he says.

"Hello, Voss." Her mouth splits into a fragile smile.

"Hello, Eve," he answers.

"I am going to to die, aren't I?"

There is another silence. Again, Voss answers. "We do not know how to treat you," he tells her earnestly. He is careful with his words, but his voice is steady. "This disease was given to you by Voran's minion, and from all I have seen there is no medicine that has yet cleansed one who was afflicted with it. Perhaps a man of the Gods could cleanse you, or a mage of sorts, but I am uncertain."

"What will happen to me?" the Captain asks.

"You harbour within yourself one of those creatures. You are its egg," Voss responds. "In a few days, or even sooner, it will be ready to be hatch."

The Captain lies silent. There is resolve on her face. A single tear jumps onto her left cheek. It glistens brighter that the beads of sweat on her brow.

"I do not want this fate," she tells them.

"I do not know what to do," Voss tells her. His voice threatens to crack.

"Kill me," she says. "I do not want any more of those creatures to set foot in my town. Take its life before that happens, please." More tears threaten to burst forth as the room falls once again into silence.

"I would not slay my Captain, nor have anyone else do it," Nineshield speaks.

"Carver," Eve says, "I am too weak to do it myself."

"That should not be your fate," the dwarf responds.

"Do not make me order you," she snaps at him. "I would prefer a friend to honour my last wish, not a soldier to honour a command."

Nineshield looks at the floor, and again, for awhile, no one speaks. Boe fishes through his satchel and pulls out some thin vials of orange liquid.

"Voss, can we step outside for a moment?" the gnome asks. The two leave the treatment room, and walk to stand near the front door. The sound of rain pounds now against the roof of the clinic, and onto the road outside.

"I have studied alchemy," Boe tells Voss. "I have samples that I made some time ago of a strong poison. I make sleeping tonics as well, quite frequently, to help me drift off. Otherwise my mind does not stop."

"How potent are the tonics?"

"If I had a burner and some time alone I could concentrate it. No one would wake under a strong Chong tonic," he tells the soldier, offering a half-hearted grin.

"Go," Voss tells him, "and return within the hour."

Boe nods and scurries out the door, pulling his hat down to block the rain.

Voss remains there. Only soft conversation seeps through the treatment area behind him. Words come in small clumps, and then allow quiet to return. He takes his mind off of Eve for awhile. He studies the metal object left by Voran. It is small, thin, and rectangular. It looks like a playing card, but made of strong steel. Upon one side is carved two peering eyes with a line between them. They are painted red, and carved horizontally.

Voss' spirits are restless, and it gives him a great ache in his temples, but he talks to them of new plans, and their discussion seems reminiscent of when they were his friends, and under his command willingly. Nhasan speaks respectfully, and when Valindra speaks Voss almost believes he can see her smile. There is still anger and pain and confusion in their voices though. In the end, they leave him waiting for Boe with no real resolution, save for an offer of their respect.

This is a minor step forward, but it does not reassure Voss very much at all. Something is gnawing at the back of his mind. Every swing of his axe alleviates some of his anxiety, every step closer to danger seems to excite him, but every time he returns to safety he is hit with an increasing sense of restlessness, boredom. He feels very far from who he once wanted to be. He shakes this thought away, favouring the task at hand over the dusk in his own mind.

Boe returns after just over half an hour later, soaked by the rain. He is holding a cup of deep blue liquid. Voss takes it from him. The glass is warm, even through his gauntlet.

"This will put her to sleep?" the soldier asks.

"If I drank that," Boe tells him, "I might not even wake up again."

"Let's go," Voss says. They reenter the treatment room where the others are standing loosely around the Captain.

"You've been gone for some time," Eve muses softly. Speaking the words causes her to grimace and cough. Small specks of blood fly from her mouth. "My stomach turns."

"Captain Shoal," Voss speaks, "we wish to honour your request."

"Good."

"We have a tonic here that will put you into a deep sleep," Voss explains quietly. He places the glass in her right hand. "Only drink it when you are ready and have said everything you need to. We will not rush you. You will not wake again from this final rest."

She nods with difficulty. "*Captain* Nineshield," she says, "you will do honour for this town."

"I will, my lady," he responds in a trembling voice.

"Thank you all," Eve says, raising the glass a foot off the bed in a toast-like gesture. She then puts it to her lips. The blue liquid pours into her mouth. She lets it sit for only a second before swallowing it. "I will go peacefully, knowing that my town is safe again, and that all our fear will fade with time. The people who survive from here on owe a debt to those who defended us. Locals and visitors alike. A pity I won't be the one to repay it, save for a genuine happiness in my last few moments." A thin smile plays across her lips before her body relaxes and her breathing steadies.

"Captain Nineshield," Boe says, "this poison will painlessly stop her heart, and should kill anything growing within her. She should be able to have a burial fit for a woman of her status."

"She will have a warrior's pyre, and we will write her a song to be sung in the house," the dwarf says proudly, with a tear trickling towards his beard. "You are friends of this town, and will not be forgotten so long as I live. You have done a service now for me personally as well, and if you ever pass this way again, you shall be welcomed with open arms."

"Thank you, Captain," Voss says. "We cannot stay long, however. I hope you understand, but we must be leaving town soon. More than likely, we will be leaving after today."

"I do understand, and I will not ask you to remain longer than you must."

"And Nineshield," Voss presses, "seek out the wizard to the south quickly if you want hope of saving the others who are sick."

The Captain nods, a stern look seizing his face.

"If you hear any news of Eralius, or if any people go missing now, then send word to Taernsby, and it will reach my ears," Voss finishes.

"That bastard would be foolish to stay here now that we know his hiding place, but we will be vigilant. Safe travels on your return."

"Your fight, I hope, is over. But if the wizard nearby cannot help them, then you will need to organize an alternative. At the very least, if you remain vigilant, you will not suffer for much longer." Voss salutes him in Dabarisian manner, by placing his closed right hand across his chest and his left arm behind his back. He turns and leaves, the other two follow. Carver pours the poison into Eve's mouth, and it trickles down her throat.

There will be much work and pain ahead for this town, as the sick will likely be doomed to death, but that is a battle that the new Captain will need to face in the days to come. Voss does not worry for the sake of Highfell now. They return to the inn and, for the rest of the day and that night, they rest in their rooms.

Chapter Eleven – A Bard's Tale

3E056, 11th of Renewal

The first three days of study have shed no light on what Evandur seeks. The paladin spent nearly the entirety of the ninth and tenth within the library, pouring over old tomes and papers. When it closed, he returned to the church and scanned through any records that Ewain and the other caretakers could find that relate to arcane study and dark magic.

On the morning of the eleventh, Evandur hears the sound of hooves in the courtyard outside. He rouses himself from slumber and begins to get dressed. As he leaves his room, he hears the doors of the church being pulled open, far below.

When Evandur has finally wound his way back down the flights of steps to the main floor, he sees one of the church's younger caretakers greeting a man that is roughly his own age. They are walking from the doors, and the caretaker is holding a large travel bag.

Evandur approaches. "You must be Douglas," he says.

The man looks up in surprise. His skin is dark and his black hair is only slightly darker. He has his locks pulled into a tight bun that sticks up behind his kindly face. His eyes are youthful, but there is something in his gaze which presents his strength as well.

"Indeed, I am Douglas," the dark man says to Evandur. "I do not believe I know your name or face."

"I am Evandur Angelthorn, full paladin of the Church of Valkronus." They shake hands. Douglas holds the paladin's eyes.

"It's a pleasure," Douglas says.

"Indeed," Evandur responds. "I have been told by Ewain that you are quite skilled in lore and research." He offers his hand forward. "Shall I take your other bag?"

"You can take the one from caretaker Jon," Douglas says, and the caretaker obliges, handing Evandur the travel bag. "On Ewain's words, I must state that I believe he is simply trying to tell you that I spend far too much time in the libraries, and not enough time in the training yard. That is partially why I have yet to earn full status," Douglas explains as they begin to walk towards the staircase door.

Even Evandur has some trouble getting beyond Douglas' looks. He acts the same as any northern man would, but he stands out against the rest of the world like a drop of paint on an otherwise clean canvas. Evandur chooses to not let that thought take root.

"Ewain seemed to praise you in his speech," Evandur says. "I truly believe he meant no insult."

"No, I am sure he did not. I only meant to jest," Douglas responds. "So what sorts of lore are you searching for?"

"That is one of the problems I am facing," Evandur explains as they reach the second floor. "I am not entirely sure. I believe it must be related to the arcane in some way, or perhaps something darker. It is a lengthy story, and I know that there is something important in what I sensed, but it is not easy to research on a hunch."

"Well, the day is early," Douglas says with a smile. "Let me put my things in my room, and then I will help you if I can. It has been four long days of riding, but I can handle a day of sitting and reading, and walk would be a benefit to my sore legs."

Evandur returns the man's smile, and walks with Douglas back to his room. After several minutes are spent in their separate rooms, they meet again for breakfast in the dining chamber on the third floor. They eat at the long table. Their meal consists of eggs and cheese. Afterward, they exit the church together and, leaving their horses behind, they begin the walk to the library.

As they traverse the City Ring Road, Evandur tells most of the tale which he found himself in. He begins when he first met Voss and the others, and ends with his departure from Taernsby for Daroonga. He speaks mostly of Voss, as he is Evandur's area of study. The paladin is not worried about speaking openly with Douglas, but he does lower his voice or stop altogether whenever they pass common-folk. Evandur trusts the church, and would be hard pressed in finding a reason to distrust Douglas so far.

They reach the library and begin to carry different books and scrolls to a large oaken table. They read much about necromancy, and Echoshan, as that is what they both think is most likely the source of Voss' abilities. Nothing seems to jump out at either of them.

Since his talk with Peren before he left home in Taernsby, he has viewed God of Death with less malice than he used to. Now, after reading deeper into necromancy, he cannot even find a sense of pure evil in the practice. Soul magic, and the bending of life essence to reanimate the dead is unholy and wrong but, as it turns out, even the God of Death is against this. The use of raw magic is more rarely used to reanimate the dead, but when it is used, it is not really any different than animating a statue or a broom. It is still immoral and illegal, but otherwise it is not unholy.

Nothing in the books gives Evandur the sense of pure darkness that he felt in Voss. It was only in certain moments that he got that sense to begin with. By the end of the day he feels no closer. In truth, he feels even less sure of himself.

He confides in Scilandra when they have returned to their rooms at the end of the day.

"Are we wrong?" he asks her.

"No," she replies. "We are uncertain. You know that you felt something in him, and I did too. We are searching for the truth, but moving on a parallel path. If we don't find a way to the one that is running beside us, we may pass by what we seek and lose it forever."

Evandur sleeps uneasily.

In the morning of the twelfth Douglas rouses the angel-blessed paladin with a swift knock on his door. Evandur throws a pair of trousers over his pale legs before answering. He is still cinching the cloth belt around his waist as he pulls the door open.

Before the shirtless paladin can offer a welcome or good morning, Douglas speaks, saying, "Tell me what you said before about the ghosts."

"Pardon?" Evandur asks, half awake.

"I apologize," Douglas says, shaking his head to focus. "I awoke this morning with a thought and I haven't brought my manners with me. Would you describe the spectral images, or ghosts, that came from master Hallehwell?"

Evandur wraps his mind around the question, nodding. "There were several of them," he says. "One was a woman, an archer, one was a dwarf who wielded a mace and shield, and two were men. They were all spectre-like, a pale, ghostly blue. Like the turquoise roofs of Daroonga if they were on the brink of death, or a blue sky wrapped in a veil of thin cloud."

"Voss had other magic, right? You said he could summon a weapon. Would you describe that as well, please, sir?"

"It appeared out of mist," says Evandur. "It would form from the same ghostly blue into his dark, steel axe."

"The same colour," Douglas mutters. "Was any magic different? Arcanum is a changeable phenomenon, but in all of my study I have never heard of a wizard using his favourite hue for all his tricks. Furthermore, the way you described this colour rings a bell for me."

"Does it?"

"Yes," Douglas tells him. "We must go to the library again. I think that we were in the right place, but in the wrong section."

On that, Douglas returns to his room, and Evandur hurries to get dressed.

"We may have found a way onto that parallel path," Scilandra tells him.

With renewed vigour, he grabs his weathered journal and throws it into a shoulder bag with some fresh breads and older cheeses, and rejoins his new companion in the hall.

They move with haste, as Douglas wracks his brain for a specific book. The squire does not speak much as they saddle their horses, opting for a faster journey. Thirty minutes since Evandur woke, and they arrive in front of the library. They leave their horses saddled, and tie them to a tree growing in a small courtyard with a wooden overhang and a low wall. The rain has started again, but the oak awning will keep the steeds dry. Guards posted on the Wessteroad corner agree to watch them, and so the pair enters the library once more.

"Will you tell me what we are searching for now, Douglas?" Evandur asks.

"I- I can't say for certain what the title is, but I may know it by the cover. It is one of Ran-Levyr's less famous stories."

"Ran-Levyr?"

The bard in question is well known throughout the world. Many travellers have written great works, but none have surpassed Ran-Levyr in fame. He has been writing since the dawn of history and, until recently, he had not stopped. He was claimed to be immortal, and never once did he say otherwise. He retained perpetual youth well into the third era. He travelled the world. Some say he has seen the continents beyond Streboya that no one else has. He has been seen as a simple bard, a scholar, a warrior, and an advisor. No matter how you view him, he has played a truly pivotal role in the development of Thrella. And now, he is gone. He disappeared some forty years ago.

"Yes," Douglas answers the paladin, "he wrote a book based in Streboya, from when he first travelled to the continent. It is a short story, and truly not one that I would usually recommend reading, for there is no happy ending or heroism. It was more of an article, in all actuality."

They scour the shelves for some minutes before Douglas comes to a subdued red cover that is faded and worn at the edges. It reminds Evandur immediately of Voss' cloak. Upon the cover is a demonic looking face, painted carefully in pale blue ink. Not quite the exact shade that Evandur believes to remember, but still it is eerily close. Even the sight of this book sends some feeling straight into the paladin's heart.

They sit together, and open the story.

Within the red bindings are twenty or so pages of thin script, with several drawings upon the corners every now and again. Another reason that Ran-Levyr's work is so popular is because he employs mages to reproduce his books. All of the writing, the fantastical nature, the mystery and excitement, appears in its original, unedited state unless he has specifically changed it later. This book is certainly not edited as, while no spelling mistakes can be found amongst its pages, it is a wandering story, with no real arc.

Evandur soaks in every word nonetheless. He takes over two hours to study the material, telling Douglas his occasional thoughts, but often remaining quiet.

The story is from a voyage that the bard took before the colonists from Estrand ever set foot on Streboya. It tells of how himself and a small crew of only five others anchored in a small bay along the southern side of the continent in order to begin mapping it. Ran-Levyr rarely writes the names of those he travels with, unless they are of great importance or a close friend of his, and so this crew remains entirely anonymous.

The first portion of the book is rather boring and tedious, but the description of the route they took and the small drawings of various maps do stand out. Towards the end of the book, when they arrive at a place that the bard writes he "was later told to be called the Whispering Grove," things begin to go horribly wrong. By the end of the Streboyan Civil War, it was established legend that the Whispering Grove, and all the woods that lie around it, were cursed and dark. At the time of the book's story, however, there was no knowledge of the land which the bard was stepping foot on.

Within the grove, the small crew made camp. During the night they began to hear soft voices in the darkness, and they could not strike a fire. As the night grew later, the voices seemed to grow closer. The crew and Ran-Levyr huddled together in a small circle. No one dared to sleep.

An hour before the sun rose, the air felt colder than it had all night, colder than it should have. Even more than that, though, it felt dry, dead, as though it were made of wisps of ice-smoke, clawing at the crew's sheets and bodies.

They prepared to leave immediately, but as they were packing, a voice rose above the other whispers until it filled the glade. It was laughter. Ran-Levyr drew upon his arcane well and a light hovered above the crew. Even the bard's magic had difficulty piercing the heavy dark around them. The sky was black, and the tree line was beyond their sight. From a pile of broken stones in the centre of grove, a figure arose. Ran writes later, in the margin of the page, that he believes that pile of stones could once have been a dark altar, but he never returned to prove himself right.

"Pain has the most excellent quality," the figure spoke to us, as a deathly, pale blue mist swam about its feet. "If prolonged, it cannot be severe, but if severe, it cannot be prolonged. There must be balance, or there must be a choice."

It was after those words were spoken that an excruciating pain entered the bodies of the crew, and of the bard as well. They were all pulled into the air and suspended there. Ran-Levyr watched as each of the crew members strained in agony.

"It seems that your pain is severe," spoke the figure. The mist around the beast rose, glowing that ghostly-turquoise. It was revealed that the creature was larger than a man, but with the same proportions. It had horns, and its entire body looked almost as though it were made from chunks of bone and black rock or metal that also jutted from it at the out-facing joints and shoulders. There was no tail to be seen. It looked like no devil or demon that I had come across, and I have seen many, but it wielded just as much power, if not more.

Suddenly, one by one, each of the five crew members gave a scream of sharp pain and the bard watched their souls depart their bodies. He saw his own leave too.

As each soul was wrenched from its vessel, it rushed to the beast in a blur of the same blue mist that it wore around itself like loose clothing. The mist shifted as the souls joined it. I saw briefly each of my crew's faces, but I could not discern the nature of it, as pain was forcing its way into my mind the whole time. I watched in horror as my own soul was pulled through my skin. I am of no weak will, and no mere mortal either, but this was no magic that I had ever seen. I cried out, both in pain and in anger and, with my own mental power, I forced my soul back inside of myself.

The beast looked shocked, and then smiled. "You are the first creature to not bend before me. I have tasted your soul, though, and it makes my mouth water."

"You have stolen the innocent souls of my crew, but you will not have mine, vermin," I said. "I will take theirs back as well." I knew my words were hollow. That being knew it too. It laughed its foul laugh again.

"You are strong," it said, "and in you I can see something that I have longed to see for some time."

"And what is that?"

"Opposition. In you it is pure. You strive for good and for light. You were put upon this earth, by a power greater than the Gods, to heal and protect. I was put here to injure and destroy. I desire only pain and suffering. For so long I have waited in this grove, taking essence, building power, waiting for the one who would stand against me, the one who would be my way to freedom. You carry a piece of me within you now, as I carry a small piece of you. It will grow heavier and, once I speak my name, you will know that you can never be rid of me."

I was lucky, though. I was blessed by the Gods, or by whatever greater power the being believed existed above them, for I found in myself a strength and determination that I have never been able to replicate. I searched deep into my soul and found the place where I had been touched by this darkness, and with a furious cry I glowed radiant and my soul was cleaned. The being cursed me as I fled. Never did I look back.

Ran-Levyr writes little more. He found his way to house Whiteguard, the home of the old elves of Streboya, and sought their aid. They told him of the legends of the Whispering Grove, and that they would double their watch of it with this new information, but they have kept the creature at bay for centuries. The elves said that the beast had no name that it had shared with any of them, and that none who had truly encountered it had even returned.

The end of the book is only a warning. He writes to be careful when you track into uncharted land, and to never enter this grove, as it was beyond even him or the strongest elven wizard's ability to cleanse.

Evandur and Douglas sit quietly for some time.

"What are your thoughts?" asks Douglas at length.

"That it was fortunate that you were brought to my attention by Ewain. I would never have turned to bardic works for my answer," Evandur responds. "Somewhere in my heart, though, I feel I am a great step closer to finding it."

Chapter Twelve - Plans in Motion

3E056, 12th of Renewal

The winds that thrash against Zyban's Rise are ferocious. The Red Hand stands upon a large metal deck that is constructed off of a natural ledge two hundred feet below the peak of the mountain. The Infinity Spire, a once-great prison complex, was built near the summit of the mountain as well. Now it has fallen to ruin, as it has sat largely unused since the beginning of the second era. Over a century later, The Red Hand came upon it, and took it for his own.

Now, on this deck, which wraps around the spire at roughly the midway point, he looks southward. From the platform, he can see over the swamps and the plains below, painted golden-white by the hot sun. He can see just to the edge of Rail Lake on the clearest day. Of course, his eyesight is also far better than the average man's, but — even so — all the members of his organization could see the glow of Marsh Hold to the south-east in the dead of night. He would have thought this beautiful, even by the standards of his youth, if he found much beauty in the world anymore. He sees past the twisted facade too well now, though.

The Red Hand is, of course, connected to the Wight's Call, the bandits' guild, the thieves and the assassins that reside now within the Infinity Spire's lower levels. He is not of them, though, nor is he their leader, despite having authority over their actions. He would call the section that he is part of "The Sanctum," for only a small percentage of the Wight's Call truly answer to him. He only presides over those with any real power. His following is still fairly great and widespread, however, as they managed to secure him an airship and get contact to a small sect of Sanctum members working in the south.

The Red Hand grins. It is not a warm grin, but one of some cruel excitement.

Beside him stands an older fellow. This man is clothed in dark-grey robes that are adorned with a patch on the left shoulder showing three red streaks running from top-right to bottom-left in parallel. They resemble claw marks, and are the symbol of the Wight's Call. On his right shoulder there is another patch, which shows two red eyes with a line cutting between them. He also wears a hood to block some wind, though his beard still blows westward in the shrill breeze. His long, greying black hair is tucked into his cowl.

"Layvaas, I am close to completing the next step in my plan," The Red Hand speaks. His empty voice does not seem to strike the man beside him in the same way that it does with many others. "I was even more lucky than I could have imagined. My intuition is more honed than ever. I have watched this world work for years beyond my memory, and so I must have learned some skill in prediction."

"I am glad for you, my liege," Layvaas responds. "I will not pry into your meaning behind that, but I can certainly feel your excitement."

"And I yours. I hear that you are close indeed to your goal as well," expresses The Red Hand. "In regards to my meaning, it is just that I found both a means to further my goal, and a person of great interest to me."

"Then that is certainly good luck, sire. And of my plan, yes, I have found a handful of willing subjects. They follow the regime of the old ones, not of the ones left in hiding on this world. They are the ones who fought man until their end, and they now swear great revenge."

"Is there a war waging in their world now?" The Red Hand asks, though he knows as well as his friend what the answer is. The Red Hand has been on this world before its history began. He aided in the slaying of the last Dragon Lord, Aercitazk. He was once a mighty warrior and mage.

"There is war, yes," Layvaas tells him, "but things are always both less and more complicated than they seem."

"Indeed, you speak truth," The Red Hand says, nodding. "I am still going to be lessened by your absence on my next journey."

The aging man nods solemnly. "You will not have need of me though. I am no alchemist."

"You are someone that I trust. That is rare, Layvaas. I do not trust fully even the God who spared me, nor the being that I serve now."

"You serve no one here, my liege," Layvaas tells him.

The Red Hand smiles again. This one is nearly warm. They stand for some time.

Thirty feet to the right of them, on the south-west side of the deck, a small airship is hovering. There are a handful of people loading boxes up a ramp into the small storage compartment.

Airships were not popularized until some years after the turn of the third era. Krunix was the first to produce an actual fleet. The most common design is a large, airtight balloon, with a living compartment and storage compartment built underneath, and sometimes even around the balloon. Many additions and different models have been made around this basic concept. Some larger ships feature multiple decks, or a higher deck built on top of thick, metal reinforcements that can wrap vertically around the balloon.

All airships are powered on arcane energy. This arcane energy was originally — and is still frequently — supplied by on-board mages and wizards. More recent ships have employed the use of arcane storage crystals. Only two different spells must be known to operate a ship, and both involve air and wind magic, so a wizard who is not very broadly learned could still make a decent living on an airship's crew.

With every airship, the balloon is first filled with air, sometimes naturally, sometimes with the aid of an arcanist of some sort. Then, the ship is suspended by magic - spells that force the air in the balloon to become lighter in weight, and move upwards. More than one mage is required at any time, to give the other a chance to rest. Most large ships employ at least three or four mages, and are equipped with backup crystals. Many ships have no means of moving forward, either, and this requires the mages to also focus on pushing the air in the balloon in the direction they want to fly. The process of piloting an airship requires great arcane strength and focus. This is why they are still rare and expensive to operate.

This particular airship was pilfered by Layvaas and another of The Red Hand's close servants, Noroviin. It was taken from a Dabarisian trade route while it was heading south. This was done by using scroll and crystal magic to cancel the other arcane energy on the ship, and bringing it slowly to the ground.

The vessel only has enough room for twelve crew members, with a separate cabin for the captain. There is also the storage space on a separate deck at the bottom of the ship, and a small kitchen and dining room. A thin deck wraps around the outside of the balloon which is accessible from the crew's quarters. Upon the deck, on either side, are large sails that are secured at many points to a metal circle that wraps vertically around the balloon and the decks below. The sails should allow the mages on board to focus more heavily on raising the air up, and not on pushing it forward when the wind is favourable. The captain has control of a wheel that turns two rudders, both in the centre of the ship, one above the balloon, and one below the storage deck. It is a heavy wheel, and locks into place at several predetermined positions.

If there is wind coming from anywhere northward, it will be easy enough to steer south. He does not expect an easy job to be made of the landing at the end of their journey, as he is aiming directly for the Beltwood. Once the ship touches down, The Red Hand finds it unlikely that it will ever fly again. Getting back for him will be easy, though, as he long ago installed an arcane gate that he alone can use from anywhere in the world.

He has not told his crew that he does not expect any of them to return after this mission.

The deckhands finish loading boxed of food and barrels of water onto the ship and wave toward the pair of silent figures.

The Red Hand nods to Layvaas. "I shall be off, then," he tells his friend. "Do not expect my return for some months."

"Understood."

"Noroviin will remain in charge of the Sanctum here. Shadow will keep things running through the Wight's Call."

"Yes, my liege."

"Good luck to you as well, Layvaas. I am certain that we both need a streak of fortune to complete our goals. I will pray for us."

"I will as well. Maltram give you speed, Crovosius guide the winds south."

"We shall see," The Red Hand speaks coldly. He turns from his companion and strides with great speed towards the loading ramp.

He throws off his black cloak to reveal, instead, dyed, leather armour. It is drawn tight against his body, and consists of shoulder-guards, chest-piece, bracers, and shin and thigh padding. Under the armour he wears a tunic with a hood and cowl sewn along the collar. The hood is a forest green, but the rest is dark browns and black. He has buckled a belt around his waist, and in a sheath has placed a gorgeous longsword. The blade is of ancient elvish make. No one would be able to guess where he obtained it.

He also has a shortsword slung on his pack, and many poisons and other supplies inside. He carries no food. He does not need it.

He walks to the base of the ramp. The storage area is packed to the ceiling with boxes and barrels on one side and, on the other, nearly a dozen people sit cramped and bound. He eyes them coolly. They look back in fear.

It used to pain him to steal life from those who have lived not nearly as long as him. He would try to weep for them, but never would tears come. He has a goal, though, a purpose that he must fulfill, and not just for those that he serves, but for himself as well. He seeks an end that none above him yet know.

The ramp is drawn away from the storage back and the doors are sealed. The ramp is then moved to the doorway above, which leads into the crew deck. The Red Hand enters first, and moves quickly to his own cabin. The wooden floor is splashed with the blood of the previous owner, but he pays the stain little attention. Piloting an airship was not something he ever had the chance to do in life. He has flown pegasi, though, and hung below a soaring dragon by an arrow-rope. After doing the things he has, a challenge rarely frightens him.

He takes hold of the wheel, looks out of the window that takes up most of his cabin's walls, and calls behind himself to his crew through his open doors. "Mages, up!" His voice floods the ship. "We cast off for the Beltwood now!" Then to himself he says, "By this time next year, I will have my revenge."

His cruel, excited grin returns to his cracked lips as the ropes are cut from the platform and the ship begins to rise.

Chapter Thirteen – Choices Made

3E056, 13th of Renewal

The morning of the thirteenth creeps in nearly unnoticed through the clouds and the rain that now pours unabashedly into the streets of Daroonga City. Despite the rapid movement of the water, there is a stillness to the air itself that seems to make it heavier than usual. There is a greater storm moving from the west, and the rain is likely to continue for some time.

Evandur wakes early. The sun has barely lit the world from behind the wall of deep grey, yet the paladin can see his room clearly enough. He has been mulling over the things he has learned in the past few days. The bard's tale still sits upon the floor beside his bed. He has read it several times since he and Douglas first scoured it together a full day ago.

"My obsession with Sir Hallehwell is not pointless, it it?" Evandur asks inwardly.

"I do not believe so," Scilandra responds. "I can offer little knowledge or guidance in this area, but truly I would not yet forsake your beliefs. You have proven that there is more to discover, and the tale in that book makes it seem that this is not yet the end of the story."

"I can only hope."

"Yes, you can. Now close your mouth and get dressed."

Evandur does as he is told. He rises, buckles his trousers around his waist, and throws a tunic over his head and shoulders. He dons a grey travel cloak to fight the morning chill, then exits his room. After descending one floor, he finds two of the lower priests engaged in excited chatter. One of them is a human woman, and the other is a man he recognizes from years ago, and elf named Aerlei.

Evandur strides up to them and gives a short wave that they return.

"What is going on that has you both up this early?" Evandur asks.

"Evandur!" Aerlei says. "It's good to see you! A royal messenger arrived early and passed a letter to Emma to give to the higher priests, but we managed to sneak a peak."

"What did this message say? If my curiosity is allowed," Evandur asks them.

"The King has asked churches to send paladins and priests to aid a military operation, allegedly," says Emma.

"No other news?" Evandur presses.

"None," Aerlei says. "High priestess Errester snatched the letter and took it away. The message said little else of importance, though. I read the whole thing."

"Curious," Evandur says. "It was nice seeing you Aerlei, but I have much to do today. I will catch up with you later should I get the chance."

They bid each other goodbye and Evandur pushes out onto the balcony and descends the next stairs, all the while being watched by the great Valkronian window.

He spends the first part of the day breaking his fast with Douglas in a family restaurant across from the church. He then returns to his room and begins to pack. He has already bundled his clean clothing, his travel gear, and some rations into his larger travel bag. His weapons are organized on his bed, and his dirty clothes are folded on the floor awaiting a wash. He is just about to fetch a washboard from the storeroom adjacent to the kitchen when a knock sounds through his door.

"Enter!" he calls.

The door is pushed open and Ewain passes gently into the room. With him is the high priestess of the Daroonga Church to Valkronus, Hailey Errester.

"Greetings, my priestess," Evandur says, bowing low. She is older and far wiser than he. She has been in charge of this church sect for more years than Evandur has lived on Thrella. Her silver hair is braided down her back, hanging almost to her hips. She is dressed in a clean black dress, which has been embroidered in a repeating flame pattern of orange and gold around the neck and bottom of the skirt.

"Stand tall, Evandur," she tells him. He straightens his back. "I wish to speak with you and Ewain in comfort. There is an important matter to be shared, but we will talk in the privacy of my home."

"As you command, my lady," Evandur says, bowing again slightly.

"Join us the lobby when you are ready and we can walk together. Bring a rain-cloak," Hailey tells the paladin, and takes Ewain by the arm. They leave the bed chambers. Evandur dresses for the weather and then meets them downstairs two minutes later.

They walk out of the front doors and into the street. The light of day floods the roads, and gleams off the turquoise roofs and the silver of the lampposts, even in the dismal weather.

It is only ten minutes to High Priestess Errester's house. It is a large, single storey home with many windows and the round architecture of many Daroonga buildings. Errester inherited it from her father, who was a priest of Valkronus for his entire life as well. The walls are a light, beige stone, and the roof is the same blue as the majority of the city, but with some red accents, which are set at equal distances around the pointed, circular roof.

They enter through the arched frame and thick, spruce door. Inside it is a lavish home, with carpets of gold and deep brown, and paintings that cover the pale walls wherever there are no windows. The main hall is separated from the entry by a thin paper divide, which light flows through.

They walk around the divide, removing their wet shoes and cloaks, and seat themselves at a round, white-wood table, taking three of the eight available chairs. Errester soon brings a plate of cheese and fruits which she sets on the surface before her guests.

They sit for some time, warming up, before Evandur breaks the silence. "My lady," he says, "what news brings you to me?" Some part of the paladin guesses already that it must have to do with the conversation he overheard that morning.

The High Priestess does not avoid the topic. "I have received, this morning, a letter from our King," she says. "He has summoned paladins and priests of the church for an important military mission. I have little doubt that you heard the excitement of the other priests already."

"I have," Evandur speaks the truth.

"I know more than they could tell you, however," she says. "It is the will of King Rory Dabaris to put an end to the speak of rebellion in The South. He is to garrison men in a fortress, in preparation for a counter-offensive."

"Such that if a rebellion begins, he can mobilize forces quickly?"

"Correct."

They think for a moment.

"You mean to send me," Evandur guesses. "I do not wish for that."

"You are a strong paladin," she says. "Not in your training alone, but in heart and soul as well. I can think of none better, and few who match. None of them are within the city, or are expected to return any time soon."

"I am on a personal errand," Evandur tells her. "I know not why, but my heart compels me to seek an answer to a question that has plagued me now for many months."

"I have little choice. The King is a good ally to have in these times, and I must send aid. You must go."

Evandur is silent. He knows better than to argue beyond what he already has.

"I am sorry. I cannot send any other, though you may take who you wish," she says. "I bid you meet with the King's Royal General who will oversee the mission. He leaves the city within the month."

"I will take with me the squire, Douglas Tumbolamew, and the priests Emma and Aerlei who initially told me of the letter's arrival," he says.

"I will have arrangements made," she responds without pause.

Evandur continues, saying, "I must ask for a time-line and for my duties. I will provide all the help I can, but if I am to hold in a fort for years then I will have my willpower tested greatly."

"You will be sent to aid in training, and in combat, if need arises. Paladins Fairblade and Orrober should be returning ere summer's end. I will have them relieve you as soon as they arrive."

Evandur's heart lightens. "Thank you, my lady," he says. "You are gracious to listen to me."

"I take council in those who have wisdom. You are an important asset to this church, and one with a stout mind, possibly even more so than a stout blade. I would be made a fool to refuse to aid you in a quest of your heart."

Evandur looks at Hailey for some time, watching her face as she takes a sip of water from a wide cup in front of her.

"I will seek the general, High Priestess, if you would speak his name and place."

"Langford," she responds. "General Barriston Langford. He will be in the Gaelsa Manor in the Royal Ring."

"Thank you, my lady. May I take leave?"

"You may go. I will be speaking with you again before you depart, I am certain, but the rest of the day is yours as you please."

Evandur bows and leaves the table quickly, but not rudely. He slips his shoes and cloak back on, and glides through the streets. He takes great, fast strides. There is frustration growing in his heart.

"How important is following orders?" Scilandra asks.

"What do you mean?" Evandur responds.

"I mean that the church is not the mouth of the Gods alone. They speak for others as well."

Evandur slows his pace, but Scilandra says nothing else.

The paladin returns to the church. By the time he arrives, he is soaked with rain to his skin. He finds the current priest on the platform and asks where Douglas might be. He is directed upstairs, as Douglas is allegedly still in his room. Evandur climbs the stairs with great speed and knocks on the door to the squire's chambers with force.

There are two footsteps that come from within the room before the door is pulled open and Douglas is standing, looking curiously at Evandur.

"I have been given a task by the High Priestess and, though I am regretful, I have been told I must complete it," Evandur tells the squire. "I would be even more regretful to take it alone, however. I am to travel south for several months. I cannot refuse this mission, but I can offer you the choice to travel with me if you would. I will not try to force it upon you, though I do long for a friend, someone I trust, to join me."

Douglas thinks for a long time. "What would we be made to do?" he asks.

"Oversee training of soldiers in a military fort and, if they have need to fight while we are stationed there, then we would aid in their campaign."

"You have never seen me wield a blade," Douglas says.

"I trust you, though, as a member of the church. Above that, as a squire who has already exceeded my expectations and, as I said, a friend," Evandur tells the dark-skinned man. "My heart does not oft lead me astray, and now it says to trust in you."

"I will go with you," says Douglas suddenly. "I would ask a request in return."

"Name it."

"If I prove to be of use, and to follow orders, I would like a recommendation for promotion given to the High Priestess," the squire says. "I yearn to be a full paladin. This one mission may not be enough, but if the thought can grace her mind, then perhaps I will be considered fairly."

"Would you not be otherwise?" Evandur asks.

"No," Douglas says quietly. "I believe that I would remain a squire for some long time, unless chance does not lean on my side."

"Then you have my word," Evandur tells him. "I will give a full mission report that will include your honour and a recommendation from myself. You helped chance lean to my side, now I will help it lean to yours."

"Thank you."

"My pleasure. Today we must meet with General Langford in the Royal

Ring. You must come with me."

Douglas' face grows stern. "I do not know if that is smart."

"It is my decision, and we will be welcomed."

Douglas nods. "Then allow me to slip into rain-boots and more elegant clothing. I will meet you on the main floor," he says.

Evandur also redresses in a clean and formal shirt and black pants. He dons his rain-cloak and leather boots. He wears his longsword in its sheath on his hip and pulls his cuirass on with its pauldrons, as the chest-plating is emblazoned with the symbol of Valkronus. When he is ready, he waits downstairs.

Douglas meets him, dressed in similar attire, but without the armour. They set off, taking their horses. Nearly an hour past noon, they arrive, riding up the Wessteroad, at the gates to the Royal Ring. This ring is the only one with full gatehouses, and guards are always stationed along the outer boundaries, both in view and out.

One guard hails the pair as they approach the gate house. She is tall, with blonde hair and a beautiful face. She is clad in shining white mail. The paladin stops and she asks him a few questions. She leaves two other guards to watch the gate and escorts the pair into the ring.

The great courtyard of the Royal Ring stretches before them. The Wessteroad, like the other cardinal roads, runs between two of the House Manors into the centre court, which lies around the Dabarisian Castle. This road happens to pass between the houses of Gaelsa and Talava. Not much farther, the road would lead them to the Castle Yard, a great stone court that wraps around the centre of Daroonga City, filled with fountains and gardens. The guard leaves them near the great metal gate to the Gaelsa yard.

The houses that make up the King's Council are wealthy and powerful. The sprawling mansions and villas — that have been long maintained — are testaments to that. Three of the four houses are made up of families chosen by the King himself, and the fourth, House Dabaris, is made up by both the residing royal family, and a collection of nobles elected by the people of

Daroonga.

Farathorn is the largest house, consisting of seven families. This house represents the King in the northern townships of Northwich and Azgul Hold, and the lower townships of Helmshire, Outton, and Rockfell.

The house with the midmost power is Talava, which is made up of four families. These families represent the Kingdom along the eastern coast of Estrand, the reef-towns, and the colonies on Streboya.

The smallest of the houses is Gaelsa, with only two families. One of these families is the Langfords, who boast a long and pure lineage. This house has overseen the growth of the colonies in Southern Estrand.

The villa of House Gaelsa is set about a wide, green lawn that is hidden by hedges and the tall, shining iron fence and gate. There are three buildings that ensnare the yard between them. All are of a circular design, with high and gleaming turquoise roofs. From each roof protrudes several chimneys. The buildings are not permanent residences for the majority of the house members, but are able to easily accommodate all of both families should the need arise.

Evandur is met at the gate by a guard. He is dressed in dark leather, fitted with steel pauldrons and cuirass, and he wears a helm. Draped down his back is a long cape that is coloured (from Evandur's right to his left) half in the green of the Dabarisian standard, and half in the dark grey of house Gaelsa. There is no symbol upon the cape.

"Hail," the guard says calmly to the visitor.

"Greetings. I am Evandur Angelthorn, paladin of the Church of Valkronus. I seek General Barriston Langford. I have been sent by High Priestess Errester."

The guard pauses for a moment before nodding courteously and opening the gate. "The General is finishing lunch," says the man. "He is holding a meeting afterward with two other paladins, and I shall put a request in for him to see you as well. Will your servant be entering the grounds?"

"Douglas, my squire, will go where I do, if he pleases," Evandur tells the guard. There is no hostility in his voice, but it is firm and commanding.

"Of course," responds the guard. "My apologies, sir. Please come in."

They begin to walk straight across the yard, in the direction of the farthest building. The walk through the courts and gardens takes them a minute. There is a walkway of level stone that leads between the two grassy fields to the stone patio that joins the three abodes. Each field has several benches and a fountain at their centre.

As they reach the end of the courtyard, the patio raises to a dark, wooden deck that wraps around the front of this building. The guardsman salutes two other guards, a man and a woman, and explains the situation. They nod in response. The woman moves to take the initial guard's position at the gate.

The first guard opens the set of two spruce doors, above which hangs the Gaelsa standard: the dark-grey rectangle hanging horizontally with a black inlay of a mountain in front of deep clouds. The paladin and his squire walk across a bristle mat, upon which they kick the rain and mud from their shoes, and then enter the building. The second man bids Evandur and Douglas to follow him, while the gate-guard leaves to seek the General. The doors have opened to a large and ornate staircase that travels forward before looping back around on either side, and meeting the upstairs hall directly above their heads. On either side of them, a hallway runs around the the whole building in a circle. The floors are made of marble and covered in dark-grey rugs. The inside walls are of panelled wood, where the outside was black brick. The inside is also adorned with a variety of paintings and weavings, lit by the natural light from the outer windows.

The visitors follow the male guard as he leads them down the right-hand hall. They curve gently around the outside of the building, past many doors on their left, and are soon led into a long and comfortable chamber, which lies beyond a set of two swinging doors. This room is filled with furs, pelts, and paintings depicting hunts. There is a large brick hearth set upon the western wall, and several wide leather chairs are throughout the room. Two chairs are in front of the fire, two are against the east wall, on either side of a small, dark table with a blue-glass topper. There are also two bookshelves that are set against the north wall, filled with history tomes, in front of which is another chair.

Their guide salutes the holy men and leaves them in the room. He exits through the swinging doors and disappears around the bend. The doors only cover half of the arched entrance, but the room feels comfortable and secluded nonetheless.

Evandur and Douglas take seats on either side of the table. They do not speak, but pass the time watching the dancing flames of their God.

After ten minutes, an elderly servant enters bearing a silver dish. Upon the platter is cheese, fresh bread, meats, smoked fish, grapes and other fruits, and two large glasses of aromatic red wine.

The servant places the platter on the table and stands patiently.

Evandur smiles at him and nods. The older man departs with a bow.

They enjoy the platter while they wait for someone to summon them. The food is all of exquisite quality. The meat is cooked to perfection and seasoned with exotic southern spice, the grapes are fresh, which must be thanks to a greenhouse or magic, and the wine is aged and was clearly not bought for a small sum.

Nearly half an hour passes. A different servant, this time a young woman, comes to the sitting room. "General Langford is able to see you now," she says. "He is upstairs and bids me to take you to him."

"We are ready, thank you," Evandur says, rising to his feet. He sets his nearly empty glass back on the tray. Douglas does the same.

The woman leads them back around the hall to the main entrance. From there she takes them up the stairway, which opens to a nearly identical hallway that wraps around the second storey in the same gentle arc. The servant woman brings them to the right, into the other side of the building. After some minutes of navigating, taking turns that lead further into the surprisingly sprawling building, the trio arrives in a smaller hall where many white doors branch to bedrooms, studies, and meeting chambers. The hall is lit by several candles, but the light does not reach the end.

The woman stops at a door marked by a golden plaque that reads 'Olar's Hall.' She knocks upon the wood.

"Enter!" comes a gruff voice in response.

The handle turns. The door is pushed open. Inside is a room larger than

Evandur or Douglas expected to see. It is rectangular, and lit by a low handing chandelier made of copper. The fixture hangs from the flat ceiling, and is suspended over a dark, circular table. Here the floor is made of thick cedar wood, lighter than stone, but heavy enough to support the weight of the table and its twelve chairs.

On one side of the table sits a stern looking man. He is bald, and a scar runs from his forehead to his jaw on the left side of his face. His eyes are a deep brown, but seem even darker in the steady flicker of the candles on the chandelier.

Across from him are two seated figures. They are covered in full suits of plate armour that is painted black. Their cuirasses, pauldrons, and the shields that lay beside them all bear no markings that Evandur can make out.

"Enter," the gruff voice repeats, coming from the mouth of the bald man. Evandur and Douglas realize they have stopped in the doorway, and shake off whatever feeling possessed them. They step into the room. "Have a seat, we were just finishing here."

The two armoured figures rise and bow slightly. They take their shields and turn to leave. They brush by Evandur as he enters, and it sends a shiver running up his spine. Once they are gone, Evandur and Douglas take the seats that were just made vacant. The paladin notes that his chair feels colder than the air in the room.

"I have been told that you are sent from the Church of Valkronus," the general says. His eyes seem to be aimed like arrows at the pair, though they rarely leave Evandur's.

"Yes," Evandur says, "I am to join the mission in The South. This is my squire, Douglas, who will accompany me, with your leave."

"You may bring who you trust," the general says, glancing briefly at the squire, "just so long as your pets remain in line." His words spark a sudden anger in Evandur, but he keeps composure.

"There will be no problems on my end. I am only here to find when and where we depart."

"I am riding to Kognear on the last of the month. From there I will be boarding an airship bound in secrecy to our location. You will join me on this trip, as will the others sent by the churches. Or, if you must, I can arrange for a ship to take you at a later date."

"We will be fit to ride on the last of Renewal. I would prefer to arrive and begin as soon as can. If I am to be of any help in training soldiers, then I would like to have as much time as I can with them."

"So be it," the general mutters. "You seem able and intelligent. I am thankful to have you on board. Meet me back here the day before we leave, as we will be setting off early in the morning. Make sure you have whomever and whatever you need ready and packed."

"Understood," Evandur responds. "Thank you, General Langford." He says the words as he stands, but there is no emotion to his tone.

Chapter Fourteen - All Banners Flying South

3E056, 19th of Renewal

Far south, in Krunix, Roger and his companions are summoned from their new chambers in the Velvet Hall. An elvish man with nearly snow-white skin and straight, black hair knocks on their door. Each room has three beds, which are draped in purple blankets and black sheets. Not much else fills the dorms of the lower-ranking order members. Roger, Helena, and Jitz have been sharing a room for the past month. They have been extremely low on coin, but have been able to eat for free in the Order Hall. They have also undergone some training sessions with various instructors and adventurers who have returned from some expeditions.

Now, they are met by this servant, whose past has remained a mystery to them. They have seem him before. He is clearly respected, as he oversees much of the order's business.

"I do not believe we are introduced officially. I am Avaciir. Master Firemark has requested to see you and your companions," he tells them in a monotonous voice. He has a clean face, and his hair shines in the morning light. His eyes view them with an odd sense of certainty, as though he knows them well.

"Do you know what for?" Jitz asks, grabbing her new, iron staff.

"I believe that your request to venture to the desert may have been approved," the elven man says.

They stand in silent shock. They had asked for leave to venture to the Great Estrand Desert to help partake in the exploration of the ruins as soon as their membership was approved. They asked on the fourth of Renewal.

"What changed?" Roger asks.

"I do not know," Avaciir responds. "I know Master Firemark rather well, however, and he did seem to be in deep thought. Something recent must have occurred."

"We shall find him, then," Helena says before the others can shoot more questions. "Thank you."

Avaciir nods and departs. He turns down a long hall and heads for the stairs that follow the outer wall of the building. That man is of the race from the Lowerlands, Krulaeji, the deep-elves and their slaves. That is certain from a simple glance at him, but who he is and what he has seen is wreathed in fog.

Roger pulls his hair behind his ears and pins it down with a black, wide-brimmed hat. Helena was dressed already, so she ventures ten feet down the hall to gather the other two members of their new guild. They quickly dress in their cleanest clothing and meet in front of Roger's room.

The passage that runs by their chambers wraps around the outer wall of the Order House, and runs to stairs on either end, both near the main entrance, that lead to the second floor. They follow the hallway leftward and, after a few minutes, they are climbing up. This storey houses more elite members, and deeper into the centre of the building there are studies, libraries, and even alcoves from which people can watch the interior training ground below. Roger and the others turn, however, and climb the next flight of steps. They rise to the third, and then the fourth level. They venture down the circular hall, then turn leftward, then right, and then finally they reach the thick, steel, double doors bearing the engraving: 'Firemark.'

Roger lifts the knocker on the left-hand door. Before he drops it, a voice comes from inside, which beckons, "You are expected." The doors are then pulled open by an unseen force.

Firemark's office space is deceivingly large. The main portion of the room is dedicated simply to the elvish man's desk and large chair. There are several cabinets on either side of the desk, and two chairs stand on the opposite side from his own. The chamber is lit by four floating white lights that sit in place, one in each corner. Upon first glance that is all one would see. Hidden, though, nearly seamlessly against the back wall is a secret door that leads deep into vaults behind the room.

Roger and Helena are the only two of their group to have seen it used, and only recently. If they had not witnessed Master Firemark use this door firsthand, then they would likely have never noticed it at all against the otherwise smooth, light wooded wall.

Now the golden-skinned elf sits calmly in his chair. His white hair is tied in a bun atop his head, and his smoldering red eyes glance up only briefly from a small stack of metal disks in front of him.

"There is no room for you all to sit, but I am in the middle of something important, and I cannot spare time to change rooms," he explains as his summons file awkwardly into his office. He waits patiently for them settle before he continues. "I have looked through the applications from adventurers wanting to be sent south to the desert and, while there are many, I have selected you."

Roger speaks next. He says, "I am happy to hear this, but I must ask why? Initially you told us we would have to wait for a different assignment."

"And I thought that would be the case. I spoke no lies," Firemark responds. "Apparently there are some new large sections of the Dusk Knight Ruins that were uncovered in the past few weeks. At the same time, we have had a call for powerful mages and their companions to head to Vruyoth for a secret matter. We are suddenly limited in our ranks by this. This is an offer that I am only making once, and you must decide quickly before I pick some other, less deserving group."

"We are willing to depart tomorrow," Helena answers.

"Very well," Firemark tells them. "Please take these medallions. They signify that you are on an assignment for us. You will travel with two other guilds that will leave tomorrow at noon. Hopefully the townships of Raeborg and Taernsby will arrive to fill in the final gaps within the month or two following your arrival. There is still much to uncover there, I feel." As he speaks he takes the disks from his desk. They are made of shining grey metal that glitters in the light. He hands one to each of Roger's party. The disks are attached to a silver chain and, despite their large size, they weigh very little.

"Thank you Master Firemark," Roger says, bowing in appreciation.

"You are free to leave. I will have arrangements made for wagons, food, and water. If there is anything else that you would like requisitioned, please tell Avaciir," Firemark explains. "The conditions for the contract, that you accept by leaving this office with the medallions, are that any valuables including, but not limited to: precious metals, gems, jewelry, and books, be turned over to the Velvet Compass for processing." He takes a breath. "In return you shall receive a base payment of two hundred gold coins each, in addition to fifty percent of the monetary value of any goods uncovered in the ruins and surrounding area."

"Understood, sir," Roger responds, bowing again.

They take their leave in a mixture of excitement and worry. They return to the first floor, but not to their rooms. Instead they opt to head further into the hall, to the cafeteria. They sit for some time, discussing anything they might wish to rent from the order. The excitement finally begins to subside and hunger moves in to replace it.

They take beans and strips of cooked hog to their table and eat it quickly. It is fresh and hot. Azgul Hold has not yet failed to impress them with the quality of its goods. Despite being located in the side of a mountain, being so far from the coast, and using the surrounding lands almost exclusively for agriculture, all trade is of exquisite quality, and all of the goods manufactured in the town are done be what seems to be the most talented craftsmen in the known world. All of this is only amplified by the limited palettes and experiences of the small-town adventurers.

They finish their meal quickly. Another miracle they seem to have uncovered in the Krunixian capital is the wonders of coffee. Coffee is mainly grown on Streboya and in The South. It is available in many towns in the Dabarisian Empire and in Krunix, but it is especially a pride of the dwarves. The coffee of Azgul Hold is a bitter and unique experience. The brewing guilds take the coffee cherries, grind them into a fine dust, and pack it into long, funnel shaped bowls. These are suspended above a counter, or even the floor, by a metal apparatus. Cool spring water is then dripped slowly through the tight mix of grounds. By the time the water finally passes through the bottom filter and into a glass, it is a dark brown, and full of energy.

They each take a glass of this, thanking the gnome behind the machine profusely.

They scramble to write a list of any specific goods they think they will need on the journey while they drink their coffees. When they are done, they track down Avaciir and give him the list. He nods and places it in a leather folder in his side-bag.

They spend the rest of the day packing and preparing their horses for the trek. They fill their travel packs with whatever think they will need daily, and leave the rest to sit in the wagon.

By the time the next morning arrives, they feel ready to leave. Excitement and anxiety both gnaw at them as they load boxes of food, and barrels of water and mead into the back of their large, covered wagon. They hitch four of their horses to the vehicle. Roger takes the lead on his own horse as the others clamber into the covered cart.

The wagon is also packed with blankets, pillows, hay, lumber, and a variety of other gear which ranges from rope to torches to climbing axes. They meet by the rest of their caravan in the lower square. Two guilds are waiting, both of which have been adventuring far longer than Roger's brand-new one. They both raise large banners, each taking to the breeze and unfurling. One is a clean white, the other is a deep lilac. 'The Knights of Jallor', and 'Storm Corps', with ten and six members respectively. The Knights of Jallor's symbol is that of a closed helm with a sword rising behind it, which reminds Roger of Voss Hallehwell. The Storm Corps' is a flash of lightening striking a dead tree. This seems ominous at first, but it is their leader who smiles and waves to Roger and his friends.

Roger then opens his own banner and, taking the pole from their wagon, holds it high above his head. A vermillion cloth flaps into the wind, uncovering the image of a slain, headless giant who lies face down. Upon its back stands a man wielding an axe.

"*Bigger They Are*," Roger proclaims, "at your service."

The leader of the knights nods and turns her horse. "We set off now, then!" she says audibly, and she spurs her horse.

The first leg of the journey takes them over the Wassterbrig, which passes over the Krunixian River on the road to Marsh Hold. They turn long before they reach that town, however, branching at the Triangle Gardens towards Wylamburd. There they restock on water and extra provisions, then continue.

From Wylamburd they ride quickly to Dragon's Rest. This is a town on the border of the Council Lands, and the last place where they will see civilization until the tent city in the desert. The landscape has slowly changed as well, becoming increasingly dry. Groves start to grow further apart, and the trees that make them are wiry and more sparse. The grass has wilted from the vibrant green of Krunix and The North into a struggling brown.

    The caravan halts at the edge of town, and they rest there for some nights. Already over two weeks have elapsed since they left Azgul Hold. The wagon's wheels will make it around the tall hills of the plains, but once they reach the desert they will still have a day or more of travel, and the wheels will be hard-pressed in the sands. There is little to be done, of course, as they are not going to leave their horses and wagons in Dragon's Rest, and so they set off again. The rest of the journey is not as difficult as they thought it would be. One of the axles breaks on one of the two Storm Corps wagons, but Roger and one of the knights help to repair the damage and only several hours are lost.

    Finally, on the sixteenth of Celabra, they come over a large hill and, ahead — maybe a day's travel — they see the sprawling mess of tangled dunes that stretch forever into the horizon. It is breathtaking for those who have not yet laid eyes here. The heat has been growing steadily now for many days and, as the sun rises far above the caravan, sweat beads on the foreheads of them all, even the many who ride in the shade of the wagons.

    They camp that night in the dying plains, at the border of the desert. In the morning they affix new wheels that are unused. They take out planks of wood as well. When the wheels begin to sink into the sand, they wedge the wooden beams underneath and build temporary tracks. It is grueling, and for the next two days they travel only from dawn until before midday. Then they rest and resume as the sun wanes. Near the evening on the nineteenth, they finally find themselves crawling over the dunes that overlook the camp, an array of white and purple tents rising from the sands, roughly an hour away.

* * * * *

    Far north, before Roger had even set off, Voss, Emari, and Boe return to the township of Taernsby. In the late morning of the nineteenth of Renewal they ride through the gates, after having stayed the night before last once more in the Aldshire Inn, and then the most recent night in the East Air. The trio does not plan on stopping long in town, so they make the most of the day. Before noon comes, they report to Mayor Brenspire and he listens with a stern expression. In the end he pays them a small sum for their efforts and agrees to send a military fortification to Highfell to relieve the injured township.

The mayor then informs them that a group of kobolds was taken prisoner by the watch not too long ago. They had marched into town stating that they were royal messengers and were seeking a man named Hallehwell. Voss agrees to speak with them.

They also take papers from him that will allow them to work as temporary members of the Velvet Compass while on the expedition to the desert. The mayor tells them of the new location where the elvish man, who initially informed them of Highfell's predicament, is staying. Harold Brenspire bids them good luck and fortune, and they set our from his manor.

They seek the elf near the docks. He is staying in a small, seaside inn where traders and sailors often go for drinks and games. It is a rowdy pub, but it is warm and clean. They find the man dressed in brown and green, with his blonde locks tied back in a bun. He smiles, recognizing them.

Emari once again recounts their experience in Highfell and, while the elf's face falls at many points, in the end he seems gladdened by their actions. He pays them each eighty golden lions, plus a good sum of silver and copper shillings, which equals about one hundred gold in value. He also gives to Emari a small wooden boat. It appears to be a very intricately carved model.

"This coin was most of what I got from my family's business, but I do not plan on returning home yet, I think," he tells them. "I think I want to travel, for awhile, and be away from there. This boat that I give you was made by my grandfather, who would travel up the Highwater River as a trader. I've never been on a boat in my life, though, even a small one."

"Well this certainly is a small one," Emari tells him.

The man laughs. "When you speak the elvish word for 'rowboat' or 'longboat', the ship will grow to the full size of either. When you speak 'model' it will shrink again. Don't try it indoors, though," he says, chuckling again. "But truly, you have done a great service to my town and you have made me feel a better man for leaving. I wish to compensate you for that. Maybe your travels will one day take you to where this is useful."

"Thank you kindly, sir," Emari responds warmly.

After this, they venture back to the East Air, and rent two rooms again.

They meet Brael by chance while he is having his lunch. They sit with him, and recount their tale of tracking and encountering Voran Eralius again to the deaf half-elf over bread and meats. Brael watches their mouths and gestures with interest, and sees their words form through their use of magic in his mind. The hunter tells them some of his personal studies into the orcish tribes of the swamps. He explains how he intends to pursue knowledge of the areas he travels, and eventually publish his writings if he deems them well-crafted enough. He then tells the others that he saw Peren, and was told that the nobleman was intending to seek an airship southward, and that he left just under a week ago.

Brael expresses that he is ready to set out with them on their next journey, if they would still like his company. Emari is not opposed, and neither is Boe. Voss is surprisingly welcoming, stating that he would appreciate a good tracker and bowman in the group again. After the conversation, Voss slinks off to have his armour polished and his axe sharpened. The rest of the day is spent making small purchases, restocking their supplies, and grooming and outfitting their horses, which Emari and Brael must purchase.

Voss goes then to the prison under the main Taernsby barracks. It a damp and cool place, where water drips from the ceilings. It is not nearly the worst prison that Voss has seen though. Torches provide light, and there are bedrolls provided for the prisoners.

There are four kobolds sitting in one of the twelve cells. Voss struggles to communicate through their vague grasp of the common-tongue. He asks them to explain themselves, and they do. They state that their king has made a decision that requires Voss' presence. Voss tells them that he will set them free if they agree to bring the king to the roadside the morning of tomorrow. They understand and agree.

Voss then convinces the guards to let the kobolds out and escort them out of town. The guards, who know Voss and his group by this point, begrudgingly agree.

Finally, as night sets in, Voss, Emari, Boe, and Brael find restful sleep once more at the East Air Inn and Tavern. They wake ready and excited to be on the road. As they ride through the west gate, Voss veers off towards the mayor's manor, reassuring the others that he will not be long. He gives a sealed envelope to Mayor Brenspire.

"Would you mail this for me with the utmost secrecy?" Voss asks him.

The mayor nods. "And without question, after all you have done for me."

"I thank you, Magistrate Brenspire."

The mayor sends the letter that same day, on a ship bound for 51 Silver Street, City of Krosa, Streboya. It reads:

Vaeus Fairwind-Hallehwell,

I received word from your mother, telling me that I had a son. She asked me if I would look after you, but I fear that my life is not one for a young boy to be part of.

This world is a dangerous place, especially for a child with no home, so I urge you to seek out Neihmen Rheisteim. He is the brother of a man named Nhasan, who I fought alongside during the war. Tell him that you are the son of Voss Hallehwell, and that I sent you to him. He will take you in, and he will train you.

During my time in this world, I have learned several things. One, is that if you want something done well, then you do it yourself. Do not be afraid to fight for what you believe in. If you can justify your actions to yourself, then you do not need to justify them to anyone else. Sometimes in life you make a wrong decision, a misstep. Even the smallest mistake can cost you, it may bring a lifetime of unnecessary pain, but remember this: to stand against pain is the truest show of one's personal strength. Pain has the most excellent quality. If it is prolonged, it cannot be severe, and if it is severe, if cannot be prolonged. If you encounter pain in life, in any form, try to find a balance to it, and that may help you.

I hope that you do not make the same decisions that I made, for they have lead me down a treacherous path. This path, I do not know yet myself. Not where it leads, nor where is passes through.

Try to keep good in your heart. That is something which not many people have these days. The world needs better people than myself, and even those around me, if it is to recover from all the wrongs it has experienced.

Try to save what's left.

You father,

Voss Hallehwell.

Chapter Fifteen - The Coming Storm

3E056, 20th of Renewal

As the group from Taernsby sets off, Voss prepares for a meeting with Scazgix of Scazgixia. It is near half an hour before the small caravan sees the contingent of draconic men and women waiting patiently by the side of the road. Two rough looking tents have been erected, and smoke rises from one.

When the horses reach the outskirts of the makeshift camp, a detachment is sent to meet them. The seven draconic figures meet the travelers and declare to Boe that the king requests their presence. They agree politely to the meeting and follow the small creatures to the larger of the two tents.

There they dismount and are walked inside to see the great King Scazgix seated atop two loyal kobolds acting as a chair.

"Welcome!" the king says in the standard-tongue, stepping down from his seat.

"Greetings, king!" Emari says. She kneels. The others reluctantly follow suit.

"I glad you agree to meet."

"We are glad to be asked for," Emari tells him kindly.

"You are go on journey?" the king asks.

"Yes," Voss responds, "we are going far south."

"Excellent," Scazgix speaks, "I come with." The statement knocks the others into shock. No one speaks for some time, so the king continues, saying, "I have thought about kingdom. You have shown that my lands are small, and that world is big. I want to see it, to learn."

"My king," Emari says, "I do not believe that it is safe beyond your borders for you."

"I am warrior," Scazgix retorts. "I will be safe. I travel with you, and I take care of self."

"If you help set up camp and hunt, you are welcomed," Voss tells him.

"What?" Emari hisses quietly.

"I wish for their continued alliance with us," Voss replies, using Valindra as a messenger.

And so it is that Scazgix takes leave of his kingdom, placing his son, Scazgix the Fourth in charge in his absence. The group from Taernsby has no extra horse, but he rides with Boe until they can buy a sickly pony for him at Eavat.

The journey is certainly a tiresome one, and Brael is a welcome addition to the group once again. He spends a large portion of every evening hunting as the others set up camp. The nights in the Kognear Tunnel are especially interesting to their newest, underground-dwelling companion, but they do not spend long there. As they continue their trip, the weather begins to grow warmer, and the sky clears . Within the great tunnel it is stiflingly hot. A respite comes when they emerge into Krunix. A gate guard recognizes them at the walls of Kognear City, and treats them to dinner. They stay the night and the next day in the city to recover from their hard ride. They set out at a fast pace, after this brief rest, once more.

It is in Kognear that Voss first begins to grow uneasy. Restlessness is not an uncommon trait of his to begin with, of course, but this is something new altogether. He finds difficulty sleeping. Every time his mind begins to rest, he is met by horrific and vivid dreams. He tells no one of this, but the ghosts in his mind see them nonetheless, and they seem to agree that they are, in fact, visions.

The first dream, that occurs in the inn in Kognear, shows a great cloud in the sky, crackling with red lightning. Voss also hears a great drumming. It is nearly indistinguishable from the torrent of wind and rain that begins to beat down upon the earth as the cloud passes over him.

When Voss wakes from this, he finds that he is still comfortable in bed, in the Gong Inn. His body feels wet, which at first he believes is from the rain, but it is only sweat.

The travel continues without any change. A week later, on the night of the eleventh of Celebra, as the party is riding through the mountain road from Lo'Dorra to Azgul Hold, the next nightmare strikes Voss. The scene is similar to the first. Voss is lying naked on his back, and above him is a great could, rolling with thunder and flashes of red light. From deep within the cloud, between the crackles of electric energy, Voss sees two points of white light glowing constantly. They begin softly, but they grow brighter and more prominent the longer he watches them.

It seems as though the thunder changes tones too, booming deeper at certain times, and then more gently at others. Always there comes a great torrent of rain, forcing him to sputter and gasp for each breath of air.

With a sudden boom, Voss Hallehwell realizes two things. The two points of light disappear, for as long as someone would blink and, when they return, he feels them staring at him. He realizes then, that they must be eyes and, for that paralyzing moment, that they can see him, lying helpless on the cold ground.

With a deafening burst of energy, the cloud volleys hundreds of bolts of energy towards him, and he feels pain surge through his entire being.

He wakes from this drenched in sweat and shivering inside his small tent. A draught is blowing through the open flaps, and it is still the dead of night. Voss leaps from his his tent. He is unclothed and uncovered. He looks wildly around the campsite. The fire has smoldered to ashes, and the horses graze calmly nearby. The area looks undisturbed, but Voss always pins his tent closed.

It isn't until two days later that each traveler, aside from Scazgix, finds a single metal card in their coin purses. Each card is identical, engraved with a symbol of three claw marks moving from top-right to bottom-left. They are coloured blood-red. It is the symbol of The Wight's Call. Nothing from their packs or coin purses is stolen, which is quite possibly the most disturbing part of the situation.

Emari quickly connects the cards to the one left by Voran in Highfell, and when Voss holds that card to the others, the resemblance is clear. The metal cards are the same shape and size, but with different carvings on their surfaces. It cannot be dismissed as coincidence and, for the weeks of riding afterward, they post a constant watch.

Finally, they arrive in the safety of Azgul Hold. Once again, the size and energy of the city takes hold of them and they are astounded by the palpable nature of it all. They have little time to explore, though, and stay in an inn near the heart of the capital, having arrived late in the evening of the fifteenth of Celabra. That night is one of the four celebrations after which the month is named. The travelers from Taernsby drink until almost sunlight. In the afternoon of the sixteenth they approach the order hall of the Velvet Compass.

The hall stands in one of the northernmost areas of the city. The main face of the great structure looks westward, over the enormous dwarven and gnomish capital, and the rolling hills of the Krunixian lowlands beyond the walls. The house is four storeys in height, and the inner keep is the same, but the tower that rises from it resides far above the highest church tower in the city and any of the guild halls around it. The house stretches out from the tower in a wide and long rectangular arm. Windows line the great hall, stained in the purple hue of the order. The roof slopes up in an A-frame that is polished in the same colour, shining with the rest of the red-gold city.

Simply walking towards the building instills a sense of just how many resources the order must possess.

People throw odd looks toward the group as they pass through on horseback with a kobold in tow. For the most part they are given space, but guards keep their hands clenched around their pikes and crossbows as they watch the visitors.

Voss thrusts open the doors. The bright light of the spring sun throws itself onto the purple carpet of the order's entrance hall. At the end of the long room are two figures. They are robed in the same violet as the floors and the banners on the walls. The people stand guard on either side of a massive golden door. The large space between the visitors and the guards is populated by several benches, many tables and chairs for meetings and lunches, large candle holders that light the walls between the banners, and a circular basin in the centre that looks to be full of wine or some other deep red liquid. This is the part of the order's complex that is used by outsiders, the large, circular keep-tower is only for members and, in the lower levels, special dignitaries.

The Taernsby party enters the building. Brael lets the doors drift shut behind them. It does not make a noise, despite the weathered look of the brown wood. As soon as the outside is closed off and the doors rejoin the stonework of the outer wall, the two figures look up.

The visitors approach, crossing through the silence of the hall toward the golden door. When they are still two dozen feet from the pair, the guard on the left speaks. She is a young, human woman. Her hair is tied behind her head so that its dark strands are mostly concealed by her hood. "Welcome to the Velvet Compass," she says.

"We seek the order master, or one who can review our papers from Taernsby," Emari says. "This is in relation to the expedition in the Great Estrand Desert."

The woman responds to her, saying, "Master Kalissa is the only order master in the hall tonight, though Firemark should be returning from a trip to Raeborg within the week." Neither of the guards seems to care about the strange group before them.

"We shall see Master Kalissa, then, if that is permitted," Emari replies.

The woman reaches into her robes around her neck and produces a small, shimmering, silver whistle. She blows into it, and it produces the sound of wind chimes that echo through the hall, and seem to drift upward toward the high ceiling. After only a brief moment, an elven man with incredibly fair skin and black hair enters through a side corridor that was nearly hidden in the darkness of the back-right corner beside the main doors, and begins to move around the keep.

"Avaciir, take these guests to Master Kalissa," the other door-guard says. He is a human man, whose head is shaved bald.

"Of course," the snow-skinned man says, and bows low.

Brael has grown very rigid at the sight of this man. The elf's ears are long and pointed, even more so than the denizens of Vruyoth or Streboya. Emari looks to Brael, and projects a question into his mind.

Brael whispers as they approach further, saying, "This is a member of the Krulaeji race. They were the elves who forsook Stren's light and sought to live underground, away from it, in the ages before history."

"I thought you hated Vruyothy elves for what they did to you. Why would you also hate their enemies?" Voss questions, overhearing, and using Torkurth as a messenger.

"They are traitors older than my own kin," Brael says. "Their treachery has long been carved into our stories. That, and all elves are cruel. We will speak later of this," he finishes as they near the man.

"Greetings," the Krulaeji speaks. "I am Avaciir. Please follow me upstairs. I will take you to Kalissa, who will be expecting you."

They follow willingly, though Brael keeps one hand resting on his left dagger, in its sheath on his belt. Avaciir leads them back along the side passage, through three thick, metal doors. The passage soon meets a thin stairwell that winds up many flights. As they climb, they grow aware of the intricacy of the craftsmanship that the building possesses. The stairs are all level and, despite their decades of age, they have remained smooth and untarnished by wear. The walls are thick, and covered with tapestries of the same grey tone threaded with black images of the order's founders and prominent members. The stair-hall is wide enough to accommodate two single-file lines of traffic. It is located between the outer wall and the interior chambers of the keep. The inner wall is just as strong as the outer one, with massive stone bricks blocking the stairs from the inner workings of the order. No doors seem to branch off from the path until they finally arrive at the third floor.

As they reach the top of the stairs, Avaciir unlocks a large metal door after producing a heavily populated, copper key-ring. Through the door they find themselves in a barracks area. As they pass through the finely furnished chamber they see more robed figures. They appear to be servants of sorts, all dressed in purple. They are resting for the most part, though one appears to be adjusting scaled armour under his robes. They are not so ill equipped or trained as Voss and the others had initially believed.

They exit the barracks area through another metal door and walk into a wide hallway. Avaciir doubles back and leads them up yet another flight of stairs that lies just through an archway on the left, set in the inner wall. An iron gate can be seen protruding slightly from the top of the open arch, made of thick, crossed poles.

Up they climb. These stairs have the same violet carpet as the entrance hall running down the steps, and runs around the circular keep in at a gentle incline. As they climb they realize that the spiral is moving them further into the building. The fourth storey is located nearly within the roof, and is smaller than the other floors, being reserved only for the order masters and the elite members that are integral to the function of the hall. The only area above them now is the tower itself, which is only used as an arcane study for individuals with permission to use it.

They reach the top of the stairs and walk through another open, gated arch into a long and wide hallway. At the end, a great metal door bars the way into the keep's vaults. Before this, on the inner wall, they pass many smaller doors bearing plaques made from a variety of metals that seem to be indicative of status. Just before the vaults, at the far end of the circular hallway from the entrance, they stop. Avaciir stands at a door. Upon this, a gleaming silver plaque is embedded. He knocks once, before the door whipped open inward.

Inside the room is a spacious chamber with very little furniture. A circle is painted onto the floor with runes written around the outside in four distinct rows. Sitting cross-legged inside of this circle is a dwarven woman. She is hovering nearly a foot above the wood, and around her are floating books that sit level with her head.

Her eyes are closed, but all who enter feel her sight.

"Welcome. You come from Taernsby, yes?" she asks.

"We do," Voss says. "Are you Master Kalissa?"

"I am. Now that we have eliminated the redundant questions, let us see to the business at hand." Kalissa's eyes open, and she gently descends to the floor along with her books. She stands and gestures to shelves on either side of the room. A folder flies from one and two quills, both soaked in ink, whip from the other. "There are some basic formalities, contracts that bind you to working for the Velvet Compass on this mission. Signing them says that you will pay one hundred percent of any damages dealt to order property on the mission, and that we will pay you a flat seven hundred fifty gold on top of whatever treasure you obtain, should there be any."

"Are there any insights into treasure?" Boe asks curiously.

"Rumour is that many guilds and groups have become quite wealthy from this expedition," Kalissa says, smiling. "I cannot offer further speculation, but the chances are seemingly high." She grabs the folder from the air and holds it forward.

Voss takes it, and replaces it with the papers they were given by Mayor Brenspire. She hands him one of the pens, flips the bindings of the folder open, and points to a box at the bottom of the first page. He signs his name clearly in the box. Emari signs 'Chablisienne Authei', Boe and Brael both sign, and Scazgix does not.

"Your kobold friend is not with your group?" Kalissa asks.

"He is a friend, not a partner," Voss responds.

Kalissa makes a note on one of the papers while nodding. She takes the folder, and writes 'Taernsby' at the top before signing her own name. She removes the sheet of parchment from the folder, closes it again, and places the signed page with the documents that Voss gave her. The folder flies back to its place, and a new one appears from beside it. She seals the documents within it and returns that and the pens.

"Excellent," she speaks at last, breaking the silence. "You may write to Avaciir or another gold-ranking servant about any requests for equipment. Food and water and drink will be provided to get you at least as far as Dragon's Rest. If you need horses or wagons, armours, weapons, or other common items, you are free to borrow them. Ammunition must be purchased, and any repair will be deducted from your final payment. Other than this, like I said, anything that can be lent, will be lent. You are acting as temporary order members, of full standing, and you will be treated as such. So, welcome home, for the time being." She smiles again. It is warm and kind.

At some point, the elf must have left the group, as Avaciir is no longer behind them. The visitors return to the outer hallway, leaving Master Kalissa to her business with many thanks.

They decide, next, to have lunch. Hunger had not taken hold of them with the remnants of ale in their stomachs and the stress of pushing ever forward, but now it seems as though they are all on the brink of starvation.

They find the mess hall in the first floor of the keep. It is a large room with many tables and many faces enjoying meals. They grab plates of warm potatoes and beef, and take tankards of fresh stream water instead of any of the fine ales that are offered.

They sit. Voss removes his helmet, but covers his head in a dark cowl, pulled from the back of his scale armour.

When they have been sitting for around fifteen minutes, Avaciir reappears, standing near their table. This causes Brael a great deal of discomfort.

"Is there anything out of the ordinary that you would like prepared?" he asks. "It is best for you to set out within the next few days, and so work should begin immediately to facilitate that."

"We have our own horses, but a small wagon for bedding, food, and drink would be appreciated," Emari tells him.

"Of course." Avaciir nods.

"I would like a suit of plate armour to be lent to me," Voss says.

Avaciir appears pensive. "I will see to it," he states. "You may be called upon for measurements within the next few hours. Do not leave the hall until we speak again if possible."

"Understood," Voss says, returning to his beef and potatoes.

The others have a few requests, including two quivers of arrows for Brael and a variety of herbs for Boe, which they both agree to pay for at market price. Soon, Avaciir has a list half a page in length, and he bids the group farewell as he strides across the room towards a large wooden door on the north wall, leading to the crafters section of the keep.

Minutes turn to hours. Emari suggests they claim a room. Even though they are not short on coin, it is still more pragmatic to spare every piece of gold they can. They talk to one of the servants and are shown to empty quarters, free of charge. They settle in, unpacking some of their belongings even though they only plan to stay one or two nights. Their horses are well taken care of by Velvet Compass stable hands.

Voss is called upon close to evening, and leaves the others for near an hour to be measured. They tell the soldier that they have chest plating, greaves, and gauntlets that should fit him near-perfectly, but they will need to stay two nights for the manufacturing of a helm, pauldrons, and the rest.

"Do not worry with a helm. Mine is fine," Voss tells the crafters. "Have everything ready by the morning of the eighteenth if possible."

"We will see to it, master Hallehwell," responds the smith. He then gives a series of instructions to a human man and a young dwarf, who rush off to the market for steel.

The next day passes much the same. A covered wagon is prepared and chefs and the culinary guilds prepare a variety of dried meats, cheeses, fresh breads, water and wine to be loaded for the trip. Brael is given quivers of arrows, and Boe receives a new bag of smoking weed, an assortment of jars with the herbs he requested, and some salves as well.

They eat excellently in the cafeteria. Pastas, sandwiches, fish, and many roasted vegetables are just some of the options that the visitors have a chance to enjoy.

In the late afternoon of the seventeenth, the smiths call for Voss to be outfitted. The armour is of good craft. It is not as pristine as the armouries of the main city, but it fits well enough and is sturdy. They explain the last minute adjustments they will make in the evening, and Voss gives them thanks.

Finally, on the morning of the eighteenth of Celabra, they repack their horses with extra foods and clothing, reorganize the bedding and tents in the wagon, hitch Sir Whore and Rosebud to the tongue, and set off. No banner is flown over their caravan, but a long silk tapestry bearing the violet colour and golden eye of the Velvet Compass is hung over the wagon cover and pinned in place.

They ride through the main streets of Azgul Hold. People give them way and look both in wonder and annoyance as the party rolls by and Scazgix waves cheerfully from the back. Soon they are back into the countryside, passing through smaller hamlets and villages, and by distant farmsteads surrounded by sprawling fields of of wheat, beans, and berry bushes.

A breeze crashes down upon the lands from the Voiceless Peaks behind them as they ride from the city. It brings back a brief feeling of winter, but soon they are days from the capital and the mountains, and are enveloped in spring air. In a week, they pass through the small town of Ashcrest, which hugs the Suedarbrig bank of the Krunixian River. For a few days after, they are rolling down a small horse trail that runs, unmarked, from the Suedarbrig to Dragon's Rest.

All the time Voss' visions persist. He sees the same storm repeated each night. Every new dream, it appears more violent, more angry. Voss tries to understand it, but he cannot. The only things that change are the colours and the rumbling. Sometimes the lightning crackles a deep red, sometimes it is a brilliant white, and sometimes, perhaps most horrifically, it is a pale, ghostly-blue. The rumblings seem to be speaking. Voss grows more and more certain of this, but he can never discern the words, or perhaps the language.

On the eighth of Sowwing they stop in Dragon's Rest to resupply and gather some civilized interaction with the townsfolk. The town has grown fond of, and used to, travelers bringing news and stories from the world to the north. They partake in a free round of beers at the local alehouse, but they do not stop for more than one night.

A week and several days pass before they reach the desert, after rolling treacherously over many kilometers of rolling, grassy hills. It grows so hot that Voss loads his armour into the wagon, and instead wraps his cloak around his head and body to conceal himself. As the grass fades, it becomes impossible to believe that the desert does not roll impossibly far into the distance, and the sand makes any movement much more difficult, but they press on. They camp for the night of the sixteenth just within the desert sands, and prepare for another full day of struggling through the dunes, dotted with small patches of struggling grass and cacti.

Voss dreams this night. It seems the same as ever, but this time there is no rumbling. Black clouds surround him on all sides, but he feels strangely calm. He hears distant crackles of lighting, but sees no light. Slowly, voices begin to reveal themselves. They speak with ancient power, and each word threatens to tear Voss' soul apart, but, for once, he understands them.

"Your goals are too small," says one. His booming words take the tone of the thunder Voss has come so used to hearing.

"My goals are to set things right. To make order for your plans to come," speaks another. This one is less powerful, and sounds hollow. There is deceit on its tongue, and the sentence evokes red energy that floods Voss' vision.

"Your goals should be the ones that I set for you, and none other!" says the first, and now white lightning breaks through the red.

Blue lightning cuts through the rest, and all fall silent. Then, Voss feels his lips move. He does not choose the words, and they do not come in his own voice. He speaks in a voice that fills him with dread and fear, saying only, "We are being watched."

Once again, Voss feels eyes on him. The rumble of thunder begins again, deafening him.

He jolts awake. He is shivering, and when he steps from his tent into the cool air of the Great Estrand Desert, he sees a crackle of white lightning far behind them, where Dragon's Rest must lie. They have outpaced a spring storm, so it would seem. Voss tries to shake the feeling that this flash means anything more than a change of weather. When his sheen of sweat begins to turn cold, he returns to his tent.

In the morning, they pack up and carry on. Voss says nothing. Somehow he feels as though the dreams will abandon him from here on out. Something has changed, and his mind has grown dark with thoughts beyond his own comprehension. He knew the voice with which he spoke in the last vision. He has heard it before, and he will never be able to forget it. Emari notices him shivering throughout their journey that day, even in the sweltering heat of the desert, and Voss rides most of the day in the wagon.

At long last, in the late afternoon of the seventeenth, they can see the tent city in the distance. Smoke rises into the fading light of the sky. They find fresh speed and begin to push through the last leg, towards their next journey, and their next challenge.

Book Three - The Siege of Dal-Gorün

Book Three of the Series: "A Splintering World"
Part Three of the Novel: "The Stillness in the Air"

By: James Lytton

Piece of Lore - The Krulaeji and The Ancients

3E056

Long before the ages and eras of history began, the race of elves was present on Estrand. They were the first of the sentient creations placed upon Estrand. They lived in peace and spread throughout the great and magical forest of Vruyoth. As they delved deep into the arcane secrets of the world, and harnessed the energy of the Gods and the arcane reservoirs that fed their homeland, they learned to make many unique artifacts and to create many powerful spells.

It was Stren the Ageless, of the first elves, who finally unlocked the power to finish an artifact that he was working on for thousands of years. He called it 'Ilis Tonnuc', 'The Black Sun', as it produced darkness instead of light. It was no larger than a closed fist, and yet it held immense power, beyond anything that had existed to that time on the world. He used it to create a ritual which would transfer its power to himself. He wanted to bring great help to his people, but the artifact corrupted all it touched and turned the kindest hearts to malice.

The Gods found out too late of his plan, and so it succeeded. Stren shed his mortal body, and ascended into Godhood. He had become a powerful being, who would see his people survive. The Black Sun had not corrupted him past the point of evil, but he also feared he would be a harsh God. As a reward for becoming a match in power to the Gods, they allowed him to oversee the development of his own people. They also punished him, though, and put certain restrictions on his power and on all the elves. He accepted their terms nonetheless and began to work magic to aid his people, enforcing their borders against dark magics, and writing a set of laws that the elves would adhere to in order to succeed against their new restrictions.

There were some elves, though, that disagreed with these laws, and a rift formed in the population. Unlike the other Gods, Stren was still able to interfere with the mortal world. He personally appointed the next king, Qinzieros, and cast out those who openly opposed his laws. He forced them into the tunnels below the Voiceless Peaks, far to the north, a show of how the corruption had eroded his compassion. With the realization of his new cruelty, the new God absolved to shrink into his own realm and cease all interference.

Since that day, thousands of years ago, the Krulaeji, 'Forsakers' in old elvish, have sought a way to return to the surface. They grew pale and gaunt, and have warred with the races above in many instances, but have always failed.

'The Ancients' are a race of beings rumoured to have come to Thrella from the stars. They arrived on great beasts made of metal in the days before history. They were not creations of the Gods, and yet they thrived for a time and fed on the other races that inhabited the world, driven by hunger and their own desires.

The Ancients saw the giants in their reign, and saw the others that the Gods made after. They prayed on early humanity and the dwarves, but by then they had grown too confident, and despite the evolution of their race in both physical appearance and mental capacity, they were defeated long before history began, in a great war. Before the Krulaeji wars, before the wars of men and elves, The Ancients were driven back, off the surface of the Estrand. Some fled on great ships to seek new races to torment, some fled underground or into other, more volatile realms. Some took their ancient metal beasts and took once more to the stars, but all were forgotten.

The Krulaeji and The Ancients lie below the world in unknown locations, allying with unknown monstrosities and with the deep-dwarves that abandoned their people during the Elf War of the first era.

These dwarves have suffered a similar fate to the Krulaeji elves after years of living in the darkness below the world, becoming vengeful and brainwashed by the elves and The Ancients. They now share the name Krulaeji, 'Uumbreich' in the dwarf-tongue.

The most prominent attack from these subterranean peoples came about at the end of the second era, during the Malachi Crisis, when they joined together with the forces of the evil wizard Malachi and his army of undeath, lead by his servants of the apocalypse. The crisis was stopped by great heroes, whose names were mostly struck from history, and the Krulaeji retreated into their darkness once again.

They are hated by most, and kept at bay only by the vigil of paladins and soldiers watching the lands for any sign of them. To most, because of this constant watch, the Krulaeji are a fear of the past, nothing more. But they still exist, sitting under the feet of the world.

- Excerpt from Kyrolin Omarona's "Proposed History of the Pre-Era Races"

Chapter One - The Desert Camp

3E056, 17th of Sowwing

The collection of white and purple and brown tents are spread about the dunes, fastened to the flatter areas using long stakes and rocks. Various standards flutter in the warm wind that rushes through the camp. It is nearing dusk, but the air has not lost any heat. There are many people moving around the tents, and even more have joined together in a large square of space in the centre-west part of camp, where a bonfire has been lit and drinks are being served. There are sounds of music and laughter in the air. Harps, lutes, drums, and a violin are bubbling joyously into the approaching night.

A lone guard, dressed in light cloth and with a purple sash crossing his chest to display his affiliation with the Velvet Compass, stands watch at the northern edge of camp. He watches as three horses — two of which are pulling a wagon — a pony, and an ass rise over a nearby dune.

As they draw closer, the guard hails them and they approach him. A woman rides the unhitched horse, and pulls the ass and pony behind her. A gnome sits at the front of the wagon and steers the pulling-beasts carefully over the sands with the help of another, slender man who sits beside him. A bulkier man sits in the cover of the canvas top, wrapped in a cloth blanket. There is another small creature in the wagon, but it is wrapped in a cloak that hides its skin.

The guard does not recognize the travellers, and they have come without a banner above their wagon, but Emari, Voss, Boe, Brael, and Scazgix approach him calmly and confidently.

The guard asks to see their order medallions or papers, and they present each a gleaming metal necklace, aside from the one small figure in the wagon. He asks where they travel from.

"Taernsby," Emari answers him warmly, "and we have had a long and tiring trek. If you could show us where we can throw ourselves, we would be grateful."

The guard nods and smiles. He leads them through the camp, around the edge, so they do not become stuck in the clusters of tents. After fifteen minutes of trudging through the sand, they arrive at the western edge, where only one tent stands.

This tent is a finely made one, with a dark-grey banner flying above it, along with the purple standard of the Velvet Compass.

"You will be staying here," the guard explains, gesturing to the empty, flat basin of the dune beside the other tent. "You have been given a section of the ruins nearby, and the Dusk Knights should be able to show you the entrance. They are in the tent beside yours." As he speaks, they bring their wagon to a stop between their own site and the site adjacent to them. It acts as a kind of visual barrier between the groups.

"Thank you," responds Boe the gnome.

The guard departs, leaving them to begin setting up their tents. The group works quickly, and soon four small tents and a fire pit have been added to their patch of sand. Surrounding their area are large dunes and several patches of tall, bleached rocks that dot their crowns and slopes.

"Emari," speaks Voss, unwrapping himself from the blanket, "start the fire, and I will unpack the cooking pot." He begins walking toward the wagon, which they have left between their site and their neighbours' tent.

"You know, adding a please once in awhile would go a long way," she responds. The mask on her face changes colour along with her mood, transitioning to a wavering red from the usual calm navy.

"Voss," calls Boe, sticking his head from his own tent, "do you need help with anything?"

Voss returns from the wagon with the large cooking pot in his hands and a collection of metal posts to make a spit under his left arm. "No," he responds to the gnome. "You could help Brael get water into the horse-troughs though."

The gnome nods. The half-elven man, Brael, has already taken the two, long, rectangular metal basins from the wagon and set them on the ground beside it. Boe has known Brael for less time than the others, but the two have grown quite close over the course of this trip.

Emari is kind enough, but during their journey she grew quieter as Voss did. Such it was that the gnome ended up speaking mostly to Brael. The half-elf is a good listener, despite having lost his ears long ago. His ability to read lips is impressive to say the least, even if he has had several decades of practice. Most of the group can utilize some form of thought-projection as well, and so communicating with him is rarely an issue.

Brael turns and smiles as the gnome approaches. "Hello, Boe," he says.

"Hello! I wanted to lend a hand."

"I will pour the water," Brael explains, heaving a barrel onto one shoulder, "you hold the troughs so they do not spill over."

Boe nods, and they begin to fill the basins.

Soon a fire is going, the horses are happily quenching their thirst, and a stew is bubbling in the large pot. The group has dragged a few empty barrels and a large rock over to their fire for seating. The stew turns out to be of average quality, but it is warm and satisfying, and better than the travel rations they have been eating for the better part of the last week.

Their other small companion, Scazgix, joins them as the meal is served. "Thank you," he says, grinning as he is handed a bowl and wraps himself in his cloak. He is the king of his own kingdom: Scazgixia. At least as far as he is concerned, he is. He is covered in red and black scales and his head is draconic in nature. He has no wings, but a thick tail does sprout from his lower back.

Emari talks with Boe and Brael about how much food and water they have left, and then about whether they would like to explore some of the camp and find the source of the music that still permeates the air in the distance. Voss remains quite silent.

They finish eating, and put their clay bowls carefully into another pot full of stagnant water from several days ago to be washed. Voss places this pot over the fire to help the dishes soak.

"Voss, would you like to come with us to the square?" Emari asks.

Voss does not look up. His brown hair hangs over his face like a curtain. "Someone should watch the camp," he says at length.

Emari studies him for a few seconds. Eventually she settles against pressing. "We won't be long," she responds instead.

The others leave Voss alone near the fire. It is not much of a chance for peace for the man.

"What did you think of the last vision?" Voss asks aloud. He is referring to dreams that have been plaguing him for the past month of travel. He speaks to the spirits in his own mind, echoes of the few people he may have called friends. The last vision he had was over a week ago, and it left him with a sense of dread that has still not departed his bones.

"I do not know exactly what to believe," Nhasan's voice responds. It hurts Voss to listen to the words of these spirits, but the more he opens his mind to them, the easier it becomes.

"I do not know either," Voss responds. "I want opinions, that is all."

"If they are visions, as we suspect," begins Valindra, the elven archer, "then they were likely happening at present time."

"I agree," Torkurth, the spear-man, says. "The last vision was the first time we heard any voices, but they seemed to notice us."

Voss thinks back to his dream. He spoke in it, but not with his own voice, and not voluntarily.

"We are being watched," Voss says, repeating the words from the vision. It was not just the sentence itself that instilled dread in him, but the voice that spoke them. He remembers hearing it once before, and each word spoken sent fear into his chest. "You have been a great help to me, all of you," he says quietly.

"Greetings!" a man's voice sounds from near the wagon and pulls Voss back into his surroundings.

Voss glances over to see a tall human with short black hair standing and watching him. "Who are you?" he asks.

"Ah," the man starts, "I am Holland Ferndash. I am a member of the

Dusk Knights. We are camped on the other side of your wagon."

"Is that not the group that discovered these ruins?"

"Yes, Dusk Knight Ruins are named after us. We are only a guild of three, but we have made our mark now. Myself; my sister, Yuriel; and our goliath friend, Jorrig. We were investigating orc movement in the desert, and stumbled upon this place instead."

Voss says nothing.

"I was wondering if you would like to share in some wine. We are not planning on staying much longer, as we have camped here for many months now, and so we were hoping to celebrate," Holland continues. He grins, and lines form around his blue-grey eyes.

"Which are you celebrating: your departure, the discovery, or something else?" Voss asks.

"Both the departure and the treasure we found. There was much gold in the ruins. Tombs held ancient weapons and old jewelry. We have found enough to buy our own piece of land and even build a small hall or some homes. This is not the end of out adventuring days, but it is going to mark the start of a long vacation, certainly," Holland says proudly.

Voss notes that the man does not wear armour now, nor does he carry a weapon, but he certainly has a similar stance to Evandur and other members of the churches that Voss has encountered. "If you would bring some wine," Voss tells him, "we have some left-over stew. You are welcome to join me, and my companions as well, when they come back from the main camp."

Holland smiles and nods. "I will return shortly," he says.

Voss manages to put his thoughts about his visions aside for the rest of the evening. Holland soon joins him around the fire. With him is a tall goliath, bald and beardless with skin like iron, carrying a barrel that is still half full of a fine wine, and an elven looking girl. She appears to be in her late teens, or at least would be certainly if she was of fully human blood. Holland is not old, at least five or six years younger than Voss. The goliath appears to be a similar age as well, but it is never easy to guess the age of a goliath.

Holland introduces Yuriel and Jorrig to Voss. The soldier initially remains reserved, but they seem to be in high spirits, and it soon begins to rub off on him.

The Ferndash siblings both have deep, black hair and light, blue-grey eyes. They are tanned, but on their palms, bare feet, and under their chins they remain quite pale. Holland has broad shoulders and a deep, commanding voice, while Yuriel is much smaller and comes across as very timid. Jorrig is a beast of a creature, with muscle that looks ready to burst from his skin. His laugh is that of a common man, though, and his green eyes gleam like they are hiding something terribly comedic.

Goliaths are descendants of giants, but those who diluted blood through the years and lost the gifts of the original creations. They no longer possess the immortality or the passed-down memory that the ancient race did. In the ages before history, when giants roamed the land, they lived in a fixed number. They did not mate, or reproduce, they only existed and, if they died, a new one would form and take on the memories of their predecessor.

When the giants found Streboya and Estrand, they did not stay long, for their race was already in turmoil. Rodath the Destroyer, of the first giants, had taken control of his predecessor and was waging a great war on all who opposed him. He scattered the giants and then abruptly disappeared with his supporters. Even so, they met with the elves who had moved to Streboya, and began to live in close proximity, and the elves shared their lineage. The giants on Streboya ended up leaving into the sea, but the goliaths and the remaining pure-elves remained.

The goliath and the others from the Dusk Knights share the wine with Voss. By the time Emari, Boe, and Brael return, all are intoxicated. Voss is openly discussing his own past adventures. He has thrown the hood of his cloak back, and his face is illuminated by the light of the fire. Holland is telling his own stories as well, and Voss nods along at the interesting details. Jorrig plays a long and wide lute with fifteen strings, and softly sings a song. The words are Streboyan, a mix of giant-tongue and ancient elvish, but the accent is not one befitting a native of the eastern continent. Voss even sings along to the chorus.

Voss' face is rectangular, with a strong, sharp jaw, and a wide nose that looks to have been broken at least once before. His eyes are a deep brown, and they listen intently, piercing into Holland as he speaks. As Emari and the others rejoin the circle, Voss looks briefly to her. There is intensity in his gaze and, for a moment they even seem to glint blue in the dancing light of the flames.

They all make introductions again, and share their excitement about the ruins beneath them. Holland and Jorrig have much to say about the ancient carvings that they saw and the old halls with collapsing ceilings. Yuriel does not say much, but, when Jorrig resumes his tune after the others join, she hums along. Emari does as well.

Scazgix seems very content with all the new faces and the stories that he hears, though he does not understand much. He grows quite drunk on the wine and passes out in a ball near the warmth of the fire. That night, after the party winds down, the new arrivals from Taernsby fall quickly into sleep, following the kobold king's lead.

Voss lies awake for an extra hour, as the sense of dread claws its way back into his heart. The fear finds him just before the wine can finish lulling him to sleep. It is a slow and persistent feeling, a gnawing thought of something inescapable, something approaching him, walking just behind him, keeping up with him despite every step he takes to out-pace it.

Chapter Two – Into the Ruins

3E056, 18th of Sowwing

The morning dawns clear and bright. The sunlight pierces through the fabric of the tents and rouses the travellers early. It is Brael who prepares breakfast. He uses the last of the meat from animals he shot on their journey through the lower council lands. The meat is boiled with some vegetables and bones into a stew that is more flavourful than the one for the previous dinner.

The others join him at the fire as he is finishing. Voss comes last, emerging from his tent in full armour, minus a helmet. He wears a hooded cowl to block the sun and his face instead.

The all eat ravenously in the growing heat. They drink a tankard of water each as well. As they are finishing, Boe begins to clean the dishes. Scazgix places himself upon a the sand and bathes in the sun.

"We should find the entrance to these ruins as quickly as we can," Voss says.

"Eager to get some gold?" Emari asks.

"We will be paid well enough regardless," Voss responds. "I want to get the job done."

"Ah, so you're already longing for the road again?" the bard jokes.

"No," is his only reply.

They finish cleaning together and return to their tents to get ready. Voss takes the opportunity to walk to the Dusk Knights' tent. Holland is awake and groggily attempting to strike a fire for their own breakfast. He looks up as Voss approaches and smiles.

"Fine suit of mail," says the man. "Did you get that from the order?"

"Yes, but for my helm, which was painted and crafted by a friend," replies Voss, holding the helmet up for viewing.

"I see. What brings you across the wagon-wall?" Holland asks.

"We seek entrance to the ruins, but we do not know where to look."

"Oh! Well if you want to wait for an hour, I could show you after we eat."

"We are anxious to get going. I am certain I could find it, if you could point the direction from here."

Holland obliges, pointing to one of the croppings of stones on the westernmost dune behind the Taernsby group's camp. "Among those rocks," he says, "is a small hole that leads down a slope. You will have to use a rope to get to the bottom, and it will be a tight fit, but if you take it slowly you should make it without trouble."

"My thanks, Sir Ferndash," Voss says, and returns to his camp.

The others have finished getting ready. It is odd to leave a camp standing when they depart, as they are so used to packing up every morning. They have pulled sections of cloth out over the horses to keep them in the shade, and Scazgix elects to watch their camp. It feels oddly homey here. They are uncertain of how long they will stay, but for the moment they decide to attempt relaxation and let the thought of staying be a good one.

Emari has dressed in fine leather armour with a black, cloth hood. She has her rapier in its sheath, and a small crossbow folded into her bag. Also in her pack is a journal and some extra provisions.

Boe has wrapped himself in a cloak, which will protect his finer robes from the sand and dust that they will be dealing with. He also has leather boots on, which are thin, but have good soles.

Brael has armoured up in leather, with steel reinforcements around major weak-points. He has his longbow on his back, and a quiver with twenty arrows strapped to his belt. Two daggers are in sheaths on his calves, and his hair is braided and wound into a bun. He wears no hood or cloak today, but does carry a pack with rope looped and pinned to the side.

Scazgix bids them goodbye in the common-tongue, and then says something to Boe that draws a laugh.

Voss places his helmet back on his head before he rejoins the others, and then bids them to follow him towards the cropping of rocks.

Climbing the dune is slow work, but they manage to scramble to the top. The rocks are larger than they initially appeared, with some standing well over Voss' height. They are jagged, with many flat surfaces carved from the wind sweeping through the cluster. After some investigation, it also becomes apparent that under a layer of crusted sand, they are a nearly black colour, which stands against the red and white sands of the desert.

The cropping takes up the whole crest of the dune, which is circular in nature and of about a twelve foot diameter. They begin to examine the ground. It takes only a minute to find the small passage, but it would have been nearly impossible without knowing where to look.

The entrance is a square, just over three feet wide on all sides. It descends into the ground at a steep incline, and the bottom cannot be seen in the darkness of the passage and the shadows of the rocks. With Voss' armour, it will certainly be a delicate process.

The soldier loops Brael's rope around the bottom of one of the taller, pillar-like stones, and ties a tight knot. Brael begins to feed the rope into the hole. After fifty feet of rope, it still does not appear to reach the bottom.

Voss grabs hold of the cord and pulls. It is secure. He steps into the passage, drawing his arms close to his chest to conserve space. The others watch as he slowly descends into the darkness.

Minutes pass with only the sound of clinking mail resonating from the tunnel. Finally, just as standing in the heat among the rocks is growing unbearable, the rope goes slack. A grating noise rises from the passage before silence returns.

"It's a few feet to the bottom!" calls Voss. "It's safe!"

The others begin to descend. They are all light enough for the rope to support them at once. Boe goes first, holding the rope in one hand, and a glowing staff in the other. Brael comes next, then Emari. As they slide slowly down, the sand quickly turns to a light-brown stone and, as light begins to back into a distant square, the walls start to show signs of ancient carvings. The bottom-most wall of the tunnel also becomes increasingly coated in sand that has drifted into the passage through of years of neglect.

They reach the bottom of the rope and, one by one, they slide the last few feet onto a pile of sand in a small room. This room is square and made of the same brown stone blocks as the passage. There are remnants of a large, stone basin beneath the sand pile, but little else in terms of furniture stands in the room. One door exits directly across from the basin and passage, and another exit — a set of double doors — leads leftward. All the doors are made of thin, rusting, blueish metal.

Voss has already lit a torch, and Emari lights one now as well.

"Remain on guard," Voss tells his companions as they stand up. "I worry that we are not alone."

"What makes you say that?" Boe asks in a whisper.

Voss points to some small marks in the sand pile and across the floor. "Those are footprints. How long ago they were left is impossible to say," he says. He then points to the door. "Those hinges look newer, or, at least, less rusted than the rest of the metal. Someone inhabited this place after its original owners."

"But it is unlikely that they are still here after the Velvet Compass has been camped above for many months," Boe argues.

"That is true. Let us not lay down the possibility yet though," Voss responds.

The others nod.

Voss walks to the smaller door, and opens it with a creak. Behind it lies a smaller room that is only four feet wide and ten feet long. Within it are petrified scraps of wood, and a few intact boxes. The soldier begins to search around for anything useful, but other than a few small pieces of old jewelry in a sealed box, and some rusted knives, nothing seems preserved.

"Check the left wall," Valindra informs Voss.

He stands and looks to the wall. It is barren and appears uninteresting. He raises his torch, however, to see that one of the stone bricks appears to have separated from those above and on either side of it. Voss pushes it, but it does not budge. He reaches into the small space above and finds a groove. He pulls, and the bricks slowly and painfully slides out. He places it carelessly on the floor. Now, in the small space left in the wall, he can see a box. It is made of old wood, and is sealed shut. He takes this and opens it, which snaps the lid at the corners.

Inside there are twelve glass vials, in two neat rows. Each row is a slightly different colour, but both are a red-orange. Six are lighter, and six are darker, but Voss cannot tell for certain what they might be. He brings the box, and a necklace and pair of earrings that still have shine back to the others. They have now placed their bags neatly beside the sand pile.

Voss shows the vials to Boe, who looks at them for a moment.

"They look like they could be healing salves," the gnome suggests. "They are more of a liquid than a salve though. Perhaps they are a drink. I wouldn't go drinking them, though, unless you want a horrific stomach ache, or death."

Voss nods, but takes one of each and gently folds them into a cloth pouch in his leather hip-bag. He leaves the rest in the box, and the box with the bags.

Brael walks quietly to the other exit, and places one hand on the centre of the right-hand door. He pushes slightly, and the door begins to swing, making no noise. Seemingly content, despite being unable to hear whether it was silent or not, Brael continues to push. It is half open before it creaks slightly. Brael stops.

The half-elf peers into the space beyond, then turns back.

"It is empty," he reports. "It is a long chamber. The floor is clear of debris, and large pillars hold up the ceiling."

The soldier holds his torch high and gives a nod of approval. Brael nods back, and walks through the doors. The others follow, and soon they have passed through into the next, much larger chamber. It is as Brael described, and with a long trough in the middle that runs from close to the group to near the doors on the opposite end. It is made of stone, and still contains small traces of water, as it is fed by stone aqueducts that protrude from the walls near the ceiling and drip into the basin. The doors at the far end are made of metal as well, but they appear to be in better condition than the others. It is difficult to tell at this distance, however, as the whole room is nearly a hundred feet long, and at least thirty feet wide. High above them is the ceiling, which is missing some chunks of stone, but appears to have remained structurally sound despite this. A section of the left wall has fallen to rubble, but, when it was clear, it may have held a passage to other sections of the ruins. As for now, however, there is no other exit than through the new doors.

The room possesses a certain chill. As the four enter, a shiver runs up Boe's spine. They leave the entrance ajar. There is sand in this room as well, though most of it has fallen over time from the ceiling and walls. There is a lingering smell of burnt coals and ash, and the ceiling appears covered in black soot that dances atop the dust and grains of sand.

Emari looks to Voss. Neither of them speak. Voss begins to walk forward. His footsteps and plate armours throw sound throughout the hall. The others follow slowly. They reach the furthest set of columns, of which there are ten total, one on either side every ten feet. Boe stops at the column on the right.

The gnome holds his staff toward the support as a light. All along the stonework are carvings and peeled paintings. They seem to depict various gatherings, and feature human-like figures, but tall and thin. The figures appear to be in discussion in some images, and at war in others. Some show a tall, kingly-looking figure. Brael and Emari begin to study the carvings as well, while Voss keeps watch.

The images all feature symbols of either the humanoid beings, riches, or blades. There is also a script of dots and elegant lines that seem to have some vague resemblance to elvish, but with very few similar letters.

Voss draws upon the spiritual energy within himself. He instructs Dadek the dwarf to carry a message to Brael's mind. Brael can hear the voice of Voss in his ears. It does not startle him. He has become used to this phenomenon when around the armoured soldier.

"Near the other pillar there is a creature on the ground. Shoot it," comes the message.

Brael reacts immediately. He slowly pulls the bow off his shoulder. Then, in one motion he spins, nocks an arrow and, after only half a second taken to find the creature, he fires.

The creature dodges however. It scuttles around the pillar and begins to rush towards the door they entered from. It is a small, wiry beast, running on short legs. It looks canine in nature, but is smaller than any common dog breed, and with no hair. Its face is more flat as well, and its triangular ears stand straight. It hugs the edge of the centre basin, using it to cover most of its body.

Brael is fast to act again. Before the others have finished turning around he has launched another arrow. This time, the projectile finds its mark, and pierces straight through the creature's left eye as it reaches the centre of the room. It collapses in a heap, skidding to a fast halt.

"Excellent," Voss sends to Brael.

"How did you see that?" asks Boe, after getting the hunter's attention.

"Voss told me," Brael responds.

The soldier crosses the room to the fallen beast, and lifts it up. It is lifeless. Its body is indeed devoid of hair, and wrinkled. It is a pitiful looking thing, but it seemed intelligent.

"Boe," calls Voss, "what do you make of this?" The soldier approaches the others, holding the creature by the nape, with his torch beside it.

The gnome studies it. "It is a desert animal, certainly. I have not encountered one in my studies before, but it does not appear to be incredibly dangerous." He opens its mouth to reveal a single set of teeth, which also resembles a dog's.

"I did not like that it was observing us," Voss says.

"It was likely just a scavenger that got caught in the hole, and has been feeding off of whatever rats or small rodents are down here," Emari decides.

Voss says nothing, but chucks the body into the corner in a way that leaves its good eye facing the wall.

"This image here," Boe draws Voss' attention back to the column, "appears to be a map, and looks similar to the section of ruins that we are in."

Voss observes where the mage is pointing with his staff, and sees a faded pattern of squares and rectangles carved into the stone that resembles a sort of floor plan. It appears that there was originally a passage that connected this area to others, but it did collapse with the left wall. There should, by this diagram, be stairs beyond the next doors. The pattern is faded, but it appears to lead eventually to another large room, where the icon of a throne has been cut into the plan.

"That could be promising," Voss states, tapping the last room with the bottom of his torch and sending a piece of charring cloth into the air.

"It certainly could," Emari agrees.

Brael walks to the next doors. He tries to open them, but they do not budge. They move slightly when pulled, but get caught on something. Upon a brief investigation, they find nothing on their side that would prevent their movement.

Boe examines the metal carefully. It is not as rusted as the other doors they have encountered, and it looks to be quite thick. "If I could see what was stopping this, I may be able to move it using arcana," he offers. "Metal as thick as this would block most conventional forms of scrying magic, and even my owl, if summoned, would not be of much use here."

"I meant to ask if that was just a trained companion, or is it something spiritual you summon at will?" Voss asks the gnome.

"It is actually a creature from the faerie realm," Boe explains. "It is intelligent, and can return to its own dimension when it is not needed. As I said, though, even if I brought it into these ruins, it would not be of much use."

Emari approaches the doors. She presses her head to the area near the handles and knocks gently. She knocks again, slightly louder. Then, she begins to whisper softly. The sound of her voice flows through the room despite its low volume.

"I think that there is something wedged in the handles on the other side," she tells them.

"Could your magic clear it?" Voss asks her.

"I doubt it. My magic is mostly used to affect people and their bodies and minds. I am not so trained in varied arcana."

They discuss for a few minutes. Other than attempting to melt through with concentrated arcane energy, or blasting the doors from their hinges, very little seems to be a realistic option.

"I believe that I could knock the doors down," says Boe, "but that would definitely leave me spent of energy for some time. I would not be knocked into unconsciousness, but I would have to lie down for an hour or more."

"We do not have much of an option other than that," Voss tells him. "We can return to the surface after, and come back when you have rested, or else I can go ahead with Brael while Emari takes you back."

"I am not missing out on the exploration," Emari retorts. "As if I would leave you to discover some great treasure and hide it for yourself!"

"You think of me as that dishonest?" Voss asks.

"I don't know," Emari admits. "Probably not, but I am not one to take that risk."

Voss shrugs.

Emari listens to the door again. "Nothing is moving beyond, not that I can hear in any case. But something is definitely blocking the door, and we are not going to get rid of it easily."

"Boe, blow it," Voss orders.

For a moment no one moves. Voss turns to look at the gnome. As the hulking figure glances in his direction, Boe nods and brings his journal from its clips on his hip. He begins to rifle through it.

"Voss, are you sure this is a safe idea?" Emari asks, backing away from the doors.

"Whatever is through that door, we can handle it," the man answers her without turning away from the gnome. His body has grown stiff.

"Something had to have blocked the door in the first place. What if it was not just falling stone? We could ask for assistance. Holland and Jorrig could help us in some-" the bard continues.

"We blow the door."

Boe stops on a page.

"I don't agree-" Emari starts.

"Now, Boe," Voss tells the mage.

Boe begins to speak a long phrase. Lines carved into his staff begin to glow bright orange as energy moves from his hands into the wood.

"Boe-" Emari pleads.

"Quiet," interrupts Voss.

Boe continues speaking, his face becoming increasingly strained as energy pours into, and is contained within, his staff. Emari glares at Voss, who finally turns from the mage and faces the doors expectantly. Blue mist forms around his hands and face.

Suddenly, a burst of bright red and orange light erupts from Boe's staff and slams into the doors. The stonework shakes and dust rains from the ceiling as one of the doors is wrenched from the sturdy hinges and thrown backwards into the space behind it. Voss' axe and shield form in his hands and licks of flame and force bounce off the metal.

The gnome falls to his knees, breathing heavily.

"Good work," Voss says as Brael moves to Boe's side.

The hallway beyond the door is shrouded in darkness, and their eyes are no longer used to the level of light their torches provide after the blast of energy. As their sight slowly adjusts, they can just make out the point, about fifteen feet beyond the door, where the hall turns right and begins to descend in a straight staircase.

No one moves. Voss is about to take a step when a sound captures all of their attention. A shout bellows through the hall, rising up the stairs. It is accompanied quickly be more voices that join in.

"We need to run," Emari states levelly.

The sound of rushing feet mixes into the shouting.

"They will reach us before we escape," Voss informs them. Then he messages Brael using Nhasan. "Take Boe to the first room and cover us from there." Brael grabs Boe and drags him backward across the room. "Emari," the soldier continues, "stay behind me, but close enough to heal me. I will have need of you."

"Voss, you moron!" she shouts, but moves to stand behind him. The footsteps draw closer. "I will not die in this forgotten place by the mistake of listening to you!"

"You will not die unless I do first, so stand your ground!" he shouts above the growing noise. Torchlight rises from the stairs, and dances into the hall behind the broken door.

There is no more time to prepare. The shouts flood the air in the large chamber and two figures, one holding a torch, reach the top of the stairs. Voss drops his own torch a few feet to his right. The rest of the room is in pitch darkness.

It is difficult to discern details about whatever is approaching. Two more figures reach the top of the stairs behind the first pair. They are shorter than an average human, but they are stockier. In the flickering of the torches it is nearly impossible to make out their specific features, though the one leading this charge certainly has a square face and nose, and his skin is a deep red. He, and the one beside him, have long hair, which is black and braided. They are all dressed in a variety of leathers and metal plates, and the first few wield blades and spears.

Before anything else can be done, they have thrown the other metal door open, and are pushing straight for Voss.

The soldier times a block, and the sound of metal against metal ricochets through the chamber. Another blow is avoided by a back-step and then Voss manages to swing his own weapon. His attack is blocked by the leader's longsword. A spear is thrown over the heads of the first attackers, which Emari barely avoids being impaled by.

Voss and Emari hold their ground. It appears that after six of the creatures reach the top, no more are following. They are strong and organized, but only the first two have approached close-quarters. The rest watch for the moment, swords and spears at the ready.

The first one lunges, and cuts around the plating on Voss' side, but the scale beneath holds firm. The other swings for the soldier's head, but Emari catches the blade with her own, and steps into the fray.

It is at this point that the other four attackers act. Two of them move around each pillar. Voss and Emari are in no position to stop them, and soon they are surrounded. Once the creatures have moved to cut off the first fight, the last two take off for Brael, who has barely reached the other doors.

One of the new opponents has a shield and a rusted mace. This one waits until Voss is distracted with blocking other blows before taking his weapon and swinging toward Voss' knees. The attack lands, and Voss falls, crouching on his left leg.

With no other options, Voss shouts orders to the spirits within him.

Valindra, the elven archer, appears between the fight and where Brael is soon to be engaged with the two others, and launches several arrows. The spectral-blue shots connect, and a cry of pain is heard above the fight. Attention is drawn away from Emari.

Voss turns to the distracted targets and cuts one deeply down his back. The other takes a step toward the archer, but Voss grabs hold of him.

A spear breaks through Voss' plating and scale shirt, stabbing deep into his left shoulder from behind. He grunts and then shouts again at the spirits. Dadek emerges from within him, shield first. The shock causes the spear-wielder to drop his first weapon and fumble slightly in switching to his blade. The spears are solid metal, and weighted enough to be a very serious threat.

Emari trips the one that Voss is holding. Valindra fires an arrow into the chest of the one who lost his spear, which causes him to fall backward. Voss takes his shield and slams it into the only one who is still collected. Before he can press the button on the handle, however, the attacker wrenches it from his arm. Voss quickly swings at the one Emari has tripped, and his axe embeds in the neck.

Brael is dealing with two at once, by himself. Boe has regained his feet, but is breathing heavily and unable to speak. The half-elf has drawn his two daggers, unable to see viability in his bow.

The attacker on the left lunges for the hunter, but Brael is fast, and easily dodges. He is about to counter, when the one on his right presses as well. Brael manages to parry the sword's swing, but is forced further from Boe.

The attacks continue to be volleyed. Brael carefully parries and steps back to avoid being injured. He waits for his chance to strike back. Soon, he is pushed nearly to the other door, opposite the entrance passage. It is at this point that the first one pulls back. Brael is blocked from any action by the other, as the first takes two, great steps towards Boe.

Brael blocks another swing.

The first attacker drops the sword from his hand, and replaces it with Boe's neck. He lifts the gnome from the ground. Brael's back touches the opposite wall.

Three things happen in less than a second.

First, Brael shoves his own attacker, having braced one foot against the wall. Using this momentum, he gains enough space to hurl his dagger towards the other.

Second, having Brael's focus removed briefly from the immediate threat allows for his initial opponent to swing his sword without a block.

Third, just before Brael's dagger connects with the space between its shoulders, the creature holding Boe plunges his spear through the gnome's stomach. The tip appears again, sticking out into the open air above their bags.

The dagger dives through the flesh of the attacker's back, and the beast drops Boe and his spear in surprise. Brael spins, only receiving a gash along his left arm.

Both Boe and the injured attacker fall to the floor.

Blood spews from the gnome's mouth, and runs into his wispy beard, as the spear is pushed from his body. The gnome's bubbling life begins to stain his face a crimson-red.

Voss has slain one of his four opponents, and the other — who was pierced by the spectral arrow — has not regained his footing. The other two have rallied, however, and stand a few feet back, protecting their frightened companion. The soldier is injured, and blood is pouring from his shoulder. Emari sings several, clear notes, which help to slow the flow and ease the pain, but in these conditions it will not heal fully.

Neither side wants to advance and, for an eerie moment, there is calm.

Finally, the one who lead the charge shouts in an unknown language, raising his spear. Voss darts to the right side and grabs his shield again. As he turns, he sees that one of the creatures which pursued Brael is rushing back.

Voss swings his shield around, between him and the three. He pushes the button, locking it in place beside the spectre of Dadek. The one behind them is running in an arc around the left side of the room, giving a wide berth around Valindra. The other attackers push up to the shield, drawing Voss' attention once more.

There is an immense throbbing in Voss' head and blood begins to leak from his nostrils.

The retreating opponent makes it nearly to the fight, before lunging toward Emari. The other opponents are holding their ground before the shield-wall.

Voss barely sees the danger on his left, but he acts fast. He jumps into action as the new assailant does. He shouts to Valindra, who launches two more arrows towards the first group to keep them at bay. The creature has both his spear and his sword in from of him. Voss grabs the spear inches from the bard's chest, and takes the force of the sword, and the weight of his enemy, with his own.

The beast, the bard, and the soldier land together on the stone floor.

One of the attackers grabs the top of the shield and prepares to vault, but Dadek's mace catches him in the chest and he leaps back in pain.

Emari is pinned, and Voss' axe lands just out of his reach. The spectral archer continues to launch arrows, but the rest of the attackers have taken cover behind the pillars.

Voss is, once again, out of options. "Nhasan! Torkurth!" he screams. Two more ghostly figures join the fight. Voss screams in pain and rage as Nhasan the assassin materializes behind the creature that is pinning them down. The spearman appears between the pile and the nearest pillar on the left. Voss' mind feels as though it is going to melt under the stress.

Nhasan's daggers cut into the back of the assailant. The creature shrieks and rolls off. Voss grabs Emari's rapier as soon as there is room and plunges it into the opponent's neck. Torkurth advances, but the remaining three are pulling back. With a loud cry, they pass through the doors, and move down the stairs.

Voss falls into unconsciousness as the ghosts return to his body.

Chapter Three - Reunion

3E056, 18th of Sowwing

The small guild, Bigger They Are, has been sharing three tents for the past month. Roger and Helena Hardwick took one tent, while Jaine, Arther and their gnomish wizard — Jitz — took another. The third has been used for cooking and, partially, for storage, just to keep themselves and their supplies out of the rising heat.

They have almost gotten used to the oppressive sun by now, but this day seems to be hotter than the rest. Roger rises from his sleeping pad and sets his feet into wooden sandals. There is a discussion nearby, and Roger can easily pick out the voice of his sister amidst the others. By his stomach, it must be late morning, maybe even approaching lunch.

He wraps a tunic around his shoulders, but leaves the buttons open. His airy trousers come next, cinched with a piece of cloth cord. He pushes through the flaps.

On the short walk between tents, the sun beats ferociously upon his already-burnt neck. Roger enters the communal tent. The others have all gathered, save for Arthur. They are sitting on empty barrels around a small, dead fire. Smells from a missed breakfast still linger in the air.

"There is cheese and potato left in the pot," Jitz informs Roger as he sniffs the air.

"My thanks," he replies.

They have done well in their endeavours here, by their own standards. It is clear, however, that some groups did much better. When the Dusk Knights discovered the ruins, they had other guilds come to do some preliminary investigating. In the first basic mapping, they found areas where more wealth and space existed. More long-term and loyal guilds within the order were given the sections with better prospects. Despite this, the amount of gold and silver that Bigger They Are found, even in the form of plates, cutlery, and jewelry, could pay for a few months of relaxation.

Spirits are fairly high because of this. Their area was not large, and fairly empty, and so for the past few weeks they have been mostly relaxing and socializing with other guilds. Their supplies could hold another week, but they plan on leaving before the end of Sowwing.

Roger takes a bowl and fills it with lukewarm cheese-and-potato stew. He sits with the others and joins in the talk about starting to pack. He would not mind heading out soon and escaping the desert heat.

Suddenly there is a commotion outside. Shouts of serious injury and calls for healers fill the air. Roger sets his bowl down and exits the tent. It is not yet midday, but the heat is fierce and biting, and he begins to sweat.

"What could it be? There has been nothing of danger in the ruins," Helena speaks, stepping out beside her brother. "Even the sparse trap mechanisms were long worn away."

"Let's go try to take a look," Roger says, grabbing her arm and pulling her along behind him. They follow a group of three unofficial looking priests in various stages of preparedness. Each of them clutches a holy medallion of some kind and one of them is also holding a large canvas bag in which glass clinks together as she walks.

They move westward through the tents, past the square that was cleared for parties, and all the way to the far-edge of camp. Over a dune lies a wagon. On the left is a single, large tent bearing the Dusk Knight flag, and on the other are a few smaller tents and a cooking fire has been set up as well.

People are hurrying about. Two have laid a large cloth tarp onto the sand. Four others are setting up another above it to create shade. The members of the Dusk Knights are directing things and trying to make space and prevent people from crowding too close to the cloth. Roger looks around frantically for a sign of any injured, and soon notices a handful of people buzzing about a cluster of rocks atop the next dune. He draws his sister's attention as well, and they see figures emerge. Some limp, and at least one is being carried. All exit from the rock cluster.

They carefully descend the slope. A trail of blood is being left, more vibrant in colour than the red-white sand.

Before the wounded pass the farthest tent, Roger is struck by a sickening realization. Among the group limps a tall figure dressed in shining, plate armour and a black helmet. The helmet's faceplate is painted carefully to resemble a grinning skull or demon. It was designed by House Ironheart on Streboya to inspire fear in enemies. Horn-like additions run up either side as well.

"That's…" he trails off.

Helena grabs his arm now, and pulls him down their own slope towards the makeshift treatment area. Someone attempts to question them, but Helena brushes by, carefully shouldering him out of the way.

Voss and the others reach the tarp. The soldier appears to be injured on his back, and is hardly standing. There is a gnome with them, who is unconscious and being carried by a large goliath: a member of the Dusk Knights that Roger has seen before.

The gnome is laid gingerly on the tarp. Brael, who Roger also recognizes from Railwood, clutches a deep gash on his arm, but he stands back for the moment.

"Voss!" Roger calls, which draws the attention of the man. The armoured figure stands taller for a moment. Another man tries to prevent his movement, but Voss steps around him. He makes it a few paces before falling to a knee.

"Treat the gnome!" the soldier's voice commands the healers around him. "Emari," he then says, and the bard moves to his side, "heal me."

Emari hums a tune. The wound in his shoulder slows its bleeding slightly.

"Not the shoulder," Voss grunts, "my mind."

Emari begins to sing gently, a song of rivers and still ponds. Voss falls backward, ungracefully, sitting in the sand. He clutches at his temples through his helmet.

The healers rush about them, desperately attempting to keep the gnome alive. Roger leaves Voss and Emari. He moves to see what is happening to their smaller companion. Brael also stands nearby, watching over the healers' shoulders. He does not move his gaze from the man on the tarp.

The gnome's clothes are drenched in blood around his midsection. A woman in brown robes kneels quickly beside him. She takes a knife and slices through the cloth. The man is unconscious, and does not show any signs of waking. The woman pulls back his blue and grey clothes, revealing a wound.

The hole in his stomach is not wide, but it is oozing blood profusely. The woman gags, but places her hand on the gnome's injury. He sputters and blood shoots from his mouth and nose.

Roger can do little but watch. He has no medical training that would be able to save this man, and even the trained healers - who hum prayers and spells - seem to only be able to slow the blood. The gnome has lost a lot already. A strange, small, dragon-kin like creature, is trying to make its way towards the scene, but Brael catches its arm and holds it back.

Suddenly, Voss stands again. He walks shakily onto the cloth tarp, and kneels beside the gnome. No one stops him. Many are beginning to finish prayers, and some are speaking words of Echoshan. Voss rips his left gauntlet from his arm and, with the exposed hand, he reaches into a small leather bag on his hip.

He pulls out two, small, glass vials, one of which is cracked badly, but both of which are full of liquid. There is a moment of hesitation. Voss pulls his helmet off his head with the armoured hand, and bites down hard on the cork of the cracked vial. He rips it free with an audible *pop*. He smells the contents and retches, throwing the glass into the sand beside him, where the liquid begins to quickly congeal. He removes the cork from the second vial and, when the scent hits his nostrils, he looks suddenly to the gnome again.

He pours the liquid directly into the hole in his companion's stomach. The gnome begins to squirm and, through the blood in his throat, he tries to scream in pain. Voss holds the gnome against the cloth. His own blood is now pouring through his amour and out onto his uncovered hand.

The hole in the gnome's stomach begins to close as a soft, red light bubbles from the torn flesh.

With renewed hope, the healers jump into action, casting minor spells to help with the pain. Voss releases his hold on the gnome, and the man's eyes close again.

After twenty minutes have passed, with no one speaking save for the commands of the healers, the gnome appears to be breathing shakily. His skin is pale, and his body is drenched with sweat, but he is alive for the moment.

Ten more minutes pass before the healers bring a wooden carrier and take the gnome away. Voss struggles to unclasp his armour. Emari begins to help him in silence.

Ten more minutes until Voss' back and shoulder plating, his helm, and his scale shirt, have been stripped away from his body. His shoulder is a mess of blood and swollen skin, but Emari's healing slows any infection from setting in.

Roger sits beside Voss on the bloodstained cloth. Helena stands nearby. Brael and the draconic creature have disappeared with the healers.

"What happened?" Roger asks.

No one responds for a long time, but Emari's mask changes to a violent red. Finally, the bard stands and turns away from Voss, walking towards the edge of camp.

"What happened, Voss?" Roger pushes.

"Something in those ruins made an enemy of me," Voss responds. The voice is strained, and sounds different from what Roger remembers. The soldier's eyes are pointed downward, and his dark, greasy hair covers most of his face. He grabs his gauntlet and shoves his left hand back into it. He picks up his helmet next.

"Where are you going?"

Voss looks up. Roger is filled with a sense of dread. The gaze pierces through any thought or feeling, and directly into his soul. Voss' eyes seem to glow with blue flame. He places the helm back on his head, but Roger can still see motes of blue light pouring through the guard.

"Voss..."

"My enemies do not last long in a war," comes the response from the armoured figure as he rises. Blood drips through his gauntlet onto the cloth, but it is slow and inconsistent. "If you want to be of help, then help me with my armour." Voss gestures to the scale shirt and pauldrons on the ground. He grabs his cloak from the sand as well.

"Whatever was down there will kill you!" Roger raises his voice.

Voss picks up the shirt and sets it over his helm. He finds his belt cinches it around his waist. Roger rises and continues to protest. Voss finishes, by clipping his banner-cloak to his fur ring, and turns to leave.

"He will die in there!" Roger exclaims, spinning to face his sister.

Helena shifts her balance from foot to foot. "We are not prepared to help," she replies.

"Find Brael and the goliath, then, and tell *them* to help!" Roger says. He takes off after Voss. Emari emerges from behind her tent at the sound of Roger approaching. Voss walks up the dune beyond her.

"He is going back in!" Roger exclaims, pointing up the hill.

"Let him!" she shouts. "It's his own fault that we almost died! It isn't my problem if he's developed a death-wish!"

"Fine, don't help!" Roger shouts back. "Give me your blade then, or another, and I will do it myself!"

Emari is taken aback. She draws her rapier and hands it to him. He takes it and begins to march up the dune after Voss, skidding through the sand with every step.

Chapter Four - The Fate of Voss' Enemies

3E056, 18th of Sowwing

Voss slides down the passage, ignoring the rope. His armour scrapes the sand from the stone, and the metal scratches the entire way down. He lands at the bottom, on the pile of sand, which is now littered with blood. He picks himself up, but falls against the stone basin for support.

"What are you doing, Voss?" Valindra's voice presses in his ear. For once, this doesn't hurt.

Voss does not reply. He rights himself before bending down and grabbing the box of vials he found earlier. He also takes a fresh torch from beside the pile of packs. He places the box on the lip of the basin, and takes one of the vials. He uncorks it and smells it carefully. It burns in his nose with an acrid, deathly scent. He summons his axe. It feels heavy in his hands. The liquid in the vial drips onto the blade as Voss tilts it slowly. It sits upon the cool metal, coagulating in the presence of air.

As he takes a few steps and lands clumsily against the main door-frame, he carefully drops the remaining five vials from the other side into his hip-bag. He places the wooden box back onto the floor, with the four vials of poison still inside.

A sound from behind him draws his attention. He turns to see a figure slide into the room, landing on the sand pile. Roger rises, wielding a thin sword, recognizable as one belonging to Emari. He wears no armour, and his footwear is wooden sandals.

Voss huffs, but does not turn fully around. Roger bends and picks up a spear, covered in blood. He swaps that into his main-hand, and moves the blade to the other.

"You will not make it far in that gear," Voss tells the man. "Return to camp."

"Unless you are coming with me, then I will do no such thing. You are not going to make it far in your condition."

"My condition is stable," Voss tells him, looking back. He grabs a vial from his bag and opens it. He uses his injured side to gently lift his helmet up, and uses the other hand to pour the vial's contents into his mouth. It tastes like metal, and burns going down, but he can feel heat begin to emanate from his wounds. He grunts, but retains composure as the pain dulls.

"I was worried you would say something of that sort. I sent my sister to the Dusk Knights and to find your other companion, the half-elf, and see if maybe they could talk some sense into you."

"I will not wait for them. If you are following me then I won't stop you. Just keep your own head on your shoulders," Voss says and turns back again.

Roger takes a deep breath and follows him through the double doors and into the large chamber beyond. The door on the other side of the room is still blown off its hinges, and no sign of movement can be seen throughout the area. No beast jumps from the shadows as they cross.

They reach the opposite door.

"Voss, stop," Roger hisses. To his surprise, the soldier listens, and turns around to face him.

"You will be slain with no armour," Voss notes. He looks to the ground, where two of the creatures lay dead. "Take a pair of boots, at the very least. If you think that one of their chain shirts would fit, or even a leather jerkin from that one, then take something for your chest." He points to the different bodies as he speaks.

"Voss, when you told me back in Railwood that you were going to fight back against the orcs that had been destroying my town for months, I believed that I would finally get the chance to destroy the beasts that had been tormenting me. I was filled with such a vengeance that I was excited by the prospect. When you told me and my militia to stay in town, I was furious. I spoke nothing of this feeling to you, but I would have thrown my life away if it meant I could put an end to those orcs. Now, though, I am grateful that I stayed. It was the smart thing to do. I was weak from months of stress, and my muscles yearned for rest. Voss, you are not thinking clearly. You are battered and bruised and injured. You can end this fight with help, maybe, and with sleep you would have an even better chance."

Voss stands still. He looks at Roger. The militiaman can see the blue light behind Voss' faceplate dim.

"You are a smart and kind man, Roger," Voss tells him, "but you cannot dissuade this course of action. I will wait for Brael or Jorrig or another - if they should come within minutes. If no one arrives, I will go alone, or with you, if you are an idiot enough to follow me in sandals." Roger cannot see, but Voss does offer a slight smile under his helmet.

Some minutes pass. Roger does trade his shoes for some ill-fitting, leather boots, tied with rough thread. One of the fallen creatures was also wearing a chain shirt that covers Roger well enough, despite not hanging below his waist.

Voss examines the opponents' corpses for signs of what they could be. Their faces remind Voss of a goblin's, with a short, hooked nose, and fang-like teeth. All of the creatures have long and black hair, and their skin is a brownish-red. They must be some sort of desert race. Peren would probably know what they were called, but Voss and Roger have never studied the denizens of this area, other than the desert orcs, which are similar to the orcs of the north, but with darker-toned skin.

Just as Roger is beginning to grow anxious once again and Voss is clearly preparing to move, a sound echoes from the first room. Through the doorway comes Jorrig. He is a tall being, but not overly so for a goliath, standing at just about nine feet. His skin is grey and, unlike others of his race, which Voss has seen on Streboya, he is also devoid of any tattoos. He has on a well fitting white tunic, under a reinforced leather vest and bracers, and a pair of linen trousers. On his feet he wears thick-soled boots that rise to his calves. On his back he has a lute, and in his hand he holds a greatsword, though for him it must feel a much shorter blade.

Behind him comes Brael, with his armour still on and his bow slung around his shoulder. His left bracer has been sliced through, and his arm has been hastily wrapped in a thick cloth, which blood is still seeping into. As the half-elf reaches Voss, the soldier holds out another of the healing vials.

Brael stops just in front of him, not yet taking the potion.

"You are a fool, Voss," Brael tells him. There is no humour on his face. The blue flame in Voss' eyes flickers, but then returns even brighter.

"You may tell that to my corpse if, one day, I fall. Until then, consider me as no such thing."

Brael takes the vial, and pours its contents along his forearm through the cloth. He then says, "I will not die here. If you are in danger, I will not hesitate in my retreat."

Voss stares for a long time at his companion without speaking.

"You are a friend, Voss," Brael tell him, emotion speckling his voice, "but I would not lay my life on the poor planning of even the best of friends."

Voss nods respectfully. "Let's go," he tells the others.

They say nothing else, and follow as Voss marches through the broken metal doorway. The soldier holds a torch in his off hand, and the flame hurls light against the walls and floor. Just eleven feet beyond the arch, the hall turns straight right, and a long, wide set of stairs leads down into the darkness.

Jorrig also lights a torch, having grabbed one from the pile near the entrance as well. No light appears to be coming from the lower level of this section of ruins.

"Brael," Voss says aloud, and sends through Valindra, "can you make out the end?"

"Barely," comes the response, "it appears to branch off in either direction, but it's hard to tell."

Voss nods, and sets his right foot on the first stair. As he continues to descend safely, the others begin to follow. Their feet send echoes up and down the passage with every step.

Roger counts fifty stairs until there is a flat landing. Then, he counts fifty more, and several dozen which still stretch ahead toward the bottom. The heat of the desert air begins to creep away, leaving them shivering. The air grows tighter as well, and quiet, suffocating them in dust and blackness. Finally, they near the end of the stairs, where the passage opens into a hall that runs perpendicular to the current tunnel. The walls beside them are still covered in odd carvings and remnants of once vibrant paints. These are more wholly intact than the ones on the pillars in the chamber above, but they seem to be similar in design. The figures in these carvings have long heads and, in some, there appear to be smaller humanoids alongside the taller, ruler-like beings.

They reach the base step. Still, it is not light here, but their torches dance into the hallway. Both directions lead to another turn; to the left the hall veers right, and to the right it turns left, wrapping around the wall of stone that lies directly in front of them. On the outside there are a series of doors, three on either side, all constructed of metal with a slight, blueish tinge. On the inside there is none, but a large, mural-like carving is engraved across most of the surface. It shows a great king on a throne, surrounded by bowing figures.

"We are in for a fight," Voss conveys to the others. He summons his to his off-hand with his torch, which takes the weight despite the wound in his shoulder. The others prepare themselves as well. Voss moves leftward, and walks three paces, so that he stands in front of the first door.

The soldier readies himself. He lifts his right leg to his chest. His foot then flies towards the metal and, with a deafening *crack,* the doorway is opened, and the door itself has been pinned against the inside-right wall.

Nothing stands within the room, save a cobbled-together stone bed with a rough looking sheet, and a wide, shallow stone box. Before the echoes have had a chance to completely fade, the sounds of two more doors opening draws attention. A war cry is sounded, and figures enter the hallway. Two of them are closer to Voss, and four are behind, closer to Jorrig and Brael.

Voss' torch is thrown ahead of him and upon the floor in a heartbeat, and his weapon and shield are readied not a moment later. Roger leaps back to stand with Jorrig. Brael fits an arrow and draws the string while moving between the two groups. They are not cut off from the stairs, but fleeing now would only leave more room for error.

The attackers rush them, trying to catch them off guard. Voss twists his shield horizontally and hits the button with his left thumb. The first creature throws his weight against it as it becomes magically fused with the air. He is repelled, and lands on his back near the torch.

Now that Voss and Brael have had even a brief amount of time to think about these assailants, they have realized much about their tactics. They fight well, with some wits and some strength, but — like orcs — they rely too heavily on offense and the first charge.

Brael's arrow streaks between Jorrig and Roger and cuts along the face of one of the attackers on that side. The war cry does not cease, but the goliath and Roger manage to lock the four in combat, trading blocks and parries.

Brael shoots two more arrows, which finish his target with precise ferocity. Jorrig manages to shove another into the inner wall, and slices through its neck with his sword. Roger spears the other in the guts and pushes it back several feet. It swings at him still, but he parries it with Emari's rapier.

Voss ducks below his shield. As the first vaults over, he cuts deep into its chest with his axe. The beast howls in pain as the poison takes effect. The other turns and bolts, as does the one that Roger is locked in combat with, and the uninjured one on their side as well. They rush and hobble as fast as they can around the corners. The sounds of multiple doors opening and feet rushing away drifts towards the group. Harsh voices in an unknown tongue mingle with the sputtering noises of the creature dieing from the poison.

As the enemies withdraw, Voss allows himself only a moment to breathe. As they fully exit his view he grabs his shield and presses the button again, taking the weight on his injured arm. He sets off leftwards, leading defensively. Two spears collide with the metal as he rounds the corner, and then the throwers retreat through another set of metal double doors on the inner wall. The soldier speeds after them and just before they can close him out, Voss shoves his shield into the gap and, once again, hits the button on the handle.

The others arrive behind him. As they pass the other rooms with open doors, they see a variety of sleeping spaces and work spaces with makeshift forges and kitchens.

Nothing can be seen through the gap of a few inches that is left between the new doors, but commotion and bellowing, harsh voices can by heard within the room. Several times something slams against the door, but Voss' shield does not budge.

"Jorrig," Voss says calmly, "on three, we push back."

The goliath eyes Voss with suspicion, but moves close to the door. Voss counts aloud, quiet enough to just be heard over the angry cries from inside. When the soldier reaches "three," he and Jorrig slam against the door. Despite some feeling of resistance, the metal is thrown aside. Voss quickly hits the shield's button and swings it in front of himself. An array of rocks and some spears clatter into the defensive wall and his plating, but nothing draws blood.

"Halt!" calls a commanding voice, belonging to a woman. The words reverberate through the room, and the red-skinned attackers stop, though most continue snarling. Voss and the others refrain from pressing an assault, but they still continue to move defensively into the room.

This is a long, rectangular hall lit by torches — five on each length wall, and three on each width — sitting in metal sconces. Voss has left his torch behind, but Brael tosses his onto the floor between them and the opposition, freeing his hands again.

They take the moment to survey the room. Opposite from the doors they entered is another set, and those are barred with two metal spears through the handles. Between the two entrances stands a large statue that stretches twelve feet upward, leaving about five feet between the top and the ceiling. The statue appears to be missing its left arm, which once would have stretched upward with the right as if reaching for something far off and above it. Its head is also cracked in some places. The chin has fallen off, and the eyes and nose have been worn down or rubbed off, as they are not visible at all. It looks now like a once powerful — now forlorn — being, reaching for something that it could once see before it, but has now left it behind.

At the farthest end of the hall, towards the woman's voice and the stairs that they descended, stands a foot-tall platform. This is bridged to the main floor by a single step. Upon the platform is an elegant, stone chair that is covered in fine;y made, but tattered cloth. There are bones around the raised floor. Some appear to be human-like, but most are clearly from animals. Around the seat is an array of polished gold plates, bowls, cups, and coins, all in large piles.

Between the statue and the platform stretches a long, stone table, surrounded by simple seats made from rough stone and covered by bits of leather.

Behind the group — opposite the throne — is a very thick, tall and wide, circular iron door. It appears similar to the door of a city-bank's great vault, nearly impenetrable and with no visible locks.

There are seven of the creatures here that they have been fighting. All of them are wearing simple leather jerkins and metal armours ranging from torn chainmail to rough plating. Five have grabbed shields instead of spears, but all wield long blades as main weapons. There is one who stands taller, and wields a great metal shield of ornate make. Surprisingly, he also seems to hold a greatsword that is slightly curved, jet black, and looks very well constructed. The blade of this sword is suspended half a foot from the floor, clenched in the creature's sturdy fist. This one continues to issue orders through the moment of pause that has possessed the room. Six of the seven fighters, all but their apparent leader, have fanned into a semi-circle with three on either side of the table. They stand defensively. They do not charge.

Sitting at the head of the table is a woman. She has long, blonde hair, which barely covers her naked breasts. Around her neck is a silver necklace with an orange-yellow gem as the pendant. Her eyes search for Voss' and he meets her gaze with little hesitation. They are not a singular colour, but neither do they appear to be more than one at any given time. In one moment they might be green, and in the next they have fluttered into purple.

She does not appear afraid.

"You are unwelcome here," she says. "Leave, or do battle with me, if you are suicidal. Those are your options for treading where you do not belong."

"Then I am the lucky one," Voss responds, "for at least I have options. Your only path is death." With these words, he begins his advance.

"Pity," the woman replies, "you are more a fool than I thought." As she speaks, the other opponents begin to shift, with one moving to the other side to strengthen their defence against the right flank that Voss is approaching along. "One of us shall die at the hands of the other." The woman rises. At first it seems that she is simply of an unnaturally tall stature, but, as she steps from the table, it becomes clear that she is not entirely human. Her body from the waist down is feline, with strong, hair-covered legs and clawed paws. As she moves, though, her form changes. Her breasts recede into her body, and her skin grows fur, which is the same golden colour as her hair and lower body. Her head grows along with her arms, until her entire body looks like that of a large lioness.

Voss is not deterred. He has fought many beasts before and, though the lions were long ago hunted from northern Estrand, this battle should be nothing special.

Roger stays in a defensive position behind Voss. Jorrig snatches a spear from the ground and moves to the left flank, forcing some attention away from Voss. Brael eyes the scene warily with an arrow in his off-hand.

Three of the goblin-like creatures ahead of Voss wield shields, one behind them holds two spears. Three, including their leader, are focused on Jorrig.

Voss is fifteen feet away now. One spear is hurled towards him. He whips his shield around to the right just in time to deflect it. The spears are all solid, sharpened metal poles. Their weight alone makes them difficult to block, and likely even more so to wield.

The soldier has exposed his left side, and one of the shield-bearers rushes him, swinging for the open area with its longsword. Voss anticipated this, however, and with unnatural speed he spins his axe so that the haft collides with the blade and shoves it upward.

Roger seizes the opportunity and leaps forward, onto the table. He brings his spear down towards the staggered opponent, and barely avoids its shield. The spear enters the creature's shoulder. With a cry of pain the shield is dropped and the figure retreats behind the others.

Brael has decided on his course of action. He springs onto the statue and begins to climb. The lioness sees this and reacts swiftly, bolting onto the table. As she barrels for Brael, she manages to also knock Roger off balance and send him falling against Voss.

On the other side of the room, Jorrig is ravaging his own opponents. Despite his relatively peaceful seeming nature, and apparent love for music, there is no disputing the goliath blood in his veins. The first attack comes for his legs, but he parries the swing with his own behemoth of a sword. He lunges quickly after, but is blocked by the shield. Jorrig throws the spear towards the one farther away, and before either can react, he grabs hold of the closer one's shield.

The creature releases his grip on the buckler and goes for a two-handed swing. Before the blade connects with Jorrig's side, the goliath swings the shield and lands a blow with it upon the attacker's head. He suffers a small gash along the back of his leg, but manages to plunge his greatsword through his first opponent's spine.

As Voss steadies himself and his ally, the other two shield-bearers leap towards him. Voss barely gets between Roger and the new attack as they clash against his defence. He manages to hold them off, but they do manage to pierce through his right greave and stab through Voss' foot into the ground.

Roger spins around the soldier and interrupts the beast. His spear impales the one who injured Voss through its throat. It gurgles and releases its grasp on the sword immediately as it fumbles for breath.

The lioness reaches the base of the statue as Brael pulls his legs onto the stone arm reaching upward. The structure holds, but the width does not make the half-elf feel very safe. The feline form begins to climb, but Brael can see her struggling. He takes the time to notch two arrows and loose them one after the other into the fray. The first strikes the shoulder of the second shield-bearer fighting Voss, and the second pierces the arm of the spear-thrower as he winds up towards Roger.

Voss stumbles on his injured foot but still manages to cut through the nearest target across the chest. This gives Roger the chance to push forward and bring Emari's rapier across the spear-wielder's throat. Voss turns toward the leader of the goblin creatures, who has backed towards the platform. The soldier begins to below a low, powerful roar of animosity.

The lioness manages to reach the arm of the statue. As she does, Brael pushes off the face. Her claws catch his chest as he jumps, however, and leave a long rend from above his navel to below his left knee. He lands on the table, rolling to avoid further injury. He attempts to stand, but winces in pain.

Jorrig narrowly dodges a spear thrown by the final thrower, but loses his grip on his sword while moving. The creature rushes towards him. The goliath blocks the first swing of the enemy's sword with the stolen shield. He turns the wooden buckler with such force that the blade is wrenched from the opponent's fingers.

Voss trades blows with the leader, neither landing a hit in the first volley. The leader swings his greatsword with surprising strength, but the blow is parried.

Jorrig grabs the thrower with both hands and raises him into the air.

Voss leads with his shield and slams the leader into the ornate throne. The spike drives through his liver. The leader drops his blade.

Jorrig bends and brings the creature rushing headfirst into the stone table.

Voss' axe slashes through the leader's skull at the same time Jorrig spills the contents of his opponent's head onto the table. Their bodies go limp.

The lioness had prepared to pounce and finish off Brael. Seeing the carnage of her allies from above, however, she leaps sideways instead. She lands gracefully near the open door.

"No!" Voss cries, blue light pouring from his helmet. He leaves his shield where it is, pinning the corpse to the seat, and takes off after the lioness. She darts from the room, but Voss is moving fast as well - despite his foot. He vaults onto the table, leaps over Brael, and continues through the door.

She is faster than he is, already rounding the next corner.

"Valindra! Get ahead of her, now!" the soldier yells. His plan is hastily cobbled together, but he is already set on it. The spectral archer bolts from his body, but for the moment he feels numb to all pain. The spirit speeds through walls and up the stairs, reaching the landing ahead of the lioness. "Bring me to you," Voss orders. Valindra cannot disobey, and begins to attempt the most difficult task she has ever done for him.

Voss' body begins to unwind into the same blue mist as his weapons. Each foot fall leaves him feeling lighter and colder. His scream of pain is soon lost in the empty air.

The lioness is almost to the landing. The archer is before her, but she does not see this as any more than an illusion. She dashes through the womanly figure. Her paws hit the first step, then the third. Her back legs suddenly give out and she lands upon her stomach on the steps. Pain erupts from her lower back. She forces her upper body back into human form, so that from the lion's shoulders emerge a human torso, arms, and head. She cranes back toward the landing.

In the darkness of the stairs, all she can see is glinting metal protruding from her back and, behind that, a grinning skull wreathed in blue flame and crystals of ice.

Voss steadies his mind. He has been thrown through an alternate realm in which he was not meant to enter. His body cries out in pain and frigid cold, but his mind ignores it. He has severed any current hope of the lioness' escape. He prepares himself to lift the axe once again.

"Wait! I was wrong!" the woman coughs.

Voss stops and responds, "About what?"

"You. Confidence is often indicative of some shortcoming, of a false ability or strength. I clearly underestimated you, and that was my undoing." Her voice is hoarse with pain.

The blue flame in Voss' eyes dims. "What were you doing in here?" he asks.

"Surviving."

"You seem more intelligent than I believed. You did underestimate me, but you are not a savage beast as you first appeared to be. Perhaps I underestimated you. Why, then, are you underground with a mob of beasts for protection? And why should I spare you?"

She looks away. "My eyes charm those who gaze into them. I warn you to avoid them as we continue to parlay, as men fall more easily under their control. Those creatures were under my sway, and made themselves useful in smithing and in hunting. We did not mean harm on anyone else, only defended ourselves when you arrived. We have been living in fear since the army arrived above."

Voss nods. "I see."

"You have beaten me. I am at your mercy. If you are to kill me, I only ask that you do so quickly, as my pain is growing. Your blade certainly has some poison on it."

Voss is uncertain on how to proceed. His anger is subsiding, and he does not feel done with the conversation. "If I chose to let you live, what would you do?" He asks her.

"I would almost certainly die without some sort of healing."

"And if you received some sort of healing?"

"I desire no chaos, nor harbour malice towards you, if that is what you are asking. I desire life, that is all I have ever sought. I bear no sadness for the loss of my servants, for they only served my spell."

Voss stares her down. She does not meet his eyes. He wrenches the axe from her back, provoking a stifled cry. He opens his hip-bag. Three more vials of the healing solution lie carefully within. He opens one and drips the contents onto his own foot, which is throbbing intensely with pain. He opens another and pauses. There is brown, murky blood oozing from the lioness section of her back, where his axe bit deep into her flesh and bone. "I do not know if I have already dealt too grievous an injury for this to heal," Voss admits. "If this does save your life, then you will remain my prisoner until I decide your fate. For now, you are too dangerous to let out of sight."

"I accept," she responds through closed teeth.

Voss nods. He pours the vial into her wound. She clenches her delicate jaw. Pain knots into her brow and face as the liquid burns her wound shut. It is not pretty, but the blood stops flowing. "The poison should at least be slowed, as there was not much left on the blade," Voss says. "Can you stand?"

"Not in this form," she responds, "at least not for now." Her body begins to change again. The fur recedes and she grows thinner and feminine. Soon it appears that a normal woman is lying naked upon the stairs in front of Voss, with blonde hair that rolls down her shoulders and back. She stands shakily. "Are you not intending to bind my hands?" she asks as she turns towards him. She still does not look at his eyes. She is beautiful, with tanned skin and a round, youthful face that still holds a wisdom that only experience can grant.

"No," he answers her. "If I believed you would betray me here, I would have killed you. If I thought that I could not handle you in the future if you betrayed me then, I would have killed you. Now come, we are not yet done, and you have injured an ally of mine. We must gather ourselves before leaving."

"Still," she says, "you cannot possibly allow a prisoner to go with you whilst armed." She reaches and draws the necklace from around her neck. Now Voss sees the gem is not only warmly coloured, but pulses with some powerful energy. "This is a weapon that was given to me by one of the men you slew," she explains with little emotion. "It if cracks, it will releases its power wherever it is aimed. Be careful with it, as it is almost certainly volatile."

He takes it, and places it gingerly in his bag. He grabs her arm then, and pulls her with force behind himself as he begins to descend the stairs again. His head aches with constant pain, and he is certain that the full strain of his actions will soon be upon him. For now, he retains his focus and leads the woman back towards what once was her hall.

Chapter Five - The Mind of The Bard

3E056, 18th of Sowwing

The sun has flown past noon. Emari's rage has subsided, but a new anguish has taken its place. She shakes her head, sitting on the floor of her tent. She has been doing nothing save for staring at the flaps as they flutter slightly in the warm breeze. The minutes smudge together.

Her mask lies beside her on the canvas bottom that fights a futile battle to keep the desert sands out. She has pulled her hair from the short bun that she keeps it in, and it now floats gently by her chin. The soft light that pushes through the fabric paints the strands almost purple and orange, as opposed to its natural blue and white. She has pixie-like features; a short, button nose, a round face with an angular jaw, and large eyes. Her soft skin is a deeper blue in the light than it usually would be. It is for her own sake that she keeps her origin a secret, for there is no one like her that she has met, and many who have seen her have given her titles that she would not call any other.

Now — for whatever reason — the weight of the thin wooden mask seems too much to bear. Maybe her tears needed freedom to run unobstructed down her cheeks.

It is not for Boe that she sobs quietly. His injuries are grave, but he may yet recover, and while she does blame Voss for their brush with death, she is not entirely angry anymore. She just feels paralyzed. There is a large part of her that has yearned only to run after Roger and Voss and perhaps help them against the unknown depths of the ruins. The other, smaller part of her has been stronger somehow, and has kept her sitting cross-legged on the floor.

There is no way for her to state with any simplicity the way she has come to feel about herself and those who surround her. She now genuinely enjoys the company of Brael and even, at times, of Boe. Voss does not provide her any joy, nor does she seem to give any to him. Somehow, though, she feels closer to him than to anyone else. It is not something that she wholly understands, nor does she wholly want to.

She trusts Voss, or she had — fully — until this morning. That is one issue: trust. She never intended to find someone to trust. He has been cruel on occasion, rude, and blunt, but he has not lied to her, so far as she can tell. He may brush off her questions, or refuse to answer some, or refuse to even talk at all at points, but he is no liar. He has honour, in a sense, above many she has met.

The only other person she ever came close to since she left home was Shae Vatorril. She made love to her the first night they met, and they spent a few days together afterward. That may have been the last time Emari truly felt happy. Since then, the only feelings that have at all mimicked joy have been the excitement she got from pulling cons and heists with the small group of bandits that she ran with and — now — the feeling she has for Voss. This is not a lighthearted joy, though, and she is not smiling; she is in tears. It is a heavy kind of joy, a feeling that reminds her of the pains of youth and the sweet little anguishes of learning the lessons of life.

It has felt like a long time since she first sat in her tent when she hears commotion coming from the east. She stands shakily and puts her mask back onto her face. She loosely bunches her hair into her hood and then pulls this over her head.

The bard steps from the tent and looks instinctively for the rock cropping. Five figures are descending the hill towards her. She is, at first, relieved, then she is confused at the increased number. She walks towards them without thinking, meeting them near the base of the dune.

Voss walks down ahead of the rest, his red banner-cloak fluttering in the hot wind. He is pulling along a blonde woman by one arm. He has also grabbed a blade. It is a greatsword with a gentle curve towards the top. It is made in an unknown style, but it seems to catch the sunlight and hold it, maintaining its unique, blue-black appearance. Brael is being supported by Roger and limping. Jorrig is carrying a large metal box and walking behind the others.

"Voss," Emari begins to speak.

"We need to talk," he responds, brushing by her and continuing for the tents. The others follow close behind. They pause briefly near the wagon. Jorrig slams the box into the back, opens it, and removes a beautiful looking silver and gold necklace with red gems.

"This is mine," he tells Voss in a deep and commanding voice, who makes no objections. The goliath nods and returns to his own camp.

"Roger," Voss says, "take Brael to the medical area, and grab something from the box if you'd like as well."

Roger nods. He takes a unique, glittering coin, and helps Brael away from the camp.

"Who is this?" Emari finally asks.

Voss looks at the blonde woman.

"My name is Hariscine," she speaks. It is a calm voice. "I am Voss' prisoner."

Emari glances between them, her mask growing pale.

"She needs medical attention, and I need you to supply it," Voss tells the bard.

"You must be joking!" Emari says, throwing her hands to either side of herself in exasperation. "You've gone off to your certain death after nearly dying once already this morning, leave me to worry and to grow guilty, and instead emerge with a beautiful, naked woman and a box of gold?"

"You had no need to worry, as you are not responsible for me," Voss tells her in a monotonous tone. "That box is only the first of many, and this woman is a more pressing concern of mine."

"Why?" Emari's voice is shrill.

"We need to see if any poison is in my body from Voss' axe," Hariscine answers.

Emari stares at Voss for a long time. No one speaks.

"Get her into your tent and I will see what I can do," the bard finally relents.

They move into Voss' tent, where he promptly shuts the flaps and pins them together. The woman sits on the small cot that has been set up for the soldier to sleep on. His tent is clear for the most part, same as Emari's, with only the bed for sleep and a small storage chest for what belongings they need daily.

Voss wraps his new sword in cloth and sets it under his cot. He then directs the woman to lay on the floor, and she obeys. She sits awkwardly, with her legs under and beside herself. It looks uncomfortable.

"Emari," Voss says, looking at the bard, "do not be alarmed." He then looks to the woman. "Show your true form."

The woman grins slightly. "I have no *true* form," she explains, "but I will change such that this healer may examine the wound."

Emari watches as the woman's lower body begins to change. It grows fur and elongates into a large, feline physique. Emari's mask changes briefly from red to a solid white, and then settles on a swirling mix of light-pink and blue.

"What *are* you?" she asks.

"I am a desert shifter. My kind are rare, but can be found throughout these lands," Hariscine replies. "In what stories are passed down, we once roamed farther north, but we were killed for our eyes."

"Do all of your kind shift into cats?" Emari presses.

"Many do, but some choose other forms. Whatever feels closer to our heart. I never learned more than one, though some can learn many."

"Where is your wound?"

"Near my hind legs."

Voss remains in the tent, but stands to the side as Emari examines the tender scarring of the axe blade. It was clearly a deep wound. She hums, and her notes push through the skin and flesh of the strange creature. She can feel her pain.

The wound may heal naturally, but at this point there is little that her magic can do. There is no poison that she can sense, but she is not trained to observe this in injuries. She expresses her findings to no comments.

"I do not think that she is in any further danger," the bard says after. "It is possible that a powerful healer could mend the scar, but otherwise I believe that, given rest, she will likely regain full mobility in a few weeks."

"Weeks," Voss huffs.

"What is the issue?" Hariscine asks.

"I will not send you to the desert to die with this injury, yet I cannot allow you to roam free in the camp with no supervision," he tells her.

"So I am to be under constant watch?" she asks, not in objection.

"I don't understand what is going on!" Emari interjects. "What happened in there?"

Voss quickly recounts the most important details. As he concludes, he clutches at his helm and grunts in pain.

"You are exhausted, Voss," the bard says.

"Yes," Hariscine agrees, "I saw the amount of strain he was under in the ruins, as you call them."

"You know nothing of my strain," Voss tells the shifter.

"Your eyes were not your own," she tells him. "Your spirit-woman must draw on something in order to manifest, and I am certain it is not some trained arcane pool in your mind."

Voss looks at her. She is not looking back. "What is it, then?" he asks.

"I am no mage, I could not say for certain."

"You seem fairly scholarly for a desert creature."

"I would guess that, being the most natural source of arcane energy, it would be drawing on your own soul," she tells him calmly. "Otherwise, your mind or blood."

Voss looks at her for some time. "Hm," he hums at length, "that seems likely, then." He is equally calm.

"Wow, it's like watching someone speak to their own reflection," Emari says. "Well, if you are going to keep monotonously bonding, I am going to excuse myself."

Emari leaves the tent and walks hastily into the order's camp. There are eyes everywhere, and many glance as she passes them. She is walking fast. Soon she is in the square area. There are tents arranged around it where people are gathered in the shade, and more cloth pieces are hung above the makeshift tables to provide cover. There is drink and food out, as lunch has only recently passed. Emari finds a table where no one else has seated themselves and begins to cry once more.

Her mask hides her tears, and she became good at stifling sobs long ago, though her mask becomes deep blue to let those who watch her know something of her emotion. She lets herself weep quietly as the hot wind picks up again.

After a long while spent sitting alone, she is joined by two young men and a woman. They introduce themselves, and so Emari does the same, giving them "Chablis" as a name, and laughing off the oddity of it. One of the men leaves and returns with large tankards of ale. Emari pulls her mask forward and quickly downs the cup to half. The others cheer and start their own drinks.

She learns that one of the men, the more attractive of the two, is married to the woman. They tell her about their great adventure northward into the Tyhamm Wilds, and she pretends to listen enthusiastically. Feigning emotion has become second nature to her. Her personality is now a defence, or an offense. It is as malleable as clay, but once she sets it to dry it becomes as hard as steel. Usually.

The other man begins to flirt with her, as she anticipated. She does not think particularly highly of her own beauty, but she has had enough time in her life to recognize the patterns. She knows of this man's jealousy. The woman at the table is quite pretty, and clearly he has had feelings for her in the past. He is looking to forget this for an evening.

She lets him flirt, but gives little in return.

He does not give up easily, continuing to bring her drinks, which she accepts. Soon she is feeling the affects of intoxication. The heat, strength of the ale, and her weakened emotions all play a role.

They spend the greater part of the afternoon talking. She says things that he wants to hear. He does the same. She tells him as the singing fades low that she has to return, but he responds by telling her where his tent is and that, if she wants to, she can find him there any time. She nods and leaves.

Back at her own camp, Voss, Scazgix, and Hariscine have joined Jorrig, Holland, and Yuriel around the extinguished fire and are having their own wines and ales. There seems to be an intense discussion going on. Whenever Voss looks away from the new woman, she looks at him.

Emari tries to feel nothing, but an impermeable wall seems to have surrounded the others and she cannot bring herself to break through. She walks to her tent. She sits and lets hours wash over her, eating dried rabbit and soft cheese.

When the sun has abandoned the sky, Emari rises again. Now Brael and Roger are at the fire as well, the flames are licking the night, and the conversation seems serious, but not ripe with anger or sadness.

Emari ignores it, and ignores her name being called by Roger as she turns into the maze of tents. She will not remember the man's name that she met that afternoon, nor will she remember the encounter that she will have with him soon. She is resolute in this, though maybe she wishes that it had some meaning for her, so that a new feeling could replace whatever is in her heart tonight.

Chapter Six - Into Darkness

3E056, 20th of Sowwing

Two sleeps have passed since the clearing of the ruins. Some smaller groups of adventurers have even begun to pack and depart north again. The major guilds; Helm of Auris, The Knights of Jallor, and The Edgewood Alliance — among others — are settled to stay another week to exhaust their supplies and revel.

Voss has enlisted the help of Bigger They Are, Roger's guild, to pack and bring many of the riches out of the chamber under the desert. He remained in bed for the first half of the day, to give his head a chance to rest, but began to help the guild in extracting the rest of the riches in the evening of the nineteenth.

Hariscine did find some of the treasure in the throne room, but not most of it, and she is not in opposition to the movement and taking of it. She advocates her own submission, stating that she has clearly lost, and wishes only to survive now that things have changed.

The platform around the great stone throne was surrounded by piles of golden items and coins. It takes several trips each to bring just the larger items to their wagon. By the afternoon of the twentieth, after nearly two full days of leisurely removing the wealth, all that is left in the room is a few scattered silver coins, a few large pieces of armour that are accented in golden lines — which have been ignored in favour of lighter items — and a sword that was clutched tightly in a skeletal hand. This appears to be of standard quality, but as Voss grabs it, along with the chest-piece of the armour set, he finds that the blade is very light. The hilt is set with finely cut gems. He swings it, and the air seems to shine around the arc. As his grip on it grows more comfortable, it also seems to shine dimly in the low light.

He looks at it for a long time. It is a shorter blade than usual, but is still much longer than a dagger. It is made of expertly folded steel. Voss taps it against his chest plating, and the sound of metal intermixes with faint harps and lyres. It is certainly magical. He takes it, along with the armour piece, and returns slowly to the surface.

He leaves the blade unceremoniously on Emari's cot. He has not spoken much with her in the past few days, nor, truly, in the past month. He goes afterward to the Dusk Knights' camp with a handful of golden lions and trades those for the help they've provided and a new sheath for the blade he found. They find one that fits loosely, made of light-brown leather with black-dyed bands at the top and bottom. It is unassuming, but well made. He returns to the bard's tent and prepares the gift in a more appealing manner by sheathing it and lying it atop the thin sheet. Her journal is lying upon the wooden chest. He glances at it. Briefly, he is compelled to open it and perhaps learn something of her thoughts. He dismisses the idea, however, and leaves.

It is during the small lunch wither Roger, Helena, and Holland, that Emari returns. She has been in and out of camp for the past two days. She sits across from Voss and grabs herself a bowl of stew. There are not many animals to hunt in the area, but some supplies have been coming down from the town of Dragon's Rest and, as such, they are having a salty mixture of rabbit, mushrooms, and potatoes.

The bard eats much faster than the others, and soon leaves her bowl in the pot of dirty water before returning to her tent.

Voss' armour is still damaged, and will not be repaired until they have returned to a town or city farther north. He has acquired a new chain shirt from another adventuring group for a small collection of gold cups and plates. He can also replace his greaves with the ones in the throne hall, but the rest of that gear would certainly be too small for him to wear comfortably.

Emari emerges with the sword strapped to her hip and sits down by the fire pit again. She sits beside Voss, still saying nothing.

Voss opens a discussion once she has settled.

"There is still the issue of the large metal door in the throne hall," he says. "We have not yet discovered a way for it to be opened, but it must be possible. I would like help in searching the room. We should prepare for anything, and carry extra torches, though there are still several in the first room down the entrance."

"The door is certainly not sealed by magic," Holland says. "I would have felt that. I dare to guess, then, that it could be mechanical. I saw no hinges, either, so it cannot be manpower alone that opens it."

For the first time in a while, Emari speaks openly to them. She says, "Unless it was meant to remain sealed."

"All doors are built with a means of opening them," Voss tells her with certainty, "regardless of the purpose. It may be built with the hope of blocking something off, but if they wanted to seal it forever, they would have built a wall."

Hariscine emerges from Voss' tent. She has spent her last two days there for the most part. If she had any malicious intent towards the soldier, she would have had a chance to act by now. It is her who speaks next.

"I cannot help but listen to your discussion," she says. "I have spent a good deal of time in those ruins. Most doors were there before me. The rooms were built by ancient beings. I do not know any way to open the circle-door, but I have also not spent much time looking for one."

"I have good luck in picking out details," Voss responds to her as she approaches to circle. "I would like to spend some time searching the room within the next few days."

"Are you not still sore and injured?" Holland asks.

"I am, but that I can deal with," the soldier responds. In truth, his physical injuries have mostly healed. His shoulder and foot are still aching, but there is no bleeding and the swelling has gone down almost entirely. His mind has taken longer to calm down than the rest of him. The voices in his head were initially excited with their freedom in the last two battles, but already they are restless again, despite seeming as exhausted as Voss does. His headache has still not fully subsided, and he has experienced intermittent nosebleeds. Today, though, he feels like he is getting better. Even since breakfast, his mind has quieted a good deal.

"I will go with you," Holland says. "We are leaving the day after tomorrow, but — should we head down again tomorrow — I am not opposed to seeing what lies behind this last great secret of the ruins."

"I will go as well," adds Brael. "I have not escaped unscathed yet from a trip below the sands, but I also have yet to be unsurprised. I would like to see the first streak ended, even if it means the second must end as well." The archer's arm has healed fully, but his leg and lower torso are still very tender. He has not helped with removing the gold, nor has he been into the ruins at all since their fight with Hariscine and her gang of desert-goblins.

"I want to see this door," says Scazgix. The small draconic king has been taking this entire trip as a chance to relax, it seems. He has been drinking in the square, and learning a variety of curses in different languages. The others have been doing their best to keep him away from any danger, and so far he has not resisted.

"No," Voss tells him, "you must stay here and keep watch." The dragon-kin looks confused for a moment, but then he takes an air of pride.

Emari has been thinking. She is still not happy with her entire situation, but the last time that Voss went into danger without her, she felt responsible. "I would like to help," she says. Voss glances at her, but does not say anything.

"I would help too, but my guild is beginning to pack," Roger tells Voss.

"We meant to be off sooner," Helena admits, "but we've postponed to help."

The others wish them varying degrees of luck, but decide that they have had enough of these ruins for a long while at least. They all join together in the square for a meal at dinner time, though, and share many drinks. The merriment of the evening passes and soon they return to their beds. Voss has had less difficulty than he thought he would in getting used to Hariscine's presence. She seems more comfortable in her human form, as her mobility otherwise would be hindered. Voss has given her loose fitting clothes, but when she is not outside she often leaves them folded in the corner on the floor.

Voss returns this night and sits on his cot, which is built with sturdy wooden legs and a woolen bag that is loosely packed with cotton and serves as a mattress. Truly, it is not a comfortable bed, but it is still slightly better that resting on the ground. Voss has even seen Hariscine laying upon it when he is not using it.

He removes his helmet and looks at the woman sitting naked on the floor.

She looks up and gasps, quickly looking away.

"I do not fear your gaze," he tells her as he fumbles with the first of his armour straps.

She rises and approaches. "You should," she responds. "Do you want help?"

"I don't need any."

"That does not answer the question."

Voss pauses. "Fine," he says.

She unbuckles his dented chest piece with ease and sets it neatly on the ground where he usually keeps it. He removes his chain shirt while she releases his greaves, cuisses, and faulds. Soon he is sitting comfortably in just a pair of tight cloth pants. His chest is covered in short hairs, and his broad shoulders are reddened by the weight of his pauldrons.

"Why do you wear it all, when you are not at war?" Hariscine asks him.

"I am always at war," he responds off-handedly, slurring slightly from the drinks he has had.

"With what?" comes her response. It catches him off guard. He thinks for a moment.

"Myself, I suppose," he mutters. He lies down on the mattress. There is no need for a blanket; he has felt warm of late.

"Well, I like whichever side is winning right now," Hariscine tells him, lying on the floor, "for that side is interesting and merciful. I think that you are in turmoil, however, and I wish you would let me help somehow."

"You sound like Emari," he murmurs.

"That is because she cares about you as well. I think she cares quite the same as I do."

Voss blows air through his nose and closes his eyes. Hariscine lets her gaze fall on his face. It is framed by a rough beard and long, greasy hair, both of which are flecked with grey despite his young age. Wrinkles have dug themselves across his forehead and around his mouth, but he does not look old, nor weak. He is — and has always been — a soldier, and he will have fight in him until he is slain in combat or is convinced to lay down his helmet and cloak.

The morning of the first of Mivosera dawns spotted by clouds. Another summer storm has brewed over the north, but none of the rains or thunder can reach so far into the desert, only the strong winds that pick up sand and scatter it against the sides of tents.

Voss is armoured with the help of Hariscine and has his bags packed full of supplies by the time breakfast is prepared by Yuriel Ferndash. Holland and Brael are largely unarmoured, outfitted in minor leathers. Holland also wears a half-cuirass with the owl of Horan engraved upon it, and has a small, dark buckler on his left arm, and a elegant longsword at his left hip. They have also brought full packs, though, and strapped torches to the sides of them. Brael has looped a long rope to the bottom of his as well. Emari is dressed in a casual grey and white set of cloth, with a dark, hooded cloak around her shoulders. She has placed leather armour over her chest, arms, and legs. Her pack is small, with only three torches bundled loosely to the top.

They eat quickly, giving hardly enough to time to savour the sweetness of the yam stew. After breakfast, they shoulder their packs and prepare to set off. Yuriel takes Holland's arm and quietly wishes him luck. They hug for a long moment before the sister releases him and her brother leaves camp.

Voss looks at the half-elven girl as she begins to clean the dishes. She is strong and observant, but he knows very little about her. She cares deeply about Holland, but he is a capable paladin. Paladin's rarely carry divine magic — if such a thing truly exists — and Evandur was certainly more powerful than most, but many are trained in expert swordsmanship and in basic arcane healing or spellcraft. Holland is leader of a guild on top of his training under the eyes of Horan, God of Wisdom and Knowledge, and seems, at least to Voss, to be a very capable man.

They trudge up the dune and into the rock cropping. The rope that was first tied to the standing stone still hangs down the passage, blending almost into the sand that it lies upon. Voss carefully descends into the darkness. Emari, Holland, and Brael follow in that order.

When they are all standing in the first room, Voss and Holland light torches. The warm flames fill the room. It is growing hotter as the day matures, but it is still fairly cool for the moment. They walk calmly through the next room, around the long basin, to the broken door. They have moved the damaged metal and leaned it against the left wall so that it stands out of the way. Next, they venture down the long stairs. Finally, once they are in the throne room, they place four torches in the sconces nearest to the door.

The door is a perfect circle, eight feet in diameter. It is covered by a layer of dust, flecks of sand, and patches of rust where some moisture has found its way to the iron-like metal. It is a thick door, certainly, as they can barely hear the echo that results from pounding against it. Their side is worked with intricate symbols and drawings. There are depictions of war, weapons, and great beasts. Emari shivers as she inspects the images. Nothing on the door itself seems to move or activate an opening mechanism. They inspect every inch of the frame as well, which protrudes a few inches from the thick stone walls, but this leads to no new information.

After many minutes of scanning the door, Voss begins to grow restless. The others pull their waterskins out and decide to sit at the table for a short break. Voss paces back and forth across the room. He pulls at the torch sconces on the walls, hoping for a miracle, but it does nothing.

He walks to the throne and sits upon the tattered cloth that covers it, leaning comfortably against the back. His head does not quite stick over the top of the large seat. His feet sit in a groove along the floor, which is the width of the throne, and sticks out for a foot ahead of it, chiseled into the stone.

"Holland!" Voss calls, standing suddenly.

The paladin jumps up immediately. "What is it, Voss?"

"Come here. Help me move this." Voss steps to the right. Holland steps up on the left.

"What, the throne?"

"Yes. Look!" Voss says, pointing to the groove on the ground. "Why would they leave a space to move a throne unless something was behind it?"

Holland straightens his back, suddenly struck by realization. He grabs his side of the seat. His hand barely fits between the throne and the back wall. Voss does the same, and together they heave the seat half a foot forward.

The wall behind the seat is no different from the rest, but Voss can now see that on the back of the throne itself is a small metal square that sticks an eighth of an inch from the stone. He pushes it with no hesitation, and the metal square clicks into the back of the seat. A rumbling begins on the other side of the room. All eyes turn to watch the iron door. After several long seconds, the circular door slides backward until the metal has passed the stonework. It then rolls leftward, and disappears into the wall, revealing a long, circular, dark, stone passage.

The torches around the entrance do little to illuminate the staggering blackness beyond. Heat also pushes into the room, warming the cold stone and flickering the flames in the slight wind.

"Well," says Brael, "I guess the surprises aren't over after all. I should hope this means my other streak is not to continue as well."

"We should get others," Emari says. She is staring down the new tunnel. The others are all doing the same.

Voss steps away from the throne. He walks past Holland, then Brael, then Emari. He grabs a burning torch from one of the sconces as he shoulders his pack again. He does not pause, walking straight through the doorway. Brael is the first to react to this, grabbing his pack as well and jogging to catch up to the soldier.

"What are you doing?" the half-elf asks him, his icy eyes burrowing into the side of Voss' helmet.

Voss projects his response into the hunter's mind using Nhasan. "I intend to see where this leads." The path that they follow seems to be gently winding left, and then right again. It is also descending at a gentle angle. The ground is uneven, but not so much as to be an issue. The tunnel was carved by skilled creatures, holding its shape after years of neglect.

"There could be any number of dangers down here," warns Brael. "This could connect straight to the Lowerlands. If that is the case, then venturing farther is an extremely dangerous endeavour. Spiders, many different tunneling beasts, and hunters that rely only on sound and smell could wait below."

Holland and Emari are coming as well. They catch up to Voss and Brael, but do not interrupt the conversation. The farther they walk, the more stifling the air is becoming.

"I am not afraid of any creatures that hide in the dark beneath the world," Voss says aloud and through Nhasan.

"You should be," Brael argues. "Do you remember in the Velvet Hall when I spoke to you about the Krulaeji man?"

"Yes."

"His kind dwell here, beneath the civilized world, in blackness, where their hatred can fester and grow. They are vicious and cruel. If they are this far south, which they may well be, then we are entering their domain," Brael pleads.

"If we meet them, then we shall slay them. It will be a service to those races who still live in the light."

"Voss, I urge you to be careful. The farther this passage leads, the closer we come to death," says the hunter. He may mean this in more than one sense, but at the very least he is not wrong in a divine sense. The farther one travels underground, the farther they move into the domain of Echoshan, God of Death and Darkness.

Voss does not give thoughts on this topic though. He walks ahead without any more words. After ten minutes of steady marching, with every step sending echoes bouncing ahead of them, they see light ahead. Around several more gentle bends in the tunnel, an amber glow reaches out to them. They are also suddenly aware of a great rumbling noise that has been ever-so-slowly growing louder.

"The sound of Thrella's heart," Holland says quietly. Voss and Emari look towards him. His face is stern, but his eyes study the path ahead with uncertainty.

As they near the source of the light, the tunnel begins to widen until they emerge into a large, open chamber. It appears to have been mostly naturally formed, with a tall ceiling and walls on either side that are a far distance off. Ahead of them is a flattened ground that stretches out for twenty or so metres before it falls into a wide chasm. The amber glow rumbles from this gap. On the other side there is another half of the chamber, with floor that stretches another twenty metres to the opposite wall, dotted with more raised structures.

Around them on the floor are a variety of old machines, long fallen into decay. There are several forges built out from the walls, and a plethora of tables and raised platforms carved from the stone ground rise up like islands. This was once an ancient smithy of sorts, likely with housing and storage, but now it is certainly inoperable.

"Explains where the metal doors came from," Emari states.

Voss nods, looking ahead. "Hariscine said that her followers smithed as well, but they couldn't have made anything more that the spears and blades at their makeshift forges." The soldier approaches the chasm, which is hardly distinguishable in the low light. The others follow close behind. They peer over the edge and into the deep ravine below. As they do, they are hit with a blast of heat. The sides of the divide are sheer and tall. The other side is not too far, just over fifteen feet, but it is also a few feet higher.

At the very bottom, at least a hundred feet down, runs a river of lava, the source of light and hot air. A single piece of rock seems to branch across about halfway down and fifteen feet to the left of the group. It looks as though it runs out of one tunnel and into another.

"That is a bridge across, I am certain," Voss tells the others. "There must be a tunnel on the left wall of this chamber.

"Voss, we cannot keep going," Emari proclaims. "We are going to run into danger eventually, or lose our way. We should be taking this venture with better preparation."

"I am prepared," Voss tells her. "You can return if you wish. I will not blame you."

"You will not find the end of this tunnel if it connects to some network of others," Brael argues. "Krulaeji cities and towns have many passages carved by their enslaved. The deep-men and the twisted dwarves they stole and domesticated in the ancient days."

"I know of the Krulaeji, Brael," Voss says spitefully, still sending the thoughts with Nhasan. "I am ready for whatever awaits. I will find something of interest, or I will turn back when the day is growing to an end. It must not even be lunch yet, and I have enough provisions on my person to feed us all a meal."

"Fine," Emari announces, "we can march until our hunger calls for a rest. After lunch, or if there are any signs of trouble, we turn around. Agreed?"

Voss turns back, saying nothing.

Brael picks out the new tunnel with ease. It is a smaller opening, only about seven feet in diameter, and runs into the left wall about halfway between the first passage and the chasm. Their torches are burning low, so they leave them at the new tunnel and strike fresh ones.

This time the slope is much steeper. The tunnel winds steadily to the right as it descends in a spiral through the rock. The walls, ceiling, and floor are all dark-grey stone, having forsaken the yellow and orange pigmentation of the desert above.

It grows hotter with every step, until they are all sweating profusely. Their skin does not burn, but it cries for cooler air. Still, they march onward, with only the light of Voss' and Hollands' torches to see by. After a five minute descent, they find themselves at the opening. Here, the light from the lava is brighter, and the heat more threatening. They can hear the rumbling of the molten river as it bubbles and flows beneath them.

Beyond the opening is the small bridge they spotted from above. It is pure dark rock, and appears sturdy enough, but it is only a few feet in width. The walls are even farther apart down here as well, standing about twenty feet from each other. The glow and heat from the lava rushes to meet them as they stand at the edge of the tunnel.

Voss steps onto the bridge and continues with no hesitation. The others follow reluctantly, one at a time. Soon, they are walking back up another winding tunnel. It is more tiring moving upward, but the heat is withdrawing now, and for that they are all grateful.

They climb back to the top in just under ten more minutes. They arrive with tired legs and parched lips. They walk out onto another large, flat area with a high ceiling and far walls. This was not used as a forge, but, rather, remnants of old camps and fortifications seem to dot the surroundings. Another large tunnel bores into the wall opposite the chasm. Voss begins walking toward it.

"Voss, wait!" Brael calls. Voss heeds the order, turning to face the others. "This is suicide! These fortifications are Krulaeji design. They are old and unused, but this is indication that they have spread this far south! Walking into territory that could still be theirs is certain death with so few of us."

"We have come this far, and I have seen no signs of recent activity," Voss projects the thought while speaking aloud.

"That is no excuse. We can return here tomorrow with more men. I am certain there are others on the surface who would willingly explore these depths, others who are as fearless and unthinking as yourself."

"Wait," Holland says. Voss looks at the paladin, which causes Brael to look over as well. "Look here!" he is pointing to one of the old fortifications near the edge of the gap. It is made of piled, dark stone. It is a square, walled area, with an open side facing away from the crevice.

"What is it?" Voss asks.

"There is something in here. It looks like a winch-wheel, but it is pretty banged up and covered in rust," Holland says. He walks into the open room and puts his hand on a metal ring protruding from the thickest wall, closest to the tunnel that they just exited from.

Voss brushes past Brael and joins Holland in investigating the structure. The metal contraption in question was certainly once a perfect circle, but it has seen much neglect. The metal, once shining iron or something similar, now is a crusted brown. The ring shape is bent and missing a section of about five inches.

"What do you suppose it does?" Holland asks.

"Nothing anymore," Voss answers, scanning the ground for anything else of interest.

"Help me turn it," Holland says. He grabs hold of the wheel and tugs. The metal grinds slightly, but does not budge more than a quarter-inch. Voss watches the man struggle for a moment before shrugging and grabbing the other side.

Holland pulls downward while Voss pushes upward, using the broken edge as leverage. Slowly, the wheel turns. After one full rotation, they become aware of movement around them. The ground below them shakes as a piece of wide rock begins to stretch through the space of the chasm. After seven full turns of the wheel, there is a bridge crossing the gap at the top. This bridge is nothing more than a flat and thin piece of stone, but it is at least six feet wide and rests atop the other side. It came from below the ground they stand on. Now it looks like a set of elongated stairs, as the drop from this ground to the bridge is about a foot, and the drop from the bridge to the other side is about a foot as well.

Voss nods at the paladin and turns once more to the new passage. "That will make heading back somewhat easier." All the area looks much the same. Every tunnel is dark and feels tight around them, and they are in no rush to enter a new one. Rather, none are but Voss, as the man walks briskly away from the bridge and the others.

"Voss!" Brael calls again. This time, the soldier does not stop. "I will not go a step further until this is settled!"

Voss sends his response to the hunter alone. Torkurth carries it, and in Voss' voice he says, "It is settled. Return if you wish, but I am not yet done."

The half-elf stares at him as he continues.

"Emari, Holland," Brael says, exasperated. "I will not go in there. Only death lies beyond this point. I can feel it in my chest."

They look at each other for some time.

"What pushes us further?" Nhasan asks Voss. "We have found enough gold to sustain us for months, and you are clearly under a great stress still. You have not been acting yourself of late."

"At what point did you become the voice of reason?" Voss asks in response.

"I have never been opposed to taking risks when they suit us. In an open area where I can watch for danger, this would be fine. This is a world I have never entered. If I could feel fear as I did in life, then I would be growing more nervous with every step."

"You have no reason to fear. I will not die here," Voss tells the rogue's ghost.

"And how it is that you are so certain?" Torkurth breaks in. "We are in the realm of death, and we — the dead — do not feel comfortable. We are something not meant for the afterlife, though I am sure Echoshan would take us here and now if he could."

"There is business that I have yet to finish. I will not allow death to claim us before all has been settled," Voss replies. "None of us may know what needs to be done, but we will find out soon enough. And when we do, we will work together to do it. Until then, I will not let us die."

They walk in silence for a few more seconds.

"Voss," Nhasan speaks again, "do you believe that your death would free us?"

"I do not know," the soldier responds quickly.

"We all feel as though only darkness and agony awaits us beyond your life. It is one of the reasons that we will work to keep you alive. None of us are certain, and it may be that, no matter what, we are all destined for oblivion, but for now we are all in this position together. Remember this while you venture deeper under the light of day. Remember that it is not only you in here."

As Nhasan finishes speaking, Voss hears footsteps approaching from behind. He turns to see Holland coming up behind him, carrying his torch high above his head. The flames lick at the ceiling. Behind him is Emari, who has lit a torch of her own.

"Where is Brael?" Voss asks Holland. He stops walking to wait for his head to shake off its ache.

"He returned. Brael was certain that this tunnel would be your demise," the man responds.

"Voss, will you at least admit that continuing is the fool's choice?" Emari asks.

"If that were true, why are you both here with me?" Voss asks.

"I swore an oath to protect those around me," Holland answers, "and to delve into the places of the world that remain unexplored. This happens to test my oath in both these ways. I agree that we should leave and return with more men. If you are set on continuing, though, then I cannot leave you to the darkness alone."

Emari gives no answer, just kicks a loose stone across the passage. Voss nods and turns around again. They follow him with no further questions. Both the paladin and the bard have reasons to stick by Voss and, whatever those reasons may be, they outweigh the fear in their hearts, if only for the moment.

Chapter Seven - The Krulaeji Camp

3E056, 1st of Mivosera

Their current course leads them further downward. The heat recedes slightly as they draw farther from the lava river, but it is still nearly as warm as the desert day forming above them. They push forward for forty minutes, following the gentle curves of the tunnel.

There is no discussion, just footsteps and heavy breathing. There is an air of fear surrounding the bard and the paladin. Voss leads on with some unnatural and unbreakable determination. They walk for another hour.

Finally, ahead of them, Voss hears something move. He raises a hand and calls for a halt. The others listen too, and they can pick up sounds in the distance. A single crackling of laughter and occasional, loud words in an unknown tongue.

"We must turn around," Emari whispers.

"If there are Krulaeji hunters this close to the camp then they could know we are above them," Voss argues. "We should make sure these scouts do not bring any message back to a town or larger group."

"That is foolish!" Emari hisses.

"I have to agree with Chablis, or Emari, rather, on this," stumbles Holland.

Voss eyes them coldly.

"They may not even know we exist," Emari protests further. "Why would we risk a possibly pointless battle with Lowerland elves on a hunch and without enough help?"

"It is no risk," Voss says. "I have never allowed your safety to be truly compromised, and that will not change." His words sound so genuine that Emari is struck silent for a moment.

"I will scout, then," she says, setting her pack down and pulling her waterskin free.

"Fine, but be fast and stay quiet. Leave your torch," Voss commands.

She nods and gives the torch to Holland. She drinks several mouths of water. The others also grab their skins. She looks back only for a moment before dropping hers back on her pack and slinking into the darkness ahead of them. After only a few steps, she has turned the curve and the light of the torches fades behind her.

At first, Emari cannot see anything. She slinks along through the narrowing passage, feeling the wall to tell her where to go. After several minutes of complete blindness, her eyes finally begin to make shapes out around her. She has moved around three curves and finally she can hear the sounds of conversation more crisply, and can see the twinkling of some weak source of light.

She can barely pick out where the tunnel opens farther on into a larger cave. Above her she can see stalactites hanging down. They range from small finger-sized bumps to large cones that reach almost to the floor. From the ground rise stalagmites and large boulders. Between this maze of shapes she can see the dancing light of arcane candles. In this light she sees what appears to be several tents, but these are nearly indistinguishable from rock, as they are made of a dark, leather-like material.

An uneasy feeling grows on her here, one that there are eyes watching in the darkness. She settles on it being her imagination. Leaving the cover of the tunnel and taking care to remember where the entrance was, she creeps to a tall rock that lies ten feet away. This cave is only about forty feet long, and maybe twenty wide. It is tall, but the stalactites make it seem less so, like the ceiling and floor are reaching to grab hold of one another.

From her new vantage, Emari can see the campsite more clearly. There are at least three tents, though more could easily be hiding in the darkness, and she can pick out four distinct beings. They are elven-kin, but with chalky skin and pitch black hair. They wear half-leather armour, and appear to be sitting in a circle and eating over a strange fire made of green and blue flames. Emari does not want to risk being seen, so she turns and sneaks back to the tunnel. As far as she can tell, she made no indication of her presence. She follows the wall again until she sees the light of torches pouring around the bend.

Voss and Holland stand waiting for her, alert.

"You return," Voss says quietly. "Good."

"There is a camp ahead. At least four of the deep-elves — Krulaeji — are eating something in the middle. There could have been more in the shadows, and maybe even more than the three tents I saw," Emari reports. "The whole area is filled with stone spikes and rocks that obstruct view."

"The hunters can be taken care of," Voss says.

"Krulaeji hunters are near as fierce as their soldiers," Holland tells the pair. "I would not expect a fair or easy fight. We are outnumbered against four, even if none slink in the dark."

Voss glances between his companions. "I fought elves for many years. After all the things I have seen, the scum of the Lowerlands do not bring me fear," he says.

"Lord Hallehwell," Holland pleads, "I will not abandon you in this cave, but I do not agree with this course of action."

"I am no lord, nor do I command you. I will not hold it against you should you turn around. This camp is as far as I shall venture today, but I will see it destroyed before I quit."

"Voss," Emari starts.

"Enough," the soldier says. He spins and begins walking down the tunnel.

"Horan, bless us with your light, and keep him from the darkness we plunge into," Holland murmurs under his breath. He raises his buckler and draws his longsword, which glows softly, accompanying the light of the torch he still clutches in his shield-hand.

Emari draws the shortsword that Voss left for her. It shimmers in the blackness of the tunnel, moonlight on rippling water.

They catch up to Voss.

"What is the plan, then?" Emari whispers.

"Holland and I will rush for the camp and throw our torches into the centre. You keep back and remain unseen. Heal us if we are injured, and watch for anything else," Voss replies.

They nod.

Voss breaks into a run. The sound of metal on stone pulses through the cavern with every step. He moves with great haste. Holland matches it. They break through the tunnel exit into the larger cavern before anyone in the camp has done more than stand. As they hurdle a low stone, they are met by two arrows that are shot from the circle of Krulaeji. One glances off Voss' left pauldron, the other sticks deep into Holland's shield.

The other two hunters have grabbed cruel, serrated shortswords, two each, and leapt forward to meet the charge. As the men clear fifteen feet, they hurl their torches forward. Voss throws one, Holland throws another. The light fills a large enough area to allow for a fairer fight. The hunters jump backward at the bright orange flame, but they hold their guard.

The two melee-defenders meet Voss and Holland head on. The clash of steel against whatever metals the Lowerlanders' weapons are made from rings audibly throughout the cave.

Emari keeps her eyes out from the rock that her companions have vaulted over. Nothing seems to come from the darkness around the camp.

At first, the battle seems to be even, with neither side getting the upper hand, but soon it becomes clear that the archers will be the key to Voss and Holland's defeat. Emari realizes this even from her removed position as arrows grind off the chain below Voss' plating.

"Gods," the bard mutters to herself, "if I live, I may regret this." With no more hesitation than that, she leaps the rock and sprints towards the back wall of the cave, with her rapier ahead of her and the shortsword behind her.

Voss is pierced by an arrow through his thigh and quickly feels a poison taking hold of his muscles. He fights through it, swinging wildly and leaving a great wound in his opponents chest. The Krulaeji man falls backward in pain. Voss takes a step. His legs buckle and he lands with his knee upon his bleeding enemy. The other hunter swings for him, but Voss blocks the blow with his great shield. One of the archers draws her bow to fire at the injured soldier, but before she can loose the arrow, Emari knocks into her at full speed. The two women land on the stone floor and the bow skitters away from them.

Holland begins to shout a prayer to Horan, and his shield-hand glows bright white. The paladin glances at his fingers in some wonder as the light spreads. This is no learned spell of his, but a channeling of his emotion into spellcraft. Voss tries to stand, but still cannot. His muscles are growing tighter. Holland throws his shield at his opponent, staggering him, and slams his hand against Voss' shoulder. Heat rushes into the soldier's body and Voss can feel some life returning to his limbs. He pushes off the Krulaeji man's chest, causing the deep-elf further pain, and then kicks his head, knocking him cold.

Holland turns back to his opponent.

Emari uses her shortsword to cut into the archer's face, blinding her in one eye. The Krulaeji screams and the other archer turns to the bard.

Holland is cut along his arm, unable to defend properly without his shield. He begins to chant another prayer, but no light seems to be coming.

Voss lunges and clears the distance between himself and the archers. His axe pierces through the final archer's shoulder, and his shot misses Emari by a few inches.

Holland plunges his sword deep into the stomach of his opponent, who spews blood in response. The paladin's hand begins to glow again finally. The light is weaker, but begins fighting through the poison in the Holland's arm.

The Krulaeji grips both his shortswords tightly. He swings his off-hand for Holland's side. Surprised, Holland catches the blade with his longsword. The deep-elf swings with his main-hand next, drawing on all of his remaining strength. The blade cuts deep into Holland's neck. With a horrific cry of anger and pain, the hunter severs all the way through the spine. Holland's brown-haired head topples from his shoulders and rolls to the ground.

Emari kills her archer by taking her rapier and stabbing it through the neck. Voss manages to whip around and easily finish off his own assailant. They both turn to see Holland's body hit the stone. The longsword bounces from his dead hand. The last hunter looks at them with seething anger in his eyes.

Voss extends a hand. "End him," he speaks in a grave voice that cascades through the room in a thunderous wave. Two ghostly arrows, a long-spear, and two daggers surround his outstretched arm. All fly at once for the deep-elf. The hunter stands no chance as he is impaled by the ghostly energy. He shakes and falls limply beside Holland.

Something slams into Voss' back. He turns to look, surprised. Emari's head is bowed, and her clenched fist is pressed against his bent plating. Voss surveys the scene again. His thigh hurts, but is not bleeding.

"One life traded for yours," the voice of Torkurth echoes in his head. Voss does not respond. Some sense of reality returns to him, like a fog being vanquished by a sudden, bitter wind. He takes a knee and, for the first time in a long while, he speaks a prayer to Echoshan. "We, in your domain, who do not belong here, ask forgiveness for our deeds," he says. "Our own from the realm of light has fallen before his time, and his soul is yours to claim. I ask for mercy on him, for he did not wish this fate, nor was he the cause for it. I ask you return him to Horan, as would be his wish." Voss then stands.

Emari has moved to lean against the wall between the two archers' corpses. "Are you satisfied yet?" she asks him.

Voss does not respond.

"That man had a younger sister, maybe more than that. He had a guild, people who love-"

"I am well aware," Voss interrupts.

"Are you?" Emari screams, her voice filling the cavern. "You didn't seem to be before!"

"I did not ask him to come with me!" Voss says, raising his voice and turning to face her.

"And neither did you ask me!" Emari responds. "And yet if either of us had left you, then you would be dead, not him! You'd have died alone, and have been left alone! Have you no respect for the sacrifices of others?"

An explosive silence overwhelms them. Voss lowers his head towards the stone floor. His weapon and shield vanish into the blue mist. "This is my fault," he says quietly.

"You are very correct in that regard," responds the bard, her voice dripping with sarcasm. "You know, I used to wonder what made me start caring about the lives I would once deem insignificant. I used to completely disregard any emotion for those I was not close to, to those who were less cunning or less beautiful. I asked myself when we first met Scazgix why on this world I would care if he lived or died."

"And?" Voss asks, prepared for a quick response.

"And it's because I used to be the one who cared least. I was always surrounded by those who cared more. I always had someone to keep my apathetic tendencies in check and remind me that it's the ones who are the least assuming that need the most protection and care."

"But now?"

"Now, I have to be that person who reminds you that Holland was not a friend or an important man to me, but his death will have ramifications throughout our lives that we will now never be able to undo."

"I am not his killer, but I am his death. I will avenge this day."

"You will take his body and return it to his sister and his friend!" Emari objects. She stomps her foot as she speaks, sending the noise ricocheting against the rocks.

"I will have whatever settlement these Krulaeji bastards crawl out from burned to the ground."

Emari suddenly places both hands on Voss' shoulders. "For the love of the Gods," she says slowly, "please, for just this day, can we drop the fight? We will argue about the reasons behind this, and the plans moving forward, and where to place the blame. We will argue about it all, but not today. Not today."

Voss looks up, and through his helmet he can see her mask swirling in a pattern of red and pink. She can see his eyes pulsing with blue light. He nods. He blinks, and the blue leaves his eyes dark and brown.

Emari pushes past him and cleanly stabs her shortsword into the neck of each Krulaeji body. Voss takes a single deep breath before turning and approaching his fallen ally. Holland's armour is untarnished, save for his left bracer. His blade is notched from the combat, but would have been salvageable with a whetstone and some care.

The soldier walks around the entire camp, grabbing a torch to make sure he misses nothing. Two of the tents are for sleeping, and each only has two patches of soft bedding. The third is a storage tent. There are a few extra quivers with many black arrows, a few jars of their deep, black poison, drying meats from their hunt of subterranean creatures, and a large, wheelbarrow-like wagon to transport it all.

Voss wheels the cart out of the tent, leaving a few boxes and barrels unopened. He piles rocks into the two front corners and wedges a torch in each. The fallen paladin is surrounded by his own blood. His head has rolled a foot away and rests, with its mouth and eyes open, staring at a small stalagmite. Voss heaves the body onto his shoulder, and lays it gently in the wagon. He takes a piece of strange, thick fabric from a Krulaeji bed and cleans the blood as best he can from the body and head, and then lays the head beside the body in the wagon. He covers the scene with a blanket from another bed.

"Are they all dead?" Voss asks Emari.

She nods.

Voss breaths in to ask another question, but falls silent instead.

"This is your fault," Emari tells him firmly. "I wouldn't tell you to not blame yourself, and I hope that you do not simply move past this and onto something else. But, that being said, do not let it destroy you, for it does not make you a bad man. What you do from here, that is what will define this. You need to be a good man to make up for it all, to prove he didn't die in vain." With that, she strikes one of her two remaining torches and begins to walk back towards the tunnel.

Voss grabs the two handles of the massive cart and lifts, walking slowly after her with the wagon before him.

Chapter Eight - Death and War

3E056, 1st of Mivosera

It is approaching early evening when Emari climbs back through the square tunnel and to the surface. She is covered in dirt, and her muscles are beyond sore. She pulls herself up the rope and into the sunlight. It is nearly blinding after hours underground. Once she is out, she stumbles down the dune into her camp. Brael is sitting in the shade, and has watched as she approached.

"Are you the only one who made it?" he asks, standing. His voice is concerned, but not surprised.

She shakes her head. "Voss is coming, though he suffered some injury," she tells him.

"Holland?"

She shakes her head.

"I see."

"The body was recovered. Voss has it in a cart at the bottom of the tunnel, but he cannot bring it up on his own, and I am not strong enough."

"Holland was a strong man. It is regretful that he was slain, but I warned you of the risks."

"We knew the risks."

"If I had have gone, he may have lived," Brael says.

"If none had gone, all would have lived," Emari responds.

"Indeed. I will help Voss bring the body up. Are you going to inform his sister?"

"No. Voss will."

"Good." The half-elf turns and walks briskly towards the dune.

Voss and Brael work in silence to get the body out of the ruins. They pull the rope under Holland's arms and gently drag him up the tunnel. Emari gathers some healers who bring a carrier. By the time Holland has been lain upon the stretcher, they have attracted the attention of several groups. Voss tells the healers that Holland had a sister, and they agree to take the body to the Dusk Knights' camp first.

Voss, two healers, Emari, Brael, and a few others march towards the wagon between the two camps.

Jorrig and Yuriel are standing together under an awning for shade. They have begun to pack.

"Finally!" Jorrig bellows as Voss rounds the end of the barrier. "You were gone a long time. Did you manage to get the door open?"

Voss does not respond. Behind him come the healers with the covered carrier. There is blood staining the blanket now, near the top.

For near ten seconds, an unbearable length of time, everything is still. Even the wind refuses to blow and disrupt the pure shock that has set into everyone's bones. Yuriel's scream finally escapes her mouth, and she runs towards the healers, who set the carrier down upon the sand. Yuriel rips the blanket back. Holland's eyes and mouth have been closed. He looks at peace, but there is still blood and torn flesh beneath his paling face, and his head is grotesquely separated from the rest of him. The half-elven woman grows silent, choked, as she stares at her brother's lifeless body. Jorrig has not moved.

"I'm sorry," Voss says. His voice flickers weakly.

"What happened?" Jorrig demands as he takes four large steps towards Voss.

The soldier tries to hold his gaze, but his eyes land on the sands instead. "He saved me."

Yuriel wails lament behind him. She throws herself on top of the body. The healers to not interfere.

"What happened?" Jorrig asks again, towering above Voss now. "Take your damned helmet off and look at me."

"I lead him through Death's Door," Voss says, pulling his helm off his head, but still eyeing the sand for security. "The Krulaeji held the blade that slew him, but it was my blindness that lead us too far."

Suddenly Voss is shoved from behind. Jorrig steps back, allowing Voss room to stumble forward. He turns around to see Yuriel's fist slam into his cheek. The sound is jarring and staggering. She swings again, but Voss catches her fist, white with anger. He holds her there, a fury burning in them both.

"Monster!" she screams. "Killer!"

Voss does not reply.

"You will never by forgiven for this! Not by me, not by the Gods above or below!"

"I swear that I will bring vengeance to-"

"You could bring all the fucking Krulaeji in the world to their knees and your actions would still not be absolved until your own damnation."

"Enough," Voss snaps. "I am already damned." His voice has hardened again with resolve. "While I cannot save myself, certainly, I can bring about the destruction of those who took his life."

"And either you will succeed, and I will gain no satisfaction, or you will die trying, and *then* maybe I will forgive you," she spits. She wrenches her hand from Voss' grasp and turns around once more. Tears are streaming from her eyes. The healers pick up the carrier. Jorrig shoves past Voss, stumbling him again, and the pair follow their fallen companion away from their camp.

Emari stands watching Voss for some time. His head pounds.

"You did the right thing," she tells him. "Maybe you could have listened earlier, but, in the end, I am glad you did."

"It is not the end," Voss says.

"For today it is," Emari tells him firmly.

He doesn't argue.

They pass most of the afternoon resting and contemplating what transpired. Voss examines the sword he took from the leader of the goblin-creatures. It is strongly made. Its blade is a dark metal that he does not recognize, that cannot seem to catch the light, but its edge is razor-sharp. He has never been one to use a sword over an axe, but he does have the skill to be able to.

Hariscine listens as he tells her openly of what happened, and she gives her opinion when he is done. It is not much different from Emari's. She is more logical than the average creature though. She talks about his determination to bring death to the Krulaeji, and openly tells him that she thinks it could be possible.

"You alone would have no hope, even against a single group of hunters," she tells him. "If you are to actually enter a war with the Lowerlanders then you need to know your enemy better. Your best hope of succeeding is speaking with Brael. If he can tell you anything about them that you do not already know, then you will have more of an edge. The other thing that you need to do is make use of these adventurers here. They are no army now, but if they are all trained for battle and you can organize them, then you would have a powerful force behind you.

"How could I do that?"

"You were a captain once, or so you said. Lead them! Appeal to their desire for war, or coin, or justice. Appeal to the thought of safety, or of good, or destiny. You are a smart man when your head is not clouded by its own single-mindedness." Her mouth flashes into a sly grin. "If you cannot do this, give me a month and perhaps I can charm some."

Emari sits in her own tent and reflects. She has seen more bloodshed in the past year than she has in the whole rest of her life. It is not a want of hers to kill or to fight. She has grown numb to it now though. She feels as though her path is leading her somewhere, and she is blindly following.

She falls asleep for the latter part of the afternoon as fatigue consumes her. In her sleep, she dreams of darkness and arrows. Then, just as she is slowly waking, a beautiful, glowing shortsword appears before her. It pulsates with light and energy, and then a timid voice comes to her ears.

"Hello?" it asks.

She wakes to the sound of approaching feet. There is a call for her in front of her tent. She opens the flaps to find one of the healers. Voss has also been summoned. They are lead to the healers' tents, which are set north of the square. Inside each there are only a few cots, and crates and chests of healing ointments and clean cloth.

Inside the smallest tent there are two bodies, wrapped in white sheets. One is tall and broad, one is small and thin. Lying atop the former is Holland's sword and shield, which Emari recovered. Upon the other is Boe's staff and his book.

"I am sorry," says one of the two healers who stands with them.

Emari and Voss stand as stones in the entrance, unmoving, rigid.

"No," Voss says.

"His bleeding must have resumed internally. We didn't know until it was too late," the healer tells him earnestly.

"No!" Voss tells him. His shoulders tense and he almost steps forward. Emari grabs his arm, but he shakes her grasp off. He turns and walks from the tent instead.

Night comes quickly. The sun, the great celestial, Matahari, rushes from the sky. The stars, fragments of his sister Estrela, begin to dance in his place. Dusk mediates the change, but seems to give way without much fight.

Voss sits at their camp's fire pit. He can hear revelry in the background, more draining of the wine and ale barrels before the long journey back, no doubt. Emari has long sat beside him. Brael lit a tall flame in the pit and boiled a stew that none of them have touched. Silence has held their tongues for hours. The weight of thought, of fear and pity, press on all of their shoulders. It seems to Voss, at the very least, that the two deaths of this day were his own doing. No one has yet disputed this opinion.

It seems as though the silence will starve them all, when a voice calls from the rear-end of their wagon. "I was wrong," it says. It is Yuriel. Her brown locks are tied in a ponytail that cascades off her shoulders. Her eyes are raw from crying. "May I join you?" she asks.

Emari and Voss nod, but say nothing. She approaches and sits opposite Voss on a wide water barrel.

"I was angry, and I have not had near enough time to grieve," she says, "but I was wrong. You are not my brother's killer, even if you admit to be. You did not wield the sword that killed him." Her words seem difficult for her to say, like she cannot yet admit to herself what has happened. "I want revenge, as I am sure you do. Your section of ruins has claimed the only life of this whole expedition, but that is not on your shoulders."

"It claimed the only two," Voss corrects, his voice dark, "and I will carry that burden nonetheless."

Yuriel sits rigid. "What happened?"

"Our companion passed this day," Emari tells her.

The half-elf nods somberly. "I am sorry."

"I led both your brother and my own friend into danger," Voss says, looking up. His helmet is resting on his head again, though Yuriel's eyes can see his. "They followed my command, and they were slain."

Yuriel flinches, but slowly she sits tall again. "My brother is — was — not a fool. If he chose to stand with you and your orders, then he did so for a good reason. It pains me greatly to think of a life without him, but we were often in danger. Death never seemed a possibility, but Echoshan always watched."

"I cannot undo this," Voss tells her.

"Then do not," she says. "If you seek vengeance, some fight against darkness, then I will fight as well. If you leave us to mourn and to return home with saddened souls, then that is what fate awaits me. My heart is bent by the pain I have suffered today, and it will not be set right for some time. Though my misshapen soul will blame you for his death, my mind knows that you should not be made to feel the same."

"I will seek revenge," Voss tells her. "There is a war. I have felt it for some time in my bones, like I was running towards a great battle. It comes closer every day, though it feels constantly as though it hovers on the horizon. It may be that I have finally found it and, if it lies so close within my grasp, I cannot simply let it slip by.

"Then you will have my bow."

"I will not have just yours, but an army of bows and blades, of men and women. I will have just what I said: a war."

He rises suddenly. He steps around Yuriel, sending sand into the fire pit so that sparks leap into the sky. No one gives chase right away. He moves through camp like a bad omen. People turn to watch and, as soon as he has passed, whisper. He reaches the centre of camp, the square, and views the scene with apathy. There are people drinking and socializing. It is revelry, relaxation.

There is a table in the centre that has been coated in a sheen of golden wine that drips off the side into the sand. The table has been abandoned, left to marinate for the night. A gentle-voiced bard with a lyre is singing a song of love and sex, and a crowd has formed to dance, mixing the arid ground with their footprints.

Voss walks to the empty, wine-soaked table. With one great bound he launches himself atop the wood, which shakes under the weight of his armoured movement. He stands tall above the rest, and already draws a few eyes his way.

"My name is Voss Hallehwell!" he calls, drawing more attention. "I have a message to deliver!" The revelers turn to observe the new spectacle. The bard stops playing. Even a few faces peer from between — or out of — tents. "There have been two deaths today," Voss continues. "Both were a result of attacks by denizens below the desert. Through a great metal door we have found tunnels leading deep under Thrella. Myself and a close friend of mine, along with a good-hearted, brave paladin, who was a member of the Dusk Knights, founders of these very ruins, ventured into the dark. The paladin, Holland Ferndash, was slain in cold blood by Krulaeji hunters."

There are some murmurs among the crowd.

"There must be a settlement nearby, and I intend to find it, and then to destroy it," Voss tells them all. Torches around the square flicker, and Voss' cloak flutters behind him as wind rips through the tents. There are some scattered, drunken cheers, but little other reaction. "If any are brave enough to follow me, I would have your swords."

A man laughs. It is a piercing squeal of a noise that bounces of the sand. He steps forward from the group of dancers. "Is he serious?" he bellows, turning around again to face the crowd. He turns back again to Voss. "Are you serious?"

"The Krulaeji nation is one that we have known to exist since our time began," Voss tells the crowd, ignoring the man. "They are slavers, raiders, and murderers. That was proven again today. We sacrificed the lives of holy warriors in the epochs past to fight them back into the dark. We fought them on the Dabarisian Plains in the wars of the Malachi Crisis. Still, we did not teach them to leave the surface to the civilized. They have pushed closer to the light, and farther south, away from our eyes, while our diligence has faltered."

The man laughs again. His hair is red and short, and his beard is curled and soaked with wine. He walks a few feet towards the table. "You expect any to stumble blindly into the Lowerlands on a task of vengeance for someone who they don't even know?"

"I do not expect anyone to follow blindly. Even the most respected general would not expect his men to fight with no plan, and there will be one before we run into danger. For someone you do not know to lead you, I understand the hesitation," Voss continues, "but for a man who was a fellow order member, a man of the Gods, a man who provided the opportunity for you to grow wealthy and fat on wines and cheeses for months? Yes, I do expect that there are those among you who are intelligent and would stand to avenge him, even if there are others who are not and would not." Voss ends the sentence by staring down at the red-haired man.

"Yeah," the man gurgles, "good luck with that, Metal Head."

Voss leaps from the table. He lands in the sand a mere foot from the man, and grabs his shoulder with a massive, gauntleted hand. Several people inch swords from their sheaths. "If you have no sense of honour, then turn and leave. I was a soldier, and a man of justice. Those who cause senseless pain in the world are part of a blight that exists everywhere. I cannot seek them out wherever I walk, but when I find them I can seek to stop them."

The man trembles before the hulking figure, but maintains a strong voice.

"You have not even found this settlement you speak of," he says.

"And when I do? Will you stand beside me then?" Voss asks softly.

The man winces in Voss' grip. "If you bring me a plan that I can approve, and a promise of gold," he says, straightening his back, "then I will consider."

"And you'll be a damned man if you don't," Voss affirms, releasing his grasp with a slight shove.

There is some laughter from the crowd, but Voss can tell he has put a thought deep in many of their minds. "All of you," he calls, "should raise your blades. We have over a hundred trained swordsmen, archers, mages, healers, more than there may be anywhere else in the world right now. We have an army before us!"

Brael and Emari have found their way to the square with many others from the outskirts of camp.

"We will send scouts into the darkness, find their settlement, and we will destroy it," Voss continues. "They have made an enemy of the surface, of our order, of us!" There is a cheer at this. "Gather here in three evenings and I will come to you with enough information to form a plan. I will meet with all the guild leaders and anyone who earns a say in discussion, and I will convince you to join me in a quest far greater than the one you have been on for months." There is a chorus of voices, shouting several profanities and many praises. Voss turns back to the red-haired man.

"My name is Dane Mills!" the man calls loud enough for the square to hear. "As the leader of Warrior's Temper, I will hear your information in three nights!"

A woman stands from another table. She is adorned in a purple sash, and surrounded by several others wearing the same. "I am Lynn Rose, leader of The Knights of Jallor!" she calls. "We will also hear this information. We make no promise of aid, but we will postpone leaving and lend open minds."

Several other guild leaders step forward and make similar proclamations.

A few of the smaller guilds say nothing and leave the square, but after a minute, as people return to their drinking, there are still over a hundred adventurers that appear to be in agreement to hear Voss' information.

"Brael," Voss sends the thought to the hunter. He approaches. "I would like you and I to explore the tunnels. I will listen to your advice and gather others if you wish. I want to find their settlement and assess it."

Brael looks at him for a long time. Finally, he says, "Fine. You will wait behind though. Your armour is too loud, and even I know that. Find me seven who are light on their feet and I will take them in the morning."

Voss nods.

Brael nods back.

Voss approaches the leader of The Edgewood Alliance. He is sober looking, and surrounded by members of his guild at a long table. They are playing cards, talking lightly, and two are dancing together to the lyre that has resumed.

"Master Frank Gilmore, yes?" Voss asks. The man turns around. He has blonde hair and no beard. He is neither old nor young. His green eyes survey the armoured man before him.

"Yes, master Hallehwell. What brings you so soon to the Alliance after your speech?"

"I have heard some tales of your guild in my time on Estrand," Voss tells him. "I know you have employed many good trackers and archers in your ranks."

"The news you have heard is correct."

"I would like to hire them."

"What?"

"We have found gold in our section of the ruins, as I am sure you have as well. I would like to pay your trackers, those who are smart, strong, and quiet, to follow my scout into the tunnels."

Frank Gilmore thinks for a time. He turns his head slightly and calls behind him, saying, "Who wants to make some more gold?" There is a call of agreement and some mugs are smashed together. "Wilkins," Frank says next, "get your squad. Get Ortiz' too, and that kid who keep hanging around!"

Voss waits while a tanned man leaves the table into the maze of tents. Ten minutes later, a sizeable crowd has gathered around the guild master, who explains the offer. Many agree, and Voss picks seven of them. Four are women, two are men, and one is a tall elf. This elf is scrawny, mostly skin and bones, but his feet do not even shift the sand as he walks. He is the size of a Streboyan elf, but, with light skin and no muscle to show, Voss is uncertain.

"Meet me at the western edge of camp at dawn. Bring your gear, I will bring the coin," Voss tells them. They agree. Some bump chests, two hug, and the elf just nods at the armoured man.

Brael watches from the other side of the square. He smiles his approval, though no one is around to see.

Chapter Nine - Dal-Gorün

3E056, 2nd of Mivosera

Boots hit the sand. Brael strikes a torch to illuminate the small room, which he has decided must have been a smithy of some sort. The entrance that they have been using was likely a chimney.

Another figure emerges behind him, and then another. They walk calmly into the next room. No Krulaeji would have found their way into the ruins within the last day. Judging by what Voss and Emari have told him, the hunters were not finished with their hunt. There are probably still many days until any alarm is raised regarding their absence and, even then, blame would not fall until bodies were found.

The tall elf appears beside him, making Brael jump. He is dressed in light leathers, which nearly match his long, brown hair. His eyes are a reddish-brown as well, but they seem to absorb the light of the torch that Brael holds before him, turning them amber and gold.

Brael's mind can accurately track the positions of around ten people at any given time, but, for whatever reason, this elf moves quicker than he anticipates.

"My apologies," the man says, smiling. His teeth are white, but not straight, and one near the back has broken off.

"It is fine," Brael responds, feeling the vibrations in his throat to control the volume. "Let's keep moving."

The group of eight moves through the large chamber with Brael at the lead. They reach the stairs before Brael is tapped on the shoulder. He turns to see the taller elf still behind him. "Should we be on guard?" he asks. Brael looks at the others, who are viewing him expectantly.

"Not yet," Brael tells them. "Once we have passed the bridge through the tunnels, we should be wary, but until then you can talk with ease." He turns but is immediately tapped again.

"You cannot hear," the tall elf tells him.

"Correct, but I can see far better, and more accurately, than anyone else that I have met, and I can make a shot from double the distance of a common hunter."

"I meant no insult, friend," says the elf. "I just want to make sure we are all informed."

Brael turns and begins to descend the stairs. Being questioned about his hearing is nothing uncommon to him, and by now he trusts his own abilities too strongly to be disarmed by simple doubts.

Travelling with an elf is not something that Brael would prefer, but this man is not from Vruyoth, nor from the Lowerlands, and so the deaf hunter does not find him as detestable as the rest. It is his attitude that will create any tension between them more than his racial background.

They reach the bottom floor and follow the hall into the throne room. Both doors are unbarred and stand open now. The heat from the lava down the long tunnel now disperses comfortably throughout the ruins.

"If you are carrying unnecessary gear, you should leave it here," Brael says, "but take all the food you have. I do not know how long these tunnels are." He takes his cloak and lays it on the stone table. Several others unload cloaks, hats, even some of the coin purses Voss gave them, and a box of dice. "It will not be a long walk until we reach the camp, little under an hour, but it could be more than a day's march before we find any other sign of the Krulaeji or whatever settlement they come from."

They set off again at a quick pace. The tunnel leads them soon to the large, open cave. They cross the stone bridge high over the lava in single file. It supports their weight with ease. They continue through the next passage, and their pace slows to maintain a quieter step. They walk in the light of torches for over half an hour more.

Brael halts the group and goes ahead to the camp. The smell of death hangs in the air of the cave and reaches down the tunnel towards the scouts. When Brael reaches the camp, he can see the four bodies lying, unmoved, on the ground. They are all surrounded by their own dark blood. He spits onto the face of one with a hole in his stomach. The hunter finds that there are two more passages that turn into parallel tunnels on the other end of this cave. He looks down each one, and his eyes only unveil stone.

He returns to the others and bids them to follow. They enter the camp and survey it. Most of the scouts gather arrows and poison from the supply tent, but Brael refuses.

They do not stop here long, as the smell of blood starts to weigh on their noses. It is difficult to choose a tunnel, though, as they both seem to lead onward for a good distance.

"We could split up, four and four," suggests the tall elf.

"No, we should keep our numbers. We are in dangerous territory now, even if being attacked is not likely," Brael tells him. He shrugs. Brael rethinks. "I will go down one for five minutes, and you will go down the other. We will meet back here and discuss.

"Sure," says the elf. He begins to jog down the left tunnel. Brael also takes a quick pace. He knows he is not loud, and he does not believe that this tunnel will be under any watch.

Krulaeji hunting parties do not stray far from their homes, but they do hunt for several days or more, usually. This is likely no more than a fringe town or fort, as the capital is known to be somewhere under the northern parts of Estrand. Little is known about the deep-elves, their slaves, or government, though, so Brael keeps low and quiet. After five minutes he has still found nothing, and the tunnel seems to continue for a long while. He turns around and speeds back to the others.

After he has returned, he has to wait another five minutes for the tall elf while he grows increasingly worried. The man returns at ease, though, carrying a handful of what looks like black lichen.

"This was burned in a fire pit not far back. It was a small section with some chairs and benches set up, but the ceiling had a hole in it where the smoke could go, unlike here," the elf tells Brael.

"Good eyes," Brael comments.

They choose the left tunnel and set off. After ten minutes of walking they come across the fire pit, seats, and a few baskets with bags in them. The bags contain smoked herbs and other cooking ingredients.

They stop for a brief time, taking use of the dried herbs and their own provisions before pressing on again. The tunnel is very winding, but, if they are not mistaken, it leads generally northward. The back of the group lights a torch, but Brael and the tall elf rely on their enhanced eyesight. They march for many hours. Finally, they break again in a small section of the tunnel where it is wider.

Brael scouts ahead for several minutes while the others set up. They eat a cold meal and rest their legs for half an hour before Brael calls them to move again. They pack quickly and begin to march onward. They walk for longer this time, and eat dinner without stopping.

Exhaustion begins to set in, so Brael calls for sleep as they arrive in a tall cavern. There is a soft rumble of water coming from somewhere, but no one can find anything more than a thin trickle running down the southern wall. The sound soothes them as they lay down bedrolls and blankets. The cave and tunnels have grown colder, but it is still warmer than The North would be. They fall into sleep quickly, hardly establishing a watch. One set of eyes does remain open at any given time, though, as Brael would not take chances.

They rise and pack again. It is probably very early morning, but under the great ceiling of stone it is difficult to say whether or not night has fully ended. This day of travel is much the same, but towards the middle they do begin to see more signs of activity, old fire pits and animal bones. A feeling emerges amongst the group of being watched. It is Brael who waves it off. He tells the others, "If we were being watched by anything that lived in these tunnels, we would be dead already." After that, they move on in unease.

Near six long hours have passed, with only a short break in the middle. They are beginning to grow famished again, when the tall elf raises a hand. They halt. "There is a great noise growing in the background. It comes through the tunnel from far away," he says. The others cannot hear it.

They gather speed and eat while walking. After another thirty minutes, the others can hear this noise. After an hour has passed, they are sure it is close.

Half an hour later, they all come to a large cavern. It is wide and quite long. There are signs everywhere of hunter activity. They make sure that nothing lurks in the shadows before creeping to the other end, into a new tunnel that is very wide, and quite flat. There were two other tunnels as well, but these lead upward and they were much smaller and devoid of any signs of use. The one that they choose has been made dirty by what looks to be feet and wagons' wheels.

It is likely reaching early afternoon. They are walking in silence and with a growing anxiety. The tall elf has been silent and staring, always with his eyes ahead. Brael looks to him frequently for signs of change.

"We're close," the elf says suddenly, when he sees Brael glance at him.

Brael does not see what he means until several more minutes pass, but eventually he does understand. Far ahead, at the edge of their vision, the tunnel has come to possess a red glow. They continue their march. Soon, the others can see the change as well.

Now they approach a definite end to the tunnel.

"There is the noise coming from ahead," the tall elf says. "It is a cacophony of sounds, pounding and ringing — like a town — but it is distorted by the tunnels, such that it sounds like a grinding or rumbling."

They come up quickly upon where the passage opens. It leads on to a large stone lip that juts from a cave wall. This cave is massive, descending for hundreds of feet, and it is mostly cloaked in blackness. The ceiling is a dome above them, and also reaches higher than they can see, though they stand over halfway up the ovular cave. The bottom is reachable by a long stairway that wraps around the outside of the oblong cavern to their right. These stairs are made of large, sturdy, metal steps that are hammered into the cave wall, and a thin, gnarled railing protects the outside and the platform. The floor of the cave is lit by lights that are spread unevenly throughout. Around these lights are what appear to be farms, but at this distance it is hard to tell.

There is one place that is clear and easy to pick out. A large stone wall surrounds a wide, cylindrical building. The roofs of other, smaller structures stick above the wall at places as well. This must be the source of the noise. Hammers ring throughout the air, and there are voices that the tall elf can barely hear on the wind. The main building is at least two, tall storeys high, and there is a smaller cylinder atop it that could be a lord's room or study.

At the base of the stairs is a small stone building with a low turret atop it.

In the very low light, Brael thinks he can make out some sort of bell or metal glinting within.

The tall elf looks at Brael. "These people would speak the low-tongue. I know some of this. If they have any maps or books in that building, we should take it and bring it to Voss."

"We would risk being caught. We certainly cannot handle a fight in this area, their territory," Brael tells him.

"Then I will not be seen. Let me try."

Brael looks at him for a long time before responding, "I will stay here and observe for a few minutes, and then I will take the others back to the large chamber for a rest. If you are not back in fifteen minutes, I will assume you have been captured or killed."

"I will look into the stone building, and will not go farther. I would have thought I proved by now that I am both quick and quiet."

"I only hope none are quicker and quieter. Good luck."

"Never needed it."

They split up. Brael watches the elf move with incredible speed down the stairs. His heart feels tight in his chest. He looks warily at the settlement. It is more of a fort than any kind of village or town. It looks militaristic, but it is possible that all Krulaeji dwellings are in this style, as no one has really seen them since the days before history.

The others scan the area as well, and whisper to each other. Some think they can see men moving in the fields below, others say they spot something clinging to the ceiling above. Brael sees none of this, but that does not make him feel any more at ease.

After a few minutes have passed, and he has developed a strong mental image of the large cavern, he instructs the group to leave. They have much ground to cover, and little time to cover it in. They head back down the tunnel with speed. After twenty minutes at a quick pace, they return to the open cave. Scarcely have they reached it, when the tall elf returns.

"That was quick," Brael notes.

"It was a small guardhouse, by the looks of it," the man tell him, not acknowledging his comment. "There were three deep-elves that I saw on my way, and two were in the building, but I managed to get my hands on this." He holds out a book, bound in a black, leather-like material. The cover is written in a mixture of elvish characters, and what looks like dots and lines. It is covered in a thick layer of dust. "I don't think they will miss it."

"Can you read it?"

"*The History of Dal-Gorün*," says the elf. "I read a few headings in the content list on my way back. I think the name refers to this place. It is a castle, of some kind, for their ruler, who was named *Jiih* in the book."

"That could be very useful in devising a plan," Brael speaks.

"Perhaps, though I saw no floor plans, nor any information on the layout other than a general drawing of the grounds near the front."

"That will be more than enough to prick at Voss' interest," Brael says. "We need to keep moving. We have less than a day and a half to reach the camp."

"I could run ahead, or you could," the elf suggests. "These are slow people, and we could make much better time than they can, but we cannot both leave them behind." Brael realizes that the elf is only moving his lips, not speaking.

"On second thought, you go," Brael says aloud. "I will lead the others back to camp. We will make as good a time as we can, but you will make better." There is some arguing, but soon it is settled, and the elf begins to move quickly down the tunnels.

Brael watches him disappear into the darkness before rousing the others once again and setting off after him.

Chapter Ten - The Army Mobilizes

3E056, 4th of Mivosera

The mid-morning of the fourth has arrived. With it comes a speckling of clouds that have fought their way through the Council Lands and won the opportunity to catch this brief glimpse of the desert. Voss grows impatient. He paces his campground. Emari tries occasionally to set his mind at ease to no avail. Yuriel also stays nearby, but spends most of the time preparing for her brother's funeral, which is to happen this evening as well, after the meeting in the square.

As the sun climbs to noon, Voss retreats to his tent. Hariscine, who is in her half-lion form when he walks in, quickly returns to her human form, sitting naked on the rug.

"How is your back?" Voss asks.

"Recovering, but slowly. How is the waiting?"

Voss does not reply.

"You could do with some stress-relief, you know. Never have I met a man so tense. Albeit, never have I met a northerner at all, nor many men."

"I am no northerner," Voss tells her.

"Ah yes, the exotic Streboyan from overseas," she says, smirking. "You can be from north or east, or west or south and I would not know the difference."

"What are you suggesting?" Voss asks bluntly.

"Sex," she responds.

Voss looks at her through his helm.

"You asked," she shrugs.

"That sounds like a bad idea."

"I don't know why you say that," she says. "My eyes can charm a man to do my bidding, and yet you search for them as though you want to prove your will over mine. Well now, I would say *that* is the bad idea."

"You are really suggesting that we have sex to relieve my stress?"

"You'd be a true idiot to think that I am not stressed as well, though we seldom speak our minds. I would not be opposed to the act, as it would certainly be mutually beneficial. One cannot go through the hardships of life without indulging in the pleasurable aspects."

"You sound like a proper Dabarisian philosopher."

"I'd let you keep your helmet on if it makes you feel better," she says sarcastically. Voss removes it and sets it atop his wooden chest. "Are you taking up my offer then?" Hariscine asks him.

"Yes," Voss responds, beginning to undo the clasps on his greaves. She rises from the ground and walks towards him. Once she has helped to remove his greaves, she stands and places his hands on her sides as she continues to release his armour, piece by piece.

The tall elf climbs from the ruins in the late afternoon. He made good time. He was lucky Brael agreed, otherwise they would not have gotten the information back soon enough. His legs are tired, and his water has run out. He heaves himself onto the sand and stumbles down the dune into the camp of the Taernsby adventurers.

The bard greets him, and he explains what he found and where the others are. The noise draws Voss' attention and the man exits his tent. He is dressed now in a grey, hooded robe, and his hair is tied back in a clean bun. His brown eyes burn intensely as he views the elf.

"Master Hallehwell," the elf starts, "I am Siegmire Vanderbell, and-"

"Come," Voss cuts him off, "sit and show me this book you've found." The soldier walks to the dead fire pit.

"I am in need of some water or wine, I am parched."

"Hariscine!" Voss calls. "Would you please fetch a bowl of water from the wagon for you, our guest, and myself, and then join us here?"

The woman emerges from Voss' tent. She smiles and nods. She is wrapped in a white robe. Her blonde hair ripples off her shoulders. Some of it stands on end, but most seems carefully placed. She walks along the hot sand without shoes and fills a large metal basin with water at the wagon. She grabs several copper mugs and takes them over to the sitting area.

They sit and pour over the book that the elf, Siegmire, has brought.

Time moves quickly until the evening begins, but Voss is determined to make the most of it. Some basic maps and passages about the overall layout are really the only useful parts of the book. References to 'The Legion of Farrash' also draw attention. It is generally decided that it must refer to some kind of government system that the Krulaeji follow. Perhaps it is equivalent to a kingdom of sorts. Nothing can be determined in a short reading, however.

Brael and the other scouts arrive as the hours push onward and the sky dims. They are dirty and exhausted. All but Brael trudge off towards their camps to sleep. The deaf hunter joins them at the fire, but there is no time to fill him in, so he simply watches.

Darkness begins to overtake the desert as they sit and discuss. Voss feels as though he has gained enough to make a hasty plan, but is determined to leave the details open to further talk. He quickly garbs himself in more proper attire, including dark, linen pants and a clean beige shirt. He drapes himself in his chain shirt, clips his cloak to his fur ring, and places his helm atop his head.

They close the book and rise as music begins to sound form the square. Voss leads the others through the camp. When they arrive at the centre, they find that the guilds have already gathered as promised. Some of the smaller groups have already set off for their homes or the order hall in Azgul Hold. Standing around the square, and sitting at the tables on the outer-edges, are nearly eighty adventurers. The masters of the larger guilds — Lynn Rose of The Knights of Jallor, Frank Gilmore of The Edgewood Alliance, Brett Scottsfeld of Helm of Auris, and Dane Mills of Warrior's Temper — and some of the smaller guild leaders are seated at a large table. The surface is made of smaller tables pushed roughly together and topped with a large, white sheet. The guild masters are joined by two elegant looking men, a bald, fair-skinned elf and a black-haired, fat dwarf, who stand near Master Rose. They all hold cups filled with golden wine or dark ale, and talk jovially as Voss approaches.

As the soldier reaches the table, silence begins to fall. A bard still plays a soft tune on his lute, and Emari hums along. It is a somber, relaxed tune that seems to draw attention directly to the table.

Voss sits at an open seat at one end. Introductions are made. The minor guilds announce themselves, and the elf and dwarf are revealed to be the only two members of Qoud Pacem, a guild thought to be most knowledgeable in arcane and healing arts. All have agreed to hear Voss' new information. Many are clearly skeptical, but some look at him with kind eyes and open minds.

"Dal-Gorün," Voss says. He gently tosses the book towards the centre of the table. It shakes the surface and slides across the cloth. "Any who can read the low-tongue may wish to view this for themselves, but I will explain what has been gleaned thus far."

The pale, bald elf from Qoud Pacem takes the book and begins to leaf through the pages while Voss continues.

"The settlement, as I had previously described it, has turned out to be a mining fort of sorts, made for — or by — a leader-figure named Jiih. It is not large, but neither is it small, and could hold over three hundred citizens at minimum," Voss explains, moving his gaze over each leader in turn. "This fort is far on the edges of their empire — The Legion of Farrash, as they call it — and it is not likely to be reinforced against an attack. Reconnaissance will be necessary before any military operation could be attempted, but I believe victory is possible."

"How so?" asks the elven man. "This fort has tall walls, and we have no siege weapons."

"Guild masters," Voss addresses them, "how many mages are among you?"

After a lengthy count, it is stated to be just over twenty in total.

"And of those, how many know teleportation spells?" Voss asks.

Another tally reveals eleven, six of which can be utilized by those other than the caster.

"And Qoud Pacem, how many men could you alone transport beyond the walls?" the soldier continues.

The elf chuckles. "Thirty or more," he says, then, "but only to a focused location. I could bring the whole of this camp if I could draw circles at either end."

"So then, we send the bulk of our attack into one area, past the walls," suggests Master Gilmore, "and smaller groups to other key points?"

"Yes," Voss says, "small groups would land in guard towers to prevent fire from above, and some others would be sent throughout the housing and trade districts to spread resistance."

There is some discussion among the masters. Some more questions are asked, but Voss responds with ease. They could first be teleported into the large cavern that lies not far from the fort, using two circles drawn by the elven mage. They could wait there for a night while he replenishes his arcane well. The next day, they would launch an assault. The whole operation would only take two days once the supplies were packed and the preparations made.

Payment would be derived through pillaging. Voss agrees to take no cut of any wealth in the town, so long as the keep is left to him and his group. There is some argument on this topic, but the soldier holds firm and eventually the guild masters back down.

"Lord Hallehwell," Lynn Rose speaks to the man, "if the Knights of Jallor offer aid to this cause, what advice would you give as the leader of the mission?"

"If any are to offer aid to this, they will experience loss of some kind," Voss says. "There will be lives extinguished under this desert in the near future. If none help me, then there may be more, or it may be mine. The more arms we have that swing blades, or loose arrows, the less danger we are in. We are trained soldiers, adventurers, archers, and mages. We all have strength in us, and — if we march as one — then we will be victorious. There will be wealth in that fort, in one form or another. No matter what, there will be singers to tell the legend we forge. We will be the men and women who struck the first blow against the Krulaeji slaver-nation that has plagued our world for years."

There is some cheering at this, especially from the outer crowd.

"Then my knights will lead your charge," Master Rose tells him.

"Alongside my warriors," says Dane Mills.

"Helm of Auris will hold any front you send us to, even one that we are unfamiliar with," says Scottsfeld.

Frank Gilmore just smiles and nods.

The minor guilds cheer and join in.

Roger Hardwick steps from the outer crowd and stands beside Voss. "My guild will stand with you as well, Voss," he says, "so long as I may fight at your side."

Voss nods.

"This is possible," the elvish man agrees. "It will be a hard fight. The Krulaeji are a vicious group, even more so under a strong leader. The only saviour of our assault with be in surprise and ferocity."

"Pack your camps," Voss responds. "We must make fast time. Stay your excitement until the day we charge, and stay your fear until the day after."

There is a cheer that is carried by the whole crowd. The guild masters raise their cups. Roger hands Voss a full mug of his own, and the soldier joins the toast.

"To legends," he says.

"To legends!" the adventurers call in unison.

The crowd thins over the next half hour, but many remain to drink. Voss rises, leaving his mug on the table, full. "Come," he tells Roger, who follows him out of the square. They walk northwest. Emari joins them, as does Siegmire and Hariscine. After fifteen minutes they are out of the main camp. Brael has appeared. He is tired, but keeps pace. They leave the tents and walk over a tall dune. At the base of this dune, they can see a pile of broken boxes and barrels arranged in a pyre.

Yuriel, Jorrig, Scazgix, and a priest have gathered there already. Voss does not know whether they were present for the meeting, but he does not mind if they weren't. They certainly had more important things to attend to.

The bodies of Holland and Boe lie atop the pyre, wrapped in black cloth. Voss and the others join the king, sister, and friend near the scene. The priest reads several long passages from a book of Echoshan's prayers. The sky has cleared of all clouds, and both moons shine brightly now above the shadowy sands.

"Is there anything you wish to say for Holland Ferndash, paladin of Horan, brother, and friend?" the priest asks when he is finished.

Scazgix kneels on the sand, with his hands on the hilt of Emari's old dagger. He mutters something in the dragon-tongue.

Yuriel looks at Voss. He has not removed his helmet, and he stands tall above her.

"When I spoke of him as a good man," the soldier says clearly, drowning out Scazgix's prayers, "I did not lie. I knew him very briefly, and yet he laid his life at risk for others far more readily than any man I have called 'good' before him. His end was as regrettable as it was untimely, and I was lucky to have met him at all. I will remain sorry for the part I played in his death, and I will stay my course in avenging him. He will not be a nameless loss, claimed in darkness."

Yuriel speaks next. She tells many stories of their adventures and of their youth. The others listen in silence. Finally, she says goodbye to her brother, and prays that Echoshan and Horan take care of his soul.

"Is there anything you wish to say for Boe Chong, mage from Fairgarde, adventurer, and friend?" the priest asks next.

"He was an invaluable member of our party," Voss says. "Without him, I would likely have fallen long before him. He was wise, kind, and pure of heart - for the most part. I also knew him only briefly, and I would have taken as much time as was given to know him longer. It was my command that created the danger he was placed in, and I take responsibility for his injuries and death. If there are ever songs to tell of his deeds, I will sing them with pride."

Emari watches Voss, searching for a hint of dishonesty, but she finds none.

Jorrig takes a torch and lights it. The flame burns bright and pure. Yuriel strikes one as well, as does Voss. In unison, they throw them to the pyre and the barrels begin to crackle and catch. The whole pyre is soon engulfed in flame, and Holland's and Boe's forms are covered in light and heat. Scazgix rises to stand beside Voss, a sadness in his eyes.

The smoke bellows silently into the night sky. They watch until the pyre is left to ash and the souls of their companions are forever sent beyond the confines of this world.

They do not sleep long that night.

As the sun rises, Voss moves from his tent and rouses Brael. The soldier is already armoured and comes bearing a travel pack.

"What is the plan, then?" Brael asks Voss.

"I will take the elf and dwarf from Qoud Pacem and bring them to the cave you found. The elf will set up a circle that we can use to bring everyone down. That will happen today and tomorrow. When everyone has arrived, we will rest and then attack," Voss affirms.

"Dal-Gorün is a fortress," Brael tells him. "Do you really think your plan is a reasonable one?"

Voss shrugs. "Any fortress is built with a purpose. Dal-Gorün was built to withstand the dangers of the Lowerlands, not an army of trained adventurers launching a surprise assault."

"We may have a good chance, but you are risking nearly a hundred lives on a chance."

"Yes," Voss agrees, "and if everyone stands by me, then we will be victorious in the end."

"You have never felt the sting of defeat," Brael tells him.

"You best watch your assumptions more carefully," Voss fires. "I have faced defeat more than you will ever know."

"I will stand by you, Voss," Brael says. "I only hope that you have thought clearly on what you intend to gain from this."

"There is much to gain. And would you truly shy away from the chance to slay Krulaeji?"

Brael pauses before responding, "No. I look forward greatly to the thrill of their deaths. That being said, I do have a request to ask you."

"And what is that?"

"Even among the cruelest of peoples, there are those who are innocent. I only ask that you exercise mercy where it is warranted."

Voss looks at the hunter for a long time. Finally, he speaks. "I do not doubt that many of the residents of this fortress will stand aside and flee. I will cut down those who stand against me. If there are soldiers who back down, they shall live. If there are children who take up a blade, they shall die. Mercy is deserved by those who do nothing to convince me otherwise."

Less than half an hour later, Voss stands at the western edge of camp with the elf and dwarf from Quod Pacem. Official introductions are made. The elf is named Ealendur, and the dwarf is Ziros. They are both practitioners of traditional arcane arts. Ealendur specializes in the manipulation of the physical realm, and Ziros specializes in the manipulation of body and mind, both for benefit and detriment.

Voss is joined as well by Emari, Scazgix, and Siegmire, the tall elf who has seen the way to Dal-Gorün. The five of them set off before the sun has fully flown into the blue sky. They slide easily down the passage into the ruins, then follow Voss and Emari down into the tunnels. Ealendur and Ziros create two floating arcane lights that trail ahead of them. Siegmire takes the lead as they pass the decimated Krulaeji camp. Brael and the others have moved and burned the bodies, which is certainly lucky for the five that stand in the camp now, as the smell still clings to the air.

They carry on down the series of tunnels, and Ealendur begins to talk of his successes. "I am actually on the forefront of teleportation study," he says. "The idea to enchant certain items with an innate, controllable teleport-field has existed for a long time now, but no one had managed to perfect it. It was myself and three others who finally devised the usage of rune-magic in an arcane circle to contain the energy."

"And you are certain that you can use a circle like this to bring everyone down here?" Voss asks.

"I am sure," the elf replies. "It will take much of my own energy to stabilize the circle, as it will lack a crystal, but it will serve its purpose. Once we take the keep, you should let me install a circle there." He chuckles. "Then, I could just send myself all the way back to the Order Hall."

"That's not a bad idea," Voss tells him honestly. "I heard they were planning on building one in Taernsby as well."

"And Azgul Hold and The City of Stren, and maybe Aebarrow and others," Ealendur says. "I would be the one building them. They don't seem to understand the risk, though, that once someone learns of the runic pattern of a circle, they could reach it without any permission. It will take allocating guards, and constructing a defensive facility around the circle with processing and all sorts of precautions..." He continues to speak as they walk through the passages.

Scazgix spends the walk admiring the stonework and prowess of whoever — or whatever — built the tunnels. He speaks in poor common-tongue to describe his appreciation of the cave systems.

After six hours of fast walking, they stop for a break. They eat bread and molding cheese, and drink enough water to replenish the sweat from walking through the heat from the lava-flow. They rest for an hour and then carry on until they grow weary and need sleep. Voss establishes a watch order and they settle down on rough-packed rolls.

In the morning, they wake and continue as before. Not much longer lies ahead of them, but they walk with speed. Ealendur had left Lynn Rose of The Knights of Jallor with an amulet of his that was enchanted to hear Ziros when he wears the matching piece. Once the circle is complete, they will be able to communicate with the guilds and coordinate their arrival.

After another four hours of fast walking they reach a large cavern. It is long and somewhat wide. There is enough space for the amount of people coming down, but not by much.

"This is it," Siegmire tells them. "Through the larger tunnel on the other side it is less than forty minutes of slow walking."

"Then we set up here," Voss announces. "We remain quiet as well. No music or revelry tonight. Tomorrow morning we must ready for an assault." The others nod.

Ealendur begins to work on an arcane circle. He takes a dark box from his pack and produces blue chalk and a bottle of liquid gold. He draws a massive circle and inscribes clean ruins around the edge. He then takes a small and sharp chisel, and breaks a symmetrical design into the floor of the cave, consisting of thin lines. He pours the gold into the cracks, filling them. After almost two hours have passed, he is finishing up.

"We can now begin to bring the others through," says Ealendur. "Once I open the circle, we cannot safely close it again until the magic runs its course. I did not build a permanent arcane well, so this is actually quite dangerous. I would not attempt it unless I had years of practice. We will only have one attempt before we have to waste another day, and more expensive supplies to make another circle."

"Understood," Voss says. "Get Master Rose in communication and tell her to start organizing everyone. They should be mostly packed by now. Tell her that everything needs to come down, as we may not be returning the same way. That includes smaller wagons, horses, and all the supplies that can be brought. Empty barrels and crates are to be left behind, we will not be lighting fires."

"Ai!" Ziros exclaims. He places a golden amulet over his head.

"Ealendur, do not open the circle until everything on the surface is ready. We want a steady stream coming through. Emari and Siegmire, I will need your help organizing," Voss continues. "Ziros, I want Roger Hardwick and Bigger They Are to come through first, as I will need their help as well."

The others nod. Ziros begins to talk with Lynn through the amulet and, after another hour, they receive the word that everything is prepared. All eyes turn towards Voss.

"Open the gate," he says.

Ealendur speaks a string of words and the circle begins to glow with a searing, deep-blue light. The gold begins to bubble. A flash of white fills the room as Roger Hardwick and his gnomish companion appear in the space.

"Roger," Voss says, "any member from The Edgewood Alliance or a minor guild needs to be moved to that side of the cave." He points to the wall on the left in relation to Dal-Gorün.

Roger recovers from the dazed look he was wearing and nods, stepping from the circle. Flashes continue to light the cave as more people arrive in groups of two, three, four, or even five. They are directed by Roger and Emari into different parts of the cave. A good deal of noise is made, but it is far quieter than it could be. For that, Voss is thankful.

It takes many hours for the adventuring guilds to find their space in the cavern. By the end, they barely fit. Tents are left in wagons, bedrolls are thrown to the rough ground, and small camps are made. Mages create arcane flames that cause no smoke and a late lunch is prepared. The guild masters meet in the centre with Voss to further discuss strategy, while the others make sure that horses and gear are accounted for and taken care of. The beasts that came into the Lowerlands are skittish in the new area, but after a few hours of fretful whinnying, they do find calm.

Brael is very good with animals, and manages to get their own beasts situated. Their wagon barely fit through the circle, and it is unlikely to make it out of the cave, but there is still hope for the animals.

Uneasiness takes hold of the camp as hours drift ever onward. Voss and the guild masters stay at a central table long into the evening, drawing battle plans and ironing out details. Finally, they call an early night. It is impossible to tell, without arcane aid, what the hour is. To the group, though, this does not matter. They set their heads down and patiently wait for sleep to overtake them.

Brael meticulously prepares two quivers of arrows and restrings his bow. Despite himself, he looks forward to the chance to put some arrows in Krulaeji warriors. The deep-elves have been searching for centuries for ways to wage war on the surface. During the Malachi Crises, they aided the legions of undead that rose to destroy the world. When the crisis was averted they continued to attack for many years until paladins of Valkronus and Horan teamed up to send them back to the dark. Now, for the first time in recorded history, there is a chance to strike back. Despite the misguided intentions that Voss certainly possesses, Brael is happy to take the opportunity for his own reasons.

Emari is writing in her journal. She has recounted the adventures she has had since the winter: travelling to Railwood, meeting Voss and the others, vanquishing the orcs, venturing back again, Highfell, Azgul Hold, the desert. She is trying to make sense of the why of it all. Why has she stuck around this long? She had a group once, made of highwaymen and thieves and con artists. She was good at any role she was placed in, and they made money. She had left that group eventually, though, believing there were better days for her elsewhere. There are certainly better days happening away from where she is now, though, and yet she chooses to stay.

Voss lies a long time awake on his sleeping pad. He goes over the plan repeatedly. Hariscine lies beside him on another bedroll. Her hand rests on his chest. He does not move it. There is no way to feel ready for the battle that the morning will bring, but he does feel excited. A real battle is not something that he has experienced since the days of the war. Voss left Streboya before the war was over. His curse was formed in the first few years, and he had to abandon his position during the early days of the battles. Despite the horrors that came with those times, he has had many dreams and moments where all he wanted was to return to the fight he left behind. There is hope that somehow this conquest will satisfy the deep-rooted craving that him and his spirits feel.

This night, Voss dreams of a dark glade. No wind passes through it, and only a darkening sky lies above, but there is a great pain that begins to grow in Voss' mind. Hours seem to pass as he stares up at the night. Suddenly, a bird flies far above, and Voss feels a hand reach up. He sees an arm, but it does not belong to him. It is covered in, or made of, stones and metal and bone. The fingers on the hand are long and sharp. The bird suddenly cries, and falls. A pale blue shape rushes into the outstretched hand, and Voss tastes blood.

He jolts awake. Morning has arrived. The troops are preparing.

Chapter Eleven - Into the Fort

3E056, 7th of Mivosera

It is Brael's job to take the guardhouse at the base of the stairs. He chooses the tall elf, Siegmire, to go with him, but no others. They leave the camp ahead of the rest, after breakfast and preparations. Voss and the major guild masters follow them on horseback to the top of the stairs to look out at the lands ahead of them, and at the fort itself, Dal-Gorün. They take in the view quickly for themselves. Ziros gives Brael one of the amulets and keeps the other around his neck. The guild masters and Voss return, taking Brael's and Siegmire's horses with them. They can hear each other speak, even with the half-elf's lack of ears.

When the guild masters have reached the camp once more, fifteen minutes, Brael and Siegmire depart, moving quickly down the stairs. There is no light but the ever-persistent glow coming from over the walls of Dal-Gorün. Even in the near-perfect darkness, though, the pair does not feel safe. They take several minuets to wind down the steps, and as they are approaching the house they slow their pace further. Siegmire motions towards the ground and they adopt a low position. They move toward the cube of a building and get under the large window that faces the stairs. The window has no pane. It is just an open rectangle in the wall. No one appears to be watching them.

Siegmire pops his head above the bottom sill and ducks back down again.

"Two are talking about ten feet back," the elf mouths. "There are probably others, but the doors are closed.

Brael nods, and nocks an arrow. Siegmire does the same. In unison, they rise and loose their arrows. The two Krulaeji men go down. A door is thrust open beside them and another man steps out. He spins towards the window, but another arrow from Siegmire fells him before a noise is made.

"Brael, to the roof. See if the turret holds a bell. If it does, do not let it ring," Siegmire whispers. Brael nods again, and leaps high enough to grab the edge of the flat roof.

Siegmire slips into the building through the window. Brael makes it to the turret. A man stands there with one hand on a heavy looking chain. He is shouting through an opening near his feet. Brael cannot understand the language on his lips. The chain is attached to a large, blueish bell.

The hunter wastes no time. He hurls a dagger at the man. It lodges in the arm holding the bell-chain. Before the pain has even fully set in, Brael reaches him and twists the dagger, completely severing his wrist and hand from the rest of his body. Brael takes his other dagger and pierces it through the deep-elf's neck. He goes down quickly.

Siegmire clears the building of two more guards. All of them appear to be dressed in tight-fitting leather and hide armours. Weapons are found on all the bodies, and some more in storage as well, but none had the chance to be used.

"Guardhouse is clear," Brael says loud enough for the amulet to hear. "There are certainly farmlands nearby, but it doesn't look like any farther opposition will meet us before the walls."

"Well done, lad," responds Ziros. "Soon we will be opening temporary gates through the arcane field to send the troops directly into the fort's grounds. It's all a very complicated sounding process, but you'd best head for the wall. We need to know which tower has the least men stationed."

"Understood," Brael tells him. He drops back to the hard ground. Siegmire exits with a quiver of their arrows slung over his shoulder, and a sturdy looking new bow. How his thin arms are even capable of drawing back a bowstring is beyond Brael's comprehension. "We are to search for the least occupied tower," Brael informs the tall elf.

Siegmire nods. "Hard to judge from here, but it's probably one that faces west or south, as those look out at cave walls and little else."

"Perhaps, yes. We come from the southeast, but is there a tunnel leading anywhere else?"

"Yes; I spotted one to the north as we descended."

"Then let us move southward," Brael tells him.

They set off, moving quickly and quietly through the cavern. There are roads of a kind that lead through the farm fields and small buildings. The farms mostly appear to be empty, but it is hard to tell in the darkness, even with their elven heritage. The buildings are devoid of any light, and appear to be little more than square hovels of stacked or carved stone. Eyes could be looking out from within and neither scout would see. The pair does not seem to raise an alarm, at least, as they run towards the keep. It is a far distance, taking nearly twenty minutes. Finally, they come within view of the towers enough to see the tops clearly.

The walls are tall and hewn of solid, rough stone. The towers themselves are made of bricks and strange, large, fungal growths make up the roofs. Most of them appear to have at least four or five archers in them. Two of them are unlit, but there are still faces within. It appears the dark ones are undergoing a change of guards. Brael relays this information to Ziros, who barks it to Voss and the guild masters.

"We are going to begin opening the portals then. This is it," the dwarf informs Brael. "If you can find a way in before we can open the main gates, your help would be much appreciated."

Brael looks from the wall to Siegmire. "We are going to have to climb," he says.

In the long cavern, the preparations have been made. In what space remains, small and large circles have hastily been constructed using cheaper chalks and liquid metals. Crystals were then placed in the centre of some circles, into carved sections of stone, and imbued with arcane power enough to open a gate for several minutes. It is a tightly packed cluster of portals. It is going to be difficult to organize it all properly, but Voss is determined to lead a strong central charge in order to buy time for the rest to get through. He has placed his dented chestplate over his new chain shirt, and let his tattered cloak hang behind him.

If all goes well, then the majority of the Krulaeji defence will be drawn to deal with the sudden appearance of Voss and The Knights of Jallor, as they appear in the central square. Once the attention has been placed on them, The Edgewood Alliance and Warrior's Temper will arrive on the main streets and begin taking fire away from the first group. The smaller guilds will be sent to various locations and into the guard towers to remove the archers. From there it should be more than a fair fight.

Ealendur begins to chant and a door-shaped light rips through the air above one of the circles. It spreads until it is about four feet wide and seven feet tall. It looks unnatural, both light and dark, and shimmering in all different colours. Voss does not hesitate. His axe and shield materialize in his hands. As Ealendur begins to give the signal, he jumps through. A rush of air pushes by him as his eyes are assaulted with a variety of shapes and lights.

Suddenly he is standing in a new place, surrounded by stone buildings and higher stone walls. It is still dark, and there are sounds coming from all around him.

As his eyes readjust to the lighting, he steps forward and feels others arriving through flashes of light behind and around him. There are footsteps moving towards him now. He forces his eyes to see. Several figures are rushing for him with weapons drawn. Most of them are elvish looking, but a few are stout and smaller. These have the same pale skin and deep black hair and eyes of the elves. Likely they are slaves or of races long domesticated by the Krulaeji, subservient until they became Krulaeji themselves.

"Shields!" Voss calls to the others, who appear just as dazed as he feels. He swings his own towards the closest advancer and manages to block an attack from a crude, metal cudgel. The others begin to engage the defence and the battle begins.

Arrows soon begin to fly down into the square. Most bounce harmlessly off the stone, but a few find their mark and Voss sees two men go down beside him. More fighters are storming through the portal, and flashes can now be seen emanating through the slits in two of the watchtowers.

The entirety of The Knights of Jallor is soon through the gate, along with Emari, Yuriel, Jorrig, and Bigger They Are. The battle is bloody for both sides. Many of the knights are slain by Krulaeji arrows and blades, but Voss and the more stalwart of the attackers deliver grievous wounds in response. As the other groups begin to arrive around the fortress' grounds, the fight begins to change in the attackers' favour. Voss dispatches two well-armoured guards and a handful of peasants wielding basic weaponry. Many of the slavers throw their weapons down and are ignored. Many peasant-folk can be seen being escorted to the gate by armed guards as well, and Voss orders that they be let through.

The fighting continues for many minutes.

Brael climbs into one of the few remaining watchtowers with Siegmire. They slay the four guards there and survey the scene from above. Voss' group has suffered severe casualties. It is possible that many of the soldiers on the ground are only injured or paralyzed by the poison of the deep-elves, but it is certain that many are also dead or dying. The other main fronts are doing slightly better, but still they are sustaining major injuries by the time the enemy begins to pull away. Most of the watchtowers are held strong by the offensive, and some minor battles in the streets prevent any redistribution of enemy men. Brael even spies Scazgix among one of the smaller guilds, shouting orders that no one is following.

After ten minutes of intense fighting, the enemy is beginning to withdraw. Brael can see the surviving guards pull away from the conflict and retreat towards the keep - the large, circular building at the south-west corner of the fort, farthest from the main gate. There is a garrison gathering there, forming a few lines of troops with bows and swords.

Brael climbs down the ladder, which is little more than handholds carved into the tower wall. He rushes forward to where Voss is standing in a puddle of blood. Emari and a few healers are rushing around, trying to save as many wounded as they can.

"Voss!" Brael calls. "They have withdrawn across the fort to the keep. They have not entered it, they mean to defend from the outside."

Voss turns to the hunter. Blue light is beginning to form inside his helm. "Then they underestimate us still," he says. "They think they can end us in open battle." They look around at the men who still stand. Most of The Knights of Jallor were overwhelmed, including Master Rose, but The Edgewood Alliance, Warrior's Temper, Helm of Auris, and many of the smaller guilds are still largely standing.

Voss dispels his shield. He jumps upon a stone well that sits in the middle of the square and points behind him. There lies two large buildings — a tavern and a blacksmith — that wall-in a wide road. The road leads toward the main keep. "There lies the remainder of our opposition!" the soldier calls to the troops. Some of the adventurers are still making their way here, but they will not be long. "We have many wounded, and we will need a place to fall back to! Brael, take the healers and Bigger They Are and clear that tavern. There will be tables and maybe beds to lay and treat the injured."

Brael nods and hails Roger's guild. Most of the healers follow them towards the stone building.

"The rest of us need to help move the injured to safety and then prepare quickly for another fight," Voss continues. "This time, the defence will be more organized, and we won't have surprise to rely on. Siegmire! I need you to see if you can get a report on numbers and the distribution of enemy soldiers."

"Understood!" the elf calls, immediately disappearing into an alley.

Voss grabs a man under his arms and lifts him onto his shoulder. Others do the same, or help limping friends towards the tavern. Soon, all of the wounded that are still breathing are laid on the tables in the cozy inn. Many candles burn along the walls and the ceiling. There is no sign of remaining civilians or guards. The healers get to work. Emari begins to hum a tune when Voss catches her arm.

"I will have need of you still," he whispers harshly to her. "Save your energy."

"These people have need of me now, Voss," she responds, unable to pull herself from his grasp.

"The healers here will save as many as can be saved. We have a greater battle ahead." There is a rumbling to his voice, like the sea thrashing against cliffs.

Emari can do nothing but nod and stare at the blue flame in Voss' eyes through his plating.

"Anyone who can still wield a sword and shield, or a bow, back to the square!" he orders.

There is a river of bodies that rush from the doors. Some look nervous, others determined, others blank. All of them are aware that, at this point, there is no turning back. They organize themselves into ranks, with swords at the front, then spears, then bowmen, then any casters that are not preoccupied with healing. Voss stands at the front, his massive, metal shield ahead of himself once more.

Siegmire returns from a different alley.

"They have just over thirty soldiers," the elf reports, "as well as around two dozen hunters and bowmen behind them, and a woman wielding a great staff in their midst as well."

Voss turns to his own army. Their numbers are similar. This is not a large fort, nor was it well defended. Even so, both sides lost nearly equal numbers, even in their surprise assault. "Shields up!" he calls. "We cannot lose hope or momentum! A strong charge could save lives. Roger, Jorrig, you will lead the charge as soon as I move. Emari, I need you close behind them. Blades and spears, advance quickly and steadily. Bowmen and mages, lay down as much damage as you can, but stay back."

Blades, shields, and fists clash against armour, creating a chorus of noise in response. Voss begins to march. The others follow. They squeeze into the wide road and move steadily toward the keep. It is a ten minute march, with the great, cylindrical building always looming before them. They walk uphill, but it is not steep.

Soon, they can see the main entrance. It is a large metal door, and it lies behind several long lines of Krulaeji and their enslaved deep-dwarves and deformed deep-men. The elven woman with the staff stands at the back, surrounded by heavily armoured guards. Two storeys above the defending army is a balcony, only big enough for someone to stand alone, but it is empty.

It is another long, open space between the adventurers and the Krulaeji. It is not a perfect square or rectangle, but it is surrounded by more wealthy looking houses and several businesses. Despite the history and location of this place, it is not so differently structured from a surface town.

The lines stop moving with about eighty feet of open stone separating them. Voss allows Nhasan to step, invisible, from his body. The spirit begins to traverse the square. With every step the ghost steps, Voss' body begins to glow with blue fire.

A proud and clear voice explodes throughout the square. It comes from the woman with the staff. She has the white skin of the Krulaeji, and the same long, black hair. Hers is braided cleanly down her back, almost to her feet. It is oiled and shines in the light of the torches and arcane lights that illuminate the square. She speaks in the common-tongue, and says, "You slaughter our people, take our lives with no remorse. You," she speaks directly to Voss, "who leads this onslaught with no hesitation, who are you to do this?"

"Charge!" Voss calls. He begins to rush forward, the others fall in tow, and the line of adventurers rush evenly toward the opposition. Voss grins wide behind his face plate, and his eyes ignite bright with ghost-fire. "I am pain!" he calls, his voice barreling towards the mage like a volley of arrows. "I am death," he whispers. His voice seems to draw life from the very air around him, and all can hear it. Nhasan materializes behind her in the thin, open space. Voss begins to scream with rage as his body is engulfed in blue mist. Suddenly, he vanishes in a burst of light. There is no pause before Jorrig and Roger take up the battle cry and take his place in the front of the charge. The woman begins to speak rapidly, her staff glowing a deep crimson. "Who are you to stop me?" Voss' voice enters her mind as the same, pale mist begins to pour over her shoulders from behind.

The soldier reappears directly at the back of her with his axe and shield ready. He clicks the button to lock his shield between him and the back-line of Krulaeji hunters, and swings for the woman. The blade bites through her left arm, severing it. She screams as blood pumps onto the stone in front of her. Arrows bounce of the soldier's shield. He spins and catches a blade with the haft of his own weapon. The woman begins to chant, trying desperately to stem the flow of blood. Voss delivers a strong kick to her right knee, and breaks the bone, cutting off her words. She falls to the ground.

The armies clash as the Krulaeji shield wall turns its attention slightly from the charge to the mage's scream. The sound of metal upon metal is a storm in the long court. Voss barely manages to hold his own ground as the Krulaeji soldiers surround him. Roger and Jorrig punch a hole through the front ranks, though, and manage to save their leader from serious injury. The fight is quick and ferocious. With their mage bleeding out, several of the Krulaeji scatter and attempt to flee the field. Most are cut down, but a few escape through side-streets. As the victor becomes more and more apparent, the defending side begins to throw down their weapons and kneel. Several are killed quickly in the heat of the moment before Emari screams for mercy. The attackers listen and pull back from the surviving Krulaeji fighters.

The adventurers escort the deep-elves to gather wagons and take their wounded and dead toward the gate. The Dal-Gorün grounds are soon abandoned of opposition, left to the adventurers to pillage. The victors cheer, and their shouts beat away the tense silence that has formed.

"We have won the fort!" Voss shouts above their voices after a few seconds of celebration. "But there is a still a master somewhere in this keep." He gestures behind him. "That battle belongs to me. You have all fought well and fought hard. Now you can take what was promised. Any gold, any metals, anything of value in the town is yours. Tend the wounded, make pyres for the dead, and maintain a watch on the gate in case the bastard-elves decide to regroup beyond the walls!"

There is another cheer and the surviving guild masters begin to organize a defence. Voss turns to Emari, who is humming to heal the bruising he sustained.

"Bard, your skills have once again proved of use," he tells her. "You may begin looting if you wish. I must take this keep."

Emari looks at him for awhile before responding, "If I were to abandon your side now, then certainly you would either die or find treasure far greater than what lies out here. I would prevent the first, and share in the second."

Voss looks as though he is about to argue, but he holds his tongue. "You may come with me then," he says instead, "I should be better off with your blade and your songs."

"If we succeed in overthrowing this fort for good," Brael interjects, "what are you to do with it? Will you abandon it? It cannot be razed easily, and once you withdraw it will surely be recaptured."

"I do not know. It would be a great power to own a fortress hidden underground. If Ealendur would carve me a permanent teleportation circle, I could soon access Taernsby from here, and elsewhere."

"You could not run Dal-Gorün alone," Roger says next.

"Nor hold it alone," Brael agrees.

"I could hire servants," Voss states.

"You could hire friends," Roger replies.

"Would you help me run a stolen fort in the Lowerlands?" Voss asks plainly.

"I would consider it," Roger says with a grin.

Voss chuckles. The sound shocks the around him. "Then I'll consider it as well," he says. "Now, I have a keep to seize, along with whoever is standing with me."

"I am," Emari tells him.

"I am as well," says Brael.

"If I am to run this keep soon, I should at least help secure it," announces Roger.

"I am coming too," a small voice coos from behind them. They spin around to see none other than Scazgix, king of Scazgixia walking towards them. He wears a new cloak around his shoulders that drags along the ground behind him. It is fastened with a circle of silver. He tosses the head of a Krulaeji man to the stonework. "He was trying to escape," the king explains.

The others look to Voss, who shrugs. "Let's go take a keep," he says.

Chapter Twelve - Of the Ancients

3E056, 7th of Mivosera

Three mages are contracted to open the doors to the Dal-Gorün keep. One suppresses an intricate arcane defence system, one weakens the metal around the hinges, and one forces the doors outward until the hinges buckle and the two great doors collapse onto the stone of the long court. Each mage is paid twenty golden lions for their service from Voss' purse, leaving it quite light. They hurry to rejoin the looting as Voss, Emari, Brael, Roger, and Scazgix turn towards the newly formed hole in the keep walls.

The walls are made of thick stone pieces, fused by either magic or very fine masons. While siege engines or continued arcane assault could have broken through them, the magically sealed door was still an easier point of entry. Inside, they can only see another wall some fifteen feet back. A small entrance hall is what greets them, abandoned by any guards. They approach the open archway.

"There will be defence left. If the keep-lord was not slain in the field, then he will not have pitted all his soldiers against us," Voss tells them. Nonetheless, he steps calmly over the metal doors and into the cool air of the keep.

Roger follows close behind. He is dressed now in formal armour, a shining chestplate over light chain and padding. He holds a mid-length spear with two sharp blades that stick out perpendicularly around the main point. His shield is the same one he wielded in Railwood.

Emari is next, wearing some minor leathers, but mostly a standard set of hooded, grey linen clothes. Her new shortsword is in hand, and her two daggers are sheathed at her thighs as well. Her rapier hangs from her hip in its thin sheath.

Scazgix steps clumsily over the door. He wears little other than loose hide and the cloak he found on the body of a Krulaeji guard. He wields the same dagger than Emari gave him long ago. He has been told specifically by the bard to stay behind Roger and Voss, but there is an anger burning in his eyes and he seems very determined.

Brael comes last. He trails a good ten feet behind, with his bow loose in one hand, and his other hand hovering over the hilt of his rapier. His eyes dart across the entrance and climb to the balcony far above them as if perhaps something horrific will soon appear. Nothing does. He slips through the door after the others.

Inside, there are three doors. One is to the left, one is on the right, and one stands directly ahead. They are all made of the same metal as the main doors were, and appear to be locked. The one directly ahead has some golden ornamentation around the edges though, looking more presentable than the others. Voss delivers a fast kick to the handle of this one, and the hinges bend. Another kick opens it. There is noise from somewhere above, but nothing leaps out to meet them.

They quickly sweep the first floor. It is comprised of a planning room— with a long stone table and several desks — two servants' chambers, a room for storing alcohol and food that is full of barrels and bottles, and a small shrine dug several feet into the floor. Brael quickly explains the Krulaeji devotion to the 'White Devil', a supposed God of the Lowerlands. There are no symbols carved into the altar, but three bowls of red liquid and a vial of white dust have been placed carefully upon the surface.

There is a stairway that starts from the back-left side of the kitchen and wraps, rightward, up the end wall. There are no trapdoors to block the top, but it appears to lead into a hallway. Voss climbs the steps into further darkness. Emari lights a torch, but it seems to do little in the confines of the dim keep.

The stairs climb to a thin passage. Behind them now is a thick wall that hangs above the stairs, where the hallway must eventually lead to once it winds around the outside of the building. Directly ahead, beyond a thin stone landing, is a thick looking door. Voss kicks it hard, but it does not budge. There is the sound of voices behind it and something weighted shifts against the metal. It is barricaded.

"We aren't going to get through that without a strong mage," Emari says.

"I am not so sure," Voss says. "Emari, was there cooking oil in the storage?"

"I do not know."

"Brael, go with her and find a large container if you can."

They leave, and return five minutes later with a tall and wide pot full of deep brown liquid.

Voss directs them into position. Brael slowly pours the oil so that it flows under the door. A strange, sweet and earthly smell runs into the air. Some of the oil trickles down the stairs, but most moves forward. As voices begin to rise from within, Voss issues the next command. Emari lights the oil and it immediately shoots flame across its surface. There are panicked shouts from within and furniture shifts audibly.

Voss kicks the door several more times. Now the soft metal begins to buckle. There is still weight on the other side. Voss waits. There is crackling. Wood has caught fire. They wait another minute. Voss kicks again. There is a grinding sound. Again. There is a crack. Again. The lock snaps and the door shifts inward. Immediately they are greeted by a shower of arrows that clatter against the door and stone wall, and then another door slams ahead of them.

The fire dies down as the rest of the oil burns off. There is a singed dresser that has toppled backward near the entrance, but the rest of the room is intact. It appears to be a garrison. A few bunks stand against the left wall, and the right is taken by weapon racks and armour stands. Another door stands at the other wall. This one looks thinner, but not by much.

"Enough of this!" Voss cries, and runs for the door. He summons his shield and meets the metal with full force. Immediately the lock is snapped and the way is cleared. His shield is thrust before him and arrows clatter off the steel.

Brael shoots three back in response. Once of them draws a cry of pain. Voss does not stop. He charges down the winding hallway. As he reaches the fallen defender, he cracks the man's skull with his axe. The defender is wearing a tight chain shirt, but little else in terms of armour. Voss chases the remaining opposition until they close another metal door before the next stairwell. Along the hallway were several other arches that led, open, into main rooms of the second floor.

Voss throws himself against the door, but this one is made of a different, silver metal, and takes his force. He stumbles back as the others catch up to him.

"There must be one more floor before the lord's chambers," Brael expresses.

"We are fighting servants. If there are any guards left, they still stand before us," Roger thinks aloud.

"We aren't getting through this door," Voss announces, ignoring the comments for the most part. "Not by conventional tactics anyway."

They stand in silence for awhile.

"If this lord had magical protection, and isn't using his main guard, then he is likely preparing an escape or a means to bring aid," Roger says next.

"We need to get to the top of this keep before that happens," Voss agrees, turning to Emari.

"What?" she asks.

"You can get up there," he responds.

"I certainly cannot."

"You can float up to the balcony. It is still a floor above us."

"Oh, of course!" Emari says. "I could just drift up there and unlock the door while simultaneously fending off volleys of arrows and, probably, swords."

"We don't have other options."

"You could come with me at the very least," Emari sputters.

Voss leans against the wall near the door. "My strength is fleeing me," he admits.

"You have enough left to either leap or mist your way to the balcony, Voss," Emari responds. "If you have pushed yourself this far, then you can push yourself a few moments longer if you plan on sending me into danger."

He stands straight again. "Fine," he says. "I will come with you. I will fend off any assault while you clear the doorway for the others. If the defenders do not further their retreat then they will meet a fast end."

The others agree to the plan. They remain beside the blocked door while

Voss and Emari begin to search the floor for a window. This floor contains a large kitchen, a sitting room with an adjoining library, and a dining area. Among these, there are only two windows. The kitchen window looks out at the cave wall for ventilation, while the library window faces out towards the left side of the long court. This is barely large enough for Voss to fit through.

"Val, you need to get up there," Voss says quietly. Emari glances at him.

"You are killing yourself, Voss. Your mind is aflame," the ghost responds.

"Pull me up after," he whispers to her, cautious of Emari's gaze.

Valindra has no choice but to obey, and her spectral form leaves his body and disappears through the window. Emari follows and begins to float outside the keep, her body growing unnaturally light. She pulls herself up the smooth wall. Voss watches his body turn into mist and then reform on the balcony as Emari's head appears over the lip. The bard lands on the flat stone beside him, her weightlessness ceasing. An open archway leads into what looks like a laboratory of sorts. Alchemy equipment and shelves of oddities take up the majority of the space. There is a large, open section where chalk marks still linger upon the floor, showing a history of arcane circles and rituals. In the centre of the room, with about five feet of space between it and anything else, is a thick, stone cylinder. A doorway on one side leads into it, facing towards the other stairs. This door leads to a spiral set of steps climbing farther upward.

Five men stand guard near the top of the first stair and two, well armoured Krulaeji, a man and a woman, stand before the cylinder's door. Voss rushes forward. His footsteps echo through the room and all attention is drawn to him.

The two, more outfitted guards immediately begin to withdraw, opening the door and sliding through it. Voss is faster than they are, though, and reaches the door before it closes. He barely manages to hold it open. The other five run towards him. He wedges the bottom of his shield into the door and presses the button. It fixes to the air. The door-guards try to kick it out, but it holds strong.

Arrows are launched at Voss, who leaps backward and lands on the floor. The volley barely misses his head, and the shafts clatter against the door instead. Voss spins back onto his feet with his axe in hand and gashes one of the chargers across the chest. His chain buckles. He goes down. They are only servants. Emari slams into another on her way toward the door, staggering him. Voss parries, then blocks with his pauldron. Another defender loses a leg and goes down. The door behind him is thrown open by the guards.

Voss shoves the three standing servants backward and turns to face the armoured guards. The man swings a long mace towards him, and he barely dodges. The woman sends forth a metal-tipped whip — made from the same black-blue metal as Voss' new greatsword — which jabs a hole in Voss' already damaged chestplate, and cracks the chain underneath. Blood dribbles from the wound.

Two arrows fly through the air. Each embeds itself in the base of a servant's skull. Brael nocks a third. Roger runs across the room and crashes into the final servant, who goes down without much resistance. Brael's next arrow lodges in the male Krulaeji's thigh. Voss gains the upper hand and slices through the woman's whip-arm.

The man swings the mace and lands a hit on Voss' shoulder. Voss swings upward and catches him by surprise, his axe embedding itself in the man's armpit.

Roger finishes the servant on the ground by stabbing his spear through the man's' throat.

Emari jumps over the fallen servants and lands behind Voss. She brandishes her shortsword and slides by her larger companion, stabbing the woman through the chest. The attack comes as a surprise, and the woman falls to the bard's blade.

Voss uses his head to bash the man's face. His axe finishes the job, leaving a deep gash in the defender's neck.

The combat is finished, and Voss grabs his shield once more. They quickly search the floor for anything useful, but it appears that all the potion vials are either empty, or have been smashed into a metal sink. Their contents mix, bubble, and pop through the keep's pipes.

"We have to make haste. Those guards were never meant to stop an army, just to buy time," Voss announces.

"Indeed. We may already be too late," Brael tells him.

"Perhaps, but it takes some time to create any arcane circle, especially under stress, even when trained." Voss responds.

"Let's go," Scazgix urges, making for the stairs. Voss overtakes him at the doorway and leads the others in their ascent.

The steps wind much farther upward than they expected. The small tower appeared, from the outside, to be no taller than any other floor of the keep, yet they climb for two minutes until finally reaching a black wooden door and a small landing. All of them fit, but barely. They can hear a strange, rattling voice coming through the door, but they cannot make out the words.

"Are we ready?" Voss asks.

"Break it down," Roger responds, nodding.

Voss foot connects solidly with the wood, and the door buckles and splinters near the centre. He pushes off the back wall and crashes through the door with his shield forward.

"Ai carithei!" a woman's voice fills their ears, and suddenly the charge is halted. Voss' legs and arms refuse to move. Emari has run in beside him, but she also seems stuck in place. Roger and Brael fill most of the doorway and cannot move into or out of the room.

This is the bed chamber of a wealthy being. It is a circular room, impossibly large for what it seemed from the outside. It is at least forty feet in diameter, and contains a comfortable bed, a long dresser, a desk with chairs, a hearth, a wide table, wooden toilet enclosed in a separate section, and a smaller, circular, metal door against one wall that begins a foot from the ground.

Across from the wooden door where the attackers are frozen, standing near the large bed, is a pale, elven woman. Her eyes are closed in focus, and she is wielding a glowing, purple staff. In front of her, near the table, is a tall creature.

It stands almost nine feet in height. Its large head sits upon a thin, spindly neck. It has no hair, and no visible mouth, eyes, or nose. Instead, the being's chin stretches nearly half a foot longer than a normal face, and ends in a point that looks as sharp as a spike. Its skin is a pale, fleshy colour, but despite its somewhat humanoid appearance, it is certainly no common race.

A voice fills all of their minds. To Voss and Roger and Brael is sounds like a deep, masculine voice. To Emari is sounds like a cruel woman's. "You have made a fatal error in this assault," it says. "The subjects of Dal-Gorün were under my protection, and it appears I have failed them. It is you who lead this tragic effort against me, the great lord Jiih," it points at Voss. "You have wounded my pride and reputation and — without your head — I will not be able to restore these so easily. Luckily for me, you have marched straight to my quarters. I did not have to raise a finger to draw you in. Your blind aggression was your own demise."

The creature begins to move towards Voss. It hovers slightly off the ground. Soon it stands directly in front of the soldier, towering three feet over him. It raises an arm in front of itself and at the end is a hand with long, sharp, bone-like fingers. They rest gently atop Voss' helmet.

"It has been awhile since I had the pleasure of a surface-dweller's flesh," the being says. "It is a delicacy that has been sorely mi- argh!" Jiih's scream fills the others' minds, a piercing noise that engulfs the entire room. Jiih looks down toward his left foot, and sees Scazgix standing defiantly there, with his dagger embedded deep into its thigh, hidden within its purplish-blue robes. "Insolent beast!" Its pain and anger radiates off the walls. The woman opens her eyes and her staff dims. Jiih backhands Scazgix. The small, draconic figure flies from the ground and crashes over the table and onto the floor.

Voss clicks the button on his shield and raises his axe as the control returns to muscles.

Jiih spins quickly back and sees his mage's spell failing. It its hands materializes a beam of black energy. Voss swings towards Jiih, but is blocked by the black rod. No noise is emitted.

Brael looses an arrow, directed at the mage, but it is destroyed by some invisible wall that appears at the last second.

The mage sends an orb of light that winds around the combatants and strikes Roger in the chest. He is thrown against the wall and begins to roll back down the stairs.

Brael shoots two more arrows, one is deflected, the other manages to pierce the barrier and lodge in the elf's hip. She screams in pain and the barrier becomes visible for a moment before dissipating.

Emari runs in and slashes for Jiih's chest. Jiih raises an arm and she is lifted from the ground and pushed away from the creature. Emari crashes into the circular metal door and is held there. Jiih takes its other arm and swats Voss' axe from his hands with the black energy. The energy then implodes, and Jiih throws Voss against the opposite wall, where he crashes with great force into the stonework before toppling to the floor in pain beside his axe. Blood bubbles through the visor on Voss' helmet.

The being flies towards Emari.

Brael launches another arrow — this time towards Jiih — but the elven woman deflects it, and his attention is forced back to her.

Jiih places its long fingers around Emari's face. Each finger reaches all the way along her skull and touches the door behind her. "It's over," the creature says. "Your mortal abilities serve no use against one as ancient as I." The creature's chin then splits into four pieces as a hidden mouth opens, stretching out wider than her head. Along each piece of chin are two rows of small, sharp teeth.

"Hey!" Voss calls weakly. "Your fight is with me."

Jiih cranes his head back toward Voss. "Imbecile! Our fight is finished, I-"

A blast of golden-orange energy meets his face. Voss' outstretched arm continues to crush the crystal that Hariscine gave to him, releasing its well of power. The beam that emanates begins to melt his gauntlet, but he does not dare let go. Emari is dropped to the floor, away from the light, though her hood is slightly singed. Jiih manages to get a hand in front of it, and the beam is diverted around it.

Jiih slowly pushes against the energy, moving back toward Voss. Emari takes her sword and plunges it through Jiih's lower back. The monster's pain explodes into the room, driving deep into the minds of everyone present. Emari continues to push deeper.

Jiih swats at her with its other arm, but Emari manages to duck in time, leaving her sword in its back. The beam of energy finally stops, and the strange being spins to see Voss. Its face is now horrifically burned and blackened, but anger still pours through the very air.

Voss is already on his feet, though, and runs forward with his axe once more. They trade blows.

Jiih dodges.

Voss blocks a swipe of its claws.

They both lunge at once.

Voss' axe embeds itself in Jiih's forehead. Jiih's sharp fingers puncture through Voss' armour and deep into his chest. Both of them fall. Jiih crashes to its back. Voss lands, wobbling, on his knees.

Brael's last arrow lands cleanly in the mage's throat before she finishes her next spell.

Voss topples to his stomach, blood pooling from his chest and helmet.

Chapter Thirteen - Months to Come

3E056, 10th of Mivosera

The days following the siege are full of work. One counter-attack is made, but is repelled by the adventurer army. The houses within the fort are ransacked, and any deep-elves still cowering within are either escorted from the grounds or killed. The gate remains closed, and wealth is moved to the main square to be sorted amongst the guilds and individuals.

Almost a full day passes before the horses and the rest of the supplies begin to be brought in by the brave and uninjured. There is a good deal of valuables littered throughout the town to add to already bursting wagons. Most of the wealth comes in the form of finely-crafted jewelry. There are also mines and foundries at the back of the fort, and within them are some refined metals that are taken as well. The ores and the tools are left largely untouched.

Ealendur and Ziros are invited by Roger and the others into the keep after the fight in the bed chamber against Jiih. The elf begins to work on a teleportation circle in the planning room on the first floor, and the dwarf tends to Voss' and Scazgix's wounds. The soldier and the king do not wake within the day following the siege. Voss' injuries are deep and infected, but Ziros is a master of the healing arts, and if anyone could save someone on the brink of death, it would be him. Scazgix is placed in a servant bed, and Voss is moved to the bed in the lord's chambers.

Roger, Emari, and Hariscine examine Jiih's body. They have never encountered or heard of anything like this creature. It bears eerily similar resemblance to the carvings and the statue in the ruins however. At first, it appears to have no facial features at all, just flat skin stretched over a skull with a pointed chin. When they begin to move the body, though, the chin splits again into four pieces, opening vertically to reveal dual rows of razor sharp teeth. If Emari had have been held in place for a moment longer, it could have easily closed its horrific maw and snapped her head clean off her shoulders. Its bones, even its thin and sharp fingers, are quite strong as well. They appear much more dense than a normal human's or elf's bones. The skull is quite thin, despite this, and the brain inside must be far larger than the surface races', and certainly than the races of the Lowerlands.

It is impossible to discern how old — or even what — this being is. In the end, they throw the body onto the funeral pyres with the slain Krulaeji and adventurers to rid them of its presence. The body count was high on both sides. Despite the losses they suffered, however, the guilds do not point fingers of blame toward anyone, or, if they do, they do so in silence.

While the mages work, and the bulk of the army celebrates and tends the rest of the wounded, Bigger They Are and Emari spend time studying the library and the bed chambers of Lord Jiih. The tomes take a long time for Siegmire to translate, and most of them are useless. There are maps in the lord's chamber, though, that seem to depict a rough system of roads connecting major cities and settlements. It is difficult to decipher, but does reaffirm the belief that this fort is on the southern edge of a much larger system.

There are some personal books that belong to Jiih as well, but these are written in a strange dialect that no one can seem to understand. The circular door in the chamber has shown no signs of opening, despite the best efforts of those proficient in the arcane. There is certainly a spell placed upon the metal, and the whole room as well, but none can uncover the secrets. The answer must lie within the books, of which there are too many to read with all else going on, and very few with any translatable phrases.

Emari and Hariscine spend much of their time at Voss' side, but when Ziros is working they leave the dwarf be. The soldier was stripped of his armour and laid in Jiih's bed with fresh bedding. His chest and back are now covered in scars and welts from their days of fighting and his weeks of pushing himself. There is no bleeding anymore, though, and his hair-covered chest has been steadily rising and falling. His long brown hair is matted with sweat, and it has not been washed since before their arrival in the desert. It is also mixed, now, with many silver strands that dance subtly within the brown. His face is calm and still for once, but crossed with thin lines around his eyes and forehead.

Roger and his guild do an earnest job of running things: organizing the cleanup of bodies and blood, the distribution of pillaged wealth, and temporary housing for all the adventurers.

There are many things that could be done in the next few months. Of the books in the library that are useful, one is about the farming of Lowerland crops. Siegmire accepts a reasonable price to translate the entire book into the common-tongue. If servants could be hired from the surface and brought into Dal-Gorün to supplement the few human and dwarven slaves that stayed behind, the farms could likely be worked to sustain a small population.

Scazgix awakens after the first night and, when he hears of Roger's plan to stay here and run the keep, he makes a surprising offer over lunch.

"A good kingdom has allies," he says clearly in the common-tongue. "I would take cave for Scazgixia, if you would give this as reward for my service, and my people would maintain the walls of this fort and keep close ties with new friends."

"You want to live outside the fort and help with maintenance?" Roger asks, confused.

"Yes," Scazgix tell him. "We will build great kobold city to celebrate victory! With new, great space and enough room to hunt and grow, we will live many golden ages."

Roger shakes his hand and agrees, seeing no harm in the deal. The king resolves to return to Taernsby and his kingdom when Voss recovers, then bring his people here. There is still unused space to the north of the fort, and also in that direction lies another, very wide tunnel that, according to the maps they found, leads north and then west and south towards other Krulaeji cities and towns.

This, of course, begs the next concern of defence as, if they have made an enemy of a vast empire, they will certainly need a military force stationed in the fort, and paying for a guard is not going to be easy with the current situation.

It is the tenth of Mivosera. Roger and Emari have come with Ziros to visit Voss in his bed. There is no dispute among the members of the adventurer army or those who went with the soldier that he is now in charge. Brael wants no part of the keep, Roger will be his steward and right hand, and Emari says she will take a portion of whatever wealth is hidden in the keep's vault and a large manor, but wants none of the work in running the show.

Yuriel and Jorrig have also asked to join Bigger They Are, and are willing to help run the fort as well. Many things are going well outside the keep, and Ealendur is nearly finished the teleportation circle. Roger is still feeling the strain, and the past few days have been far more stressful than the fighting. More stressful, even, than leading the militia in Railwood. His back is sore and he has had a headache since the seventh.

"Voss," Roger says as Ziros emits a warm light onto the soldier's chest, "you need to wake." This is the first time since the hours after Jiih's death that Roger has seen the man. "We have done what we can, but there are too many things that I cannot decide for you."

There is quiet in the room as Ziros calmly whispers spells.

"Do not die, Voss," Emari says next. "As much as my life was safer before meeting you, I have come to terms with the fact that I do not plan on abandoning your side until I am ready. For whatever idiotic reason, I am not ready yet. You are far from a cautious man, and I have warned you time and time again about your recklessness, and about the danger involved. Despite all of that, you are resilient. More resilient than anyone I have met, and I do not believe that you are going to fall here. On top of that, if you do die now, it will have been to save me, and I do not need the burden of your life on my shoulders."

"No, you don't," Voss says, his eyes flickering open and his mouth curling into a smile. The others are struck still. Ziros steps back. "Ziros, leave us, please, and thank you greatly. I hope you have been paid well for treating me. If not, I will see to it that you are. Someone help me up."

Ziros bows and begins to cross the room to the door. Emari goes to help Voss sit.

"No," Roger commands. "You must stay in bed until you have had much water and hot soup. You have been unconscious for days."

"And still, I have not been idle," Voss responds. "But fine, bring me soup and water, and when I can stand we will search the vault."

Ziros' footsteps fade down the steps beyond the room.

"The circular door stands closed. We cannot open it," Emari tells him.

"Var-hyzek," Voss speaks. An audible click sounds from the metal door and it swings slightly ajar. "No one outside this room may know this command."

"How did you learn that?" Emari asks in wonder.

"A friend of mine was a scholar, as well as a damned good archer," Voss grins. "One of the books on the bookshelf was written by Jiih's mage, and held the Lowerland translation of the opening command."

"You studied the books while you slept?" Roger demands.

Voss explains that as he slept, he found himself within his own mind. He was able to communicate with the spirits there and do a limited amount of work from the bed. Every second he used to search through the books hurt him, but he could not sit idle while everyone else toiled.

"What are these ghosts of yours? Why are they within you?" Emari asks him suddenly.

"Unimportant for now. Go and get me soup and water. I would like to see what we have gained in this conquest, and I am tired of lying down," he tells them. Roger and Emari oblige, leaving him to wait while they fetch him a two-day late breakfast.

Voss drinks several tall tankards of water, and takes two bowls of soup slowly. His stomach feels as fragile as his mind and chest do. When he has finally finished, he is helped to his feet by Roger and Emari. They cross the room to the metal door and pull it open together.

Behind the door is a bright, large room made of grey stone. There are orbs of light floating about, and nothing seems to cast a shadow. There are piles of coins and crates of refined metal bars. Most are the same odd, blueish metal, but some are a pitch black as well, and many are gold and silver and copper. Apart from this are barrels of water and wine and pickled vegetables, and stacks of cheeses and dried meats, but the majority of the floor space is taken by wealth and metals.

"This is a fortune," Emari mutters under her breath.

They bring Jitz to the vault and, together, they all begin to count. It takes hours of work, even between them all, and even with the notes from the previous owner's journals to help them. Finally, they have translated the mage's book and counted the unmentioned sections of the vault. Within the clearly-magical space, are just about twenty thousand gold lions worth of gold and silver and copper, in coin and bar form together. There is almost double the combined amount of the strange blue metal, referenced as 'essum' in the journal, and a small amount of the black metal, which is said to be 'adamant'.

Once it has all been categorized, and Ealendur and Ziros are paid for their magical workings, and Emari has taken roughly four thousand lions worth of gold as a cut, Voss calls a meeting. Bigger They Are, Qoud Pacem, Scazgix, and Hariscine join him in the meeting room to discuss the best course for the fort.

They gather around the table, beside the newly constructed teleportation circle. The circle is raised four inches above the rest of the floor, and made of expertly sanded black stone. The inlay is done in liquid steel, and the inscription is written in alchemical paint made with diamond-dust. It was a very expensive project, but the results appear beautiful as well as functional.

The meeting is opened on the discussion of civilians and work in the fields. Voss agrees that a supply of food will become increasingly important, and tells Roger to send messages to both Taernsby and Azgul Hold. Ealendur has provided them with the arcane codes for the Velvet Compass' circle, as well as the codes he will be using in the Azgul Hold and Taernsby proper official circles in the next few months. The elf agrees to carry the message with him to Magistrate Brenspire. Voss asks that Ealendur take a second message to Brenspire, asking the magistrate to pass the message to the southern townships as well.

There is then a discussion of guards, and of a wizard. Roger brings up the first, and Voss the second. They agree that a guard will need to be established, and so the messages taken regarding immigration will include the job possibility of guard as well. The issue of the wizard is more of a personal one for Voss, as he realizes now — more than ever — the versatility of magic. There are things in the keep that someone with a good knowledge of arcana could help with and, when Voss inevitably leaves again for whatever reason, having a wizard with him on the journey would be a great help.

And so the messages are transcribed, one bound for Azgul Hold, and two bound for Taernsby, then one to The South.

Lord Voss Hallehwell of Dal-Gorün is offering an opportunity for affordable land ownership in a newly-discovered, underground fortress. There is much to be done, and many houses to fill about the town. So, if you seek land of your own, with a steady, paying job, look no further.

Citizens are being sought with abilities in farming, mining, smithing, brewing, leather-working, tailoring, management of business, or with experience in a guard or military force. Lord Hallehwell also seeks a trained wizard or strong mage to help in study and who is willing to travel around the known world for various reasons.

The area of Dal-Gorün is underground, as mentioned, but it is spacious, and has so far proven defensible. There is danger involved in living here, and it is a drastic change of scenery, but, to compensate that, the plot of land or house you receive will come free of charge, and a daily wage of one silver will be alloted to manual professions, or two silver alloted for crafters and guardsmen. You will also be able to leave the fort via arcane means on rest days to see sunlight and to visit other cities and towns.

If you are interested in this endeavour, send a letter to the nearest Velvet Compass order hall and it shall be passed on to Lord Hallehwell.

The last parts, of course, are made possible through discussion with Ealendur and his assurance that it will be okay. He agrees to speak with the order masters on Voss' behalf. For this, Voss is very grateful as well.

Voss does decide to go with him, however, as he has errands to run in Azgul Hold, and returns to give the Velvet Compass. His armour is badly damaged, but he can afford to pay the fee for having it repaired, and the wagon they borrowed must be broken down as well. Most wagons have to be left behind by the adventurers, but they made enough coin on this journey that they do not mourn their lent transportation.

Finally, on the afternoon of the tenth, the guilds begin to leave through the circle and return to Azgul Hold. Voss takes Hariscine and they go with them, leaving the others to watch the keep for the moment.

The sickening feeling of weightlessness and assault of light in their eyes leaves them blinking in the order hall. They are in a smaller, circular chamber, and ahead of them is a line of adventurers being slowly let through by a pair of dwarven guards.

Voss heads first for the smithies of the city. The best smiths, foundries, and mines in the known world are in Azgul Hold, and the best of those lie closest to the northern end of the city, where it is actually borne into Mount Azgul. The walk is long, but flat, and welcome after days of lying down. The sun feels nice upon Voss' skin as well, and the cooler, summer wind makes him shiver pleasantly.

Before they reach the smithies, Voss calls for lunch. They find a small restaurant off the main street that is not too busy, and sit at a sturdy table. Voss orders them coffees and roast lamb and cheese on fire-bread.

"I am healed," Hariscine tells him while they wait for their food.

Voss looks up at her. He is wearing his hood, not his helm. "That is good news, I suppose."

"I am sworn as your prisoner still, so I am not going anywhere," she tells him. The coffees are brought. They are cold and bitter, but welcome.

"You have proven yourself to be both loyal and useful," Voss tells her, "and kind." He sips his coffee again. "What would you do now, if you were free?"

"I do not know," she says. "Even freedom has limitations."

"Pretend, then, that you have no limitation. What would you do?"

She thinks. "I desire power. I think there is little secret there. The most power I could hope to hold would be sharing in the running of an underground fortress. At least, for now. Perhaps I could return to the ruins, enchant new passers-by to work for me. I could be an ally at arms' reach."

"My bed would be the worse for it, then," Voss muses.

Hariscine laughs aloud, drawing attention from a few other tables. "I apologize, Voss. I didn't know you were capable of jokes."

"They come rarely, but, when they do, they are very funny." He smiles.

"If you were to set me free, I could consider living in the keep or returning to the ruins. I will say that the ruins are less comfortable, but if you visit me occasionally then I suppose I could stomach it."

"I will make you a deal," Voss says, his tone serious once more. "I will set you free, on the condition that you maintain a regular watch on the ruins. Make sure nothing else makes it a home. As long as this job is done, you are welcomed in my keep and in my bed, and are welcome to leave and explore Azgul Hold and Taernsby when we establish a circle and permissions there. Only if you enchant no citizens of my fortress or of the free north."

"I like that deal very much," she responds. The lamb and bread arrive. The scent of it makes both their mouths water. "I will only enchant who you wish me to, no one else."

They eat ravenously and talk little else. Afterward, when they are back on the street, Voss officially shakes her hand. She embraces him afterward, and kisses him. It is the first kiss they have had, even when making love. It feels foreign to Voss, but not unwelcome.

"Thank you," he mutters.

"Do not thank me, idiot," she cackles, shoving him playfully. "Let's go talk to this smith about armour. Explain again what we are doing here."

"I want to know if anyone has heard of adamant or essum, or if they know how to make armours and weapons with it," he explains as they walk. She has heard the plan, but she likes the animated nature that Voss possesses when he describes his interests. "Adamant proved to be a very strong metal — if not brittle under some conditions — and one that I have never seen. I believe the new blade I found was an alloy of sorts. When I read the journal of the mage I could feel the potential it had, so I grabbed a bar of each and..."

They walk up the road and into the shadow of Mount Azgul. The large mountain looms far above them, with dark clouds now brewing at its peak.

Manufactured by Amazon.ca
Bolton, ON